# ROCCO

THE ITALIAN CARTEL #8

## SHANDI BOYES

Edited by NICKI @ SWISH DESIGN & EDITING

Photography by GOLDEN @ FURIOUS PHOTOGRAPHY

Illustrated by SSB COVERS & DESIGN

# COPYRIGHT

# DEDICATION

*For my boo.*

*I love you.*

*Shandi xx*

# ALSO BY SHANDI BOYES

** Denotes Standalone Books*

## Perception Series

Saving Noah *

Fighting Jacob *

Taming Nick *

Redeeming Slater *

Saving Emily

Wrapped Up with Rise Up

Protecting Nicole *

## Enigma

Enigma

Unraveling an Enigma

Enigma The Mystery Unmasked

Enigma: The Final Chapter

Beneath The Secrets

Beneath The Sheets

Spy Thy Neighbor *

The Opposite Effect *

I Married a Mob Boss *

Second Shot *

The Way We Are

The Way We Were

Sugar and Spice *

Lady In Waiting

Man in Queue

Couple on Hold

Enigma: The Wedding

Silent Vigilante

Hushed Guardian

Quiet Protector

Enigma: An Isaac Retelling

Twisted Lies *

**Bound Series**

Chains

Links

Bound

Restrain

The Misfits *

Nanny Dispute *

**Russian Mob Chronicles**

Nikolai: A Mafia Prince Romance

Nikolai: Taking Back What's Mine

Nikolai: What's Left of Me

Nikolai: Mine to Protect

Asher: My Russian Revenge *

Nikolai: Through the Devil's Eyes

Trey *

Wicked Intentions *

Sinful Intentions *

Devious Intentions *

Deadly Intentions *

# WANT TO STAY IN TOUCH?

Facebook: facebook.com/authorshandi

Instagram: instagram.com/authorshandi

Email: authorshandi@gmail.com

Reader's Group: bit.ly/ShandiBookBabes

Website: authorshandi.com

Newsletter: https://www.subscribepage.com/AuthorShandi

# PROLOGUE
## ROCCO

**Fifteen**

*I* startle when an ice-cold hand slithers across my midsection. It's far too small and dainty to excuse the ruckus it causes my heart, and I'm in a house far too elaborate to be my family home, but old habits die hard. It's been over two years since I've been awoken by unwanted hands touching me, but the fear never ends.

And neither will the anger.

Most kids around these parts get an inappropriate uncle or a pastor promising them a one-way ticket out of hell. I got a fucked-up father who thinks fucking with his kids isn't a metaphor.

Don't misconstrue what I'm saying. The sick fucker didn't rape me, but I had no clue the other shit he did was inappropriate until the girls at my school wanted to do the same.

I like when they touch me.

I fucking hated it when he did.

So, once I became the same height as him, I put an end to it.

You won't believe what you can get away with when your father fears you. I'm dying for the day Dimitri, my best fucking friend in the world and number one ally, reaches the same level of independence.

He's come a long way the past three years, but he still has a way to go. I'd be a lying prick if I said I didn't understand his hesitation. My father is a beer-guzzling, wife-beating soft cock who works in a factory when he gets his lazy ass out of bed. Dimitri's father is the head of the Italian Cartel. That not only makes him real fucking impenetrable, it also means there are rules Dimitri must follow.

He can give his father lip, he can flip him the bird before telling him to sit on it and spin, and he can skip school to hang with me and the flock of girls we're never without, but under no circumstances can he press the muzzle of a gun to his head and threaten to blow his brains out if he dares to touch his cock or his mother one more time.

Only I had the privilege of doing that because my father isn't mafia royalty. I'm sure it will eventually come to a head for Dimitri, especially if he discovers the real reason behind his sister's frequent visits to my room.

Ophelia isn't tiptoeing her finger across the bumps in my stomach because she is attempting to rile a response from me like the senior girls in my school. She's seeking something to cling to, to tether her down while she rides out the storm.

She's *avoiding* a sexual confrontation, not instigating one.

How do I know this? Her skin has the same clammy feeling mine got every time I caught my father's drunken footsteps creaking up the stairwell of my childhood home. Once I hit twelve, I didn't wait around to see what he had in store for me. I climbed out the window, scaled down the trestle mounted to the paint-peeled cladding of my home, then piss-bolted it to Dimitri's place.

Dimitri never gave me hell for my somewhat regular sleepovers. He tossed a pillow into my chest, nudged his head to the floor, then told me to wake him if I needed him. I won't fucking lie, I prefer to save them for the people who really need them, but there are over twelve spare rooms in the Petretti residence. Dimitri could have given me a bed. He didn't because he knew I was too ashamed to admit I was scared shitless to sleep by myself.

It was only when my drop-ins went from once a month to almost every weekend did Dimi switch things up. On the agreement I keep my mitts off his fourteen-year-old sister, he gave me my own room, right next to his.

We share a bathroom, which makes it really fucking hard to ask Ophelia if she's okay without alerting Dimitri to her visit, so instead, I weave my fingers through her damp hair until the frantic thrusts of her lungs from running from her perpetrator soothes to a lulling stillness.

She feels safe with me, and it puffs my chest out with pride. I'm an anarchist who craves carnage, but I get an equal amount of satisfaction knowing I helped weather her through the storm. Only damaged people can fix damaged people because only we know what the other has been through.

After adjusting Ophelia's position so her cheek no longer rests on the section of my shirt that caught her tears, I tighten my grip around her waist before balancing my chin on the top of her head. I'm bigger than most fifteen-year-olds—taller and bulkier—but right now, I feel about the size of an ant. I know who's hurting her. I have the means to make it stop, but since that ax isn't mine to swing, I have to sit back and watch her nightmares unfold before my very eyes.

I'm not even talking about the rules Dimitri and Ophelia are forced to live by. I'm referring to the pledge Ophelia made me agree to the first night she snuck into my room. She begged me not to mention her visits or the reason behind them to neither Dimitri nor anyone in her father's crew.

I shook my head in an instant. If Dimitri knew the full extent of his father's crimes, I was confident he could use them to revoke the rules. Monsters lurk without leashes, but some type of regulation always collars them. Sexually abusing your children is an instant fucking out as far as I'm concerned, but Ophelia didn't see things the same way as me.

Shame had shackled her.

She said if I told Dimitri what her father was up to, she'd deny everything before shifting the focus back to me by outing my secret. I wanted to hate her that night. Instead, I took a step back to work out how she knew my secret. It was buried so deep, only my father and I knew about it.

It was then I concluded that damaged people also attract damaged people. That's why Ophelia seeks me in the darkness of the night. I can't take away her pain, but I won't hammer her to tell me what's wrong either. I help shelter her shame by holding her how she doesn't think she deserves to be held and promise to take her secret to the grave as she will mine.

Within minutes of Ophelia falling into a restless sleep, I join her.

When I wake the next morning, she's gone. That isn't unusual. If it weren't for the scent of her shampoo embedded in my shirt, I'd question if I had hallucinated our exchange. Drugs fucked up my father's head, so I don't want to consider the damage they're doing to mine. I'm not an addict by any means, but drugs make the blackness inside of me not as obvious. It's no different than the painkillers Ma was forced to pop anytime my father beat into her like she was a punching bag. My pain relief of choice just isn't distributed by a pharmacist.

I stop smirking about how pissed Col, Dimitri's father, will be if he ever discovers how much capital Dimitri and I slice from his profits each run. I don't turn sixteen for another three weeks. I don't even have my learner's permit yet, but that hasn't stopped Col from ordering Dimitri and me to courier drugs town to town. He has more law enforcement officers in his pocket than he does criminals, so a minor charge of unlicensed driving wouldn't be a challenge.

My grin disappears from my face when Dimitri enters my room. His nostrils are flaring like I'm not the only one smelling floral perfume in the air. Gangbangers have always been popular with teenage girls wanting to rebel against society, but Dimi knows that isn't the case this time around. I'm not quiet when a preacher's daughter wants to get back at her daddy by sucking my dick. I want the world to hear her moans because that's the only way I can stop my father's drunken grunts from bellowing through my ears long enough I can come.

I shake off the tight grip of my jaw when Dimitri asks, "Was Ophelia here?"

He doesn't sugarcoat anything.

Not even shit he should.

I bob my chin, incapable of lying to him but adept at prettying things up with a little bit of shine. "She was. She just left." When all six foot three of him enters the room with steam billowing out of his ears and clenched fists, I talk faster. "She wanted me to pass on to you that your father is looking for you."

That isn't necessarily a lie. Col rides Dimitri's ass twenty-four-seven. He even rocks up at our school unannounced when he needs an urgent matter taken care of. Not that Col will ever admit this, but the Petretti entity would have gone to shit years ago if it weren't for Dimitri and me.

Dimi folds his arms in front of his chest when he stops at the end of my bed. "If that's the case, why didn't she tell me that herself?"

"Because you were in the shower. *Duh*," I hit back when it dawns on me that his hair is wet.

He doesn't get the night sweats like me. He's so accustomed to mafia life, he doesn't even perspire while burying bodies in the woodlands.

I scoot off the bed and swagger partway across the room before asking, "Once I've hit the head, will you be good to head out? I wanna get shit done early today. It's Finlay's birthday." Finlay is my baby sister. She's eight going on twenty-one and has more attitude than Dimitri and me combined.

Dimitri jerks up his chin before unfolding his arms. He can't maintain his aggressive stance when we're talking about family who doesn't share his blood. "Are we still taking them to Petretti's?"

Finlay isn't his sister, but since he saw her born on the floor of my parents' kitchen, he treats her as if she is. Back then, there was no Obama Care the people are gloating about these days. Since Ma couldn't afford the cost of delivering a baby at a hospital, she did it at home instead. It wasn't all bad. That day taught me that no matter what, women will always be superior to men. I don't care how old you are, you can't watch a woman go through labor and not be in awe of her strength.

My ma picked the wrong man to marry, but she's fought to fix her mistakes ever since the day my father left a mark on my cheek, unaware the sexual abuse had started months earlier. She moved Finlay, herself, and me from his house before the blood on my cheek had dried, then filed for a divorce a month after that.

Sadly, the court believed my father had the right to see his children. They granted him overnight, unsupervised weekend visits at his house. It was during one of those visits that I threatened to blow his brains out. For some reason, he annulled his parental supervision of Finlay and me the following Monday. Now Finlay only sees him for two three-hour visits a month. He gets an additional visit tossed in for special occasions such as Christmas, Easter, and birthdays. Excluding a run-in at a pep rally earlier this year that saw me do a two-month stint in juvie for battery, I haven't laid eyes on him for almost two years.

Ma has no clue why her prick of an ex-husband suddenly grew a conscience, but she's used it to her advantage the past two years. She salvaged Finlay's grades out of the dumpster and reconnected with her parents. Now her focus is on me. She'll never beg me to come home, but no amount of eye rolls will stop her from dropping one hundred hints a minute.

There are days where I wish I could tell her what happened, but the fact she lets me stay at Dimitri's without too much grievance has me wondering if I need to. Ma is more clued in than she lets on, but just like I wish I could erase Ophelia's pain, she knows her endeavors to protect me have come years too late.

After working my throat through a brutal swallow, I answer Dimitri's question, "Yeah. I told Ma we'd cruise by and pick them up around five." I don't mention the fact we're eating before the sun sets so I can avoid seeing my father. Since today is Finlay's birthday, he gets an additional unsupervised visit this month. It would also be a waste of breath. Dimi knows how much I despise my father because he hates his father just as much.

The older I get, the more I'm convinced I should have compressed the trigger when I held a gun from Col's stash to my father's head. He pissed his pants while swearing he'd never touch me again, but it's a little too late to apologize after you've damaged someone beyond repair.

I attempt to drag my thoughts from the negative. Today is meant to be a good day, and I won't have my father ruining it for Finlay. "Do you want to invite Ophelia? It would be good for Finlay to have some females in her life who ain't her mother."

As I said earlier, my ma is doing everything right. She works hard and loves her kids with every inch of her soul, but since she was the only one contributing to putting food on the table back then, she missed things she shouldn't have.

I don't blame her for what happened to me, but I do wonder how differently things could have been if she had heard my sobs just once.

Mistaking my expression as disappointment that I only get to spend two hours with my baby sister on her birthday, Dimitri says, "I can get us a run closer to home. We could do lunch *and* an early dinner."

I'm about to rile him about getting soft in his old age, then I realize he's only sixteen.

Fuck me, this life ages you. Even my walk to the bathroom is stiff. It has nothing to do with Ophelia being snuggled in my side all night and everything to do with all the heavy lifting we do.

Bricks of coke aren't weightless, and neither are dead bodies.

"Can you believe that fucking guy? *Listen here, son,*" I impersonate, "*I don't know who you think you're talking to...* pow-pow *fucking* pow!" I mimic the noise of a gun's pop. "He's minus two kneecaps and a left nut."

"He's lucky I left him with a functioning nut," Dimitri replies with a murderous grin. "I was aiming for both, but he had bigger balls than I realized."

My laughter howls into the cool afternoon air. Our baby faces often catch the eyes of the plumper fish in the pond, but it only takes an insult or two for them to unearth Dimitri's short fuse. Even though he only turned sixteen a couple of months back, his kill count is already higher than his age. It has me cautious not to piss him off, although I feel like I could get away with more than the average man. It's the perks of knowing someone since the first grade.

My hyena-like laugh dulls to a windless rustle when the back door of the Petrettis' Hopeton compound pops open, and Ophelia steps out. In a tight-fitting shirt and a pleated skirt, she looks older than her almost fifteen years, and I'm not the only one noticing.

The air in my lungs evicts with a chuckle when Dimitri throws his fist into my stomach. "Eyes forward, fuckface. You can have any girl in Hopeton *except* her."

For a second, I wonder if our friendship is as solid as believed, then I realize if Ophelia were my sister, and Dimitri was eyeballing her like a horndog with his tongue hanging out, I'd slice his tongue right out of his fucking mouth.

There's no way in hell I'll ever allow Finlay to end up with someone like Dimitri and me. She'll marry a man smart enough to know he'll be a dead man if he ever hurts her.

"Make a wish." Finlay's green eyes pop up to mine before she blows out the eight candles on top of the cake the Petretti's staff members carried out while singing happy birthday.

Tonight's festivities have gone off without a hitch. Finlay gushed over Ophelia's presence like her insides are as sparkly as the sequin top she's wearing. She told me I'm the best brother she could have ever wished for when I gifted her a bedazzle gun—the top item on her birthday wish list. Ma only glared at me for the quickest second when I told Finlay she could use it to gem up the cell phone I hid in the bottom of her giftbag so Ma couldn't confiscate it before she saw it.

It's been an awesome couple of hours, only soured by the fact if Finlay and Ma don't leave now, they'll be late meeting my father. As much as I don't give a fuck about him and his measly six-hours-a-month visitation rights, for every five minutes we go over, he gains an additional hour.

That alone has me wanting to push Finlay and Ma out the door.

"I'll get this boxed up so you can take it with you," Dimitri says to Finlay, his tone sheepish.

He isn't eager for them to leave like me. He's unaware of the custody orders. He merely wants to get away from my glare before I fry his brain cells. I warned Finlay she'd have to kiss the closest boy to her if her knife touched the cake platter. Instead of stopping before the tip got near the base, she jabbed her knife down so fast, I'm reasonably sure Ma's crystal platter chipped before she planted her lips on Dimitri's cheek.

My sister has her first crush, and it's for a teen with insides as dark as mine.

*Fuck it!*

While fiddling with a pendant around her neck, Ophelia shifts on her feet to face me. "Your mom invited me over for cake. Would it be okay if I go with them?"

Sometimes my sheer brilliance even blindsides me. I thought dragging Ophelia to Finlay's birthday would be good for my baby sister. I didn't consider the positive effect it could have on Ophelia. She's been without a female influence since her mother was killed during a botched FBI sting. She was so young I doubt she even remembers her.

"If Dimi is okay with it, I'm fine with you hanging out with my mom for a bit." When she nods, announcing she's aware she'll need Dimitri's permission before she can leave, I hand her my cell phone. "Give me your number. That way, if he says yes, we can swing by and pick you up when you're ready."

Her fingers fly over the screen of my phone as she punches in her number. Once she adds a love heart emoji next to her name, she hands it back to me, then dashes in the direction Dimitri went. While watching their exchange through the swinging door of Petretti's Restaurant, I replace her heart with an eye-roll emoji. I'm not stupid. I like my dick, and so have the handful of girls I've bedded, so I'd rather it attached to my body and not dangling off the rearview mirror in Dimitri's ride.

"He said yes," Ophelia informs me after arriving back at my side. The shock on her face is as evident as mine, then reality dawns. If she's with my mother, she won't be anywhere near me.

*Well played, Dimi. Well played.*

With the night early and Ophelia and my family on their way home, Dimitri and I cruise past a handful of house parties. Senior year wrap-up parties have started popping up all over Florida. They're usually good hook-up locations, but today, we're paying more attention to the male half of the attendees. We have merchandise to move, and the rich schmucks in this part of the state are too stupid to realize we're up-marketing the product by two hundred percent.

"This one looks like an easy row."

Since he agrees with my statement, Dimitri lowers the revs of his muscle car before he pulls it into a vacant spot a few blocks up.

"Is that Stacy?" I ask when I spot a cheerleader from Seaforth Academy. She has waist-length red hair and the ability to do the splits —two of Dimitri's favorable traits.

I smile a toothy grin when Dimitri grumbles under his breath, "I fuckin' hope not. That girl is a clinger." He twists around his phone to show me the screen. Tonight alone, he's had fifteen missed calls from Stacy.

"There's a quick way to get her off your back." I peel out of the passenger seat of his jet-black Cuda before finalizing my sentence. "Take her home to meet Daddy. That'll scare anyone off."

"It didn't work for you," he shoots back, shocking me with his wit.

A belly full of food has done wonders for his personality. He's usually a bear with a sore head on the weekends because his father works him to the point of exhaustion.

After low-balling me with a whack to the nuts, Dimitri pushes off his feet to fleece some rich fuckers of their inheritance. They're so stupid, they think you can't get addicted to heroin after one hit. He'll go for the preppy boys first. If that doesn't work, he'll use his charm on their girlfriends.

Me, I just smile and wait for the needy fuckers to come to me.

"Hey, hold up," I say to Dimitri before he's halfway up the driveway.

My cell phone is hollering. Considering only three people have my number, and the only one who doesn't share my blood is standing across from me, I can't let it go to voicemail.

It dawns on me that four people now have my number when Ophelia's name flashes across the screen. I swallow, real fucking grateful I switched out her love heart emoji when Dimitri peers at my phone's screen after returning to my side. His arched brow reveals he's curious as to why Ophelia is ringing me instead of him, but not enough to rib me about it—yet.

I slide my finger against the screen of my phone before squashing it to my ear. "What's up. Are you ready to leave already?" I say my comment with the hope it will tame the beast standing next to me, but when the fretful screams of my sister bellow down the line before a word leaves Ophelia's mouth, I realize that was wrong for me to do. "What's happening? Why is Finlay screaming like that?" She sounds like she's being murdered.

"She was fine, then your mother suggested she get changed before your father arrives to collect her. That's when she went into hysterics," Ophelia answers, her voice on the verge of sobbing. "She's locked herself into her room. She won't come out."

When I drift my eyes to Dimitri in preparation to tell him it's time to go, I notice he's already sprinting for his Cuda. "We'll be there in thirty, if that. Try to keep her calm."

After promising to do exactly that, Ophelia disconnects our call.

Just as quickly, I strive to work out what flipped Finlay's switch. I haven't seen her shed so much as a tear the past two years. Despite her attitude, she was an ideal baby, leaped over the terrible toddler years with only a handful of instances, then became the little lady she is today. She's so much like our mother, I have no doubt she'll grow into a wonderful, well-adjusted woman.

"Do you think this has something to do with your father?" Dimitri asks after pulling down a familiar-looking street. I've been so zoned out I didn't realize we've traveled over twenty miles.

It's the fight of my life to nod, but I get there, eventually. Dimitri knows how my father beat my mother when he wanted to throw around his authority. He backed up my campaign to teach him some manners when we unexpectedly bumped into him in the dim parking lot at our school. But this feels like something more than that. Ma has been off my father's radar for years. She wasn't even placed back on it when he had me locked up. But since he is always the center of every event that knots my stomach, I'm reasonably sure he's the cause this time around as well.

Upon spotting my nod, Dimitri leans across the cab of his car to lower the glove compartment. He isn't weaponing up. He is reminding me I don't have to follow the rules like him. I can take matters into my own hands.

I'm hoping he's overreacting, but our arrival at my mother's modest rented home exposes that isn't the case. My mum is five foot four. She'd be lucky to weigh one ten wringing wet, yet she's walloping into my father like I didn't inherit my bulky weight and height from him. She throws her fists into his body while screaming in his face that she should have killed him when she found out what he had done to me.

Worry that Dimitri will decode her statement for what it really is flies out the window when my dad retaliates to my mother's violence with a back-handed slap. He doesn't stop at one hit. He never does. He hits her a second and third time before he pins her to the ground by her throat.

When her face instantly whitens from his tight grip, I fucking lose it. While memories of the times my father viciously beat my mother during their marriage play through my head like a movie, I dive out of Dimitri's car, sprint across the sun-damaged grass, then ram into my father's side like I'm a defensive end homing in on a quarterback.

While he grunts out his shock with a handful of curse words, I wallop into him as I've dreamed of doing for the past three years. My fists, my knees, my fucking head, they all get in on the act. I punish him for hurting my mother and me, then I destroy him for stupidly believing he has the right to put his hands on a woman he no longer has a claim to.

She gave his children life, for fuck's sake. He should worship the ground she walks on.

My thrashing loses steam when my father stops fighting back. There's no fun beating a man who knows they're going to lose, so they don't bother trying. Ma always says it's better to walk away than waste your strength on someone unworthy of your time.

Although that's hard for me to do this time around, I'll face the injustice for her. I want her to know I'm *nothing* like my father. I may look like him and have his build and height, but I will *never* be him.

"I fuckin' hate you," I seethe into my father's ear before standing so I can lay a boot into his ribs. Once he's coughing up blood, I add, "And if you touch my mother again, I'll fucking kill you."

I can handle the shame he forced on me.

I can brush it off that it was more a consequence of his fucked-up head than mine.

But I will *not* stand by and watch him abuse my mother. I'm older now and wiser. The shit from the past ends now.

Adrenaline surges through my veins, making my body shake, but no number of tremors will stop me from taking in the fear in Finlay's eyes when she stares down at our father, writhing on the ground. She isn't peering at him with concern because his face is bloody and already bruising, she's looking at him as if she's afraid he'll get up, that his lungs will continue pumping air instead of collapsing to death like our mother almost did when he choked her. It's the same panicked glint Ophelia's eyes have every single time she tiptoes out of my room. She's petrified, but instead of her monster being the boogeyman hiding in her closet, it's her father—her flesh and blood.

My gut twists when I realize how fucking stupid I've been. I thought my father touched me because I had something neither my sister nor mother had, that I was targeted because I was a boy. I never once considered the fact he molested me simply because I was easy prey.

As my head reels with sick, heart-clogging information, I lock my eyes with Ophelia. She takes a step back, aware of what I'm asking her but unsure how she feels about it. I'm seeking confirmation of sexual abuse from a girl who's been sexually abused. That's a bitter pill for any victim to swallow, but she still seems willing to help. She just wishes it were being done without her big brother watching on.

If I could protect my sister and keep her secret under wraps, I would in a heartbeat. Since I can't, I wordlessly promise to make it up to her in any way possible. She can sleep in my bed for eternity if she does this one little thing for me.

After clearing the fret from her eyes with rapid-fired blinks, Ophelia moves close enough to Finlay she can pull her head into her chest when her faintest nod sees me yanking the gun Dimitri recently reloaded out of his hand. While staring down at the monster from my nightmare, I aim the barrel at a crinkle running down the middle of my father's head. He tries to fire off an apology and lie his way out of a situation that can *never* be excused, but I pull back the trigger of the gun before a single word leaves his mouth. I end his tormented reign like I should have years ago, and I do it while smiling.

He molested my sister—my *baby* sister. There's no coming back from that. An apology won't fix it. He needed to die for his crimes. In the eyes of the law, I may not be a man just yet, but I'm man enough to take care of business the way the courts failed to do.

While screaming like I'm possessed, I drop Dimitri's gun to my father's chest before firing in rapid succession. I get off three or four rounds before a police officer called to a disturbance mistakes me for a criminal. He's kind enough to aim for my shoulder when his multiple requests for me to lower my weapon go unanswered, but not kind enough to make sure my ma and sister aren't witnesses to my maiming.

They cry more about the bullet that ricochets through my shoulder than the one that blew my father's brains out, and they do it while kneeling at my side, pleading with the officer that they're arresting the wrong person.

To them, I'm not a monster.

I'm their savior, and I will continue to be until the day I die.

# 1

## ROCCO

**Twenty-Seven**

*I* stop striving to get a bit of shut-eye when the heated body plastered to my side tiptoes her fingers down my abs. Her breathy giggles fan my cheek when she believes my cock is twitching in response to the teasing movements of her hands. In reality, it's from recalling the fact there's more than one naked female in my bed.

I'm using a second blonde's tits as a pillow.

*No wonder my sleep was shit.*

*She's got as much silicon on her chest as she does in her lips.*

While chuckling about my witty inner monologue, I roll over to pop blonde number two's puckered nipple into my mouth. She responds as she did last night when I suggested she invite her friend into our three-day-long theatrics. She projected so much excitement, she shouldn't suck dick as well as she does. I guess even closet bisexuals exist these days, which is a shame. I've always been about love who you want and have no qualms about it. If that happens to be a chick without a dick, so be it. A man loving another man, go the fuck ahead. There are only two relationships I won't tolerate—adults fawning over kids and non-consensual ones.

If a girl says no, back the fuck up. I won't tell you twice.

My sister's pinprick for a dick of a boyfriend learned that the hard way.

With my mood now sour from memories of my past tainting my head, I release blonde number two's nipple from my mouth with a pop before rolling off the bed. Her friend, who I think name starts with an S, pouts when I stand next to my bed butt-fucking-naked. My dick is hard enough to bounce a quarter off. That isn't unusual. He has no shame, but my head isn't with the program, so that's an instant out for me.

If the woes of my past are messing with my head, I can't be sure I won't fuck up like my father did time and time again. Considering I'd rather blow my brains out than *ever* become him, the woes of my cock will be ignored.

"Do you want to shower before heading out, or are you good leaving like that?"

It takes me tugging on a pair of jeans and putting away my half-stiff cock before their eyes land on my face. They're disappointed the festivities are over, but they also know they have no say around here.

With things oddly fucking complicated for Dimitri, we've spent the last couple of weeks shacked up at his family's compound. Drugs are running rife, and whores are in abundance, yet I still can't kick them out like I only rate their value by how well they ride my cock. My ma raised me right. Even with it being her fault, she'd roll in her grave if she caught sight of the revolving door of women in my life.

I lost a part of who I was when she died. I was two years into my second stint in juvie when I received a letter from her. Although that was nine years ago, I still recall every word she wrote.

*To my sweet baby boy,*

*I'm sorry I cannot do this in person. The doctor's diagnosis took me by surprise. I wasn't expecting everything to happen so quickly. I thought it was just a headache, but by the time my vision started blurring, I had left it too long.*

*My time on this earth with Finlay and you is being cut short, but I will carry with me many cherished memories. Not all of them were good, but every one of them that included you was perfect.*

*I'm sorry for not hearing your cries sooner and letting that monster hurt you the way he did. It was my job as your mother to protect you and Finlay. I failed, and this is my punishment for that.*

*My brain tumor is inoperable. The doctors are unsure how much time I have left. It could be days, or it could be weeks. They're truly unsure. I can only hope by the time you read this, I am already at my final resting place. You've experienced enough pain. I do not want to cause you more.*

*I love you, my dear, sweet boy.*

*Forever and a day.*

*Ma. xx*

When my glossed-over eyes read the last words of my mother, I leaped to my feet and raced for the guard's hall. She had signed her letter three weeks earlier, so I was confused as to why it took so long to reach me.

My brutal speed slowed when my eyes locked in on a pair of remorseful blue eyes. Dimitri was standing behind a partition in the reception area. He was wearing a black suit, and his usually unruly hair was parted and gelled down. Ophelia was standing at his side. Her dress was also black.

"No," I whispered with a shake of my head, denying the obvious. "She wouldn't have left like this." I tossed her letter to the floor like it wasn't dotted with the tears of a woman who loved her children with everything she had. "She wouldn't have left *us* like this!" I thrust my hand to a door like Finlay was standing on the other side.

"She made me promise," Dimitri muttered, his voice cracking halfway through his comment. "She wouldn't let me take care of Finlay until your grandma arrived if I didn't promise. She would have gone into foster care, Rocco, so I did what I thought you would have wanted me to do."

Even now, it kills me to admit that Dimitri did the right thing. I would have killed him if he knowingly let Finlay go into foster care. That's what fucked with my father's head, so it's the last place I wanted my baby sister to be raised.

Regretfully, the only other option wasn't much better.

I thought my mother picked the wrong man to marry. In reality, she followed in her mother's footsteps. They say abuse follows a pattern. They fail to mention women raised in abusive situations often find themselves in abusive situations. My ma was stronger than her mother, but the cycle recommenced after her death. I was three months shy of my eighteenth birthday when Ma died. Since I was also doing a second stint in juvie, I wasn't eligible to adopt Finlay. My father's parents didn't want her—*thank fuck*—and we have no known aunts and uncles, so they shipped Finlay to live with my grandparents in Seattle.

With my grandfather passing away before Finlay was born, I was disappointed with the judge's order but hopeful it would give Finlay the fresh start she needed.

I was so fucking wrong.

Like all orphans, Finlay went off the rails. She mixed with the wrong crowd, got knocked up at sixteen, then tried to hide the bruises her punk-ass boyfriend left over her face and body when I visited her in the hospital. He beat her so badly, she miscarried, hence her hospital stay.

Finlay told me I didn't need to take care of it, that she had a 'handle' on things. Did I listen? Fuck, no. The fucker stupid enough to touch her is fish food at the bottom of the ocean, and his murder saw me going away for a third stint in lockup.

A lack of body, evidence, and witnesses meant I could have avoided conviction that time around. We only mixed things up when the Governor of Mafia Law let slip on the massive operation occurring behind prison bars. Ezra wasn't talking about a million-dollar empire. It was in the billions, and it presented the perfect opportunity for me to get Dimitri out of his father's clutch.

People often believe drugs, whores, and money dominate the underworld. That isn't true. It's all about power. The more you have, the higher up the totem pole you are.

My first year at Wallens Ridge State Penitentiary took Dimitri off the bottom rung and placed him at the very top. His father couldn't shit on him anymore, and his enemies saw him more as an equal instead of a target.

Then it all came tumbling down.

With my thoughts too murky to keep a rational head, I throw on a shirt, then head out to grab something to eat. As I weave through the dark corridors of the Petretti compound, I recall how the attorney assigned to my case when I killed my father wanted me to plead out.

She said I could get a lesser charge than murder if I were upfront with the judge as to why I killed my father. I told her I'd rather rot in jail for eternity than let that happen. If my best friend didn't know about my shame, you can be assured as fuck I wasn't going to share it with a stiff in a suit.

I also promised Ophelia I'd take her secret to the grave. I couldn't exactly do that if I said I killed my father solely on her word. That wouldn't make any sense unless I bared her as a sexual abuse sufferer. I wasn't going to do that even if my sentence had been death by lethal injection. Fortunately for me, it was seven years with the eligibility for parole when I turned eighteen.

My pace slows when I reach a familiar-looking door. It's the room Ophelia snuck in almost every night before my arrest. It's no longer filled with boyish crap teenage boys thought was the shit back in the day. It's brimming with perfume bottles, makeup, and slutty outfits I'm shocked as fuck Ophelia got away with.

Before I killed my father, Dimi and I rarely fought. We threw the occasional punch and said shit we didn't mean, but it was good-natured more than it was to maim.

The same can't be said for the day I was sentenced. He wasn't pissed I had refused his numerous offers to get me off my charges with a slap on the wrist, he was up in arms about my request for him to move Ophelia into my room. He took things in entirely the wrong manner when I asked him if he'd rather her sleeping in the room next to him or sneaking into one of their father's goons' rooms like she had mine every night for the prior three months.

He pinned me to the wall by my throat like the bailiff wasn't whacking his baton into his back. I don't know what he saw in my eyes when he was choking me to death. To this day, I assume it was my wordless pledge that I had kept my hands to myself, but I can't be sure.

Things were awkward for us when I left juvie for the second time. Ophelia was almost of age and more touchy-feely than she had ever been when she snuck into my room, and her father's quirks were growing weirder by the day.

Col had always been a little fucked in the head, but it grew worse when his brother killed himself. He's a man of many secrets. I have a feeling not even another decade-long investigation will have Dimitri unearthing them all.

He still doesn't know what happened to Ophelia. As far as he is aware, she died in a car accident six years ago. Up until two and a half years ago, I believed the same, and as fucked as this is for me to admit, I was glad she had gone on her terms instead of the way Col had planned when he believed she had betrayed him by dating a man she was supposed to be targeting.

Although Col kept the details on the down-low from anyone associated with Dimitri, it was apparent to every gangbanger in a twenty-mile radius of Hopeton that he wanted to punish Ophelia in a way no woman should ever endure, much less at the hands of her father.

Ophelia's 'death' saved her life, and it's one of the reasons I haven't told Dimitri about the time I spotted her in Seattle when I went to visit my sister. Her eyes were void of the fear they held every day since her eighth birthday. Her smile was bright, and a little boy with identical eyes and lips had his arms curled around her thigh. She appeared genuinely happy, so I snapped a sneaky picture for proof of her existence, then went on my merry way knowing one day I'd have to come clean with Dimitri.

I don't know if it's a blessing or a hindrance that he's yet to have a moment of peace long enough to share my secret with him. It's been one thing after another for him the past two years, so the last thing I want to do is add a steaming pile of shit onto his plate.

Although he'll never admit it, at the end of the day, all Dimi wanted was for Ophelia to be safe. Since she's nowhere near her father, I can confidently declare she is. Add that to the fact I promised Ophelia I'd do anything she wanted when I begged her to confirm my father had molested my sister, and I find myself in quite the pickle. Dimitri is my best friend, but Ophelia helped me fix an injustice. I owe them both so much.

I stop reminiscing on the past when an accented voice sounds out of the pocket of my jeans. "If you're stalking the corridors, waiting for the blonde bimbos in your bed to leave, you'll be waiting a while."

As my dick twitches, my brow arches. "Did they continue without me?" I don't know whether to be disappointed or excited by the prospect, so my voice relays both.

Smith's—Dimitri's techy genius and all-around fucking snoop—healthy chuckle barrels out of the cell phone in my pocket. "No. They went back to sleep."

I twist my lips, unsurprised. It's my mission to deplete my bed companions of energy to the point of exhaustion. I'm glad to see a crazy few months didn't mix things up. "What the fuck am I meant to do now, Smitty?"

My tongue peeks out between my teeth when Smith murmurs, "I could think of at least one thing." Everyone thinks he's a dorky fucker who's never got his dick head wet. I know that's far from the truth. Computer nerd or not, he brings the ladies to their knees as often as I do. I've even had to compete with him on an occasion or two—not that I'd ever tell him that. "But since you've already gone down that route, you can always pay a visit to your old stomping ground with Dimitri and me."

"Dimi is going to Wallens Ridge?" I was born and raised in Hopeton, so the only other stomping grounds I have are the prisons I've been incarcerated at. Since juvie doesn't count, that only leaves one maximum-security cooperation in their wake.

My heart beats double-time when Smith hums out an agreeing murmur. I'm not just shocked by Dimitri's sudden early-morning decision, I am also stoked as fuck he's finally going to see Maddox. Neither of them will admit it, but they have a shit ton in common. There's just one noticeable difference. Maddox openly admits his feelings for his girl. He'd shout it from the rooftops if given the opportunity. He went to hell and back for Demi—*he's still there now*. Dimitri would do the same for Roxanne, but he won't tell a soul how crazy she makes him.

I can't say I blame him. Maddox's inability to shelve his emotions has seen him played time and time again by Col. He flashes Demi in his face like a neon sign, unaware Col sees the words 'don't touch' as a challenge.

Dimi helped them as much as he could, but when it became apparent his assistance was behind his daughter being torn from his grasp for an agonizing six months, he yanked back funding.

Oh, did I forget to mention that part? I didn't keep quiet about Ophelia's resurrection because I'm a cunt who loves meddling in other people's business. It was because I was tossed out on my ass when I told Dimitri I wasn't just smelling a rat about being paroled after only three years for manslaughter. His new 'girl' was wafting up a stink.

Don't misread me. Audrey seemed as sweet as pie. She had the red hair Dimitri loves and drove him fucking nuts when she refused a single advance. It was the fact she changed her mind so fast that caught my attention. She went from telling Dimitri she was engaged with the hope it would get her off his radar to getting knocked up with his kid and marrying him in under a month.

Dimitri may have a magic cock, but I've got one of them too, and not once has it worked a spell that fast before.

I smelled a rat, and all the stench was coming from Dimitri's gushing new bride.

When Dimitri didn't listen to me, which isn't unusual—he doesn't listen to anyone—I pulled back on the reins and told him to have a great life. It was my inability to realize a lack of parental influence in his childhood was behind his decision that commenced his downfall.

My step back saw Dimitri undertaking his own. He didn't just step away from our friendship at the request of his wife, though. He pulled back from everyone. Smith was new to our duo, so he took it less harshly than me. He called Dimitri a few names, packed up his things, and went back to his corporate position where he crunched numbers for fat fuckers in three-thousand-dollar suits. The rest of his crew were either recruited by Dimitri's father or demoted to positions within Dimitri's multiple businesses. He was still making money, plenty to live off, but his wish to overtake his father had been placed on the back-burner.

He had given up, and I wasn't ashamed to tell him precisely what I thought about it. If he had kept fighting the good fight, Ophelia wouldn't have needed to hide, and he wouldn't have had to keep his wife and daughter locked up like prisoners to ensure their safety.

You can imagine how a hothead like Dimitri reacted to my vicious tongue. We had more than words that day. Everything was laid out for the world to see, including my admission that I had taken his sister's virginity to ensure it couldn't be sold.

Dimi didn't give me the chance to explain how Ophelia begged me to help her before she reminded me of the silent promise I made when I pleaded for her to tell me the truth about my father. She had heard rumors circulating amongst Col's men, and she was desperate to rid herself of the one thing her father could use against her.

Because I had heard the same, I agreed to her request. I don't know how Dimitri missed the gossip about me messing the sheets with his sister. It circulated throughout the Petretti compound like a wildfire, and it had the outcome Ophelia was aiming for.

Col spat at her feet, then he put a bounty on my head. As far as I'm aware, it's still there today. No fucker has been stupid enough to attempt to cash it in yet, although I'm sure Dimitri will if he ever discovers the number of times Ophelia and I fooled around after I claimed her virginity. We had a natural sexual connection that only faced an intermission when she shacked up with some smart fuck at a university a couple of miles from here. She still snuck into my room almost every night she was home. We just kept things friendly—a hard fucking feat for a man as sexually promiscuous as me—but I did it for Ophelia because for once, she seemed truly happy.

A rarity in this industry.

I wasn't born into the cartel like Dimitri, but I've been around it long enough to know all the ins and outs—although I never anticipated Dimitri's wife to be kidnapped and his daughter to be ripped out of her stomach in a botched home birth situation.

That was a new type of low, and it's had everyone scrambling ever since.

I'll never be a mind reader, but I'm reasonably sure Fien, Dimitri's now almost two-year-old still-missing daughter, is the reason behind his visit to Wallens Ridge this morning. All the information we've been hit with the past couple of years has had us chasing our tails, but even mangy mutts eventually reap the benefits of perseverance.

You've just got to keep moving.

After digging my phone out of my pocket so I can have a conversation like a normal person, I ask Smith, "Who's driving?" When he groans, I smile. "I'll meet you out front in five."

## 2

───────

# CLAUDIA

My cellmate is jarred awake by Officer Black shining a flashlight into her face. He gives O'Doyle a couple of seconds to roll over and face the wall before he commands for my cell door to be opened. "Open doors for cell D4284."

His voice is husky, but unfortunately, his breathless state barely dims the number of heated breaths that hit my nape when he leans in to unlock the shackles wrapped around my wrists. The scent of his breath makes me sick to my stomach in general, but when it's added to the taste of his cum in my mouth, you've got me seconds from barfing.

Officer Black thinks he has everyone fooled, but even the inmates who fried their brains with drugs during their youth know he doesn't volunteer for the suicide watch posts for no reason. Not only does his station give him the right to strip search each of his victims as she enters and exits the isolation cells the suicide watches take place in, but he's also left alone with them for up to three hours at a time.

He's supposed to talk them out of self-harming themselves. Our time together once a month for the past seven months has me wanting to do the opposite. It wouldn't be a consideration if every decision I make were solely about me. I have a little boy to think about, a eight-month-old baby boy who I didn't get the chance to name before he was ripped away from me and handed to my mother-in-law as if he was my atonement for killing her son.

Neither of us would be in hell if it weren't for her. Juana Sánchez isn't a caring mother who raised her sons with morals. After a 'rival' killed her husband, she became the head of the Mexican Cartel. She raised her sons in a violent, bloody world with no real grasp of reality. They're a menace to society who take what they want without asking and issue no apologies.

I thought Juan was different from his brothers. He was always the politer one of the quartet, and he used his manners as if his mother had raised him right.

It only took three weeks for him to remove his cloak. By then, it was too late for me to get out. According to his mother, I was his property.

He owned me.

I'm not ashamed to admit I fought a good battle for the first eighteen months. The beatings hurt, but since they were the consequence of me refusing to 'serve' certain high-up members of the Sánchez entity, I tolerated them. Besides, my father hit my mother in front of me, so I thought it was part of a normal relationship.

I could have put up with the abuse for longer if I remained the only one being hurt in the process. Everything changed when I discovered I was pregnant. Juana spotted numerous indicators of my stowaway before me—the expanding of my chest and my increase in appetite. She watched me like a hawk when I peed on the test she'd purchased for me in her master bathroom.

She was so chuffed by the positive result, she told Juan before I had the chance. I should have been mad at her, but all I felt was relief. She didn't simply order Juan and me to get married, she also instructed Juan to keep his hands to himself until her grandson was born.

I didn't have the gall to ask what would happen if our baby was a girl. Juana learned early in her reign how fierce she had to be to gain respect from her peers. Beheading an entire family was a quiet day for her. She was merciless, but at that stage in my life, my only life raft.

Juan adored his mother. He'd rather disappoint me than upset her. That's why he became clever with his assaults. He rarely struck me in the face, and when the temptation became too much for him to bear, he hired a professional makeup artist to hide his slip-ups before we went anywhere near his mother.

He thought he had it all figured out, but then I got a little teary-eyed at the baby shower Juana organized for our son. Forever the doting grandma-to-be when we were in public, Juana wiped away the salty blobs like I was a child incapable of taking care of them myself. She didn't bat an eyelid when her first wipe had her stumbling onto a mottling of bruises under my right eye. She merely spun to face the procession of people hanging off her every word, made a joke about how my mascara was clearly not waterproof, then told them she'd be right back after taking care of me.

That's when panic truly set in.

Juana doesn't take care of people the way normal, everyday civilians do. Anytime she had said that in front of me, the people she was talking to were never seen again.

There was only one way I was getting out of that situation alive, and I milked it for all it was worth. "Look, he's kicking," I said after grabbing Juana's hand and placing it on my swollen stomach. "He must have recognized your voice."

Rumors were that Juana was so determined that my child be a boy because she had given birth to a stillborn son almost a decade earlier. She tried to conceive again, but with both her age and suitors against her, she never achieved her dream. Instead, she shifted her focus onto her sons. She had four grandchildren by then, but since all of them were girls, they weren't the replacement child she was seeking.

"We're so close, Juana. We're almost there," I stammered out, saying anything to get her on my side once more.

"Yes, we are," she replied.

Neither her words nor her eyes were for me.

They were for my unborn son.

It was in that instant I realized my child would never be mine. I'd give birth to him, and he would have my DNA, but he was always going to be Juana's son.

The recollection of that is why I ran when Juana left me in the kitchen to wait for Juan to come collect me. While she went to tell my guests I'd been hit with a sudden bout of tiredness, I bolted out of the restaurant like I could make it back to my hometown of Ravenshoe without incident.

I almost made it home. Max, the Doberman puppy one of Juana's goons gifted me when they found out I was pregnant, and I was on the outskirts of Hopeton when a highway patrolman pulled me over. Max wasn't happy about his presence. He had a knack for knowing who I should and shouldn't trust. He wasn't a fan of the officer, and his unhidden growls to announce his dislike saw the officer writing me up for a heap of false citations.

Only once he had me convinced matters couldn't possibly get any worse did he request that Max and I exit my vehicle so they could tow it.

"I just purchased this car. It has a safety certificate," I huffed out in frustration when he told me we either walk the last mile to Hopeton or be arrested.

Confident his ruse was nothing more than a money-grabbing scam, I gathered up my handbag, suitcase, and the baby seat I packed in a hurry, clipped on Max's lead, then exited my vehicle.

We didn't even make it two steps away from my car when the truth smacked into me. The patrolman's SUV hid Juan's low-riding sports car. He had found me, and I knew precisely what that meant for Max and me.

We were dead.

I'm sure the motorists eyeballing me on the freeway found my seven-month pregnant sprint to get away from Juan hilarious, but I hope their opinion changed when he tackled me to the ground, unconcerned that our combined weight was squashing our unborn child into the rocky bedding on the side of the road.

Even Max couldn't hold back his annoyance that time around. The usually placid puppy turned into a sadist killing machine. He gnawed on Juan's ankles before he used the firmness of his bite to drag him off me.

He would have saved me that day if it weren't for the police officer. He whacked his baton into Max's back so fiercely, when Juan lifted me from the ground by a brutal clutch of my hair, I thought Max was dead. He laid perfectly still, unmoving, and seemingly unbreathing, so you can imagine my shock when I saw him three days ago, right outside these prison walls. He was healthy and alive, and his miraculous recovery assured me I'll make it out of here in one piece.

I just have to remain vigilant.

The facial expression of the dark-haired woman who begged me to stay away from Max exposed things aren't perfect outside prison walls, but I doubt matters could get any worse. The numerous faces I took in when marched to Juan's car like a prison escapee were confronting, but not a single person came to my aid. They watched Juan forcefully place me into the passenger seat of his BMW M5, then scrutinized his walk to the officer to thank him for his help with a bundle of greenbacks.

It's from there that things get a little hazy for me. I remember maneuvering myself behind the steering wheel, and that my struggle to find the keyless start button gave Juan enough time to dive into the passenger seat before I took off like a bat out of hell, but I don't recall our accident, nor the words Juan shouted at me leading up to it. I didn't even realize he was dead until I woke up cuffed to a hospital bed with Juana standing over me.

If she could have cut my son out of my stomach then and there, she would have. Thankfully, our exchange occurred in front of a nurse, a doctor, two prison officers, *and* my roommate. A petite blonde with ruddy lips was cuffed to the bed next to me. She appeared to be asleep, but for some reason, her presence had Juana acting as if she was a regal princess. Her eyes continually strayed to the blonde while she whispered how I'd pay for killing her son and that she would do it slowly and painfully, starting with my unborn child.

There was a gleam in her eyes that announced she wouldn't kill my son. I just wish it could have been seen without the humiliating blaze her children's eyes are never without.

Juan and I weren't close. He barely spoke to me as it was, so there was no way he'd confide in me the reason for the pain in his eyes, but we women are intuitive beings, and that intuitiveness doubles when you become a mother.

Something was off with the way Juan was raised. All Juana's sons are extremely chummy with her, but Juan's relationship was by far the oddest. Even as an adult, he rested his head on his mother's lap while watching television. She would rake her fingers through his hair and whisper things in his ear that made him laugh. I was uncomfortable watching their exchanges, but since the focus was off me, I never said anything.

Over time, it became the norm. Everyone was so accustomed to it and paid it no attention. I can only hope I get out of here long before JJ—Juan Junior as named by Juana—is subjected to the same thing. I've been working with the only lawyer willing to back my case pro-bono and doing all the necessary steps to improve my chance of being paroled at my first parole hearing scheduled for three years from now.

I'm still worried, though. O'Doyle doesn't act ignorant solely to be in Officer Black's good books. She reports back every move I make to Juana. She's a snitch, but since I need to be on my best behavior, there isn't a single thing I can do about it.

The anger bubbling in my veins gets a boost when the freeing of my ankles from the shackles sees Officer Black's hand sliding up my thigh. The long crotch in my jumpsuit ensures he won't get near my private parts, but he isn't touching me to warn me what will happen if I snitch about our one-on-one isolation sessions, he's making sure I remember that I am sans panties.

He took them during my first strip search, and no matter how many times I told the second officer who walked me out of the isolation cells that I had underwear on when I arrived, he acted as if I never spoke. I was only given four pairs of panties when I was sentenced. Now I'm down to the final pair. I could get more, but they'll cost me more than I'm willing to give.

I suck Officer Black's dick so I can eat.

He can keep the rest of his bargaining chips.

"Close cell D4284's door," Officer Black commands a second after shoving me into my cell.

"Cell D4284 door is closed," responds the person in control of the electronic locks.

I wait for Officer Black to whisper his usual, "Sleep well, ladies," before I bolt for the vanity sink squashed above a lidless toilet.

After snatching up the toothpaste and toothbrush, I squeeze a generous dollop of minty goop onto the scrubbed-smooth bristles.

"Shut up," I warn O'Doyle before a single snicker can leave her mouth. "Or I'll hand your meal pass onto someone else."

That shuts her up real fast. She doesn't have access to the perks I do. Not just because she has man's hands that give the guards a complex that they've entered the wrong half of the population at Wallens Ridge State Penitentiary, but because her name also isn't O'Doyle. She's called that because she looks like the O'Doyle characters from *Billy Maddison*.

She's a bully like them too. I'd feel sorry for her if she weren't such a bitch. Since she is, I remember the pledge I made when JJ was raced out of here with no chance of a cuddle. No one comes before him. Not even me.

# 3

## ROCCO

*A* grin tugs my lips high when Smith mumbles his frustration about Dimitri's poor driving skills in between strokes of his beloved keyboard. Dimitri was driving years before he had his permit, but he never got a handle on the rust buckets Smith likes to get around in. He tries to shave corrosion off the gearstick chamber every time he changes gears. It drives Smith batty, which has me wondering if that's why Dimitri does it.

Dimitri isn't close to the man he was before he met Audrey, but I've seen snippets of him resurrecting the past year. His girl has been good for him. He just needs to pull his finger out of his ass and acknowledge that before it's too late.

Roxanne reminds me a lot of my mother. She brings fairness into a game that's rarely fair and doesn't take shit from anyone while doing it. I did real fucking good when I forced her back into Dimitri's life a couple of months back. He'll thank me one day. I don't see it occurring while pulling into the dusty lot of a maximum-security prison, though.

While Dimi grinds his way from third to second, I suck in the smell of money, corruption, and the desperateness of the fuckers willing to do anything to get it.

It's the equivalent of coming home to fresh sheets on your bed after an all-night orgy.

Pure.

Fucking.

Heaven.

My grin doubles when Dimitri stalls us to a stop. "You need to update this piece of shit. Your laptops are more valuable than the junk you're carting them around in."

Smith makes a 'duh' face while I give a reason for his scroungy ways. "That's the idea, D. Who'd suspect a rusty van would be holding half a million dollars' worth of equipment?"

If the arching of Smith's brow is any sign, I undercut the value of the equipment in his van by a trillion. I'm not shocked. Name one computer nerd with millions in the bank, but only a startup laptop. Not fucking happening. Smith has the finest equipment money can buy, and since most of it is used to search for Fien, Dimitri paid for it.

Since he's slowly learning to back away from fights he won't win, Dimitri climbs out of the driver's seat of Smith's van without a word escaping his mouth. I work my jaw side to side when his clamber is chased by three red dots lighting up his chest. The guards at Wallens Ridge won't kill him—they might be paid a pittance and have shit for brains, but they're not completely brainless—but I don't see Dimi being too kind to their off-hand shake-up. Even hundreds of miles from home, he has highly distinguishable features. If you don't know what they are, it will only take one introduction to learn otherwise. That's why Audrey's shock about his involvement in the underworld made no sense. Cartel leaders are known across the globe. Dimi may stand next to his father instead of in front of him, but everyone except Col knows who's really running the show around here.

In case you're as slow-clicking as these guards, it ain't Col.

Dimitri's jaw works through the same stiffness mine did when the annoying-as-fuck voice of Warden Mattue crackles out of the speakers hanging above our heads. He makes a show out of announcing to his officers to lower their weapons, but I can hear the shit-stirring timbre in his tone. My voice is rarely without it, so you can be assured I'll never mistake it.

"Here he comes, Mr. Ass Kisser himself," I mutter under my breath when Warden Mattue races across the parking lot like his stubby thighs aren't rubbing together with every stride he takes.

"Dimitri, good morning." He thrusts his hand Dimitri's way, revealing its brutal shake. "To what do we owe the pleasure?"

I snicker like a prick with no morals when Dimitri leaves his greeting unanswered. Instead, he slants his head, cocks a brow, then asks, "Do I need a reason to visit?"

"No, n-not at all. We're pleased to have you," Warden Mattue stammers out as the fear encroaching him from all angles flares my nostrils.

He wasn't the warden during my incarceration. I had an old guy with a silver mustache and a poor attitude. Last I heard, he was having a much-needed break in Miami. He may have even floated as far as Cuba by now.

When Warden Mattue gestures for Dimitri to enter the prison before him, Dimi snaps his eyes to Smith.

"One sec..." Smith chews on the corner of his lower lip while tapping out his frustration on a silicon keyboard stuck to the hood of his van. Within a handful of keystrokes, the parking lot at the front of Wallens Ridge plunges into darkness. Smith tries to hide his shit-eating grin before returning Dimitri's stare. He shouldn't have bothered. His efforts are woeful. "Okay, you're good to go."

Dimitri gives him a head bob of appreciation before shifting on his feet to face Warden Mattue to give him one final threat. "We wouldn't want news of my visit getting out, would we?"

"Not at all," Warden Mattue repeats, his voice exposing he's on the verge of peeing his pants.

We barely get two steps away from Smith's van when a witch from Dimitri's past flies in on her broom. Theresa Veneto thinks the badge on her hip makes her invincible. She's dead fucking wrong. I can hear Dimitri's head ticking over a million miles an hour as he strives to hold back the urge to pop a bullet between her brows. He's short-tempered with women as it is, but Theresa knows how to push all his buttons. I'm shocked she's lasted as long as she has. Perhaps some of my can't-hurt-women neurosis has rubbed off on Dimitri. Or perhaps he's willing to alter the rules now he's a father to a little lady. He'd fall on a knife before he would let anything happen to Fien, and he hasn't even laid eyes on her in person yet.

Theresa's slanted eyes snap to mine when I mutter, "I thought only vampires roamed the planet at dusk. Who knew witches got around, too? Do you fly above the houses to avoid collisions with your sister witches, or do you prefer the sewer network?"

Theresa was part of Ravenshoe PD before she up and left town a couple of years back. Although she kept the news of her transfer on the down-low, Smith kept Dimitri up to date on how Theresa was run out of town by none other than Isaac Holt—the very man Ophelia was dating when she 'died.' Isaac's ability to see through Theresa's bullshit had me wondering if Ophelia could have stuck around, then I found out Theresa joined the FBI specifically to take down Isaac, so I stepped back from that notion. Hell has no fury like a woman scorned, and Theresa has been scorned more than once.

Like I need more proof Theresa is a snake in designer threads, she hisses at me. That's as far as her rile goes, though. She's too busy defending herself against Dimitri's claims she's here to conceal all the shady shit she does on behalf of Col. "Cover what tracks, Dimi?"

Dimitri looks close to blowing his top, but he keeps his annoyance under wraps. "Oh, I don't know. How about putting a man away for a murder he didn't commit? Or falsifying police records to conjure up a fake victim? Then we also have the fact you left an unstable woman to defend for herself."

Like a woman who has no clue about the number of times Dimitri has fantasized about slitting her throat, Theresa steps closer to him. "The fact your focus centers around me shows how far off the mark you are. I was merely upholding my end of our agreement."

"*Our* agreement?" Dimitri asks, as interested in the honesty in her eyes as me.

Dimi said he cut ties with her years ago, so why the fuck is she acting as if they rolled in the sheets last week?

"You're a Petretti, aren't you?" When she attempts to thrust a pile of paperwork into Dimitri's chest, Smith snatches them out of her grasp. It frustrates Theresa to no end, but she keeps her annoyance out of her voice while advising that they're transcripts of conversations she had with Dimitri's father. "Their seal should prove their legitimacy, but in case they don't, I forwarded links to the original files to your email."

Smith does some fancy shit on his laptop before he backs up Theresa's claims. "Imagery is shit, but the audio is first-class. Your father approached Theresa." He waits a beat before pushing on, "He didn't want Megan killed. He had her admitted for a psych workup. That kept her under lock and key for over a year."

Megan is the girl Maddox took a row for. He was set to do a seven-year stint but lucked out when the judge chose to make an example out of him. That sees him facing a lifetime behind bars.

Well, until Dimitri makes him an offer too good to refuse.

Proceedings were delayed because Dimitri was pissed as fuck when a little birdie whispered in his ear that the relocation of his daughter to another country and Maddox's confrontation with his father occurred too simultaneously for it to be a coincidence.

I don't know who that birdie was, but I wanted to snap its fucking neck. Maddox might be a little gung-ho when it comes to his girl, but Demi is a Petretti, so she should be protected accordingly. Furthermore, I can't be guaranteed the same shit Ophelia went through isn't happening to Demi. It's why I've kept an eye on her the past couple of years. Col feeds off fear, so when his daughter, who happened to fear him more than anyone, 'died,' he needed a new target. An orphaned niece seemed like his ideal candidate.

It wouldn't have taken me so long to convince Dimitri to seek a third opinion if Maddox hadn't already used his daughter to get Dimitri on his side. It lowered Dimitri's trust, and when you're out of his good books, you are pretty much dead to him.

I only clawed my way back because I wouldn't take no for an

answer. When I heard what had happened and saw the footage of Fien being cut out of Audrey's stomach in an unsterile room by jacked-up goons who didn't give a fuck about her safety, I was going to be a part of the operation to find her no matter what Dimitri's ruling was. Unsurprisingly, he was in a world of hurt, so he welcomed me with open arms. Which, in case you're wondering, is the equivalent of him only issuing one threat of death.

Everyone has a price, and from what Ezra exposed to Dimitri the past couple of nights, Maddox's could very well be out of his reach, but he'd be a fool not to try.

Ezra believes Maddox holds the key to unlocking Col's biggest and darkest secret. It's the reason Col was so eager to get him locked up for so long. Although the rules state Ezra can't tell Dimitri what the secret is, he can push him in the right direction. He's been nudging Dimitri this way for months, and I'm so fucking relieved he finally listened.

Don't misconstrue. At the moment, Maddox is where he needs to be. I don't believe he deserves to be locked away for life for a crime he supposedly didn't commit. But if he is the reason Dimitri lost contact with his daughter for six months, a twelve-month stint in a maximum-security prison is a far better punishment than how Dimitri would usually respond.

When it comes to Fien, nothing is off-limits.

Just uttering her name in the wrong manner will get you killed.

My thoughts shift back to the task at hand when Dimitri seeks answers for his father's weirdness. "Why? What possible benefit would my father get from keeping her alive? Why wouldn't he just kill her?"

Assuming his questions are for her, Theresa shrugs. "I didn't ask questions. That isn't the way I operate."

"That's right. I forgot the only time you exert any kind of normalcy is when you're flat on your back being served a healthy dose of dick." I would have spat my drink if I had one. Dimitri isn't overly good with the one-liners, but when he brings his wit out to play, you're guaranteed a fun-filled morning. "Is that why you keep showing up? Does the big gaping hole between your legs still need filling?"

Theresa tries real fucking hard to act unaffected by Dimitri's scorn, but the briefest trek of his finger up her forearm undoes her ruse. *If her nipples bud anymore, I'll have to check Dimitri for a fatal chest wound.*

When Dimitri mocks her inability to deny him with a chuckle, Theresa huffs before folding her arms in front of her chest, mercifully hiding her puckered nipples. *I was close to barfing. Theresa is attractive, but I can sniff out a psychopath from a mile out. She has the scent of a bat-shit crazy woman.* "I'm here to cash in the favor your father is refusing to bequeath."

Dimitri *tsks* her. "As I've told you before, if your favor was issued by my father, he's the only one who can grant it."

I have to wipe Theresa's spit from my cheek when she shouts, "He's refusing!"

"And how is that my problem?" Dimitri snaps back. His tone is brimming with anger, but there's a touch of amusement behind it.

"Because everyone knows you clean up your father's messes. It's what you do! You've done it for years."

*Although I'll never have any respect for Theresa, I can admit she hit the nail on the head with her statement.*

"For clients I deem worthy. Dried-up old hags who should have gotten out of the game years ago don't count." *Smith and I hiss in sync when Theresa attempts to slap the disdain off Dimitri's face.* He catches her hand before it gets close to his cheek, then he uses it to bring her to within an inch of his flaming-with-anger face. "You might have Isaac on the back foot with your tricks, but I don't play by those rules. When you are no longer of use in this industry, you're as good as dead."

"Are you threatening me?"

*Yes, ma'am, he is,* I'm tempted to reply, but before I can, Dimitri croons out in a smooth, unyielding tone, "No, baby. If I were threatening you, you'd already be on your knees, saying your final farewell." He curls his hand around her face, his grip deadly, before adding, "Now get the fuck out of my face before I send Clover over for a visit. He's been waiting years to mess up that pretty little face of yours."

He pushes her away from him, grinning when she stumbles in her stilettos. While straightening her blouse, Theresa bounces her eyes between Dimitri, Smith, and me. She looks like she wants to keep pushing but bows out of a fight she'll never win before blood is drawn. "This won't be the last of this," she warns before she darts to her Bureau-issued car at the far end of the lot.

She's barely slipped behind the driver's wheel when I begin to wonder if we're in a mafia remake of the movie *Ghosts of Girlfriends Past* with Matthew McConaughey. Theresa's taillights have barely dimmed from her removing her foot off the brake when Dimitri is confronted for a second time. Since this interrupter has done wonders for Dimitri's personality the past couple of months, I sit back and let her work her magic. Roxanne knows how to push Dimitri's buttons, but she does it to help him, not maim him. She's the first person in his life to do that.

Roxie's brisk strides falter when Dimitri issues a threat to Warden Mattue I know he'll execute if it isn't immediately followed. "If I find out your guards' fingers got within an inch of their triggers, I'll gut you where you stand."

Warden Mattue's throat works hard to swallow when he takes in the red dots highlighting Roxanne's chest. He flaps his arms around like a beheaded chicken, wordlessly demanding for his men to stand down, but it does little to dampen the anger lining Dimitri's face. He's pissed as fuck. I can't say I blame him. He put a very impressive thirty million dollars on the line to ensure Roxanne's safety. I already knew she was 'it' for him, but his response to a bounty being placed on Roxie's head all but sealed the deal for me.

"Go!" Dimitri roars out in a brittle tone. When Warden Mattue ignores his directive, it takes everything Dimitri has not to add his fists into their conversation. "Go!"

If he's holding back for Roxanne's benefit, he shouldn't bother. I've noticed the way the vein in her neck throbs extra hard when he's being an ass. Why the fuck do you think I goaded him so much at the start of their relationship? They both got benefits out of it, and I got to remind Dimi that he's human.

The warden kicks up dust on his shoes when he scurries for the entrance of Wallens Ridge. Once he's far enough away we can no longer smell the fear slicking his skin, Dimi shifts on his feet to face Roxanne. If Smith's commentary yesterday afternoon is still accurate, this is the first time they've seen each other in weeks. Dimitri denied Smith's offer to rig Roxanne's grandparents' estate with surveillance. He's running off the theory it can't be hacked if it doesn't exist. Since I agree with him, I kept my mouth shut. I know he's watching Roxanne. He's just doing it from a distance.

"What are you doing here, Roxanne?"

Proof she knows Dimitri's mindset better than anyone is exposed when Roxanne says, "This isn't Smith's fault."

Even though he denied Smith's surveillance offer doesn't mean he didn't want Roxanne watched every second of every day. It was just to be done in an old-fashioned way by good old movement sheets.

With the walk of a woman who knows how to make men's dicks throb by doing something as simple as breathing, Roxanne saunters across the dusty lot. Once she stops in front of Dimitri, Smith, and me, she mutters under her breath, "Infrareds have their faults."

My brow cocks when she presses a kiss to Smith's cheek, then my lips tug into a grin when she throws her arms around my neck, doubling the murderous glint in Dimitri's narrowed eyes.

I hug her back.

*What?* Dimitri left her hanging for six weeks. He deserves a bit of riling.

After inching back, Roxanne drags her finger over the shirt clinging to my tattooed pecs. "Is this new?" she asks, her touch lingering. "I don't recall seeing it on you before. It's cute and body-hugging." She hits me with a frisky wink. "I like it."

Dimitri doesn't nibble at the bait she's waving under his nose. He attempts to wholly fucking devour it. "Get your ass in the van, Roxanne. Smith will take you home."

She spins to face Dimitri so fast, her floral perfume whips up around us. "No."

"I beg your pardon?" If the prisoners weren't already awake, they'll be bright-eyed and bushy-tailed now. That's how loud Dimitri's voice is. "I wasn't asking."

"It wouldn't make a difference if you were. You can't boss me around anymore, Dimitri." My jaw hits the floor. I knew she had gall, but I had no fucking clue she was this feisty. "You lost the chance when you abandoned me."

Dimitri steps back with a scoff. "Abandoned you? I didn't abandon you. I set you free."

Roxanne folds her arms in front of her chest, denying Dimitri's comment with a prima-donna attitude before she adds words into the mix, "In the house my uncle, aunt, and quite possibly my grandfather were murdered in, with three snipers outside the door, and shitty-ass cell reception inside it! You may as well cut off my wings."

When she pushes off her feet with a huff, Dimitri is left reeling. "Where the fuck are you going? I'm not done with you yet."

I'm about to tell him to settle it a bit when he digs his nails into Roxanne's arm, but Roxanne shrugs out of his hold before I need to. "We came here to visit my friend. Since you seem to have pull with the warden, I guess we don't have to wait for visiting hours anymore." She tosses her head to the friend Dimitri stupidly used to force Roxanne to eat before she continues on her way.

She makes it to the reception area of Wallens Ridge before Dimitri's focus shifts from her ass to me. "Go with her. Make sure she sees who she came here to see, then load her into my car."

"What car, D?" It's the fight of my life not to rile him more about the lusty rage on his face. He looks torn between wanting to strangle Roxanne's attitude with his bare hands and suffocating it with his cock. "Do you wanna drive your girl home from your first date in Smith's beat-up van?"

I make it out of our confrontation alive since he's still pissed at Smith for his earlier slip-ups. The fact Theresa handed him information he didn't already know has his hackles up, much less Roxanne's unexpected arrival. "The car Smith is going to get here A-S-A-fucking-P if he wants to keep his job."

Smith subdues the heat of Dimitri's wrath by holding his hands in the air before putting them to work. It's amazing what that guy can achieve with a keyboard and an internet connection in five minutes.

"All right." After hitting Dimitri with the same wink Roxanne bestowed upon me, I twist my torso to face the car Roxanne nudged her head at during her comment, motion for Estelle to follow me, then take off in the direction Roxanne just went.

# 4

## ROCCO

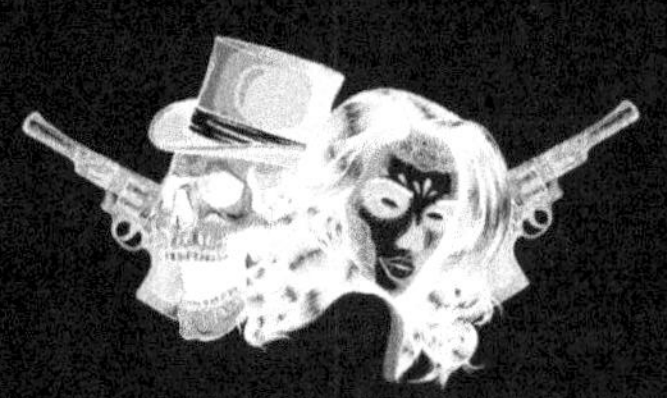

*I*'m not surprised when my entrance into Wallens Ridge has me stumbling on Warden Mattue ogling Roxanne's tits. He has to drool because he knows not in a million years would someone like Roxanne take his shriveled-up old dick between her lips. Although, if he's anything like his predecessor, he most likely wishes he could have first dibs on the female inmates. Drugs and money laundering aren't the only operations you can run out of a prison. The sex trafficking craze currently running rampant in Hopeton was founded here.

"Clearly, you didn't learn your lesson out there." I nudge my head to the parking lot where Dimitri and Smith are chatting before joining Roxanne on the non-criminal side of the reception desk. "She wasn't asking to see her friend. She's *telling* you that's what she's doing." I hear the brutal swallow of Roxanne's friend when my hand creeps around my back to brace the butt of my gun. "If you're having a hard time hearing, I can clear the blockage for you."

Warden Mattue is smarter than he looks. "N-no. That isn't neces-sary. I'll have her brought to the visiting room now."

When he picks up the receiver of a landline phone on the recep-tionist's desk, I reluctantly return my hand front and center. I'm not like Maddox. I have no hesitation shooting the stupid fuckers who think they can pull the wool over my eyes. The fact I didn't hesitate when I killed my father should clue you onto this, let alone the prolonged torture I hit Finlay's punk-ass boyfriend with. There are no judges or jurors needed for my executions because I found out a long time ago that there's no such thing as fairness.

I begged the people of the court not to let my father have visitation rights to my sister and me during my parents' custody hearing. When they ignored the cried confession of my nine-year-old self on the stand, I lashed out at my mother like my sister did on her birthday. At the time, I didn't realize what was happening wasn't her fault. She did everything right, yet the courts failed her. That's why I eventually took matters into my own hands. It was years later than it should have been, but that was more because my dad was cautious about everything he did the first couple of months of visitation. He was on his best behavior, but it didn't take long for him to fall back into his old ways.

I scrub at my jaw to loosen its tight grip when Dimitri joins Roxanne, her friend, and me in the reception area. His presence isn't solely acknowledged by Roxanne's hooded gaze, Warden Mattue gets to work on licking his boots clean with a healthy dose of ass-kissing. "Prisoner 9429 is waiting for you in my office." When Dimitri slants his head to the side, curious as to how Warden Mattue knew which prisoner he's here to see, Warden Mattue sinks like a narc weighed down with bricks. "I assumed he was who you were wanting to see, considering you've seen him once a month since his conviction."

I watch Dimitri's response when Warden Mattue thrusts a visitor's ledger under his nose. We all know Maddox's girlfriend has been the only Petretti visitor around these parts the past twelve months, but Dimitri keeps his cards close to his chest. He doesn't trust Warden Mattue, and neither the fuck do I. His ratty stench is as strong as the smell that smacked into me when I met Audrey for the first time. He's a fox in sheep's clothing, and his fleece is about to be sheared.

"You can wait here." Dimitri doesn't reach for his gun when

Warden Mattue attempts a rebuttal. He puts him in place with a vicious sneer. "Did I sound like I was asking permission?"

I stray my eyes to Roxanne when the heat of her wanton gaze scorches my ear. I think she's a kick-ass woman, and I have no doubt she is Dimitri's other half, but she needs to tone down her give-it-to-me-Dimi vibes. She's far too much like my mother and only a year older than my sister for me to appreciate her needy scent—not that I'd ever tell Dimitri that. I get great pleasure out of riling him. It keeps the adrenaline in my veins so well stocked, I only dip back to my old calming methods once a day instead of two or three times.

Drugs won't fix my issues, but it's a whole heap better than wallowing in self-pity.

After showing Dimitri the way to his office, Warden Mattue returns to the reception area to advise Roxanne the inmate she wants to visit is ready.

"I'll wait here," says Roxanne's friend, Estelle. She's still too rattled about Dimitri sending Clover over for a visit to act nonchalant about my presence.

Clover is a hired hitman. He shacked up with Dimitri's crew a couple of months after he accepted a bounty for Dimitri's head. Don't ask me how that went down. I've been dying to hear the story, but since Dimitri's every focus before Roxanne entered the picture was on his daughter, I haven't had the chance to pry it out of him.

Sympathetic to Estelle's reasoning to stay behind, Roxanne rubs her shoulder in a comforting manner before she pushes off her feet to follow the warden. I shadow their walk minus a gun in my hand. The only weapons these guards have are bribery. I can't be bribed. You need something to lose to worry about losing it. My ma is dead, my sister is far away from here studying under an alias, and the only other people I care about are capable of taking care of themselves. Even Roxanne is learning the skill, much to Dimitri's disgrace.

"Claudia, hi," Roxanne squeaks in a high-pitch tone when a prisoner in an orange jumpsuit is guided into a room a couple of spots down from the warden's office.

Claudia is shackled like her tiny frame is ten times larger than it is. Although she appears a couple of inches taller than Roxanne, they look to weigh about the same. So much so, not a snippet of orange peeks out when Roxanne wraps her up in a welcoming hug.

Some of Warden Mattue's game plan for Wallens Ridge is exposed when Roxanne's fierce clutch flattens Claudia's jumpsuit to a body I can't help but peruse more than once. She isn't wearing any panties, and although the knowledge has my dick twitching like she isn't an inmate in a maximum-security prison, it also makes me peeved as fuck. I didn't send Long John Silver to early retirement because the cooks at Wallens Ridge made the porridge too chunky for my liking. It was because he had a partiality for young, barely-of-age women.

When I saw a girl who would have only been a couple of months older than Finlay being snuck out of his office during my release with torn clothes, a tear-stained face, and a visibly absent panty line, I lost my shit.

Warden Jacobson didn't make it home from his shift that day.

Although Claudia is a little older than the inmate I defended, it wouldn't be by much. From the quickest glimpse I caught of her face before Roxanne's vibrant red curls hid it, I suspected Claudia had youth on her side. Now I have no doubts. She'd be lucky to be twenty.

Her youthful face has me confident that if I find out Warden Mattue has similar tastes to his predecessor, today's ruling will be parallel to the verdict I reached two years ago.

I hope he kissed his family goodbye this morning because it may have been for the last time.

After scanning Claudia's body for the third time, I work my jaw side to side. There's no bra outline in her jumpsuit either, which is surprising considering how high her tits sit. Their perkiness adds to my belief she's too young to be caught up in the shit Warden Mattue is running behind Dimitri's back, but before I can seek additional evidence to my theory, Dimitri's reasoning for ordering me to be Roxanne's shadow comes to light.

"I wouldn't if I were you," I warn the officer standing at my right. He was about to remind Roxanne about the no-contact rule at

Wallens Ridge, but the way his hand hovered over his baton exposes he had no intention to use words. "I just got these shoes. I don't want them splattered with your blood, but I'm willing to face the injustice if it's the only way I can get my point across."

He swallows before shooting his eyes to mine. "R-Rocco. Heyyy," he croons like I should know him by name as well.

I don't and I'm more than happy for him to know it.

After slapping away the hand he's holding out in greeting with enough force to give him the hint I'm not his '*brotha*,' I growl out, "Step the fuck back and let them do their thing."

I shove him in the chest firm enough, the rustle of his movements gains me the attention of a pair of blue eyes. In case you're wondering, Roxanne's eyes are green like mine.

With her chest rising and falling in rhythm to mine, Claudia darts her eyes between my face and the tattooed hand I'm pinning the unnamed guard to the wall with. She watches me for several long seconds, giving me plenty of time to drink in all the features of her ball-clenching face before she shuffles toward the table at a third guard's request in preparation to be shackled.

"Let her be," I demand when her hidden watch has me experiencing that weird sensation soft cocks say they feel in their heart, but real men admit is closer to their balls.

There's not much of her to see in the bright orange getup she's forced to wear, and her eyes are holding a whole fucking heap of pain that should detract from her allure, but there's no doubt she's attractive. She has meaty lips, a flawlessly perfect face, and a stare that has me forgetting we're with company.

Regretfully, my watchful stare doesn't award her the same level of comfort. Even with Roxanne fussing over her like she's lost as much weight as her the past six weeks, she forever drifts her wary eyes between the guards circling her. I'm unsure if she's seeking answers from them for Roxanne's bombardment of questions or needing constant reassurance that they're sticking to their side of the room. It could be a combination of both.

Needing confirmation, I pull out the chair next to Roxanne, drag it back until it sits halfway between the guards and the table the girls are chatting around, then take a seat. To make sure I get my point across, I balance my elbows onto my knees. It looks like I'm eavesdropping on the girls' conversation. In reality, I'm making sure the guards see my beloved anodized gold Desert Eagle pistol. It's a big heavy gun that the girls love authenticating its impressive weight with their hands.

They do the same with my cock.

My gun has magical powers with the guards too. It has them backing away like I told them Roxanne and Claudia have the clap. They stop eyeballing them like thirsty motherfuckers who have never had their dicks sucked. Instead, they do their fucking job.

Who would have thought that was so hard for them to do to begin with? All they do is hang around all day pretending they don't belong in the pond with the rest of the criminals. You don't need a degree to do that. You don't even need a brain.

Within minutes of losing the officers' watch, Claudia stops fiddling with a button in her jumpsuit. Instead, she assures Roxanne that she's eating well before solemnly shaking her head to Roxanne's question on if she's had any updates on JJ yet.

*Who the fuck is JJ?*

Considering we've only just met, it's fucked for me to say he better not be her boyfriend, so I'll keep my mouth shut. Jealousy isn't a go-to emotion of mine. I know what it is—I use it against Dimitri far too often to pretend I don't—but it's never bothered me before today.

*It's Dimitri and Roxanne's reunion fucking with your head,* I try to convince myself. *Besides, she's far too young for you and locked up. How far are you expecting to get, fuckface?*

Pissed at both my inner monologue and the undeniable scent of a woman in fear, I convert back to a coping mechanism I always use when I'm feeling snowed under.

I prepare for bloodshed.

"Is it just the warden fucking with you? Or are the guards in on it too?"

**5**

---

# CLAUDIA

s Roxanne's eyes snap to the unnamed gentleman sitting wedged between Officer Black and me, my throat dries like a desert. The man with colorful tattoos peeking out of multiple areas of his dress shirt rolled up to the sleeves hasn't spoken a word to me, yet he seems to know all my deepest darkest secrets.

*How is that possible?* I thought I was pulling off the ideal inmate ruse to perfection.

Clearly, my acting skills are in need of a polish.

My eyes float up from my balled hands resting in my lap to the man with an outrageously handsome face when he mutters, "Because you seem skittish around them all, but you've focused on this half of the room more often than the two guards behind you, so I'm leaning toward it being the warden *and* one of these pricks." He nudges his head to the officers standing behind him like he can't feel them glaring at me, wordlessly warning me to keep my mouth shut.

I obey their orders like I've been punished to do. "No one is... *fucking* with me." Even with the pause in the middle of my confession to gulp down a much-needed breath, there's not an ounce of dishonesty in my tone. Officer Black doesn't fuck me. Not only do the female inmates undergo regular pelvic examinations by an in-house doctor, but several correctional officers learned the hard way that condoms only have a 98% protection rate. Since almost all of them are married, a court-ordered paternity test isn't something they can easily hide from their wives. "I was just admiring your tattoos. You have quite the collection."

I bat my lashes at him. I'm sure I look like a wreck. I can feel the knots in my hair Officer Black's rueful clutch caused, and I'm not wearing an ounce of makeup since Roxanne's visit was hours earlier than planned, but I've got to do something. Officer Black is glaring at me so much, I may not eat for a week once Roxanne and her male friend leave.

My head bobs up and down like a bobble-head toy when the stranger asks, "You like my tattoos?" He stands to his feet, once again commanding the room with the impressive height I couldn't help but admire when I was ushered into the room by four officers like I'm a serial killer. "Do you have any?" Before I can nod, he presses his finger to his chunky lips, wordlessly requesting for me to remain quiet. "I bet one of them can tell me." He stops in front of Officer Edgar before slanting his head to the side to better align their eyes. "Does she have any tattoos?"

Officer Edgar is the tamer of the four officers in the room. He knows what happens to the female half of the population at Wallens Ridge, but he neither participates nor stops it from occurring. In a way, that makes him just as bad as Officer Black.

"I don't believe so," Officer Edgar replies after a lengthy deliberation.

The tattooed stranger takes just as long to authenticate his answer before he moves onto Officer Black. Even with my stomach in knots, I watch his approach as if not the slightest flutter can be felt. If I were to look away now, who knows how bad Officer Black's punishment will be. Not from the unnamed man, but to me for tattling. Officer Black made it very clear multiple times the past seven months that I'd lose more than meal privileges if word ever got out about our secret meetings.

"What about you, *Officer Black*?" the stranger spits out his name as if it is trash. It's clear they've met before. "Do you know if Claudia has any tattoos?"

I almost choke on my spit when Officer Black nods. He isn't lying, I do have a small collection of ink, but I never thought he'd be stupid enough to admit he's seen them.

It dawns on me that the only fool in this room is me when Officer Black locks his eyes with the cross tattoo on my right wrist. "She has a cross on her wrist. I notice it almost every time she's cuffed." He doesn't mention the small section of script tattooed on my ribcage. It's just below my breast, so admitting he had seen that means it would have meant he had seen me naked.

He would never do that.

The tension in the room boils over when the stranger asks, "Is that it? Is that the only tattoo she has?"

When I attempt to back up Officer Black's lie to save my ass, Roxanne's hand shoots out to cover mine. She knows as well as I do that her tattooed friend has sniffed out a conniving rat, and she's more than happy for him to punish Officer Black for his crimes. "The final verdict will be yours. Rocco just needs to ensure all the facts are presented first."

I'm lost to what she means until Rocco repeats his question by screaming it into Officer Black's face. "I asked you a fucking question. Is the cross on Claudia's wrist the only tattoo she has?"

When Officer Black stupidly nods, too cowardice to express his lie with words, Rocco slams his fist into his stomach, folding him in two. After pulling a gold-plated gun out of the back of his jeans, he directs it at Officer Edgar's head. He wasn't racing to assist his colleague. He was bolting for the exit. "Get word out if Claudia is touched again, for *any* fucking reason, I'll come back here and exterminate the lot of you!"

There's so much protectiveness to his statement, I can't help but push the boundaries of his offer. "Not just me. All the women." When Rocco's furious eyes swing to me, I squeak out like a mouse, "Please." I'm not special, so I don't expect to be treated as if I am, but if he can make my years here more comfortable, surely he can extend that branch to the other female inmates as well. "All we want to do is serve our time and get back to our lives. We can't do that without food."

Although my underhanded comment as to why I jump on queue doesn't wholeheartedly dump Officer Black into the deep end without a life jacket, Rocco sees it as that.

After granting my bid with a lift of his chin, Rocco slams the butt of his gun into Officer Black's temple. Blood flows out a two-inch gash in an instant, but it doesn't slow down Rocco's campaign to teach him a lesson. With a roar that exposes he isn't playing, he lays his boot into Officer Black's writhing frame while reminding him a position of power doesn't give him the right to forget the rules.

"A woman gave birth to you, you stupid fuck, so how about you remember that the next time you're forcing one to suck your dick against her will."

He raises Officer Black's head from the floor by his hair before he sends it crashing back by punching him in the face. He does this over and over again, only stopping to demand the officers watching the beat down in stunned silence to bring him the warden.

When Officer Edgar scuttles off to do as asked, Rocco locks his eyes with Roxanne. "It's time for you to head out."

"Rocc—"

"I ain't asking, Roxie."

I find their dynamic a little hard to read. It's obvious they're close, but I don't get boyfriend-girlfriend vibes from them. I would have gone with brother and sister if Roxanne hadn't told me she was an only child during our time together in a prison hospital.

I settle on friends by association when Rocco mutters, "Dimi will blow a gasket if I get a droplet of this prick's blood on you, so it's time for you to go." He gestures his head to Officer Black sobbing on the floor like a baby during the 'prick's' part of his comment

Ignoring my silent begs for her not to leave me alone with a man in the middle of a murderous rampage, Roxanne leans over my half of the table to hug me goodbye. "It will be okay," she whispers in my ear. "He hurt you first, so only you can choose his punishment."

I follow the direction of Rocco's slanted gaze when he says, "Roxie is on her way out. Meet her in the reception area." He stares at a camera mounted in the corner of the room. "Oh, don't worry, Smith, I'll add a stomp for you."

A sickening crunch booms through the room when he stomps on Officer Black's head, although it has nothing on the restrictive hold Warden Mattue's arrival causes my heart. If he thinks I'm too blame for Officer Black's punishment, he'll have even more excuses to deny my numerous requests for JJ to be a part of the prison's nursery program. My son could be here, with me, but Warden Mattue has denied every single application I've made.

Warden Mattue's eyes stray from me to Rocco when Rocco asks, "Did you know about this? Are you aware your guards are fiddling with female inmates... *again*?" Bile burns the back of my throat from the way he says 'fiddling,' but I don't let it show on my face. I need Warden Mattue to believe Rocco reached his own conclusion on matters, and that I have no say in anything happening. "Because I thought I made it abundantly clear when you overtook from your predecessor what would happen if shit like this continued under your watch." I breathe for the first time in what feels like minutes when he supplies evidence to his claims without the slightest glance my way. He pulls my underwear out of Officer Black's pocket. "I don't know about you, but I'm reasonably sure they're not his size. What do you think, Warden?"

Warden Mattue is smarter than I give him credit for. Instead of answering Rocco's first question, he keeps his focus on the last one to ensure he doesn't suffer the same fate as Officer Black. "Ah... no, they don't appear to be his size." He steps closer to Rocco like his heart isn't racing a million miles an hour. "And I assure you I was *unaware* any of these antics were occurring in my cells." Technically, that isn't a lie. The suicide watches occur in the mental health side of Wallens Ridge. It's branched off this penitentiary but is funded by private benefactors, so his comment is honest. "You have my word, this will be immediately stopped, and those in the wrong will be prosecuted to the full extent of the law."

Rocco doesn't want to believe him any more than I do, but I have a feeling he only made his pledge because he's cooking up a much more lucrative scheme.

I stop striving to work out what that could be when Rocco locks his eyes with mine. He doesn't speak. He doesn't need to. The questioning look in his eyes is very telling, much less Roxanne's promise that any verdicts handed down today will be solely my choice.

I'm Warden Mattue's judge, juror, and possibly, his executioner.

After a couple of seconds of deliberation, I shake my head. Relief engulfs Warden Mattue's face. Rocco looks straight-up disappointed, but it clears somewhat when I say, "But I may change my mind if my applications are continually refused."

"Bail?" Rocco asks, his tone somewhat hopeful.

A strand of the dead straight hair I tossed into a messy bun while waiting for the door of my cell to pop open falls into my eye when I shake my head. "My son. I haven't seen him since he was born."

I'm unsure if it's a relieved or shocked mask that falls over Rocco's face. We've only just met, so I can't be sure. Whatever it is, he clears it away before he shifts his focus back to Warden Mattue. "Get onto that." When Warden Mattue's lips twitch in preparation to respond, Rocco shouts, "Now!" The scuttle of his boots on the polished concrete floor is still sounding in my ears when Rocco asks me what I want Officer Black's punishment to be. "He hurt you, so only you can sentence him."

I peer down at Officer Black, confident I don't have what it takes to be a cold-blooded murderer but too curious to discount Rocco's offer immediately. If I hadn't been such a rule follower, I wouldn't have needed to put up with Juan's abuse for so long. There were guns in every drawer at the Sánchez compound. I would have merely needed to point and shoot. I just didn't have the stomach to view murder so nonchalantly.

When Rocco recognizes my struggle, he says, "He won't hurt you again either way, but by taking him out, you'll never have to look over your shoulder."

"But he will if I don't. A better lesson might be taught this way."

Rocco shuffles side to side to hide his ghost-like smile before doing a one-shoulder shrug. "Perhaps, but only you have the choice to decide if that is enough."

I breathe out slowly before twisting my lips. "Could you tell his wife?"

"Tell her what? That her husband is an adulterous rapist who doesn't know how to keep his dick in his pants?"

The murderous glint in Rocco's eyes dims a little when I mutter, "He didn't rape me, but I'd like her to know the rest." I wet my lips before continuing, "Then she can choose whether he lives or dies. It's only fair considering he hurt her first."

He doesn't hide his smile this time around. It's as ridiculously handsome as his face. Not even the droplets of Officer Black's blood on his cheek can deter from his sexiness. I won't mention how bloody his fists are, though. I'm acting as if they don't exist.

"Are you sure that's what you want, Claudia?" I could almost forget the seriousness of our conversation from the way he purrs out my name. There's no doubt he was born into violence like Juan, but Juan would have participated alongside Officer Black. He would have never punished him for degrading me.

"I'm sure," I reply with a faint nod. "Thanks, though."

I inwardly curse my dimness. I couldn't sound more naïve if I tried.

Rocco doesn't seem to mind. After chuckling a laugh that does stupid things to my insides, he locks his eyes with Officer Peters. "Get this cleaned up…" When Officer Peters jumps to the command in his tone, he stops his hustle with a straight-up order. "*After* assuring Claudia and every other inmate in her half of Wallens Ridge are fed and given unlimited access to toiletries, personal hygiene products, *and* clothing."

"Yes, sir. Of course, sir. I'll get onto that right now, sir," Officer Peters stammers out before he races to the door I was pushed through only minutes ago to open it for me.

After shuffling to the exit like I'm not stark naked under my jumpsuit, I crank my neck back to Rocco, smiling when our eyes lock and hold. "*Thank you,*" I mouth.

He accepts my unvoiced gratitude with a dip of his chin before he hits me with a frisky wink that will keep me warm throughout winter even if Officer Peters doesn't follow through with his pledge.

6

---

## ROCCO

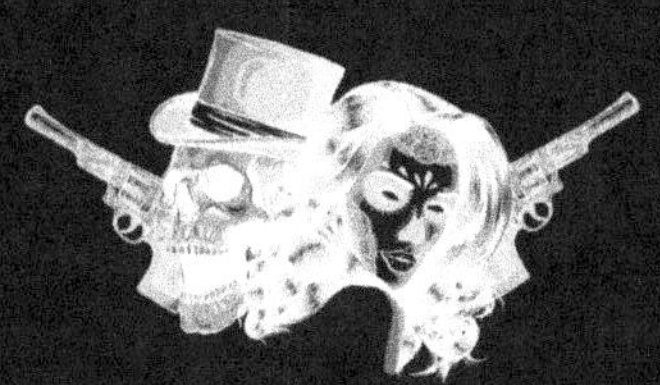

It's a fucking hard feat to walk away from Officer Black curled in a fetal position at my feet, but since his crimes aren't mine to sentence, I have no choice. Doesn't mean I can leave without laying my boot into him another handful of times, though. He knew the rules. He was one of the pricks in Warden Mattue's office when Dimitri gave him a rundown on how things were going to operate since we took care of the last Nazi who wrongly believed he was running the show around here.

There's nothing I hate more than fuckers who make you earn everything you want even with them not being the rightful owner. If you want to buy a colt, pretty it up with some slick new paint, then sell it for a profit, go ahead. But if you steal *my* colt, then try and sell it back to me like it isn't already mine, I'll take it from your hands and kill you with it.

I'm skeptical Officer Black can hear me. Blood is pooling out of his ears, but I can't help but bob down and issue one final warning. Threats are a part of who I am. "I really fucking hope the inmates worked your dick good because if your wife doesn't cut off your johnson for being a cheating prick, I'll do it for her."

I push him back with force, kick him in the ribs for the hundredth time, then make my way to the corridor lined with correctional officers too scared to impede my brisk exit. I'm partway out when Smith chimes in, "I'm sending details of Officer Black's residence to your cell as we speak, but for now, you need to hear the shit Ox is spilling. He wasn't just the key to Col's secrets. He was the treasure chest as well."

I increase the length of my strides, my pace only slowing when Roxanne tosses a rag from a gleaming Mercedes-Benz G-Class into my chest so I can clean the blood on my hands. I have one just like it, so I check the plates to make sure it isn't mine before guiding Roxanne to its passenger seat by her elbow.

It isn't mine, in case you were wondering.

Roxanne pulls away from me, pissed I'm excluding her from the festivities. Her temper cools a smidge when I hand her one of Smith's tablets before opening the Notes app. "Jot down everything you know about Claudia's case. When it happened, who it happened to, and everything in between."

The frantic beat of her heart is heard in her question, "Dimi agreed to look into her case?"

"Yes." My lie holds out for two measly seconds. "Well, he will when I tell him we're looking into her case." She looks at me like I underhandedly told her Dimitri loves her. It wouldn't be the first time I've expressed that, so I let her run with it. "But for now, we need to focus on Fien. We're so fucking close. I can feel it."

When she nods in agreement, I hit her with the same frisky wink I gave Claudia before shutting the Mercedes's door with her on the inside.

"What have you got so far?"

Smith waits for me to toss the bloody rag into his van before updating me on Dimitri and Maddox's conversation. Since he shut down all the cameras, he only has audio transcripts of their exchange. The elementary way their conversation is transcribed doesn't dampen the information shared. It went from a macho showdown to a free for all.

"Maddox hid Megan?" I ask, confident I heard him wrong during the playback.

When Smith jerks up his chin, I ask, "Where?"

"He's updating Dimitri now." He fiddles with some buttons on the makeshift command center he built on the hood of his van before their conversation streams through my earpiece in actual time.

"She's at a mental health facility one hundred clicks from here. Col wanted her to get a workup." Rustling sounds down the line, most likely Dimitri yanking his cell phone out of his pocket. "Right there," Maddox adds a couple of seconds later.

"She's at 2876 North Druid Hills Road, Decatur," Dimitri breathes out heavily before the stomps of his boots boom into my ears. He does three big strides before he suddenly stops. "Thanks." His mumble is barely legible, but I'm confident Maddox heard it. Even if Dimitri weren't wearing a listening device, I would have heard Maddox's shocked gasp from here.

In under a minute, Dimitri charges across the barren lot like a swarm of bees are chasing him. "Did you get that?" he asks Smith, more than aware a complete lockdown wouldn't have kept surveillance out of Wallens Ridge.

While Smith's fingers fly over a silicon keyboard, he lifts his chin. "I'm hacking into the hospital servers now."

As Smith works his magic, Roxanne slips out of the passenger seat. Dimitri forever has his eye on the pie, but since Fien is very much a part of that, he misses Roxanne handing me the tablet. After squeezing my hand, wordlessly thanking me for my assistance, she leans into Dimitri's side to help him scan the footage Smith is playing at three times the speed.

"There," Dimitri shouts a couple of seconds later.

Smith homes in on the petite female with mousy brown hair and crazy eyes he pointed out. The footage is grainy, but she looks a lot like the images Smith has included in his many dot-point presentations of Megan the past couple of days. I swear that guy would get a hard-on over a spreadsheet.

"Is that her?"

"Give me a sec..." Smith blows me away with his computer skills when he takes the blurry image of Megan on the screen and uploads it to a secondary program to confirm the woman on the screen and the picture on Megan's driver's license are one and the same. "Bingo. We have a match."

Confident he's now tracking the right person, Smith follows Megan's digital imprint back to the days leading to Maddox's arrest for her murder.

"There," Roxanne shouts, scaring the living day lights out of me. While smiling about my skittish jump, she points to a reflection seen in the admission glass mounted to keep the crazies on the other side of the reception desk. "Do you think it's the woman you were talking to earlier?"

Dimitri takes a moment to consider the possibility Theresa is behind his daughter's kidnapping before he shrugs, truly unsure. "Can you clean up the footage?"

For the first time in half a decade, Smith shows hesitation. "I'd have a better chance with wired equipment. The upload speed is as slow as fuck out here."

"Then head back to the compound." Dimitri takes an updated photo of Megan with his cell phone before peeling Smith's equipment off his van and tossing it in the passenger seat like it's worthless. "Forward anything you find directly to me."

Someone's a little eager to leave.

I can't help but wonder why.

"Are you not heading back to the compound?"

Dimitri balls his fists before answering me through gritted teeth, "I've got to take Roxanne home first."

"I can do that for you. You don't have to go out of your way." If he's not willing to be upfront about his feelings for Roxanne, I have no issues forcing him to do it.

Roxanne glares at me with pleading help-me eyes when Dimitri guides her walk to the Mercedes with a firm grip on her arm. He doesn't handle her quite as roughly as he did Smith's equipment, but I'm unsure if he knows how to be gentle. Ma gave it her best shot to teach him chivalry when she was around, but Dimitri found it more creepy than endearing.

Once he has Roxanne's seat belt in his hand in preparation to buckle her in, Dimitri shifts his focus back to Smith and me. "We need to find out what information Megan has that makes her invaluable to my father. If we can do that without needing to travel to her, I'd much appreciate it."

He freezes halfway across Roxanne's body when Smith says, "Megan could come to us."

"How?" Roxanne asks before either Dimitri or I get the chance.

Smith wiggles one of his prototype phones in his hand. "She's all types of crazy... but not enough for a permanent placement. She could be signed out to a guardian."

Smith's voiceless chuckles heave in his chest at the kissy-gaga face I make when Dimitri seeks Roxanne's thoughts on Smith's suggestion. He's so fucking under, a crane couldn't pull him out now.

I miss what Roxanne replies. I'm too busy staring at the lights of Wallens Ridge, confused as to why watching Dimitri fall dick first in love causes more ruckus to my veins than a near murder. Usually, I live off the hype of a kill for days. Officer Black's beatdown didn't keep my veins thrumming with euphoria long enough to reach the lot. I could blame the fact he's still breathing for the slump in testosterone, but that would be a cop-out.

I'm not a man who will sit and watch a woman be abused in public. If you're stupid enough to smack your girl in front of me, I can assure you you'll leave with more than a black eye. But there was something more than fear in Claudia's eyes that set me off. She was so quiet about it, so fucking calm. If my years in this industry awarded me anything, it's the fact I can spot an abused woman from a mile out. Roxanne's ghosts were old and faded. They weren't right up in your face like Claudia's. Hers were so glaringly obvious, I'm fairly sure Officer Black's attention was merely a sprinkle on top of the cupcake—barely consequential—and the thought has me itching for a bloodbath.

I get the commotion I was seeking from Officer Black's beatdown when Dimitri instructs Smith to tag Megan before she's released, but it's nothing close to the bloodbath I'm craving. "We don't want her location falling through the cracks."

"You can't microchip her like she's a dog," Roxanne fires back, forever on call to reiterate the rights not many women have in the cartel. Her stand on equal rights is why she's a good fit for Dimitri. Fien needs someone like Roxanne on her side.

"I can't? Since when?"

Dimitri steals her ability to answer by slamming her door closed. It pisses Roxanne off, but since her eyes have locked onto the tablet in my hand, she acts as if her back molars aren't grinding together.

I try to get my head back into game mode when Dimitri stops to stand in front of me. "Maddox asked me to get Demi out." I jerk up my chin, unsurprised. He's done as much as he can the past twelve months, but he doesn't have the means to protect her when he's behind bars. "I'm going to head to her last known location now with Roxanne." I begin to wonder if he heard my confrontation with Officer Black when he says, "While I do that, hang around here for a bit. Some fishy shit is going on, but I can't quite put my finger on it."

"Do you think the stench is coming from Ox?"

He twists his lips before shaking his head. "But it could be happening to him. He's gaunt and as white as fuck."

"Is that unusual? Everyone goes a little pasty when you show up."

He looks torn between laughing and shooting me, so he goes for somewhere in the middle. He flicks me in the nuts before hitting me with a stern finger point. "Keep communication lines open." I realize he's neither a mind reader nor a man with super strength hearing when he points to his ear. The fucker is wearing a listening device, meaning he heard every word I spoke while defending Claudia's honor. "Fien first, Rocco."

"I know," I reply without hesitation.

As much as I want to believe happy endings are more than a non-itemized order on the menu of a seedy massage parlor, I can't. There's no Prince Charming on a white horse riding in to save the damsel in distress, no Viking sailing across dangerous waters to find his one true love, and no such thing as love without carnage. Life is fucking messy. Only a rare few get their happily ever after.

Will I be one of them?

*Un-fucking-likely.*

But that won't stop me from helping Dimitri get his.

With that in mind, I drag my eyes away from Wallens Ridge and get to work on unearthing a way I can sign Megan out of voluntary incarceration at a mental health facility without the shrinks locking me up for my own psych evaluation.

7

———

## CLAUDIA

’m eyeballed by as many inmates as I am guards when I enter Wallens Ridge's commissary. They did the same thing when the guard manning the breakfast station this morning handed me an extra piece of fruit. You're lucky to get a piece without bruises and gouges, so you can picture my surprise when he gave me a perfectly ripe banana. I was so excited by its freshness, I gobbled it down before it could be plucked from my tray like my food is most days.

Shockingly, I not only made it through the line without being elbowed and bumped like I usually am, but my tray was also left untouched until I went to scrape it clean.

It isn't as you're thinking. Another inmate offered to put it away on my behalf. I left the mess hall with a full yet uneased stomach.

I had no friends before I went to prison, and things didn't improve with a change of scenery. The inmates think my one-on-one meetings with Officer Black sees me being handed a heap of favors. Little do they know, the bristles on my toothbrush are so squashed, even if I wanted to test O'Doyle's theory that the tongue cleaner on the back can replicate a man's tongue, I wouldn't be able to. That part fell off ages ago.

That's why I'm here, milling around the commissary with the hope the second half of Rocco's pledge this morning will be upheld like his first one was. I had access to *all* the items on the breakfast menu. That hasn't happened since I arrived here.

Inmates are served the standard three meals a day, but those lucky enough to have an account loaded with funds from family members or friends can purchase additional products such as hygiene items, snacks, writing instruments, and limited internet access at the commissary.

I accidentally bump into a blonde from a cell block next to mine when my heart rate fluctuates from my eyes locking in on the electric toothbrush I've been eyeing the past four months. A law passed a few years ago that commissaries can't exorbitantly markup the prices of their items, but it doesn't seem to have been implemented here. A toothbrush like that would cost around forty dollars at Walmart. Here, it's over a hundred.

"I'm so sorry. I got a little flustered."

She smiles when I fan my face before she hides her arched lips with her hair. I discover the reason behind her embarrassment when she asks, "You wouldn't happen to have a spare two dollars in your account, would you?" We're not allowed cash in Wallens Ridge. Funds are to be deposited into an online account by family or friends. If you don't have any of them, like me, you're out of luck. "I almost have enough. I'm just a little short."

"I'm sorry. I don't have anyone to put funds into my account."

That isn't a lie. My mother died at the hands of my father before he shot himself. That's how I ended up living with the Sánchezes. When Child Services was around, Juana was my foster care mother. When they weren't, I was her cook, cleaner, and all-around slave. Since I was grateful for a roof over my head and food in my stomach, I followed her orders.

I should have moved out when I turned eighteen, but that was when Juan took an interest in me. Despite no longer receiving federal funding for me, he convinced his mother to keep me on. I didn't get paid a dime for my time, but my accommodations and meals were supplied, and that was more than I had gotten in my family home.

"Okay," whispers the blonde inmate before she sets down the item she was hoping to buy.

My heart falls from my ribcage when I realize what it is.

She's purchasing a pregnancy test.

"How long have you been here?" I ask, too meddlesome for my own good.

The stranglehold on my heart increases when she lifts her head enough, I see her eyes. They're as youthful as her face, but one of them is circled with a bruise. It looks fresh. "Coming up to a year."

"Did one of the guards do that to you?" Assuming my question centers around her black eye, she shakes her head. The shame in her eyes is all too familiar, though, and it answers the rest of my question on her behalf. "They don't understand that nothing we do to them gets us any favors, do they?"

She almost bursts into tears.

She must have thought she was the only one.

"It's okay," I promise while tilting into her side. I'd give anything to hug her, but since that would cause even more trouble, I rub my shoulder against hers. "I had a friend visit this morning. She brought a man with her..." when she shudders, assuming I'm sharing a horror story instead of good news, I talk faster, "... he promised to make everything better. I don't know about you, but breakfast seemed a lot nicer this morning."

With a giggle, she drags the sleeve of the long-sleeve shirt she's wearing under her jumpsuit across her nose before muttering, "It was nice. I had two pieces of fruit."

"Me too," I admit, laughing for the first time in a long time.

We giggle amongst ourselves for the next couple of seconds before she announces she's due to start her shift at the laundry. "If I get my hours up, I might be able to afford it by the end of the week."

I forgot you can earn credits if you don't have any family members who can come to the plate for you. I signed up for a prison job my first week here, but my application was rejected because I was heavily pregnant. I don't see them being able to deny me this time around.

"What was your name again?" I shout before she can leave, hating that I know a huge secret about her, but I don't know her name.

She spins around to face me, smiling when she says, "Jodi. It's nice to officially meet you, Claudia." She absorbs my shocked expression for the quickest second before she wiggles her fingers, then dashes toward the laundry by taking a detour through the mess hall.

I stare at the pregnancy test she was hoping to buy for barely a minute before breathing out my nerves and walking toward the person behind the counter at the commissary. It's operated by a private firm, so not only is Laura in a stuffy, protective box, she also has a guard at her right.

She watches me approach with sympathetic eyes before seeking an answer to my unvoiced question by tapping on her keyboard. I do the same thing every week. I arrive with the hope Juana has kept her promise about placing funds into my account before I leave disappointed. Not a single penny has been placed into my account since JJ was ripped away from me. I even had to use the scratchy, prison-supplied sanitary napkins after I gave birth. It was horrible.

I freeze when Laura twists her lips instead of hitting me with her usual response. She doesn't shake her head at all. She bobs it up and down.

"How much?" I ask a little too desperately. Before she can answer me, I add, "Enough to get a new toothbrush?"

"Yes," she answers with another nod. "You could buy every toothbrush in stock if you want."

I almost squeal in excitement before I race to the far side of the commissary to yank the sole electric toothbrush from its stand. I have it in my hot little hand just as the pregnancy test Jodi wanted to purchase creeps into my peripheral vision. I stare at it like I have the possibility of acting ignorant, where in reality, I knew the instant I spotted it, I would swap the electric toothbrush for a standard one. I don't need fancy things. I simply want a toothbrush that brushes my teeth instead of scouring them.

"Oh," Laura pushes out with a shocked breath when I place a standard brush into the purchase slot along with the pregnancy test. "You can go to the infirmary to be tested. You don't have to use your credit for that."

"I know," I reply. "But I don't think she wants to do that."

I'm hoping my hint that the test isn't for me won't have Laura reporting its purchase to the warden. I understand it's her job to document purchases like this, but if the warden truly trusted his staff, why would he allow the commissary to stock condoms?

Remaining quiet, Laura places the pregnancy test into one white paper bag and the toothbrush in another. Her silent assurance my secret will remain between us sees me issuing her my biggest smile to date.

"*Thank you*," I mouth to her like I did Rocco only hours ago.

When she returns my gratitude with a wink, I skip out of the commissary like I'm not in one of America's most gang-related prisons. Instead of heading back to my cell to catch up on some sleep I lost from Officer Black's early morning visit, I go to the laundromat.

The smell of freshly laundered clothes and sheets has me wishing I had let Laura answer my first question. If I hadn't been so impatient, I could have discovered I have enough funds to purchase new underwear.

Alas, happiness isn't about getting what you want. It's about appreciating what you have. I have a brand-new toothbrush and a full stomach.

That's far more than I had this morning.

Jodi notices my entrance almost simultaneously with me spotting her near the massive presses. She waves at me before gesturing for me to come over.

The closer I get to her, the more nervous she becomes. I learn why when she says, "There are rumors going around that Officer Black was taken to the hospital this morning. He was in a horrific accident. They don't know if he'll make it."

"Oh, that's terrible," I lie while struggling not to show relief on my face. "For his wife's sake, I hope he pulls through."

"Or not," Jodi interrupts, grimacing. "First responders found a heap of incriminating evidence in his car." She leans in close and whispers, "And hotel room receipts for his hometown." She locks her eyes with mine like one of them isn't black. "We all know what that means."

"We do," I agree. *Unfortunately.*

Hating that memories of my past are sullying my excitement about my new toothbrush, I hand Jodi the fatter of the two white paper bags.

"What's this?" she queries while ripping it open, then she says, "Claudia..." She looks like she wants to hug me as badly as I did her earlier, but since she can't, she meets her watering eyes with mine. "Thank you, I truly appreciate it, but I thought you said you didn't have anyone who could issue you credit."

"I didn't... *until this morning.*"

She takes a little while to click onto who I'm referencing, but when she does, she looks torn between high-fiving me and warning me to be careful. "The man who arrived with your friend?"

I nod. "I think so. Roxanne doesn't have any money, so it had to be Rocco."

"That's cool." She overemphasizes her last word with a long Texan drawl.

"It is... *I think.*" Jodi bumps me with her hip when I hesitate. It can't be helped. I've never been anything without having some type of clause attached to it, so I can't help but wonder what this will cost me. "Anyhoo, did you want me to hang around while you... you know..." I point to the bag she's clutching onto for dear life.

"Ah... no," she replies matter-of-factly. "I'm not sure we're close enough for me to pee in front of you just yet." Her laugh halves the embarrassment flooding my face. "But thank you. I truly appreciate it."

I smile, thankful for her praise even with it not being necessary. "Will you let me know the result?"

"Of course," she replies with some hesitation. "Let's pray for a negative."

I rub her arm, wordlessly assuring her it will be fine no matter the result before heading toward D Block. Although I don't have the fancy toothbrush I've been admiring the past couple of months, I did a good deed. That alone makes up for possible furry teeth.

There's a hint of excitement in the air when I make my way down the gangway of D block. Chatter fills the usually docile space, and a handful of women are squealing like they were informed *Master Chef* is filming a prison episode at Wallens Ridge.

I discover the reason for the excitement when I enter my cell. O'Doyle isn't the most attractive lady I've ever seen, but she looks swanky in her new jumpsuit and thermal undergarments.

"Wow, O'Doyle, you went all out this month." I remove the smidge of jealousy in my tone before adding, "I'm glad Juana finally made true on her promise. You deserve it."

"I'm not the only one in her good books." Burnt orange hair falls into O'Doyle's eye when she nudges her big head to my cot. If we were a cartoon, my eyes would pop out of my head when I spot three new jumpsuits, two thermal sets, and multiple pairs of underwear and socks.

"They're new?" I gabber out in shock, stunned by their fancy packaging. Only the new fish get freshly packaged stock. The rest of us live off hand-me-downs. "Oh my god, they smell so good."

The surprises keep coming when my dig through my new clothes has me stumbling onto an electric toothbrush. If I'm not mistaken, it's the same toothbrush I had in my hot little hand only thirty minutes ago. "Did you get a new toothbrush?"

Smirking, O'Doyle spins around to face me with a standard brush held out like it's a diamond tennis bracelet. "I sure did. It even has the tongue scrubber on the back." Her wink makes my breakfast curdle in my stomach. "What type did you get?"

"*Saaame*," I lie while tucking my electric toothbrush behind my back. It has four vibration settings—*four!* It's such a hot-ticket item, I'd strangle O'Doyle before I'll ever let her steal it.

"Cool." After stuffing her toothbrush into the holder above the vanity sink, O'Doyle tells me she's going to see what everyone else got.

She almost knocks over an officer on her way out, but since it was an accident, she gets away with their almost collision with only the briefest warning. "Tone it down, O'Doyle." My heart sinks when Officer Maroni's focus shifts to me. "Sánchez, I need you to come with me."

I should have known nothing comes without a price tag attached to it.

After hiding my second most valuable possession under my mattress, I slowly trudge toward Officer Maroni. I'm tempted to warn him what could possibly happen if he touches me, but since that would switch the story of Officer Black's injuries from a traffic accident to an attempted murder rumor, I keep my mouth shut.

It's for the best. If I had spoken, I may have missed Officer Maroni requesting that I bring my belongings with me.

"You want me to take my things?" I ask, confident I heard him wrong.

When he jerks up his chin, I mumble, "Okay," before I spin around to do precisely that.

I don't have much to pack—just the items someone recently purchased for me, my electric toothbrush, and the only photo of JJ I have. It's from when Juan, Juana, and I found out we were having a boy. The ultrasound paper has faded over the months, but I can still see the outline of his adorable face. He has my nose and cheekbones, but regretfully, the rest of his features were inherited from Juan.

I can only hope looks are the only Sánchez feature he has when he's grown.

With my steps reduced by helplessness, it takes longer to walk from D Block to C Block than it should. I usually make it to the mess hall by now, and you have to walk through C Block to get there.

"Here we are. Open cell three," Officer Maroni requests after stopping in front of a cell branched directly off the recreation room of C Block.

"Cell three open," returns the officer in charge of the cells.

"In you go," Officer Maroni says with a grin when I remain frozen in place. "This is your new cell."

My knees knock when I enter the space that isn't bigger than my last cell but appears to be since there's only one bed. "Where will my cellmate sleep?"

Officer Maroni laughs. I'm glad he's amused, however, I am anything but. I don't get a choice of beds with O'Doyle. She changes her mind on top bunk and bottom bunk multiple times a month. Then there was the time she made me sleep on the floor because she was afraid I'd fall through the mattress and squash her.

I wish I had the courage to tell her that isn't possible, considering I weigh half of what she does. Regretfully, I still haven't learned that bullying isn't okay.

When it dawns on him that my question was serious, Officer Maroni stops laughing. "You don't have a cellmate." He hooks his thumb to a group of female prisoners playing board games in the recreation room. "Free time is still for another twenty minutes. You can either join them out there or stay in here, the decision is up to you."

"I'll stay in here." When fret is the dominant emotion in my voice, I try to hide it. "Everyone knows unpacking is the worst part of any move."

"All right," replies Officer Maroni. "But if I were you, I'd take in the last bit of that sunshine before it disappears behind the clouds." He nudges his head to the window in my cell.

*I have a window!*

Holy cow.

My internal dance-off suspends mid-hip grind when Officer Maroni mutters, "Enjoy the rest of your morning, Sánchez."

"I will. Thank you."

He isn't even one step away before I hoist myself onto the rim of my toilet to peer out the tiny crack someone left in the protective tint covering the barred window. My somewhat dream-like morning makes sense when my eyes lock in on a figure balancing his hip on the driver's side door of the Mercedes Warden Mattue didn't stop bragging about last month. It's Rocco, and he's peering straight at my window like he knows this cell is now mine.

When I wave with the hope he'll see the shadow of my hand through the tint, he salutes me with his index and middle finger before he slides into the driver's seat of the warden's car and skids out of the parking lot.

I can't help but laugh when I hear the warden's frantic cries about his car being stolen only a couple of seconds later. He shouldn't be complaining. If I were honest with Rocco, he could have lost way more than his fancy ride today.

It will do him best to remember that.

## 8

## ROCCO

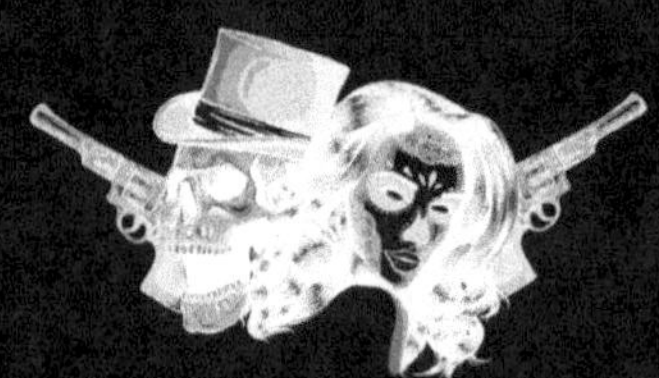

Fifty minutes later, I'm still grinning about the way Warden Mattue's thighs rubbed when he chased me by foot for 'borrowing' his ride. I could have told him I was taking it, but where's the fun in that? The prick owes me for keeping him alive after he lied to me. Organizing a new cell and threads for Claudia only sliced a few thousand off his ledger, so you can imagine how minuscule the payment will be for borrowing his ride.

I would have loved to have seen Claudia's expression firsthand, but the promise I made to Dimitri about keeping Fien first commenced ringing in my ears when Smith's computer-hub-on-wheels hooked me up with a swanky new license for Maurice Shroud, Megan's long lost and only living relative.

I put my inability to sit still and the flat landscape to good use the next thirty miles of my trip. After scanning my eyes over the background search Smith did on Claudia, I read the dossier of information Roxanne supplied. The first couple of lines follow the same basic prose the background search had. It mentions Claudia's full name, age, and approximate height and weight. Claudia's last name is Sánchez. Although she's only older by three years than my guess, I was right about her weighing the same as Roxanne even with her being a couple of inches taller.

With preliminary stats out of the way, I shift my focus to the juicier stuff—the reason behind Claudia's incarceration. Her angelic face and the fact she let Officer Black live had me anticipating numerous arrests for petty theft or perhaps a case of racketeering or insurance fraud, so you can picture my shock when my eyes stumble over the word 'manslaughter.'

"No fucking way," I mumble to myself while scrolling up so I can take in a second page of information.

My earlier assumption that Officer Black's abuse was only the tip of the iceberg for what Claudia has endured is proven without a doubt when I read the paragraphs of the statement Roxanne prepared. She spells it all out. How Claudia's black eyes weren't the only bruises she had when Roxanne and her met in the criminal wing of a hospital. The numerous visits she had from a lady whose every move was cloaked by armed men, and how even with multiple witnesses coming forward to say the man Claudia was accused of killing had his hand on the steering wheel at the time of their accident still didn't see her escaping a conviction.

Her court hearing only lasted three days. She was denied the chance to defend herself when her attorney failed to put her on the stand, and when she gave birth to her son behind bars, his custody was immediately awarded to the mother of the man she supposedly killed. She hasn't seen him since.

That's fucking bullshit. I don't know what pisses me off more. Her attorney's sloppiness, her unfair trial, or the fact her son is being raised by a woman who did such a piss-poor job the first time around she cultivated a wife-beater.

That shit isn't born into you. It's just like racism. It is rammed down your throat until you stupidly think it's the norm. And don't get me started on what Claudia has faced since her incarceration, or I'll turn my fucking car around and slaughter the lot of them like I warned earlier.

I'm so worked up that when I arrive at Oaks Valley Psychiatric Facility ten minutes later, I park in the 'doctors only' bay, stomp up the stairs, then slam my license against the partition erected to keep the loonies away from the staff. "I'm here to check out Megan Shroud."

"Did you say Megan Shroud?" asks the lady behind the desk while batting her lashes at me. She isn't seeking a bed companion for the night. She wants to butter me up with the hope her big tits and pouty lips will have me overlooking her daftness.

If it were any day but today, I may have cut her some slack. Since it isn't, I nod my head like she's slow. "I'm down on her file as her next of kin. You can check my credentials." I push my license through the slot, aware Smith hacked into their system hours ago to add me to Megan's file that was once buried with bureaucratic tape.

While he did that, I set to work on upholding the promise I made to Claudia when she bartered for fairer equality for the female inmates at Wallens Ridge. Warden Mattue's eyes will water when he sees how much my generosity cost him.

My smug grin only lasts for a second, interrupted by the receptionist's lips forming an 'O.' She continues punching my credentials into her computer before she eventually says, "I'll be just a minute."

Not waiting for me to reply, she darts to a closed door on the other side of the reception area to talk to a stout man who looks like his position has aged him by decades instead of years.

He joins me in the reception area after a brief word with the receptionist. "Mr. Shroud, I'm Dr. Faletti. You must excuse our shock. We've been searching for the contact details of Megan's next-of-kin for some time now."

I shuffle side to side while rubbing my hands together. "That's understandable. I didn't know she was admitted here until earlier this week. I raced down as soon as I found out. She doesn't belong here. I want to take her home."

"Yes, I understand, but that's where we face an issue."

While guiding me to a row of chairs like sitting down will weaken my annoyance, Dr. Faletti explains that Megan escaped from Oaks

Valley several weeks ago. She hit a guard over the head with a chair and stole his keys.

"Why weren't the authorities informed?"

"They were," Dr. Faletti explains. "And that was when we were told not to mention Megan's... *time* at Oaks Valley." He pats my knee like I'm a child. It has me wanting to sever several of his fingers. My father used to do the same until he eventually raised his hand several inches higher. "News like this can be very hard to absorb in an unfamiliar environment. If you'd feel more comfortable, you're more than welcome to gather your thoughts inside."

I leap to my feet and bolt for the door like he told me I knocked up his daughter. "I'm good. Pretend I was never here. It seems to be a favorable trait of your facility."

My speed slows partway to 'my' car when I spot a correctional transport van pulling into the back entrance of Oaks Valley. "Why are they here?" I ask the receptionist who followed me out to return my license.

She waits for me to place it into my wallet before answering, "Inmates can have as many mental issues as regular folks. It's Dr. Faletti's job to determine if they're claiming a mental health disorder for a reduced sentence or if they're truly insane."

"If they're fraudulent?" I ask, my curiosity too high to contain.

The receptionist twists to face me, but not before ensuring her gigantic tits are front and center. I was wrong when I said she wasn't seeking a bed companion. She is, but I don't have the time to work out if Oaks Valley does an employee work program like most prisons or if she works here legitimately.

In all honesty, it wouldn't matter what her title is. When you're interested, you are interested. Not even the threat of death will stop you from pursuing it.

In this case, I'm not interested—not the slightest bit—which is shocking, considering she's *exactly* the type I usually go for. Blonde hair, big tits, and plenty of hips to grip while fucking, but her eyes are too dull. They expose she isn't fucked-up enough for me.

I hear the disappointment of my silent rejection in her voice when she says, "The fraudsters get shipped back to jail." Before I can ask what happens to the real nut cases, she points south and discloses, "They transport the legitimate cases to Drakes."

"Drakes?" I query, my interest piqued by the shiver she released while mentioning Drakes.

"An asylum for the criminally insane."

I realize she's most likely a patient at Oaks Valley when she startles me with a 'boo' before she pivots on her heels with a witch-like cackle and tootles away.

"Fucking weirdo," I murmur to myself while sliding into the driver's seat of Warden Mattue's hot-wired car.

I've only just reversed out of my parking spot when Smith's name flashes across the screen on the dashboard. With multiple frustrations bombarding me at once, I spit out his name like its venom.

"Jesus... are you sure you got your dick sucked last night?" Even though he's asking a question, I don't get the chance to reply. "The last time you were this worked up was when Dimitri put Roxanne's virginity on the line for a bunch of sleazy fuckers to bid on."

Don't screw your nose up like that. If you haven't worked out by now that Dimitri is a surly bastard, you need to go back and reread his story. He doesn't hide who he is, and neither do I.

"Yes, I got my dick sucked last night... *twice!* But I didn't realize twelve hours could feel like twelve years until now."

Smith laughs before telling me the real reason for his call. "While I was waiting for Ravenshoe PD's slow-ass facial recognition program to fire up, I conducted some searches on the names Roxanne mentioned in her write-up."

I'm about to call him a snoopy fucker, but then I remember all his tablets are synced. If you write a note in one of them, it's forwarded to every device automatically. "Did you find anything interesting?"

A hum vibrates down the line. "An address popped up near Oaks Valley. It's literally two minutes away. I was thinking if you've got a minute or three to spare, perhaps you could do a drive-by to scope the premises before collecting Megan." His reply makes it obvious he read Roxanne's write-up in the same manner as me. Claudia wasn't just fucked over by the law. Child Services let her down when they placed her into a foster care home unsuitable for a child whose father had killed her mother. Then it continued going downhill from there. She had no one on her team—*until now.*

"That would be a solid plan if Megan was here. I'm leaving Oaks Valley now with an empty passenger seat." Smith groans out his annoyance but remains quiet, granting me the chance to speak. "Megan escaped a couple of weeks back. She knocked a guard out fucking cold." I shouldn't smile, but after the morning I've had, I'm going to. Women are usually passive beings until they're pushed to the brink. Then you better watch yourself, especially those momma bears who are protecting their cubs. "Send over what you have, though. Since I can legitimately drive it like I stole it, I have plenty of time to spare." An address for a rural property pops up on my ride's dashboard before all my sentence leaves my mouth. "Is this for Juana or one of her sons?"

"What do you mean?" Smith asks, his voice breathless like he's struggling not to laugh. I realize that is the case when he says, "Are you supposed to move out of home once you're thirty?"

I scrub at my cropped beard. "Well, I can't talk for society, but a good indication on the right time to move out is around the same time you start smearing the sheets with more than your cum."

Smith no longer bothers to hold back his laugh. His chuckle barrels down the line before he suggests for me to pass on my knowledge to the Sánchez family. "None of Juana's birdies have flown from the nest yet, and they're all over the age of thirty-five."

My lips twist more in shock that Claudia was married to a man fifteen years her senior than confirmation the Sánchezes are a bunch of soft cocks. You can't have much gasoline in the tank if you need to beat women to get your rocks off.

My already piqued interests grow even more when Smith murmurs, "I've only experienced one family with a dynamic as weird as the Sánchezes, but I don't tell them how weird I think they are since they pay my bills."

"Are the Sánchezes part of the cartel?"

Smith's hum is neither agreeing nor disagreeing this time around. "Their pull dipped when Alejandro was killed a few years back."

That makes no sense. Dimitri is younger now than Alejandro's eldest son would have been when his father died, and he's more than ready to overtake Col, so why the fuck wasn't Juan capable of doing the same?

When I ask Smith that, he gives credit to my theory Juana Sánchez is whacked in the head. She has to be to take a child from a woman immediately after she's given birth. Even babies born to crack addicts get skin-to-skin contact with their mothers. "Juana wanted to take over the reins. Juan let her." My silence makes Smith chuckle. "That isn't the half of it. The original coroner's report on Alejandro's death was buried so deep it took me reaching out to Hunter for help to find it." That makes me grin. Smith hates admitting he can't do everything, but he fucking loathes when he has to admit that to his idol. "Foul play was suspected. A blood work-up was ordered, but the lead coroner at the Bureau seized Alejandro's body before blood could be drawn."

"Of course, he did."

Smith continues talking as if I never interrupted him. "As you know, restrictions come into play when the rules are broken. The Sánchezes lost a ton of contacts. With other cartel groups refusing to purchase their products, their stockpile of weapons and whores soon dwindled to a pittance. They're more petty thieves now than cartel members. They just remain protected by the rules. We can't touch them."

I'm not stunned by his 'we' comment. If one of us takes an interest in someone, we all take an interest in them.

After taking a moment to consider my options, I ask, "Do they have any stock left to move?"

"If they do, it'd be no good. It's well past its shelf life."

"Shelf life?" I *pfft* his belief that cocaine, meth, and heroine have an expiry date. "The potency drops if they're not stored correctly, but they don't have an expiration date. Any real-life gangbanger knows that, Smith."

He tells me to fuck off before he floods my phone with a heap of articles that discredit my claim. I don't have the heart to tell him my knowledge is firsthand. It wasn't cooked up by a bunch of federally-funded scientists hoping to scare cartel groups into lowering the amount of product they manufacture.

As I punch in the address Smith supplied into the GPS in the console of my borrowed ride, I make sure my reach out to an old sanction won't tread on anyone's toes. "Have any friendlies been in contact?"

You don't have friends in this industry. Everyone is an enemy, but mafia wars can be avoided with some basic common courtesies, such as making sure you're not buying another entity's stash.

When Smith assures me the Sánchezes haven't been approached by any entities on the Petrettis' level for at least the past three years, I shift my focus closer to home. "What about Dimitri? Has he found Demi yet?" That's my way of asking if Dimi needs my services yet. I'll never class Dimitri as my boss, so I'll never straight-up seek orders from him, but that doesn't mean I won't give it my all to find his daughter.

I imagine Smith shaking his head when a woosh sounds down the line. "They're still a hundred miles out from Hopeton." I scan the cab of my car for surveillance points when Smith responds to my screwed-up nose as if he witnessed it firsthand. "Dimi stopped to feed Roxanne. They just got back on the road now."

"Can you see me?" I ask when I fail to spot a single device he could be viewing me through. I know the sneaky fucker can log into the camera in my iPhone, but that's why I keep it in my pocket.

"No." I can barely hear him through his breathy chuckles. "You grunt when you're confused."

"I do fuckin' not."

"Yeah, you do." He steals my ability to continue denying his claim by playing a recording of our conversation back to me. It's faint as hell, but there's no doubt there is a *huh!* grunt a second after he advised me Dimitri hadn't reached Hopeton yet. "You also rub your hands together anytime you're scheming, bite your lip when you're struggling to pick between a sweet or savory snack, and when you're showing off in front of the ladies, your punishment of choice is laying the boot into your opponent."

"It is not." It fucking is, but I'm as sure as hell not telling him that. Nosy prick. "It's turning their brains to mush with a bullet."

"If only she had agreed to your request, then you would have had the trifecta."

I'm about to tell him to fuck off, but his trifecta comment has me going in a different route. "What was the third item?"

"So you're admitting the first two is how you flirt?"

I smack my back molars together before working them through a solid grind. "Smith..."

"You laid the boot into him, almost blew his brains out, then..." he leaves me hanging like I won't whack him in the nuts for it later, "... she googled you."

I sound like a prepubescent teen when I ask, "Claudia googled me?" It's all forgotten when Smith hums an agreeing murmur. "Yow-fucking-ie, I went and got myself a crush. I hope you left up that picture of me in the shower as I asked. That shot has gotten me more pussy than last season's Super Bowl quarterback."

I push aside my showboating for a growl when Smith asks, "Can you have conjugal visits with a stranger? It would bring new meaning to Tinder. Swipe left if you want a black widower, right for a little ol' attempted murder wrap."

"Shut the fuck up, Smith."

He mimics my dreary tone but switches his name for mine before he disconnects our call. I'd be upset about his lack of a goodbye if he didn't tack on an offer that I could call him for help at any stage. That's his way of telling me to be careful without acting as if he cares. The last person he cared about shit on him, so I can see how he'd rather pretend he doesn't give a shit than put his heart on the line.

It's all good. I know he loves me.

How could he not?

I'm fan-fucking-tastic.

I'm still pushing tickets off myself when I pull down the street the

Sánchezes' compound is on. Smith mentioned that their assets had dwindled since the death of their founder. You wouldn't know it from the grandeur of the street. There's nothing much out this way but farming land dotted between cities that were once towns, but it's the ideal location to stay off law enforcement's radar.

The outbuildings nestled around the large brick and steel construction reveal the Sánchezes are still manufacturing drugs. They're just servicing the less respected cartel groups instead of the big-wigs.

I startle like a bitch when Smith's accented voice breaks through the speakers of Warden Mattue's Mercedes. "You can drive right up to the gate. I got you a meeting with Jose. Told him you were only in town for an hour. Fucker nearly creamed his pants."

His breathy chuckle halts ringing in my ears when I glide up to the manned security gate, verifying he can see me.

A man with a seedy mustache and an AK-47 greets me with a wonky grin. After tossing his cigarette to the ground, he moseys to the window I've just slid down. "When I saw your name pop up on the visitor list, I told myself they were fucking liars. The only time a Petretti comes out this way is to cause trouble. Then I remembered that's your specialty. Are you here to start shit, Rocky?"

His nickname makes sense of his early identification of my face. We must have spent some time together in jail. If his botched sleeve is any indication, I'm going to assume it was in juvie.

"Depends on what you class as trouble. If you purposely lower the weight in the bricks I want to purchase, then yeah, we'll have issues. If you don't, we'll be solid."

He pops his head through my window. "Ma won't do you wrong. She's been waiting for this day for over a decade. She won't fuck it up for anything."

"When did your last name become Sánchez?" I could be completely off the mark, but when I think of the name Sánchez, I don't imagine a pasty white fucker with freckles and burnt orange hair.

My theory is proven correct when the guard chuckles out, "I ain't no Sánchez, but Ma is adamant as to how we're to reference her." Flashbacks of a teenage boy with buckteeth and braces roll through my head when he nervously shuffles side to side. "It's best to keep her happy."

Wanting to test a belief, I ask, "Have you been here since juvie?"

My hand stops creeping for my gun resting in the middle console when he lifts his chin. "Ma took me in when I had nowhere else to go."

*And let me guess, you've been in her debt ever since?* is what I want to ask, but since I can't, I bob my head like I understand his plight. I don't because it wasn't just Dimitri waiting outside the gates of Hopeton Juvenile Correctional Facility for me after my first brief stint there. Ma and Finlay were there as well.

Although I feel sorry for him, I don't have time for idle chit-chat. I'm already stretching Dimitri's level of understanding with a pop-in visit of the Sánchez empire. I don't want to entirely eradicate it by delaying the process of having a chin-wag with an old inmate.

"If you're ever down Hopeton way, look me up." I could hand him my business card, but since that's asking for trouble, I pretend I don't have one.

"I will, man. Thanks." He smiles like I offered him an unlimited number of whores before he walks back to the security box he's manning to push the button that opens the electronic gates. "Go past the first two buildings, then follow the driveway to the right. Jose is in the main house."

I lift my chin in thanks before gently pressing my foot down on the gas pedal. As suspected, the Sánchezes are still manufacturing. The topless women dotted throughout the brick and steel warehouses leave no doubt to this, much less the vinegar smell in the air.

When I turn right as directed, I spot a man with a black satin shirt and black pants moving down the stairs at the front of a massive home. His hair is as shiny as his shirt, and it is slicked back off his face that looks like it's never not glowering.

"Mr. Shay, I am Jose, these are my brothers, Alej and Frances, and my mother, Juana," Jose introduces after opening my car door for me.

"Please, call me Ma," says the lady I'd guess to be mid-fifties while breaking away from her sons standing one step back from her. Jose assists his mother down the final two stairs like her bones are frail before he steps back to join his younger brothers' line. "We're all family around here."

When Juana holds out her hand liked a mafia don wanting me to kiss the ring on her pinkie, I stamp my authority in the same manner. I'm pissed she wants me to call her Ma like she gave birth to me. My mother raised me, so she is the *only* woman I'll ever call Ma. "I don't have long, so how about we get down to business."

Juana pulls her hand back in shock, scorned by my rejection before she signals for Jose to commence proceedings. It's a standard exchange between a drug manufacturer and a distributor. They walk me through the manufacturing sites, flash their fleet of transport vehicles, then give me a rundown on their schedule from manufacturing to distribution. There's only one difference—our walk-through is constantly interrupted by the coo of a baby from a baby monitor.

"Do you need to get him?" I ask Juana when the baby's happy blubbering switches to a wail. "I'm fine with negotiating with Jose if you have more pressing matters to attend to."

Suspicion flares through her eyes before she asks, "How do you know he is a he?"

She's smarter than she looks, but so the fuck am I. "I made an assumption based on the fact you've raised an army of men. I find it a little hard to imagine you with granddaughters."

Jose's lips twitch, but before a word can spill from his mouth, his mother jumps back into the conversation. "*Grandchildren*? How old do you think I am?" She doesn't give me the chance to reply. She isn't stupid. She knows she wouldn't like my reply, so instead, she loops her arm around my elbow and guides me inside. "JJ is not my grandson. He's my son, Juan, reborn. I'll raise him as I did his father," she says like I should be proud of her. In case you're wondering, I'm not. "Would you like to meet him?" She doesn't wait for me to answer her, she just *tut-tuts* an elderly lady with wiry silver hair.

While she jumps to her command, Juana takes a seat in a chair with rolled arms and royal tapestry. It's similar to the 'king' chair I have in my living room. It just has a matching 'queen' chair next to it.

"I hope you don't mind," Juana says when the nanny returns to the room with a baby I'd guess to be around eight or nine months old. "He's very hungry. It won't take more than a minute to feed him."

I dart my what-the-fuck eyes between her three grown children when she finalizes her statement by pulling out her wrinkly tit. They act as if it's perfectly normal for their mother to breastfeed their nephew. I want to puke. I've seen some fucked-up shit in my life, but this almost takes the cake. How is it even possible for her to do that? Isn't that why boobs shrivel and sag? Because they ran out of milk?

I'm so uncomfortable about the situation, my gun feels real heavy in the back of my trousers. I'd pull it out, pop a bullet between the old bitch's eyes, then flee with what I'm guessing is Claudia's baby if it wouldn't cause more grief for Dimitri. He's already in the midst of a war, and the enemy is his father. I can't add more shit onto the pile he's been shoveling the past two years. Instead, I make an excuse to leave the room.

"While she does... *that*, why don't we go discuss logistics." Although I had no intention of purchasing any of the Sánchezes' stock, they're selling it way below wholesale. I'd be a fool to give up this opportunity. Furthermore, I've always believed it's better to have your enemy in your back pocket than standing in front of you with a loaded weapon.

When Jose agrees with my plan, his mother un-suctions JJ from her tit, tosses him into the nanny's arms, then races across the room with her boob still hanging out. "Why, thank you, darling," she praises Frances when he tucks her boob into her shirt like he didn't have to touch his mother's tit to do it.

There's something seriously fucking wrong with this family, but I'm in too deep now to sprint for the exit like I couldn't stand up for myself since I was twelve. I have to suck it up, which is exactly what I do for the next forty minutes.

"Have them load half into my trunk, then I'll send coordinates for the rest later tonight."

Stoked about the massive order I just placed, Jose shakes my hand before galloping down the stairs to commence filling Warden Mattue's Mercedes with bricks of coke. I almost follow his descent, but the quickest gurgle of a baby stops me. JJ sounds like he's in the room next to where I'm standing.

"Come to think of it, maybe I should have it delivered at the same time. My lead foot will most likely get me pulled over by an eager state trooper." I rub my hands together before tacking a fake smile onto my face. "We all know how that will end."

Alej grins when I make a pew-pew noise with my mouth like my mental age is as low as his appears to be. "Do you want me to tell Jose about your change of plans?"

"If you could, that would be awesome. Thanks, man." I point to the door opposite to the one I hear JJ in. "Is it okay if I hit the head before I head out?"

He nods so fast, I'm confident his brain is rattling against his skull. "But not that door. That's Ma's room." He pulls a face like I'll be in trouble if I go into her room without permission. "You want the third door on the right." He stops, checks his hands to see which one shows the L, then corrects himself, "The third door on the left."

"Cool. I got it. Thanks, man." I whack him in the shoulder for a job well done before spinning to face the bathroom.

I have my hand curled around the brass doorknob before Alej jogs down the stairwell to update Jose on my plans. I sprint for JJ's room just as quickly. Juana could be inside, lying in wait, but I've got a story at the ready as to why I entered the wrong room. She'll be so flattered thinking Alej got his left and right mixed up again, she'll stop fantasizing about her sons for thirty seconds to set me straight.

The churning of my stomach weakens when my entrance into the room is done without spotting a middle-aged lady confused as to why the love you have for your children is different than the love you have for a partner. JJ is alone, happily playing in his crib.

When he spots my approach, he rolls over until he's on all fours, then he uses his crib to pull himself onto his feet. I nearly tell him how clever he is, but his excited squeals registering on the baby monitor at the side of the room stop me. Instead, I let him gnaw on the finger I had planned for him to shake.

In case you're wondering, he has teeth—a couple of them by the feel of it.

Once I've freed my finger from his vicious mauling, I drag my hand over his mousy brown hair, fixing it into place, then I yank my cell phone out of my pocket to snap a couple of photographs.

The more images I take, the heavier my guilt becomes.

Even Smith can sense it.

Well, so I thought.

SMITH:

Move on, Rocco. An army of confused
Mexicans is about to sweep the halls.

After inwardly cursing about his silent message popping up on the screen of my cell phone, I stuff it into my pocket, whisper a promise to JJ that he won't have to live with the weirdos for much longer, then bolt for the door. I wait for my phone to vibrate for the second time—Smith's way of announcing the coast is clear—before lowering the handle and breaking into the hallway.

I make it to the landing of the stairwell in just enough time. Juana, Jose, Alej, and Frances are halfway up it. Excluding Alej, all of them are carrying weapons.

"We thought you had gotten lost?" Jose questions while swiveling his assault weapon around so it's hanging off his back instead of being aimed at my chest.

"No. I needed to use the bathroom. Did Alej not tell you?"

I feel sorry for Alej when Juana whacks him up the back of the head. She isn't gentle, and neither are the words she screams at him in Spanish. I don't know many languages, but I made it a mission to learn as many foreign curse words as I could during my first stint in juvie. Juana uses a lot of them during her tirade.

"Sorry," Alej apologizes on a sob while scuttling by me.

"It's all good," I assure him before getting my head back into game mode. I usually blaze in without a thought for anything or anyone. I can't do that this time around. Not only would it put an innocent baby at risk, Fien's life could be on the chopping block as well.

For that reason, and that reason alone, I give proof of payment for the drugs I purchased before farewelling the Sánchezes with a dip of my chin.

"I'll see you soon," I assure before slipping into the driver's seat of Warden Mattue's car.

*It just won't be for what you're expecting.*

9

———

## ROCCO

One of Dimitri's understudies—*don't ask me his name because Dimitri goes through understudies like he does briefs, and I can't keep up with who's who*—tosses the keys for my Buick into my chest when I jump down the final stair of a private jet. I had every intention of driving back to Wallens Ridge not only to return Warden Mattue's car but also to drop off a printout of JJ for Claudia, but urgent matters altered my plan.

Dimitri found Demi. She wasn't living it up in a Petretti residence rent-free. They found her in the living room of a derelict property, beaten up and barely conscious. If that isn't fucked-up enough, it's been unearthed that the man she killed when he tried to rape her was a Ravenshoe PD police officer. That can only mean two things— Demi's uncle, who also happens to be Dimitri's father, organized the attack, or he has a rogue fucker floating free in his arsenal of corrupt cops.

Neither scenario sits well with me.

Order is all the Petrettis know. When it gets scrambled, people start dying. I don't mind if that person is Col, but I'm too fond of the fuckers below him to let them drop like flies. I'm also particularly fond of Demi. She reminds me a lot of Ophelia. There's just one difference between them—Ophelia got out, and Demi is still trapped here.

I don't see that being the case for too much longer if Maddox and Demi fall for the ruse a female agent approached me about mid-flight.

If you haven't worked this out yet, let me spell it out for you. I'm not a fan of law enforcement officers. They're untrustworthy, corrupt, and think because the law says it's right, it is. Not everything is black and white, and it's the poor pricks who get stuck in the gray who are hurt the most—people like Finlay, Demi, and Claudia. They were trapped in a big void with no way out. Finlay is slowly finding her feet. Demi will if she gives Agent Machini a trust I'm not sure she deserves, so that only leaves Claudia.

Yesterday afternoon, I would have said she isn't my problem, but our stories are too similar to ignore. We're both orphans, compliments to our fucked-up fathers, and we were both abused. I can hide the shit that happened to me with a heap of attitude and a swagger that hides my broken insides. Claudia can't. She spends a majority of her day in a cell, eating food that tastes like fish even with seafood never being on the menu while her son is miles away being groomed to be the next lap dog of a lady I'm reasonably sure has her metaphors confused like my father once did.

Ma will roll in her grave if I walk away from this like my stomach isn't twisted up in knots. When she was alive, I never wanted to disappoint her, so I won't in her death, either. I'll help Claudia, and she won't owe me a thing for it because helping her could very well be the only way to fix me.

I loosen my grip on the Buick's steering wheel when the flashing of lights reflects in my rearview mirror. My speed was a little excessive, but the Petrettis own this town, and my Buick is well known, so why the fuck am I being pulled over?

When it dawns on me that I'm being tailed by a first responder truck, I stop reaching for my gun. Agent Machini's undercover operatives are generally conducted in the medical environment. Smith rattled off some shit about her being a decorated medic in the military. I didn't pay much attention to what he said because, unlike him, I never have and never will shack up with a woman in law enforcement. That's just asking for trouble.

With my mood not knowing which way to swing, I go for my usual cover. Humor keeps everyone's suspicions on the down-low. "If you think you're going to give me a prostate exam, you have another thing coming."

Agent Machini should have smiled when they snapped her picture for her Bureau identification card. It's a nice asset I didn't realize she had. She never smiled anytime I saw her with Tobias, and those by-the-seat-of-her-pants visits stopped right around the time Tobias was killed. "Don't act like you wouldn't like it, Rocco."

Since I deserve the jab her reply hit me with, I take it on the chin like a man.

My lack of retort sees Agent Machini filling the gap with a hefty dose of shock. "We need to swap rides."

"Like fuck we do. The only time I'll be carted around in an ambulance is when I'm dead."

With her head tilted to the side and her brow arched, she acts as if I didn't speak. "I need a car Maddox feels comfortable with. One he wouldn't hesitate to steal."

"And you think he's stupid enough to steal from me?"

"Yep," she replies, popping the 'P' for good measure. "Just like he'll take this as well."

My jaw falls to the floor when she holds up a gym bag identical to the ones I use for drug runs. Don't read that the wrong way. I don't run drugs for the Petrettis anymore. I organize the runs. That's an entirely different field of expertise.

It's also a brilliant money-maker.

Conscious time isn't in Agent Machini's favor, I ask, "What am I getting out of this again?"

"Nothing," she snaps out, shocking me with her honesty. After opening my car door, she undoes my seat belt, hoists me out like she's double her size, then drops the keys for her jacked-up ambulance into my hand. "But doesn't it feel good knowing you're contributing to your community in a helpful manner?"

"Nope," I lie, preferring for her to consider me as a straight-up murderer than a regular joe. It's all well and good now, but one too many flirty lines, and she could turn into a dark-haired version of Theresa Veneto. The thought alone would make any man's skin crawl. "I'll expect a check for the damage to my Buick on my desk by close of business tomorrow."

Agent Machini drowns out her chuckles by slamming shut my Buick's door and cranking the ignition. Regretfully, no number of revs of my baby's sweet engine conceals what she says next, "Class the ambulance as a trade-off. I'm sure you'll have a use for it one day."

"Agent Machini..." I follow her down the freeway like Warden Mattue did when I borrowed his Mercedes. "Be gentle on the gear-stick," I beg when she crunches through gears. "She's an old girl. Don't tug it like you do a cock. Gently maneuver it into gear."

I only stop blurting out instructions on how to drive the first car I ever owned when Smith's crackling voice booms from my pocket. "She's got you played."

"Shut the fuck up, Smith."

With my bottom lip protruded like I'm a child and my Buick long gone, I stomp back to the ambulance to continue with my travels, confident a healthy dose of mafia disdain will eradicate my wish to go on a bloodbath.

I pull into the driveway of Roxanne's family's ranch forty miles later. Smith is already here, and Dimitri is speaking with him as if his eyes aren't continually drifting Roxanne's way. He has it so fucking bad for her that I look forward to ribbing him about his backpedaling when we're not surrounded by half of Ravenshoe PD's most corrupt cops.

My mocking grin sags when I spot Demi entering the living room via a door in the far corner of the outdated home. She's as white as a ghost, but her face is all shades of purple. Whoever got to her fucked her over good. Roxanne was run over—twice—yet her injuries weren't quite as extensive as Demi's.

"Did they find the second perp?" I ask Smith when he stops at my side.

He lifts his chin. "Dimitri took care of him... personally."

See, I wasn't lying when I said Dimitri can't look at Demi without seeing his daughter. Those Petretti genes are strong. That's how I knew the boy wrapped around Ophelia's thigh was her son, and it's why I'm confident Juana's 'son' is Claudia's baby. He had the Sánchez look, but his eyes and lips were identical to his mother's.

After dragging my eyes over the heavy presence of police at the front of Roxanne's grandparents' ranch, I angle my head so only Smith can see and hear the movement of my lips. "Did you tell Dimi about the purchase I made today?"

"Yeah."

"That's it? Just a yeah." When I whack him in the stomach, he almost drops the tablet he's balancing with one hand. "I need more details than just a fucking *yeah*." I impersonate his accent when I quote my last word.

Dark hair falls away from his face when he glares at me. Yes, you heard me right. He has to tilt his head because that fucker is only six-foot-one, whereas I'm closer to six-foot-four or five with the right boots.

"He was so impressed with the figures, he suggested we double your order before they realize how much they're undercutting themselves."

I fucking knew that would be Dimitri's answer. That's why I didn't hold back.

"Did you double the order as asked?"

"No," he replies while he continues fiddling with his tablet. "I haven't had the chance."

Suddenly clueing in on the fact he wouldn't disobey a direct order unless it were for something more important, I ask, "What are you working on?" I answer my question by peering down at his screen. "Is that the dark web?"

He hums out an agreeing murmur before moving closer to a group of police officers on the patio of Roxanne's family's ranch, talking like they're at a training conference. "I picked up a ping just before you arrived. Someone logged in while here."

"For what reason?" The desire to kill thickens my veins when Smith angles his tablet so I can see the website where he's running searches. It's a date-rape fantasy site. "That's the address of Roxie's apartment building." I should know. I camped outside it for days on end the past year. "Does Dimitri know what you've found?"

Smith shakes his head before his focus shifts to a stream of police cars blazing down the driveway. With everyone's focus on the arrival of fresh blood, Agent Machini slips a gym bag full of marked bills under a side table Smith and I are standing next to before she tosses the keys for my Buick onto the coffee table.

When she pushes her finger to her lips, telling me to be quiet, I flip her the bird.

It doubles her smile.

We discussed logistics during my trip here, and the remembrance of our conversation pops a brilliant idea into my head. "Go show Dimi what you've got," I suggest to Smith.

For Agent Machini's plan to work, she needs Maddox and Demi to make a break for it. They won't be able to do that if they're being eyeballed by over four dozen police officers. Dimitri is a hothead in general, but he doesn't care who steps onto the canvas when it comes to Roxanne. He'll slaughter him in front of the President if it's the only way he can get across his point that Roxanne is untouchable.

I'll do the same for my girl—*when I have one.*

Smith sighs heavily. "I will *once* I've pinpointed the culprit."

"How are you going to do that?" I ask while Maddox makes his way to Demi, who's now sitting on a single sofa chair in the middle of the living room.

I flick my eyes back to Smith when he advises, "When he posts again, I'll track the device he uses. Even if he's the size of an ant, I'll find him."

"You need him to post again so you can pinpoint his location?" When he nods, I whack him in the stomach for the second time. "Do you really think he'll do that with you right there, eyeballing every move he makes? Give a brotha some room to make a mistake."

I make a mental note to buy him some glasses when he perfects the stupid nerd expression. He hadn't considered how his hovering would dampen the perp's enthusiasm until I spelled it out for him. "I'll go give Dimitri an update."

"Good idea." I pat his head like he's a good puppy before moving closer to Roxanne.

I've been Dimi's friend since I was five. Even with Fien's disappearance making him the surliest bastard I've ever met, I know his first port of call before he flies off the hinges will be to ensure Roxanne's safety. Since that became my priority after we stumbled onto her on an off-ramp battered and bruised and with tire marks on her thighs, I may as well position myself in an area that requires less legwork.

Like a perfectly timed skit, while Smith updates Dimitri on his findings, the perp uses Dimitri's lack of attention to his advantage. His two-second update sees Smith unearthing his location in three heart-thrashing seconds.

I grin like I'm getting my dick sucked when Dimitri's big burly tone booms across the room. "Rocco, take Roxanne to her room!"

The only part of my plan that doesn't go off without a hitch is Roxanne's impressive sidestep. She whizzes past me like I haven't played a game of football in my life—*I haven't*—then races in the direction Dimitri took off to after voicing his demand.

"Roxie..."

I'm not annoyed about her agility. I love a woman who isn't afraid of a bit of gore, but I can't express that to Dimitri while he's gunning for blood, or he'll have more than one perp to contend with.

"Dimitri!" Roxanne shouts when Dimitri pole drives an officer in the middle of the group to the ground.

As Dimitri throws his fists into the face of a man with dark hair and a now bloody suit, I ask Smith, "Is that him?"

Smith nods before giving me a quick rundown on everything happening. It's worse than first perceived. The officer Dimitri is brutalizing didn't just place Roxanne's credentials on a date-rape site, he put Demi's there as well. The johns who assaulted her were supposed to sodomize her with the bat after beating her black and blue with it. The sickening details Officer Packwood added to her 'rape plan' have me wanting to join Dimitri in issuing his punishment. There are sick fuckers in the world, then there are people like Officer Packwood.

"Whose address is that?" I ask when my scroll of the page has me stumbling onto an address for the flashy side of Ravenshoe.

My eyes snap to Smith when he gabbers out. "Justine Walsh."

"Justine *Walsh*?" I parrot, my tone higher and more ear-piercing than Smith's.

When he nods, I stray my eyes in the direction Maddox and Demi were standing. Unsurprising, they've used Dimitri's beat-down to their advantage. The bag of cash Agent Machini stuffed under the side table is gone, but the Buick's keys remain.

After working my jaw side to side, confident Maddox is in the process of hotwiring my baby, I return my focus to Smith. "How long ago were Justine's details put up?"

He points to a date at the bottom of the date-rape site. Like the fuckers could get any sicker, they added the desire of being mauled by a dog onto the bottom of Justine's supposed 'fantasy wish list.'

My brow cocks when the date on the website registers as familiar. "Wasn't that around the time Dimi bought the Walsh family home?"

Smith bobs his chin. "The day before."

A grin tugs at my lips. "So technically, Dimitri could claim he saved Justine's life. If he hadn't purchased their home, she would have been raped."

"Rape isn't murder," Smith objects.

"Perhaps not for an average person, but for a woman who was mauled by a dog, it could have turned out that way." I hold my hand so it replicates a gun, press the barrel to my temple, then pretend to blow my brains out.

"You think Justine is suicidal?"

I shrug while muttering, "Aren't all rich fuckers?"

Before Smith can answer me, Dimitri's burly baritone roars across the room for the second time. "Get her out of here!" He motions his head to Roxanne, who is in the process of watching Dimitri hoist Officer Daniel off the ground by a child's swing hanging out of a tree in the front yard.

*Good improv, Dimi.*

Uneager to test Dimitri's patience for the third time today, I curl my arm around Roxanne's tiny waist before spinning away from Dimitri going to war on the officer's stomach. In case you're wondering, he isn't using his fists this time around.

Roxanne's fight slackens when her eyes lock with the screen of Smith's tablet partway to the room I'm guiding her toward. He left it at the screen he showed Dimitri. It has a copy of Roxanne's license front and center. It paints everything in horrifying detail, including just how close her roommate came to experiencing what Demi went through three days ago.

My shins get battered when Roxanne screams a couple of seconds later, "Let me go!" She kicks, wails, and screams before she seethes through clenched teeth, "I'm gonna pull his insides out of his nostrils."

Aww, her malicious mouth almost makes me hard. It's a pity she reminds me too much of my sister for that to ever happen. "You're too late, Princess P," I inform with a chuckle. "He's already met with his maker."

Daniel's head is flopped to the side, but if I were the coroner assigned to do his autopsy, I'd cite the removal of his cock via a blunt object as the cause of his death.

# 10

## ROCCO

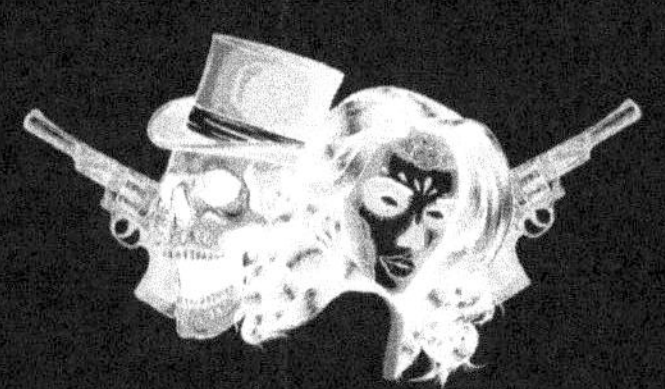

"Cute kid. Is he yours?"

I glance up at my questioner like my eyes aren't being propped open by three lines of coke. With Officer Daniel's body needing to be disposed of and Agent Machini's plan to permanently ostracize Demi from the Petretti entity going off without a hitch, this is the first chance I've had in over twenty-four hours to scratch my nuts. But instead of doing that, I pulled out my phone and scrolled through the multiple videos Smith plucked from Wallens Ridge's surveillance server at my request before I glanced over the pictures I snapped of JJ yesterday afternoon.

There's still hope for him yet. Claudia has been fucked over more ways than Sunday, yet she can still smile about the simple things in life. Like a fresh banana, a new toothbrush, and a cell designed for only one occupant. She also isn't selfish like most women are when they're denied their every want. I put enough credit on her prison account she could have purchased every item in the commissary, but instead of doing that, she put back the electric toothbrush she so desperately craved and purchased a fellow inmate a pregnancy test.

In my eyes, that makes her a decent human being.

It's just a bonus that she's also really fucking cute.

I've never had an instant interest in someone like this. Ma always said one day a girl would rock up and knock me onto my ass. I thought she was full of shit, but I can admit now that she wasn't too far off the mark. Even with us only meeting a little over twenty-four hours ago, I have an immense amount of respect for Claudia. She did what any good mother should do. She fought to protect her child. The cracked bones she got from sheltering her stomach before a collision that could have killed her unborn son is proof of this, not to mention the fact she was only in that accident because she was endeavoring to flee from the man who had abused her for years.

I won't lie. When I read Claudia's recollection of the events that occurred the day she was arrested, I was about ready to dig up Juan's body, piss on his face, then hang his corpse from the chandelier in the Sánchezes' home, but I was turned on as well.

Not that Claudia was abused but from how fucking hard she fought to get away from him. Her son wasn't even born, yet she was willing to go against an army of men to protect him. That's as sexy as fuck, and it has me tempted to scroll past the video of her shaking her booty while cleaning her teeth with the electric toothbrush I had the warden personally deliver to her cell yesterday morning.

I wouldn't hesitate if the beady eyes of my interrupter weren't absorbing every move I make. Alice doesn't like being ignored, especially if a lack of concentration centers around another woman.

"Why don't you tell me if he's my kid, Alice. From what I've heard, you're all up in Petrettis' *business* lately."

Alice was married to Col's number three. They didn't get divorced. I just say 'was' because I'm reasonably sure Jayde will divorce Alice when he finds out how she's keeping herself in favor with Dimitri's crew. As far as Jayde is aware, Alice sells Dimitri's women to sexually deprived men from Arabia. He has no clue before Roxanne showed up that she was also serving Dimitri's dick. To Alice, blowjobs don't count. I don't play by the same rules as her. If you're married and any part of your body touches my cock, you're a cheating whore.

Since Agent Machini is waving me over to the room Demi was placed in last night, I only hear Alice's scoff instead of seeing it. Since

I'm being honest, I'll admit, after last night's efforts, I have no clue which side of the fence Agent Machini's morals stand. She isn't exactly rogue like many of her coworkers, and I'm reasonably sure she'd bust my ass in a second if she saw me snorting the coke I did earlier, but she lets a lot of shit slide as well. It's like she's stuck in the gray with Demi and Claudia, but she doesn't have the means to get herself out just yet.

With her arms folded in front of her chest and her brow raised, Agent Machini waits for me to reach her before she whispers, "I never thought I'd see the day there's a woman you don't like."

I *pfft* her. "Please. You've been hanging around like a bad smell for a couple of months now, so I'm confident you've seen the look I gave Alice at least once." When she throws her head back and laughs, I continue being surprisingly honest for the early hour, "I don't know what it is about Alice. She just—"

"Sells women for a living, and that rubs you the wrong way?"

Do you see what I mean? She knows all the bad shit we do, but she doesn't bust our chops for it. She could be waiting for something that will put us away for life, like the murder of a fellow officer, but she'd need to be in the right place at the right time for that, and she hasn't been that lucky just yet.

"Is there something you want, Agent Machini? It's kinda early, so I'm struggling to remain standing."

She nudges her head to the room I placed Demi in yesterday afternoon. "Our flight leaves in an hour, but she's still sleeping, so I need to have a word with a fellow officer about an alternative mode of transport."

I almost blurt out like a dweeb that *there's more than one of you here?* but I hold back—barely! "You want me to babysit Demi for you?"

I give myself a mental pat on the back when she answers, "I have a barely conscious girl in an unknown room surrounded by mafia recruits. You seem like the logical choice."

She hardly knows me, but she trusts me.

What did I tell you? My ma raised me right.

"I won't be long," Agent Machini promises while opening Demi's door for me.

Demi is *exactly* where I placed her when Agent Machini rocked up a little after eight last night. Her eyes are shut, and a massive groove is running down the middle of her forehead.

"Take your time," I say to Agent Machini while bypassing her in the doorway.

Dimitri may trust her, but Smith and I still have a little way to go, hence the reason Smith synced my listening device to the bug he planted on Agent Machini late last night. We'll hear every word she speaks for the next twenty-four hours.

Fingers crossed it doesn't cause too much of a distraction. My head is already overloaded with information. I can't possibly fit in anymore.

I've only just coasted up to the side of Demi's bed when she commences blinking. "Hey there, baby girl, welcome back."

Bile burns the back of my throat when Demi mumbles out, "Caidyn?"

"Close." I take a breather to make sure I don't gag before saying, "But I'm ten times better looking..." I've heard of Caidyn Walsh, and although he and his brothers are popular with the ladies, I would have shot Col in the head before I would have ever torched my business to 'even the score. "...have at least a dozen more tattoos, and let's not get me started on my cock."

A chuckle rumbles in my chest when Demi stammers out, "All right, Rocco. E-Enough showboating. Can you help me up?"

With how badly slurred her words are, I'd rather she stay down.

When I say that to her, she replies, "And I'd r-rather you not talk about your cock, but w-we can't always have what we want, can we?"

She's more like Ophelia than I thought, except I would have made Ophelia recant her statement by measuring the length of my dick with her tongue.

After helping Demi into a half-seated position, I prick my ear, shocked Agent Machini's conversation with one of her crew is loud enough to cause an echo through my listening device. "She's badly concussed. We can't move her now."

"If we don't move now, we will lose the opportunity. Is that what you want, Macy? Do you want her stuck here for eternity?"

*Macy?* That's a pretty name for a ball-crunching bad-ass.

"No, of course not," she fires back. "But I don't want to compromise her health for her safety."

"You're a trained trauma nurse—"

"Who is advising you that moving her now could end disastrously."

Demi's eyes snap to mine when they move out of the hallway. She can no longer hear their conversation. I'm not facing the same issue. I don't know who Macy is speaking with, but the longer they talk, the more he sweet talks her into being his bitch. She's all but putty in his hands.

I stop smirking at the thought when Demi asks, "What's t-that about?"

I rub my hands together. It's a telltale sign I'm about to start trouble, but since Demi's eyes are too cloudy to see two feet in front of her, I get all my reply out with my life intact. "They're worried about how much you're sleeping." My arm feels her wrath when I add with a chuckle, "I told them to buy you a couple of pregnancy tests."

The situation goes from playful to tense when she asks, "Has a-anyone heard from Maddox?"

"Yeah. He's okay. He did spend the night in the hospital, though."

She almost stomps on my foot when she jumps to her feet. Her eagerness to get to Maddox almost sees her kissing the floor. She sways like a leaf on a hot summer's day when I guide her back to bed. "He isn't hurt... physically." I remember how lost I felt the months I grieved Ophelia's 'death' while saying, "Those Petrettis are hard to get over. Even an ox needs a moment to gather itself."

I'm saved from explaining myself when a knock sounds at Demi's bedroom door. Smith already told me Agent Machini was on her way back, so I'm not as surprised by her interruption as Demi.

"I'll see you around?"

I wait for Demi to nod before I make my way to the door to let Agent Machini in. When my bypass causes my listening device to pick up interference, I curse myself to hell. If she's wearing a similar device, there's no doubt she could have missed the static.

"What are the chances she heard that?" I ask Smith once I'm in the clear.

He taps his keyboard a couple of times before replying, "Buckleys to none. I'm testing out the prototype on the wrong side of the law before selling it to the Feds with a massive markup on the ticketed price. Then—"

"Not only will you make a bundle of money, you can hack into every federally protected system in the country."

I grin when he impersonates me in his reply, "Bing-*fucking*-o!" He takes a moment to relish my breathless chuckles before telling me we're close to game time. We're not about to watch some dumb fucks chase a ball for a living. Dimitri has finally accepted Roxanne's offer to help. He's throwing her into the deep end, and it's my job to ensure she doesn't sink.

Fingers crossed I don't fuck it up, or I won't just leave Dimitri up at the plate swinging the bat alone. Claudia will be left defenseless as well.

For some reason, that annoys me even more than the time Dimitri handed me Roxanne's soiled panties. I knew I was pushing him to the brink, but I had no idea just how fucking close to the edge he was until that night. It cooled my turbines by a smidge, but I'll never stop riling him. He knew what he signed up for when he caught me taking out my anger about my parents' first physical fight on an ant hill in the playground a couple of blocks up from my house. I singed those bastards to hell as I wish I could have my father. Dimitri stomped the ones brave enough to crawl away from the scold of my magnifying glass. Excluding those couple of months when Audrey was in the picture, we've been inseparable ever since.

"How long until we roll out?" I ask Smith after arriving at his makeshift command center in the middle of Roxanne's grandparents' living room.

He checks that the video button in Roxanne's dress is functioning right before raising his eyes to mine. "Twenty, if that. Roxanne's appointment is scheduled for ten this morning."

I lift my chin, acknowledging I understand him, before watching Demi's solemn walk to a fleet of cars lining the driveway. Agent Machini went all out with her transport. Not a single dime has been spared.

"She'll be better off," Smith says, mistaking the relief on my face for worry.

His error is understandable. I went along with Agent Machini's plan solely to ensure Demi isn't forced to endure time behind bars. Maddox is having a hard enough time, so there's no way Demi's incarceration would have been a walk in the park. Demi's cock-thickening face would have seen her facing the same injustices Claudia is currently dealing with, and then I'd have more reasons to set Wallens Ridge on fire.

If it weren't such a good money-maker, it would have been ablaze months ago.

While rubbing my hands together, I shift from side to side. "Smith—"

"An up-to-date inventory of the commissary at Wallens Ridge has already been forwarded to your cell."

I could tell him to get the fuck out of my head. Instead, I place him into a headlock before musing his hair with my knuckles. He doesn't seem to mind. Dimitri has been working him to the bone, so he still had the bed-hair look girls seem to appreciate. I can't say the same for Dimitri. He looks set to rip me a new asshole.

Smith calls me a chicken under my breath when I gabber out, "We should head off soon to avoid traffic."

After lifting his chin, Dimitri shifts his focus to Roxanne. I don't hear a word he speaks, but his actions ensure every man within a hundred mile radius now knows Roxanne is off the market. He kisses her like he isn't being eyeballed like a freak at a circus.

"I didn't think you had it in you, D, but I was wrong. You can *totally* make me hard," I say when some of the pimple-faced fuckers around Smith get a little too doe-eyed for my liking. Unlike Smith, they have the computer nerd look down pat, so I'm confident in saying they've never had their dick close to anyone's mouth, let alone a chick's.

Although Dimitri cuts off the grab of my crotch with a wickedly evil sideways glance, I can tell he appreciates my attempt to defuse the tension in the room. He'd kill a man who dared to look at Roxanne for longer than half a second, so I can only imagine how murderous his thoughts would be if he saw the gaga gleam their eyes got when they imagined she was kissing them instead of him.

He hits me with a second wordless thanks before he shifts his focus back to Roxanne. "If at any time you feel something is off, signal for us to move in. Rocco will be in the pharmacy next door. Clover and a team are one block over. I've got as many men on this as possible—"

"I know, Dimi," Roxanne assures, smiling when he fails to cite an objection to her interruption. He's so dick-first in love, I guarantee he'd stop a blowjob mid-blow if she wanted to have a deep and meaningful conversation. *Pussy.* "We've got every base covered. Now we just need to get your daughter back." While clearing Dimitri's spit from her lips, she twists her torso to face me. "Ready?"

"I was born ready." I pout like a child while plucking a set of keys for a spanking new truck off the coffee table. It's all fancy and shit, but it doesn't have the classic lines my Buick had. After squeezing Dimitri's shoulder in silent support, I head for the back entrance. I have to tail Roxanne's drive instead of helming it. When my squeeze does little to soften the groove between Dimitri's brows, I say, "She's got this, D. She was run over *twice.* She can handle anything."

I hit Roxanne with a frisky wink when she wiggles her fingers at me before sliding into the driver's seat of a beat-up Honda. I can hear how fast her heart is raging in my earpiece, but I'm still as confident as fuck in saying she is a kick-ass lady. Who in their right mind would set themselves up to be kidnapped by maniacs who'll cut an unborn child out of a mother's stomach without anesthetics? Only someone as tough as Roxie. She'll put herself in danger just for the chance to save Dimitri's daughter from the miserable childhood she had. As far as I am concerned, that makes her top-fucking-dog.

After checking the coast is clear to pull onto the freeway, I ask Smith to plug me into one of the many surveillance devices he rigged into the car I purchased for Roxanne at three this morning.

"What for?"

"Just do it, Smith, then log the fuck out."

He murmurs something about me having rocks in my head before he does as told. I wait for the familiar click that announces he's left the feed. When it doesn't come, I tell him I'm going to torch his van *after* forwarding the names and numbers of the women he's slept with the past two years to his ex-flame's email.

That sees him logging out quickly.

"Hey, Roxie. It's your brother from another mother."

Although her breathy chuckle is echoing in my ear, the quiver of her lips is still heard in her reply, "Are we being followed?"

"No, we're good. I just wanted to make sure you're okay." I punch myself in the thigh, hating that I'm lying to her when she's been nothing but honest with me from the get-go. "And ask if you know what Claudia's favorite food is."

"Her favorite food?" she asks, genuinely stumped as to where I'm going with this.

"Yeah. The prison menus aren't set. They're changed every couple of months, so I thought if you knew what her favorite food was, I could have a word with the warden to make sure it's placed on the menu."

She remains as quiet as a church mouse. That doesn't mean I can't hear her loved-up sigh, though. It's rumbling in her chest way too loudly to act as if it doesn't exist.

"Rox?" I mutter a couple of seconds later, needing to move our conversation along before we get near Dr. Bates's office. Dimitri will murder me if he thinks for a second my focus wasn't on Roxanne's safety.

"Umm..." My teeth grit when she pauses again. "That's a really difficult question to answer. From what Claudia has told me, she hates fish, and that's all everything tastes like in prison." I laugh, assuring her she's on the money, "But if you discount that, I'm going to say a big juicy heart-attack burger."

"A burger?" I ask, certain I heard her wrong.

I didn't. She hums out a murmur of agreement before adding words into the mix. "She's never really eaten takeout. Her parents couldn't afford it, and her foster mother wouldn't allow it." I don't know whether to glower or smile when she adds, "I tried to smuggle in some contraband when we were roommates, but she was transferred to a county jail to await trial an hour before Estelle arrived with the goods." I go for the latter when she asks, "While we're asking questions, can I ask you one?"

"Shoot."

I'm anticipating for her to ask if I think she's crazy putting herself in danger for a child she's never met, so you can picture my shock when she states matter-of-factly, "What are your intentions with my friend? If it is anything less than stellar, Mister, I'll have no hesitation whatsoever in ordering the removal of your cock."

With a huge grin stretched across my face, I grab my crotch and hiss. "Warn a man before referencing the dismembering of his johnson. He needs time to prepare."

"That wasn't what I heard," Roxanne interjects, her tone a unique mix of pride and suspicion. "Officer Black's screams echoed all the way to Erkinsvale."

I shouldn't laugh. It will have you convinced I'm a sadistic prick, but it can't be helped. I didn't think Jose would have the balls to go through with my request. I doubt he would have if he knew who he was defending. I would have cut off Officer Black's dick myself if Dimitri wasn't counting on me. He'll never admit it, but he struggled as much as I did the months we were out of contact between his marriage to Audrey and her kidnapping.

When Roxanne coughs, announcing I've yet to answer her question, I say, "She needs a friend—"

"A friend? *Hmm...*"

I grin like a fucking idiot, loving how tapped into my inner-workings she is. "You have heard of friends with benefits, right?" I slam my foot on my truck's brakes to avoid rear-ending Roxanne's Honda when she locks up the brakes. "Fuck me, Roxie. I was joking."

I realize Smith is as sly as perceived when he mutters, "I wouldn't accept his offer if I were you, Roxanne. You don't want to know where his dick has been."

"Hey!" I shout when Roxanne grumbles, "That's what I'm worried about."

Acting more pissed than I am, I tell Smith to get the fuck off our line before demanding Roxanne to continue en route. "We don't want you late for your staged kidnapping. They might pick another redhead to steal... *again.*"

My ill-timed reply dampens the mood for the next couple of miles, the silence only ending when Roxanne murmurs, "For what it's worth, I think you'd be a good match for Claudia, Rocco. She needs someone like you on her team."

I silence her for the second time when I say, "Just like Dimitri needed you."

This time, it's a good stretch of silence. It brings everything back around full circle and gets our heads into game mode.

Roxanne's plan would have gone off without a hitch if I weren't distracted by another urgent situation blasting through my ears.

"What the fuck is an acute subdural hematoma?" I ask Smith just as Roxanne is ushered into a private bathroom in Dr. Bates's office by the whack job himself.

As news of an emergency situation with Demi sounds through the earpiece lodged in my ear, I watch Roxanne uncap a plastic canister before it disappears under her dress. While she pees into a cup so Dr. Bates can conduct an onsite pregnancy test, I shift my focus to the ruckus occurring in my ear. I thought Demi looked a little off this morning, but I had no clue her brain was experiencing enough pressure to force Agent Machini to operate while thirty thousand feet in the air.

My stomach gurgles when Agent Machini requests someone to bring her an instrument capable of breaking through Demi's skull. I'm confident she's pranking me but lose the chance to investigate further when Dimitri's deep timbre roars out of the speakers of my phone, "Get her out!"

With the noises of Agent Machini setting up to operate on Demi mid-flight distracting me, I don't notice a goon sneaking up on me until it's too late. He slams the butt of his gun against my head before pinching my temple with a second gun, momentarily halting my sprint out of the pharmacy.

"This will be your *only* warning," I seethe through clenched teeth. "Walk the fuck away now."

I don't even give him a second to respond. Patience isn't a strong point of mine as it is, but it's even more woeful since I can hear Agent Machini performing chest compressions on Demi. I've got one girl dying and another one in the process of being kidnapped, but no matter how many times I tell my head to stick with the program, it continually drifts to the fear in Claudia's eyes every time she was ushered out of her cell to the area mental health watches are conducted.

The goon takes two staggering steps back when I remove my gun and pop two bullets into his stomach as if he is responsible for Claudia's pain. Since he has some extra flab around his midsection, my bullets don't take him down as quickly as they would someone much smaller than him. After pushing me back with force, he fires off one shot. His aim is thankfully pitiful. The bullet whizzes past my scalp instead of imbedding into my brain as intended.

The close call pisses me off even more. With the roar of a deranged man, I pop another bullet into his chest before ripping a fire extinguisher from the wall to crush his nuts to smithereens. I don't have a knife to slice his cock off like Jose did to Officer Black, but I can make sure even in the afterlife, this fuckface won't have the use of his cock.

With my level of understanding at an all-time low, it takes me a couple of seconds to realize the bead-size listening device in my ear dislodged during my assault. It's at my feet, teetering back and forth between the man happy to die so he doesn't have to live without his johnson.

"I fucking warned you," I snarl into his face just as van doors being pulled open sound over the grinding of his balls. A white pedo van is parked in the loading bay of the Publix Supermarket. There is a naked female lying lifeless in the back—a female I recognize even with her clothes being shredded off her slumped form.

"Roxanne!" I scream before sprinting for the untagged van.

This was Dimitri's plan. Roxanne was meant to be kidnapped this morning, but there was nothing in the dossier that said her tracker would be removed from her arm by a goon in a seedy van.

He digs out the rice-size device, uncaring if he hurts Roxanne before he tosses it onto the asphalt. With a grin of a madman, he orders for the driver to go.

"Smith!" I scream while tailing the van on foot. My earpiece is still in the alleyway along with Roxanne's bloody tracker and the goon who impeded my spring to get her, but Smith doesn't just snoop with listening devices. If you have anything electronic on you, he can track you down.

"Smith." My scream isn't as loudly voiced this time around. Not only have I lost the van through the backstreets of Ravenshoe, but I also discover the reason for Smith's lack of response. My cell phone cracked from the stranger shoving me into the brick wall. It isn't functioning.

*Fuck it!*

With my annoyance at an all-time high, I gather up Roxanne's tracker, stuff the bead-size listening device back into my ear, then drag the man I would have happily tortured for hours on end if I had time under a security camera mounted above the loading bay of the Publix Supermarket. He's dead, but that doesn't mean he's useless.

Smith unearths my location only seconds later. When I hold

Roxanne's tracker into the air, the direness of the situation dawns on him. "They removed her fucking tracker."

"What do you mean?" Dimitri asks, his voice unlike anything I've ever heard. "No one knows she was wearing a tracker, so how do you know they've removed it."

I hear the whoosh of a finger point before the thump of Dimitri's heart overtakes the ringing of the bullet that whizzed past my head.

He took a gamble, and for the first time, the chips didn't fall in his favor.

# 11

## CLAUDIA

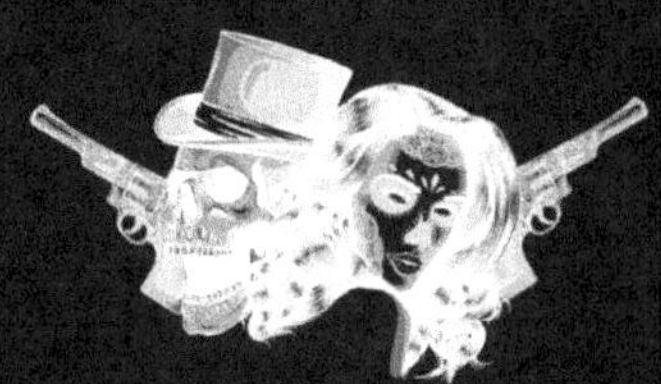

*I* roll over with a groan, frustrated about my inability to sleep of late. The guards have kept their word. They've done precisely everything Rocco asked them to do. My stomach is always full, modest yet clean underwear covers my backside, and I've not had one suicide watch the past fifteen days, yet here I am, in my solo cell staring at the ceiling instead of sleeping.

I'm unsure exactly what the time is. I am guessing around midnight. There's an eerie quietness associated with this time of the night that can't be discounted. It would be perfect for pacing if I weren't trapped in a six-by-nine-foot concrete cell.

With a final huff, I flop my legs off the lumpy mattress and rise to a half-seated position. As my eyes stray to my son's ultrasound photo, I recall the meeting I had with Warden Mattue earlier this week. He seemed more interested in learning about my relationship with Rocco than discussing the possibility of JJ joining the nursery at Wallens Ridge. Even when I was honest, he didn't believe me when I said Rocco and I had never officially met and that I only learned of his name in passing as he did mine.

While I'm being honest, I'll admit I'm not entirely sure why Rocco went to bat for me the way he did. The search I did on him with some of my commissary credit didn't unearth anything about his private life. I'm not overly surprised by a lack of information. The number of restrictions they place on the computers at Wallens Ridge is the equivalent of putting a parental lock on a child's YouTube account. You'll never stumble onto anything remotely interesting. I could have asked Warden Mattue, and it would have evened the number of interrogative questions between us, but since I don't trust him, and for some strange reason, respect Rocco, I didn't.

It could cause a heap of trouble, and that's the last thing I want.

After dragging my index finger over the outline of JJ's profile, I set to work on unearthing if the world is more alive outside of Wallens Ridge's walls than it is in them. I've perfected my acrobat routine the past couple of days. My skills are so impressive, I no longer remove my socks for the fear they'll get wet if I miss the rim of the toilet.

My heart beats in an unnatural rhythm when I drag my eyes across the parking lot at the front of Wallens Ridge. The staff has a fenced lot at the back, so I'm surprised by the number of vehicles in the visitors' lot for the late hour. Two cars appear to be government-issued. I've seen them come and go multiple times the past month, but the Range Rover parked in the disabled bay near the warden's Mercedes is new.

When lights float over the dusty ground a couple of seconds later, I contort my neck at an odd angle. Wallens Ridge is lit up like a Christmas tree at night, the rays beaming through my window every evening is one of the reasons I've struggled to sleep, but this is a different type of light. It's low to the ground like headlights or hand-held torches.

I realize it is the former when my stretch has me spotting the hood of a first responder truck. It's parked super close to the loading bay, and its engine is running. I love a good murder mystery with a touch of romance, so several scenarios run through my head when I consider the possibilities of what is happening. However, none are quite as imaginative as what occurs next.

A tall man with broad shoulders breaks through the front doors of Wallens Ridge like they're not locked at precisely five each evening. If his ability to come and go as he pleases doesn't already announce the mysterious stranger's identity, the quickest glance he directs at my window most certainly does.

Rocco has returned to Wallens Ridge, except I'm no longer on his visitors' list.

*That sucks.*

We're not technically friends, but I would have loved the chance to thank him for his generosity with more than mumbled words.

Even though Rocco appears to be in a hurry, he salutes me like he did the last time he spotted my watch, slips behind the Range Rover's steering wheel, then hightails it out of the parking lot. His speed is so fast, the fat tires on the Range Rover spray Warden Mattue's Mercedes with rocks.

Serves him right. He's been extra edgy the past couple of days. I thought his arrogance centered around Wallens Ridge being investigated, but now I'm not so sure.

I stare in the direction Rocco went for the next twenty minutes before the voice of the woman in the cell neighboring mine breaks through the silence surrounding me. "What can you see?"

Jodi loves to gossip about anything not related to her pregnancy scare. It was just that, a scare, but the more gossip she instigates, the fewer questions she faces about how she could have a pregnancy scare while incarcerated for over a year.

After straying my eyes back outside, I whisper, "Nothing." I maintain my lie for two seconds before it eats away at my insides, forcing me to blurt out, "An ambulance is idling near the loading bay. That doesn't necessarily mean anything, though." Suicide rates are extremely high in this region as it is, not to mention at a maximum-security prison.

Although I was arrested near Hopeton, I was sentenced to Wallens Ridge at Juana's request. She wanted to be close by so she could assist in the raising of her grandson when he was born.

Truth be told, she didn't want to travel far after stealing a newborn baby from his mother.

Jodi must have her face squished between the bars of her cell because she sounds like she's right behind me when she asks, "Is anyone in the ambulance?"

I shake my head like she can see me before withdrawing my non-verbal denial. "I can see shadows. Two are large, one is of a medium build, and I think the other is a child."

"A child?"

I shush Jodi when her loud shriek bellows through the adjoining wall of our cells, only speaking again once I've ensured the stomp of an officer's boots isn't racing our way. "It isn't a child. It's a woman. She was being carried by a guard, so I mistook her *height*." My last word comes out with a squeal from the warden's eyes suddenly snapping to my window. I was so enamored taking in the woman's bloody hands and disheveled clothing, I didn't realize Warden Mattue had joined the party of five.

When my balk away from the window causes me to lose my footing, my foot slips into the toilet bowl. I silently squeal my frustration into the cool night air before clambering down so I can remove my drenched sock.

Once I have it wrung out and hanging on a makeshift clothesline, I move toward the bars of my cell to pacify Jodi before she has a fit. She hates being left out of the loop. "A woman in professional-looking clothes was placed into the back of an ambulance. She had bloody hands, and her clothes were torn open like she had been assaulted."

"Was she a guard?" Although her voice is barely a whisper, there's no denying it's piqued with concern.

I shake my head. "No. She wasn't wearing a uniform."

"Wow," Jodi breathes out slowly. "I hope she's okay."

"Me too," I reply, my heart suddenly pained.

With both of us in shock about the unexpected turn of events, we sink back toward our beds, then eventually fall into a restless sleep.

The next morning, the rumor mill is running rife. I haven't experienced this much gossip since time in the yard was cut short over two weeks ago so a helicopter could land on the flat surface. Tales ranged from the Federal Bureau of Prisons popping in to visit a death-row inmate attempting to escape via a tunnel he burrowed under Wallens Ridge.

We never found out the answer because we were confined to our cells for over twenty-six hours straight, and my window doesn't face the yard.

"What have you heard?" I ask Jodi after planting my backside onto a bit of a bench seat next to her. It's breakfast time, and since I was up a majority of the night, I'm starving.

She peels back the skin of her banana like half of it isn't mush before replying, "All I've heard was that a coroner was brought in from outside prison walls."

"So someone is dead?" I hear my skyrocketing heart rate in my question.

Jodi nods. "We just have no clue who."

While she continues gossiping with other inmates around the table, I ponder what possible connection Rocco could have with the incident that occurred last night. He was here at the exact time the event unfolded, but he didn't have an ounce of blood on him.

Not that I took in every inch of him or anything. I merely would have noticed the blood splatter associated with a violent prison murder.

*Yeah, right.*

I'm so desperate, I forked over an exorbitant ten commissary credits to have the only photo I found of Rocco on the internet printed. It was from a few years back, but since I was convinced his colorful tattoos and handsome face would make my dreary cell seem not so bland, I splurged.

It should embarrass me to admit his photograph combined with the tongue cleaner on my toothbrush has convinced me multiple times over the past nine days that I'm at a country club instead of a maximum-security prison, but it doesn't.

Happiness comes in many forms. Mine just happens to be compliments to a toiletry product with a vibration setting and the wickedly immodest grin of a stranger.

12

———

# ROCCO

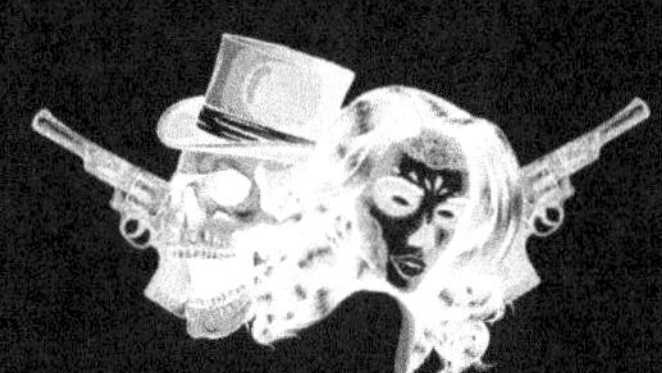

"Are you sure you're comfortable? You don't look comfortable, especially if his big-ass head takes up all the space." I step back from a row of three seats in a private jet with barely a second to spare. Dimitri's fist almost crushed my nuts. Considering I haven't used them in three weeks, that's the last thing I want. "Don't be like that, Dimi. I'm just making sure your girls are comfortable for their trip."

No, you didn't hear me wrong. The day has finally come. Dimitri is taking his *girls* home. It was a close call, one that may not have occurred if Maddox hadn't presented me with evidence that proved the person Dimitri has been chasing the past two years was, in fact, India, Audrey's best friend and roommate.

I knew I was smelling a rat back in the days Dimitri was wooing Audrey. I just had no clue I needed to extend the perimeter of my sniff.

It's been a fucked-up couple of weeks, but it's all done and dusted now. Fien is home, Roxanne and her unborn child survived being accidentally shot by Dimi, and even with India being on the run, I've got a little breathing space to delve deeper into how everything bad that's happened of late appears to center around Wallens Ridge

There's some murky shit going on there, and none of the cloudiness is coming from the prisoners.

Once Dimitri has Fien strapped into her seat, he spins on his heels to face me. "Once you've visited Maddox, are you heading back to Hopeton?"

I half-nod, half-shrug.

It frustrates Dimi to no end. "Rocco…"

"I've got a couple of matters I need to attend to first." I whack him in the shoulder before shuffling side to side. "Why? Do you need me to slice the knife I sharpened on your behalf this morning?"

There are rules we're governed by.

Rules we cannot ignore if we want to remain a part of the Cartel.

Rules that were voided the instant the extent of Col's crimes were unearthed.

Two weeks ago, FBI agents stumbled onto a corpse in the wall of a family ranch a couple of hundred clicks from Hopeton. I won't lie—Dimitri shit bricks when the child's age was unearthed during a preliminary autopsy. Although badly decomposed, she was the same age as Fien. Dimitri pretty much gave up hope, but I knew the world couldn't be so cruel to one man. I forced him to continue, and continue he did. With the help of Henry Gottle, Sr., the boss of all bosses, we stormed the fuckers who kidnapped Roxanne within seconds of her pregnancy test returning a positive result. Our showdown saw Roxanne and Fien brought home relatively unscathed.

Then shit started hitting the fan.

Audrey was found alive, India was using Dimitri's guilt to fuck with his head, and no matter how many times I tried to tell Dimitri she was a scheming bitch, he didn't listen.

It took Dimitri sending Roxanne away for her to say she'd had enough. The same evening Maddox requested an emergency meeting with me, Roxanne played Dimi's game with the ruthlessness that seeded her place as Dimitri's queen. She gave as good as she was getting, and it was that gall that saw her survive both a bullet wound to her stomach and a ruptured appendix.

Just as things started to settle down, Dimitri was hit for the third time, but instead of it centering around his daughter and his girl, it was for a relative he didn't know existed until he was handed DNA proof.

The toddler found in the wall was Dimitri's *and* Demi's half-sister. Col was unaware when Monica, Demi's mother, was gifted back to his brother, Demi's father, that she was eight weeks pregnant with his child.

When Col took Kaylee to teach Sean a lesson, he had no clue she was his daughter. In all honesty, from what I know of Ophelia's childhood and what I've heard about Demi's, I don't think the knowledge would have made any difference to Col's mindset when he killed Kaylee.

The coroner's report cites that Kaylee died of asphyxiation. Col didn't use his hands to choke her, nor did he suffocate her with a pillow. He used the very thing Dimitri has sworn to remove from Col's body before he's returned to the earth from which he came.

Kaylee's true birthrights changed everything. Since Col killed a direct heir to the Italian Cartel throne, he too could be killed. Dimitri took out the trash within hours of landing in Hopeton three days ago, and if the news circulating from all sides of the mafia world is anything to go by, he couldn't have left it a second longer even if he wanted to.

Col was making costly mistakes. So many, if Dimitri hadn't dibbed the honor of taking him out, I would have put my hand up.

After licking my lips, I say, "When I get back, there are a few things we need to discuss."

Dimitri has the killer glare down pat but looks like a big doe-eyed puppy when he slants his head and cocks a brow. "Anything urgent?"

"Nope." I pop the 'P' for good measure, confident my news can wait for a couple more weeks. "All you need to worry about right now is taking care of your girls. I can handle the rest."

Roxanne gives me a look I could mistake for her wanting to suck my cock if I knew she wasn't head over heels in love with Dimi, whereas Fien grins at me like she understands every word I speak.

While Dimitri made sure Roxanne had everything she needed at the hospital and his fly-in, fly-out visit to Hopeton, Fien's care was my responsibility. Our time together had Claudia's situation entering my head more and more often.

Dimitri got updates on Fien with every ransom he received. Claudia doesn't get a single fucking thing. From what I've seen in the surveillance footage I've watched—yes, I'm a fucking creep who likes to keep watch from a distance—the only photo she has of JJ is an ultrasound picture.

That's all set to change once I get Dimitri and his family in the air.

"Take care of them, Dimi. If you don't know how, I'll come back early and show you how it's done."

I only just make it out of the jet with my life intact. Dimitri is reaching for his gun. He did the same thing after following me to the airport I dropped Roxanne off at last week. He knew I was only playing when I let Roxanne slide her hand into my boxers. We wanted to spark a reaction out of him. At the time, Roxanne thought we lost our wager, but when I saw Dimitri slipping into his ride when I jogged around the Range Rover the valet had brought to the front of the club, I knew the big green monster on Dimitri's shoulder had been activated. He just kept it hidden from his enemies so they couldn't use it against him.

As the stairs of Dimitri's private jet are pulled up, I join Smith by a flashy sports car. "Is everything ready?"

He bobs his chin. "Being prepped as we speak." After handing me a fat envelope, he adds, "They're not the best quality, but under the circumstances, I'm sure she won't care."

I grin the smile of an insane man when I take in the contents of the envelope. "Thanks, Smitty. She'll love them."

He pushes me off him when I complete my man hug by humping his leg like a dog on heat. His deflection is all a ruse. I can smell how horny he is. That might have more to do with the fact a certain federal agent is sitting in the passenger seat of his car, preparing for their seven-hour drive back to Hopeton, but whatever. I'm certain some of his horny scent is for me.

After regaining my footing from his shove, I say, "If you didn't want to hear Roxie and Dimi fucking, you could have hired another jet. I've seen what Dimi pays you. I'm sure you can afford it."

A side of Smith I rarely see shines brightly in his eyes when he hits me with a frisky wink before he slides into the driver's seat of his low-riding car. I'm still staring at the taillights of his sleek ride when his murmur spills from the earpiece in my ear, "If you don't want to hear anything freaky, stay off this frequency."

"Smith, you dirty fucking dog," I bark out with a howl before he disables our connection.

13

———

# CLAUDIA

*I* roll my eyes when the inmate in front of me says, "I don't care what Marissa said. That skank knows nothing. She shanked his ass here because she wanted to pin her murderer on one of us."

"But that makes no sense," Jodi interjects like she's a part of their conversation instead of being at my side, feigning that her legs don't work because she's so hungry. The mess hall usually opens around eleven thirty for lunch. That was almost an hour ago. Even my stomach is protesting about the delay. "Inmates don't have access to the underbelly of Wallens Ridge like the staff and law enforcement."

"Says you," spits out a black-haired woman with crooked teeth and a spiteful sneer. "Do you really think only the guards' *playthings* get special visitations around here?" She wiggles her finger in Jodi's face when she says 'playthings.'

When Jodi attempts to slap the disdain from her face, I hold her back. "She isn't worth it."

"Oh, I know," Jodi agrees. "And so did the guards. That's why they *never* looked past her butt-ugly face."

It takes me and three of the original aggressor's friends to keep them apart, and even then, two guards have to intervene.

"That's it, Priscilla. I told you one more incident would see you in the hole. Let's go." When Priscilla tries to argue with Officer Marconi, he hovers his hand over his baton. I doubt he'd use it, but it gets Priscilla's legs moving remarkably fast.

Regretfully, her stomps don't hinder her flapping gums. "This won't be the end of this."

I balk when she mans up to Jodi like she has a loaded pistol stuffed down the front of her pants. Jodi stands her ground. She's done the same thing many times the past two weeks.

"You need to stop doing that," I whisper under my breath while dragging her into the mess hall. "Fighting will only gain you more attention from the guards, which disregards your whole tough-chick act."

The scared, timid woman I formally met while she was endeavoring to buy a pregnancy test returns full force, proving my comment hit the nail on the head. I understand the change in her personality. She either stands up to her bullies or gets eaten alive by them, but she needs to time her skits better. There are guards here who will see her newfound attitude as a challenge they'll do anything to break.

How do I know this? It was what gained me Juan's attention. His mother had every intention of kicking me out the following morning, so I left with guns blazing. *Figuratively.* I told her the way she was with her sons was weird, and that if I ever had a son, I would raise him differently than she had her children.

You all know how that turned out.

With my mood diving off a steep cliff, it takes me a little longer than normal to identify the smell filtering through my nose. "What is that?" I ask Jodi, certain my nose isn't smelling what it thinks I'm smelling. It smells like real meat. Like actual meat from a cow, not the manufactured crap they try to pawn off as meat every mealtime.

"It smells like..." Jodi takes a prolonged whiff before moaning on a growl, "Philly cheese steaks and Arby's curly fries." My stomach grumbles along with hers when she adds, "With a side of fried chicken and corn on the cob."

Too hungry to discount, I loop my arm around Jodi's before dragging her to the end of the very long line. "I really hope they don't run out before we reach the bain-marie. I'm so damn hungry, even if I'm imagining the delicious smell, I am going eat every portion of food on my plate."

"Me too," Jodi agrees.

For how long the line is, it moves remarkably fast. Before we know it, we've reached the first food station, and it's better than anticipated. The food isn't just replicating every fast-food restaurant you could possibly imagine, it is *from* every fast-food restaurant you can imagine.

"Oh... my... god." Jodi squeezes my arm while bouncing on the spot when the attendee at the fries' station places a large serve of curly fries onto her tray.

"Thank you," I whisper in gratitude when she does the same for me.

"Chicken or beef?" asks a second attendant while waving a set of tongs over some mouthwatering burgers from Wendy's.

"Umm. Chicken, please. No... beef." I don't get enough iron, so I should stick to meat even with the chicken patty looking mouthwatering.

My indecisiveness is pushed aside for shock when a sexy male voice says, "Give her one of each. There's plenty to go around."

I stare at Rocco in absolute shock, unmoving and unspeaking. It gains me the scorned rile of the women still waiting to be served, but I don't care. How can I be expected to move when my legs have turned to Jell-O? Rocco isn't wearing the hideous hairnet and baby blue apron the rest of the food staff is donning. He's wearing fitted trousers and a partially done-up shirt that showcases his impressive collection of chest tattoos.

He looks so smoking hot, I ruin my fries with drool.

"Go on," Rocco encourages after grinning about me dragging my hand across my mouth to check for spittle. "I brought it here for you, so it's only fair you enjoy it."

Missing his comment that he did this for me, Jodi plucks up two burgers, one chicken and one beef, loads them onto my tray, then does the same for herself. After thanking Rocco's generosity with a glance that goes way too long for my liking, she pushes me toward the dessert station that consists of sundaes, milkshakes in all the colors of the rainbow, and coffee that smells like it wasn't brewed in a toilet bowl.

My mouth falls open when Jodi mutters, "Take one of each."

"I can't take one of each. That will be greedy."

"You *can* take one of each, and you *will* take one of each."

The products she overloads my tray with almost fall to the floor when she drags me away from both the food stations and Rocco.

"Meals are to be eaten in the rec room of your cell block today," advises Officer Parkes, impeding our beeline for our favorable table.

After nodding in understanding, I take a sharp right. Since I'm paying more attention to the area I just left with the hope I'll be awarded a peek of Rocco before he disappears for weeks on end again instead of where I'm walking, Officer Parkes's extended elbow knocks my hot fudge sundae over before it rolls off my overloaded tray.

"I'm so sorry," I apologize, horrified by the goopy white substance coating Officer Parkes's once-polished black shoes. "I wasn't watching where I was going."

I take a stumbling step backward when he replies, "It's fine. Nothing a napkin won't fix." Officer Parkes isn't any better than Officer Black. He treats the inmates like scum, and on more than one occasion, I've heard about him making the male inmates clean up their spills with their tongues. "Why don't you go fetch yourself another sundae?"

While licking my suddenly parched mouth, I stray my eyes to Jodi. When I notice her narrowed gaze is holding as much suspicion as mine, I shake my head. "It's fine. I have plenty on my tray to eat."

"No," Officer Parkes replies, stepping closer. "I insist." My heart drops to my stomach when he removes my tray from my hands so he can dump my food into the bin next to him. After meticulously removing the smears of ice cream from the stainless-steel material with a handkerchief from his pocket, he holds it up so I see my whitening cheeks in the gleaming material. "There you go. Just like new."

"Thank you," I whisper, even though I'm feeling anything but grateful.

When I attempt to remove my empty tray from his grasp, he pulls it out of my reach before motioning his head to the half-empty mess hall. "Ladies first."

I swallow the brick in my throat before briefly nodding, advising I understand what he wants. Officer Black's 'retirement' must have awarded Officer Parkes access to the storage closet key or the blueprints to the kitchen that shows every hidden nook, and he has every intention of utilizing his new 'superiority' within hours of gaining it.

When I spin on my heels to face the entrance of the mess hall, Jodi attempts to follow me. She only takes two steps before I shake my head, slackening her stride. For one, I stupidly didn't look where I was going, so it's only fair I face the consequences of my actions alone, and two, I'm not exactly scared. I am too curious pondering what Rocco's response will be to me returning to the mess hall to feel an emotion as cheap as fear.

Jodi isn't happy about my request, but when another guard tells her to move on or face time in isolation for disobeying orders, she has no choice but to accept it.

"*It's okay,*" I mouth before I recommence my trek.

I only make it partway through the mess hall when a voice that keeps me awake for hours on end the past three and a half weeks snaps out, "I'll take it from here."

I slant my head to hide my smile, pleased by Rocco's swift response.

Officer Parkes's response is nowhere near as happy.

When he tries to tell Rocco what he thinks about his plan, Rocco stares him dead set in the eyes while asking, "Did that sound like a suggestion?" He snatches my tray out of his hand before he sends him on his merry way with a two-fingered brush-off. "I'll use more than words if I'm forced to repeat myself."

Officer Parkes's annoyed huff hits the back of my neck before the stomps of his ice-cream-stained shoes boom into my ears. He pushes through the latecomers arriving at the carnival-like gathering a mere second before Rocco signals to a newly assigned guard standing next to the last bain-marie to go after him.

"Who's that?" I ask, too curious to realize I'm being nosy. Furthermore, I should be thanking him for his assistance, not grilling him about it.

My eyes drift over Rocco's ridiculously handsome face as he says, "A friend."

After taking in my face as rigorously as I did his, he drags his eyes down my body, his perusal only stopping when he reaches my wobbling knees. Just because I'm not feeling fear doesn't mean my body won't respond to what could possibly happen once Rocco goes home. Some of the officers here are so pigheaded, they think they're untouchable.

I begin to wonder if Rocco can read thoughts when he mutters, "My *friend* will ensure nothing like *that* ever happens again." He nudges his head to my knees during the 'that' part of his reply.

"Thank you," I murmur, truly grateful but having no better way of showing my appreciation than with pointless words.

After scrubbing his hand across his cropped beard, he asks an extremely insensitive question in a weirdly sensitive way. "Has anything like *that* happened since I was last here?"

It isn't what he says that relays the sensitivity of his question, it's the gleam his eyes got while asking. I won't be in trouble no matter how I answer him. I doubt the same could be said for any culprits I point out, though.

Fortunately for all involved, I don't have any news to deliver, neither bad nor good, so instead, I shake my head.

Rocco's inflated chest deflates when he breathes out a shallow, "Good."

With my tray in one hand and his other curled around mine, he hits me with a frisky wink before he helms our walk back to the delicious-smelling food. He doesn't move us to the end of the line to wait our turn. He just gathers up one of each item before he guides me to the tables usually filled with the backsides of hard-ass criminals.

He lays out the food in front of me as if there isn't enough to feed an army before locking his eyes with mine. "Go on. Dig in before it gets cold."

"Are you not eating?" I'm starved but too embarrassed to eat with an audience. Additionally, Juan would have made me eat out of a dog bowl if I dared to start before him. Although I'm highly skeptical Rocco would stoop to those lows, there's no such thing as being too cautious. I thought Juan was my savior. In reality, he was my tormentor.

Past horrors are the last thing on my mind when Rocco leans in close. He smells more delicious than the greasy food in front of me, and the closeness gives me the chance to drink in his deliriously handsome face. "Would it make you feel more comfortable if I did?"

When I sheepishly nod, he smiles, killing me further. He picks up the first item in front of him, which happens to be the burger I was eyeing, then shreds his teeth through the meaty product.

Since he's eating, I creep my hand toward a serving of French fries, but before I can stuff a single one into my mouth, Rocco tilts the burger he's eating my way. "Your turn."

The hands holding his loaded burger together are the same hands that nearly bludgeoned a man to death, and they're the same hands that most likely just ordered the beating of Officer Parkes. But instead of being scared about bringing them near my face, I curl my hands over them, inch them toward my mouth, then take a bite out of the burger with the same viciousness Rocco used.

"Oh... my... god." I'm not sure if I voice my praise or moan it. It may be a combination of both. "That is so..." I can't talk. I've died and gone to food heaven.

"Good?" Rocco asks with a laugh before taking another bite.

With my hand covering my mouth so I don't look like a pig, I nod. "So good. I've never tasted anything nowhere near as delicious."

I choke on a piece of lettuce when Rocco twists his lips while saying, "Yet."

I'm pretty naïve when it comes to being propositioned by handsome men, but I know exactly where his thoughts strayed, and for once, I don't feel frightened by the prospect.

"You good?" Rocco asks with a grin that will highlight my dreams for months to come when silence invades our exchange for a couple of seconds.

I swallow the food in my mouth to ensure I don't choke again before nodding for the second time. "But next time, can you warn me before you put thoughts like that into my head. My memory bank needs time to prepare for the visual overload you're about to award it."

Since my mouth is empty, I choke on air when he mutters, "If only the servers at Wallens Ridge weren't so restrictive, then you'd have more to *work* with than a six-year-old photo."

I don't know what shocks me more—the fact he knows I printed a photograph of him or that he appears stoked about it.

"How do you know I have... *that*?" My last two words are spaced by a worried breath.

There's no cause for fret. Rocco isn't the least bit confronted by my interrogation. "I see the purchases you make with the funds I placed into your commissary account."

"You put money on my account?" I've known all along it was him, but it will be nice to have confirmation directly from the source.

He waits for me to take another bite out of the burger he's holding to my lips before he jerks up his chin. "I get an itemized account emailed on the thirtieth of every month. It tells me everything you bought the previous four weeks."

My cheeks only heat to half their potential from the cocky wink he hits me with since the truth smacks into me not much later. If he knows about the image I had printed of him, does that mean he also knows about the pregnancy test I purchased for Jodi?

Worry highlights my tone when I attempt to dig myself out of a very deep pit. "The test wasn't for me."

"I know," Rocco says while still grinning a smile that could stop traffic. "Wouldn't have made a difference if it were, though." He stops, furrows his brows, then corrects, "Well, it would have. Just not to you." He tilts in close before confessing, "I would have had to add more men onto Marshall's hit list." He nudges his head in the direction the new correctional officer went before he tells me to take another bite of the burger. "Your bites aren't even half the size of mine, so it's only fair you take two."

Fair isn't a word I've ever had access to. Nothing in my life has ever been fair, but it sounds honest coming from Rocco. Don't ask me why. I'm just being as upfront with you as the promising gleam in Rocco's eyes when he watches me devour another chunk of the burger.

Over the next forty-five minutes, we go turn for turn on the food that's currently being distributed to the male half of Wallens Ridge. Aware of the rarity of our lunch being sourced from outside prison walls would have inmates taking more than needed, Rocco bought extra. Jodi and I were greedy with our selections, and we're half the size of some women here.

Even though my 'date' with Rocco is being eyeballed by many high-up personnel at Wallens Ridge, Rocco has acted as if we're alone. I do the same when awarded his utmost attention. The world fades away, and every bad thing I've experienced doesn't seem real. Our instant connection is weird, but since we have a mutual friend, it isn't as off-putting as I imagine a first date would be.

He updated me on where he's been the past couple of weeks and shared the news that Roxanne is expecting a child. It was cute how large his grin was when he revealed his last tidbit of information. He gleamed when sharing stories about the carnage men in his industry crave, but it had nothing on the pure bliss his face gets any time he mentions his friends. Even with him being an orphan, he has family values.

That's a sexy trait I can't help but admire.

My thighs stop squeezing together when Rocco dangles a French fry ladened down with soft-serve ice cream in front of my face. "Come on, Claudia. It's half a bite... at most."

I shake my head before slouching as low as I can without slipping off the shiny bench seat. "If I eat another morsel, I'll barf." While recalling his playfulness the past almost hour, I add, "For all I know, your shoes could be new. I don't want to ruin them."

I roll my eyes like I'm years younger than I am when Rocco replies, "These old things? They're so last season." He drinks in my laugh like it isn't as husky as it is before he double-checks I don't want the last ice-cream dipped French fry. "Are you sure?"

When I nod, he pops the odd yet delicious concoction into his mouth before mimicking my slouched position. He only stays down for half a second before he jackknifes back up. I hate myself when I flinch about the quick movement of his hand toward my face, but it can't be helped. I've been around domestic violence my entire life. I don't know any different.

With his hand suspended mid-air, Rocco assures, "I won't *ever* lay a hand on you to hurt you." He points to a section of my bangs that has something stuck in it. "You've got a bit of gherkin skin in your hair. May I?"

He waits for me to nod before he moves his tattooed hand back toward my face. Once he has the offending product removed, which he extracts with careful precision, he shows it to me before dumping it onto the mess wedged between us.

I'm hoping my inability to keep my food in my mouth is the end of my embarrassment, but it soon dawns on me that I have a lot to learn about this man. "Is that why you ran? Because he beat you?"

I don't usually talk about my personal life. It isn't because I am ashamed about what happened to me—Juan is the only one who should be embarrassed—but more because before Roxanne came into my life, no one cared enough to ask why my face was rarely seen without a bruise.

Gratitude that his interrogative question didn't end our conversation floods Rocco's eyes when I lift my chin. "I could have handled it, but there was no way I was going to raise JJ in an abusive household. If I wanted to break the cycle, I had to take the first step."

Since we're sitting across from each other, Rocco issues me comfort by tapping the toe of his boot against my ankle. We're not technically allowed to touch each other, so that's about as good as his comfort can get.

I don't mind.

Just the fact he wants to comfort me is soothing.

After giving me a couple of seconds to regather my composure, he asks, "Is that what you wanted to call him?" Confusion must cross my features as he sets to work on relieving it extremely quickly. "JJ. Is that the name you chose for *your* son?"

I smile at his overenunciation that JJ is my son before I shake my head. "I didn't pick his name. I didn't even know what Juana had called him until the warden handed me a heap of paperwork to sign."

"Adoption papers?"

Rocco's tone exposes I don't have to answer him if I don't want to. The choice is mine.

Since I feel comfortable with him, I give him my complete honesty. "No. Despite what the warden tells you, I signed papers for JJ to join me in the nursery. I would *never* give him up for adoption, especially not to Juana." I bite the inside of my cheek in warning to my eyes that they better not release the dams pooling in them before saying. "Being raised behind bars isn't ideal but compared to that family, it would be like living at Disneyland."

Rocco laughs like he fully understands where I'm coming from before asking, "Is there anything I can do to help you get JJ..." He swallows the remainder of his offer before asking a question no one has ever asked me, "What did you want to call him?"

"JJ?" I know what he's asking. I just need a moment to gather my emotions again before I sob like an idiot.

When Rocco jerks up his chin, I say with a ghost-like smile, "I had planned to call him Dillon."

"Dylan? As in Bob Dylan."

I shake my head. "No, Dillon. D-i-l-l-o-n, as in my mother's middle name."

Rocco's grin matches mine when he says, "It's a nice name. You should call him that." He stares at my arched lips long enough for my cheeks to heat before he finalizes his earlier offer. "Is there anything I can do to help you get Dillon back?"

His offer is both unexpected and generous, but regretfully, it comes months too late. "I've been fighting to have the custody ruling overturned for months now. Every petition I've lodged has been denied. There's nowhere left for me to go."

"You went the legal route, and it fucked you over." He grumbles something about that not being unusual before suggesting, "So maybe it's time to look at other avenues."

"Such as?"

It dawns on me that we're not alone when Rocco floats his eyes over the guards now hovering in super close. If they get any nearer, they'll replace the scent of Rocco's aftershave with their own, and I'll be as pissed as hell.

Once his watch has the guards concerned they'll be added to Marshall's hit list, Rocco returns his eyes to mine. "Give me a couple of days to get some things together, then I'll get back to you."

"Okay. Thank you." My praise has barely left my mouth when the head guard of this section of the prison advises me it's time to return to my cell.

As I stand, my bottom lip involuntarily drops into a pout. I was having so much fun, I completely forgot I'm an inmate at a maximum-security prison.

When Officer Clarence seizes my elbow to guide my walk back to C Block, my first thought is to thank Rocco for his generosity for the hundredth time the past hour, but there's a burning question too hot to ignore, and it blurts out of my mouth before I can stop it. "Why me?"

"Why not?" he answers without pause for thought.

If I weren't put on the spot, I could think of a number of things. But since I've never been overly good with pressure, I shrug before mouthing a final thank you.

Officer Clarence tugs me back partway through the door when Rocco shouts, "One last thing."

It's stupid of me to admit I'm hoping he will end my first and most likely last date with a kiss, so I won't mention it. In its place, I wipe the hope from my eyes, then spin around to face Rocco. His staggered walk ensures there's no chance in hell I'll remove the lust it instigates in my eyes within the next decade. He's already outrageously handsome, but his confidence catapults it to never-before-reached heights.

"What's this?" I ask when he hands me an envelope.

When I attempt to open it, he curls his hand over mine, doubling the spasms in the lower half of my stomach. "Keep it for when you're in your cell." The hairs on my nape prickle when he leans in to whisper in my ear, "They're not suitable for public viewing."

The kiss I was praying for doesn't occur, but it's pretty damn close. The corner of my mouth catches the smallest snippet of his meaty lips when he presses them to my cheek.

"Step away from the prisoner," booms out Officer Clarence.

With his hands held in the air and his smile revealing he's not the least bit worried about the anger in Officer Clarence's voice, Rocco steps back two paces before he mutters, "Can you blame a guy for trying? Look at her. She's gorgeous."

Officer Clarence almost falls for his trick. His eyes only land on my face for the quickest second before he darts them away with a fretful bob of his Adam's apple. Other than his slip-up, none of the officers surrounding me dare to peer my way.

"They're slowly learning, but just in case they still haven't gotten the point about who's running the show around here, how about we show them." I'm lost as to what Rocco means, but I get an idea of his ruse when he curls his hand around mine to tug me nearer. "I'm going to kiss you. I need to see if these sparks fizzle with sexual contact or fucking explode like Roxie bid on. Don't tell her, but I'm leaning toward fire-*fucking*-works too."

Although he's telling me what he's doing, he doesn't act on his statement until my tongue delves out to wet my lips in preparation for our kiss. That's my way of telling him I'm more than happy to be the guinea pig in his experiment.

"Don't go moaning on me, Mama," he whispers against my lips after pulling my body flush against his and tilting my head to better align our mouths. "With how hard your ghostly grins make my cock, I don't know if I'll be able to hold back if you do."

I'm already panting over his nickname, so you can imagine how impossible it is to hold back my moan when he swipes his tongue over my parted lips before he plunges it inside my mouth. We shared every snippet of food he purchased today, so his mouth is as flavorsome as mine, but there's something more scrumptious about his taste, something distinct and addictive. It has my hands leaving my sides to weave through his recently trimmed hair and my tongue dueling his as if our kiss isn't being eyeballed by men who may want me to do the same to their cocks.

His mouth is so kissable, I can't help but get carried away. It's a sweet, lush embrace that has me craving so much more. It's also full of promise. Not just on what is yet to come, but what could possibly be. It has me wondering what sex would be like with him. Would it be rough and gentle like his kiss? Would he take the lead, or would he leave that up to me? And would it move the land beneath my feet like this earth-quaking kiss?

Not even during sex did I experience this all-encompassing range of passion. There were no tingles of excitement with Juan, no lovemaking, and I never orgasmed. I've often wondered if he found our once-a-week forays more of a chore than a pleasure. Now I'm confident in my assumption. He hated when I touched him, and in all honesty, it was the same for me. I didn't want to please him in the many ways I'm imagining pleasing Rocco now. I never craved Juan's touch, but even now, with one of Rocco's hands groping my ass and the other holding my mouth hostage to his, I beg to start our exchange all over again so then I can wish for it never to end.

"Ah, fuck, woman," Rocco growls out after pulling back, his voice husky from our kiss. "You've got me so damn conflicted." He fists my jumpsuit as if I'm not the only one with wobbly legs. "Those sparks have me wanting to walk you right out those doors, but if I do that, there's no chance you'll ever get your son back. There are rules we must follow." His comment should dampen my mood, but since he's quick to re-clutch the bat he's been swinging for me since the moment we met, it doesn't happen. "I've just got to be patient, and let Smith do his thing, *then I can kiss your cunt like I just did your mouth.*" His last sentence is barely a whisper, but my body can't help but respond to it.

*Sweet.*

*Baby.*

*Jesus.*

Can you still go to heaven if you die from multiple orgasms? Because I'm reasonably sure that's what will happen to me if Rocco's plans transpire. I'm already on the verge of climax, and all he's done is kiss me. I've also never had a man go down on me before, so I'm squirming just at the prospect.

The uncomfortable press of my thighs doubles when Rocco slants his head to the side and arches a brow. "No fucking way. Tell me it isn't so?" He must read his answer from my face as he grabs his crotch before he shuffles side to side. "You need to hurry the fuck up, Smith."

I'm not sure who this Smith is that he keeps mentioning, but I hope he's as good as Rocco implies because after our kiss, the remaining six years on my sentence now feels like seventy—even more so when Rocco pats my backside before he wholly removes his hand. "Reach out if you need me."

When I nod, he playfully bites my lower lip, kisses the tip of my nose, then shifts his eyes to Officer Clarence. He doesn't speak. He doesn't need to. He just silently warns him what will occur if his request isn't upheld. If the heat beaming out of him is anything to go by, the punishment will be worse than what Officer Black faced because Rocco will see it through to the end this time around—as will I. You can't have a kiss as explosive as the one we just shared, then act nonchalant about other sexual contacts. It isn't possible.

Once Rocco is confident the officers understand his point, he jerks up his chin, granting Officer Edgar permission to cuff me. His knowledge that I need to be guided back to my cell in cuffs to lessen the inmates' suspicions as to where I've been the past hour has me wondering how many years he spent behind bars. He's too intimate with the prison's inner-workings not to have been in one before, but his lack of respect for the guards ensures me he's never donned an officer's uniform.

I could ask, but in all honesty, I don't want to find out about his life from anyone but him. The rumor mill is one of the worst parts about being incarcerated. It is second only to the prisoners who retaliate to their belief they're being unjustly treated on the inmates who'd give anything to swap places with them. They have no clue prisoners like Jodi and I don't want the guards' attention. It isn't a privilege to be sexually abused. I wouldn't wish it on my worst enemy.

I pop my head back into the mess hall when Rocco calls my name. "Hey, Mama?" He takes a moment to authenticate the genuineness of my smile before he says, "Fireworks." He spans his hands through the air like he's fanning out a massive billboard. "Big-ass, ball-tingling fire*works*!"

His commentary about our kiss puts me on cloud nine. I practically float back to my cell. I don't hear the patters of my feet or the ruckus of the inmates in C Block asking Officer Clarence how many dicks they need to suck to get a meal like that again tomorrow. It's a heavenly beautiful time that grows more amorous when I discover what's in the envelope Rocco handed me within a second of being left in my cell.

They're photographs of my son, JJ. Sorry, let me correct that. Photographs of *Dillon*. Almost all of them are grainy and snapped from a distance, but they show him doing a range of things—crawling, pulling himself up on the furniture, and making a mess in the kitchen I was once in charge of.

He looks happy and healthy, especially in the final image that's so crystal clear, I recognize the 'L' tattoo on the finger of the man who took the shot. My son is chewing on the index finger of a known gangster, but for some strange reason, I couldn't be any happier.

The loneliest people are usually the friendliest.

The saddest people are usually the most giving.

And the people who have been hurt the most are usually the last person to hurt someone the same way.

Rocco has been hurt. I don't know how, and I don't know when, but I do know that's what draws him to me. As Wayne Dyer said, "You do not attract what you want. You attract who you are."

I am an abuse survivor, and if my intuition isn't leading me astray, so is Rocco.

## 14

---

## ROCCO

With my nuts still tingling with the urge to sink balls deep inside of Claudia in any manner she's willing to tolerate me, it takes a little longer for vengeance to heat my blood when I join Marshall in the underbelly of Wallens Ridge. He's worked Officer Parkes over so good the past hour, he can barely stand when I direct him to, but like the good foot soldier he is, Marshall saved the final act for me.

I've often wondered the past three weeks if Warden Mattue weeded out all the bad officers from his patch as claimed. The loss of eleven officers, two kitchen staff members, and a janitor made it seem as if he did, but you can never be too cautious. If you cultivate your team with nothing but broken promises, you'll grow nothing but weeds.

If my intuition is anything to go by, Officer Parkes is a weed in need of eradicating.

Smith placed Officer Parkes on my radar three days ago. He hasn't worked in the women's section of Wallens Ridge since Claudia was sentenced, but footage of him dragging Demi into the visitor's area a couple of weeks back grated my last nerve. He was rough-handling her like Maddox didn't have a sworn statement from the Governor of

Mafia Law that she wouldn't be touched in any way whatsoever during his incarceration.

Despite what people believe, no one is born an abusive piece of shit. They become one after being surrounded by the wrong people. It's why I ordered the warden to post Officer Parkes back to his station today. I wanted to see how he would act when his aggression wasn't directed at gangsters who wouldn't hesitate to pop a bullet between his brows the instant their sentence is over.

What did he do within minutes of his shift starting? Hit Claudia up like her ass was on the menu along with the food Smith organized.

My annoyance at his ill-advised assumption is heard in my tone when I say, "I thought Warden Mattue made it clear to *all* members of his staff my thoughts about fuckers who want their dicks sucked by women unwilling to do it." I step closer to Officer Parkes, spread my feet to the width of my shoulders, then slant my head to the side. "Let me guess, you were sick that day?" Mindful a bullshitter can't be bull-shitted, I act as if I never asked him a question by asking another. "Where were you taking Claudia, *Officer* Parkes?"

Blood dribbles out of his bruised and swollen mouth when he mumbles, "To replace her sundae. S-S-She dropped it."

"I did see that." I rub my hands together before stepping even closer to him, my glare murderous. "But I'm a little confused because the dessert station was at the end of the bain-maries, and you directed Claudia to the beginning of the line." I stand across from him chest to chest, eyes to eyes. "A line that just happened to be next to the storage closet Warden Mattue gave you a key for at the start of your shift."

"I wasn't aware of that. I was merely making sure C-Claudia didn't face any wrath from the other inmates about cutting the queue. T-They would have seen it as her getting favors. They w-would have given her hell about it."

"Oh... I know. Why do you think I bought enough food for every-one?" Once again, I don't wait for him to answer me. "If I hadn't, it wouldn't be just the guards I'd need to warn to stay the fuck away from Claudia. I'd have to repeat my threat to over three thousand inmates as well."

He nods like he understands my plight.

I don't believe a single fucking thing he says.

"But the thing is, *Officer Parkes*..." I spit out his name so it reflects the weasel he is, "... you only knocked Claudia's sundae off her tray. The rest of her food was untouched... *until* you dumped it in the bin, meaning you not only wasted *my* money, you wanted Claudia's only meal today to be the skanky spunk you were hoping your dick would spurt into her mouth."

Dark hair falls into his eyes when he shakes his head, commencing his lie without words. "N-No, no. Not at all."

His audacity to lie to me for the second time has me reaching my hand into his mouth to grip the very thing responsible for the alteration of my heart rate. It was thumping like crazy from the teasingly yummy taste of Claudia's mouth. Now it's pulsating with rage.

Usually, the change-up wouldn't bother me. Up until two minutes ago, I always chose carnage over covetousness. I'm not reaching the same conclusion today. I am so fucking pissed about the change-up, I don't give Officer Parkes the chance to issue a final plea. I accept the knife Marshall is holding out for me, then slice the lying prick's tongue straight out of his deceit-spilling mouth.

While Officer Parkes gargles on the blood pissing out of the nub he used to call his tongue, I wipe his blood from my hands with a rag before removing my pistol from the back of my jeans. I could take him out with a straight mafia hit, but where's the fun in that? This fucker wanted something he has no right to have. The memory has me aiming my gun at the crotch in his pants instead of the crinkle between his brows.

Marshall chuckles like a psycho when the bullet that shreds through Officer Parkes's dick sees him falling to the floor with the howl of a wolf. He grabs his crotch like his pinprick of a cock, balls, and portions of his ass aren't splattered across the padded wall behind him before he lifts his watering eyes to me.

"Please," he begs, his one word a sob.

Aware he'd rather die than live without a cock sees me offering a leniency I rarely give. I leave the decision of his fate up to Marshall. I don't know if his father fucked with his head like mine did, but I'm reasonably sure he's faced some sort of sexual abuse in his life.

You don't have the tenancies we do if you haven't experienced the hurt and shame of sexual abuse firsthand. It's why we can punish abusers without remorse. They'll never understand how much they hurt their victims until they're maimed the same way.

When I break into the parking lot at the front of Wallens Ridge, I suck in air like it's the lines of coke I'm desperately craving. I need to chase away the ghosts of my past, push them to the back of my mind, but when air doesn't cut it, I yank out the steel canister I'm rarely without, scoop up a decent chunk of white powder onto the micro spoon glued into the lid, then bring it to my nose. A bump of cocaine won't give me the same hit a line or two would, but it will tie me over until I have somewhere more suitable to subdue my habit.

Just as I snort a second bump into my left nostril, I spot a shadow moving away from a window at the far-left side of Wallens Ridge.

*Fuck!*

I was busted snorting cocaine at the front of a maximum-security prison by the girl I'm trying to woo. *Could my life be any more fucked?*

If a familiar-looking car didn't just pull into the lot, I would have said no chance. Now, I'm certain matters are about to get worse.

"Smith..." I wait a beat before calling his name again, louder this time. "Smith!"

"I'm busy," he growls down my earpiece a couple of seconds later.

"Then get unbusy because shit is about to get *real* complicated. Theresa-fucking-Veneto just rolled up to Wallens Ridge. She has as special guest in her passenger seat."

"Who?" Although he's seeking answers from me, he's also chasing his own reply. His fingers punishing his keyboard drown out the disappointed groan of a breathless woman. "How the fuck did she find her? We had her in lockdown."

"Probably the same way she skipped bail at Oaks Valley. She flew out of the cuckoo nest... *again*."

As Theresa coerces Megan out of her car with a bag of candy like she's a child, Smith says, "What are you going to do?"

"I'd like to kill the bitch."

Not Megan.

Her placement on the Petretti family tree means she's as untouchable as Claudia.

No, you didn't hear me wrong. Megan isn't one of Col's many illegitimate children, but she could be classed as Dimitri's cousin in a twisted, warped way. Demi's mother and Megan's mother were sisters. Monica wasn't quite as batshit crazy as Megan's mother, but from the stories I've heard the past two weeks, she was pretty damn close.

When it dawns on him who I'm referencing, Smith says, "Dimitri may grant your wish when he finds out Theresa can't take a hint about backing off. He specifically told her to stay out of this."

"Her inability to listen has me wondering why she's not letting it go. It isn't for Maddox's sake. If he wants an out, we'd create one. He doesn't, so why the fuck is Theresa rocking up to the prison he's incarcerated at with his murder victim in tow?"

Smith's silence is very telling. He's only ever quiet when he's stumped.

"Come on, Smitty, I need something. They're a minute from the door, if that."

A normal person would have bypassed me by now. Megan is far from normal. I thought her mental issues were because she was dropped too many times as a baby, but after spending a couple of hours with her, it's clear her issues go way deeper than developmental. She's all types of fucked-up, which is a pity because without her crazy eyes, she could make my dick hard.

I stop reprimanding myself for my inappropriate commentary when Smith groans out a prolonged, "Fuck..." I wait, praying his eagerness to get back to his breathless companion will have him filling in the gap without delay. Mercifully, my hunch is right. "We found out this week that Col kept Megan alive because she knew massive secrets about his competitors and how he used them to keep them in line. One of them was Kaylee's true lineage. What if another one of those secrets was about Theresa?"

I'm lost as to where he's going with this until my phone dings, indicating I've received a text message. "Cute kid, but what the fuck does he have to do with *anything*?" I stumble over my last word when the boy I'd guess to be around four or five ages before my very eyes. His metamorphosis goes all the way from his current age to around mid-thirties. "I've seen that face before."

Smith hums out an agreeing murmur before slicing my screen in half so he can pop up an image of Jose Sánchez next to the now-aged child. "Same butt-dimple chin, same eyes, and the same FBI agent assigned to investigate both the murder of Alejandro Sánchez and Megan Shroud."

"Huh?" I'm usually more clued on than this, but the coke I snorted must be fucking with my head. I have no clue what Smith is trying to tell me.

I call Smith a dirty dog in my head when Ellie overtakes the reins. "The first photo is Theresa Veneto's son."

"The kid she's trying to pin on Isaac?"

"Yes!" Smith and Ellie reply in sync.

"Col had Theresa jumping on cue because Megan knew Jeremiah wasn't Isaac's son."

Although impressed by Ellie's claim, something doesn't make sense. "How could Megan know that? She isn't the sharpest tool in the shed." I blurt out like she isn't close enough to hear my scorn.

Ellie's tone dips when she answers, "Because Jeremiah was born at the baby farm on the Shroud family ranch."

"We *suspect* Jeremiah was born at the baby farm on the Shroud ranch," Smith interjects. "We don't have proof."

"There are no photos of Theresa's pregnancy. She didn't attend a single antenatal appointment, and it was noted in the doctor's report that Jeremiah's fontanel did not present as a newborn when Theresa *finally* rocked up to the hospital to have his birth recorded." When Smith attempts to interrupt again, she pushes out, "She also refused a gynecological exam. How much more evidence do you need, Smith?"

While they argue a possible connection between Theresa, the Sánchezes, and the Shrouds, I twist to face away from the entrance of Wallens Ridge to ensure neither Theresa nor Megan spot me. I have a highly recognizable face, but my getup is about the same as every other gangbanger around these parts. Midnight black pants and a black button-up shirt.

Once Theresa and Megan are inside, I interrupt Smith and Ellie's heated exchange for the second time. "Nothing you're saying makes any sense. Juana is a fucking psycho. Even if Jeremiah was conceived via immaculate conception, there's no way she'd let Theresa keep him." My face screws up when Smith's big burly laugh swamps my words. "What the fuck are you laughing about?"

"The fact you think Theresa is a doting mother is fucking hilarious." When it dawns on him that I'm still lost as to what he's on about, he asks, "Where do you think I got the photo of Jeremiah from, Rocco? I don't pluck random images of kids from the net. I'm not a perve like Juana."

As unease spirals in my gut, I glance down the original picture of Jeremiah, cursing when I pay more attention to the background. The feet of the king and queen chair in the living room of Juana's house is seen in the far righthand corner.

"Juana loans Jeremiah to Theresa when he's needed. Those favors see Theresa offering up similar courtesies, such as..." I'm going to hang him out to dry by his nuts for his delay, "... a detour to a maximum-security prison to authenticate claims a new member of the Sánchez entity has been conceived." This delay is to breathe out his annoyance. "You weren't the only one emailed Claudia's commissary receipts. Even with her not putting a dime into Claudia's account the past eleven months, Juana opened her account, so she receives itemized invoices every month."

"She knows Claudia bought a pregnancy test, but she has no clue it wasn't for her," I breathe out slowly, finally clicking on.

"Bingo," Smith says. "Theresa popped into a drug store twenty clicks out from Wallens Ridge. Can you guess what she purchased?"

"A pregnancy test," Ellie and I answer at the same time.

I take a staggering step back when Smith discloses, "I'm blocking correspondence about a possible hit. If I let it through, and Claudia's test comes back positive, she won't make it out of the shower cubicle without multiple stab wounds to her stomach. Juana has no issues stealing kids, but she has no interest in any that don't share her lineage."

I work my jaw side to side, pissed Smith left his big reveal for the end, but understand why he did that. By laying out all the facts in front of me, the urge to go in with gun's blazing isn't as potent as it would have been if he straight-up said a bounty was on Claudia's imaginative unborn baby's head. This way, I can assess the situation with due diligence, which will ensure Dimitri's family won't be dumped into the deep end again after only just being rescued from tumultuous waters.

I do a final workover of my jaw when Smith asks, "The warden just ordered the collection of Claudia from her cell. Do you want me to patch you into his office?"

An ordinary person wouldn't see the lifting of my chin, but Smith will because he's such a fucking snoop. He would have hacked into the camera of my phone the instant I pulled it out of my pocket.

It dawns on me that the warden has his finger in many pies when Theresa mumbles, "You know what Juana is like, Neil. It's easier to appease her than argue with her."

Warden Mattue isn't happy with her comment, but he doesn't let her know that. Instead, he shifts his focus to another target. "Is that..." He leaves his comment open like he can't bring himself to say Megan's name.

"A constant pain in my ass? Yes." Theresa folds her arms under her chest before saying with a huff, "I thought I would have been rid of her when Dimitri discovered her connection to his family. Instead, he did the opposite of what I was planning."

"Make sure Dimi sees this."

Smith murmurs like he's sending footage to Dimitri as we speak.

Not a pin drop is heard when the warden asks, "Where are you taking her?"

Theresa glances at Megan sitting in the foyer of Wallens Ridge for the quickest second before she huffs out, "To a subsidiary of Drakes. They've assured me multiple times the past twenty-four hours that they'll fry her brain so well, she'll never slip their noose."

"Stop Ellie grinding her teeth, Smitty. If she has nubs for teeth, how will she chew your chunky cum before she swallows it?"

Smith tells me to fuck off before he patches Dimitri into our feed. Even with him not speaking a word, I can tell how pissed he is. His pulse is so loud, if I couldn't hear Fien in the background, I would have assumed Smith interrupted him fooling around with Roxanne as I did Smith with Ellie.

After taking in the setting for a couple of seconds, Dimitri asks, "Are you not seeing what I'm seeing, Rocco?" I'm not surprised when I pick up Roxanne whispering something in his ear. I don't see Dimi letting neither Roxanne nor Fien out of his sight for years to come.

I lick my dry lips before replying, "If you're talking about a traitor, I see what you're seeing."

"Not Theresa," Dimitri replies without pause for thought. "The woman who's had your head in the fucking clouds the past two weeks."

I act as if I have no clue what he's talking about. "Megan?"

My brows stitch when he says, "And her. Now go back to your girl." As Smith switches the surveillance from Claudia in the doorway of the warden's office to Megan sitting in the foyer over and over again, my heart races a million miles an hour. "You want a way to get her out, and to me, it seems as if the solution is right in front of you."

I bounce my eyes between Claudia and Megan another two times before I call myself a cockhead. Same color hair, build, and height. Megan is just all types of crazy, and we all know where they end up.

My grin is heard in my words. "Are you good with this, Dimi? You did put a 'do not touch order' on Megan."

I startle like a bitch when Dimitri's face suddenly fills the screen of my phone. They should warn a guy before doing that. I was having a wickedly naughty daydream about a woman who looks remarkably similar to Claudia when all of a sudden Dimitri's ugly mug was front and center.

Talk about a killjoy.

"Megan needs help. She won't get it in Hopeton, and I don't have time for her crazy antics. I've already got one loon I'm trying to lock down."

I smile a full-tooth grin when a pillow from the couch in Dimitri's office lands in his face. "I'd tell you to suffocate him in his sleep, Roxie, but knowing Dimi, he'd probably get off on it."

Roxanne's giggles fill my ear a second before Dimitri's deep voice gobbles it up. "Make your decision and make it quick, Rocco, your girl is about to pee on a stick."

When it dawns on me what Dimitri is watching, I scream, "Cut the feed, Smith." When my demand is answered by group chuckles, I repeat, "Cut the fucking feed!"

I'd apologize to Dimitri for using Roxanne to rile him numerous times the past twelve months if I had no intention of doing it a hundred more times to make up for the severe bout of jealousy he just smacked me with. A year ago, I would have shared a girl with him. Today, I want to cut his nuts off just for seeing Claudia's bare knees.

*What the fuck did I snort earlier?*

This isn't like me at all.

After taking a moment to remove the riled expression from my face, I muster up a friendly grin before entering Wallens Ridge for the third time today. My first was to visit Maddox while waiting for lunch to be prepped, the second was my 'date' with Claudia, and this time is to ensure I'm not a one-hit-wonder.

Megan's face lights up like a Christmas tree when she spots my entrance, but before she can blurt out an overzealous greeting, I press my finger to my lips.

When she nods, signaling she understands my request for her to be quiet, I wave her over to my side of the foyer.

She comes, albeit hesitantly.

"Hey, Rocco. What are you doing here?"

As memories of our brief conversations the night I babysat her before she was admitted into a mental health facility, I say, "Didn't you hear? Rise Up moved their recording studio an hour from here. I'm heading there now." She's obsessed with Rise Up's lead guitarist, Nicholas Holt. "Did you want to come with me?"

"Oh... ah..."

She looks desperate, and it grows more rampant when I add, "I heard they moved locations because Nick filed for a divorce this morning."

Her eyes almost pop out of her head. "He did."

"Yep! So you better hurry if you want to get your hooks into him before anyone else."

I almost feel bad for her when she follows me to my car so briskly, she misses me stopping by the trunk to soak a handkerchief with chloroform.

## 15

———

# CLAUDIA

I breathe out a heavy sigh when a guard shouts, "Lights out in ten."

I'm as tired as hell, but I'm also extremely confused.

Today has been a rollercoaster of emotions. My 'date' with Rocco was out of this world, and the kiss we shared blew any sexual experiences I've had out of the water, but then little negatives started seeping through the cracks.

The most dominant, Rocco's affiliation with narcotics.

I thought his super cruisy personality was compliments to a rough childhood. A lot of men use cockiness to deflect the anguish of their sullied childhood memories. I had no clue part of his personality was because of an addiction.

I'm not overly disappointed to learn he uses drugs. I just wish the time we'd spent together gave him enough adrenaline to make it through the rest of his day without additional additives. It has kept my veins thrumming with so much euphoria, even being demanded to undertake a pregnancy test in front of a woman I've never met before only saw it registering the slightest dip.

It's lucky I don't get stage fright. Juana ensured that could never be a possibility. When I said the way she is with her children is weird,

I wasn't lying. She didn't guide the loss of my virginity from the sidelines like a mother would. She was in the room with Juan and me. I don't know if her presence was the reason Juan didn't come or the fact I had no clue what I was doing. I laid there like a mannequin—unmoving and unspeaking. I didn't even cry, which isn't surprising. I'm not overly good with my emotions. There's only one time I've cried the past couple of years. It was when Dillon was ripped away from me.

That hurt—it hurt a lot.

My thoughts shift from the weirdness of my past to the present when a strange ping dings around my cell. It reminds me of the rattle the pipes in my old cell made anytime O'Doyle clogged the toilet.

Talking about O'Doyle, she was super clingy during shower time this evening. She was glued to my side like she was in the days leading to Dillon's birth. She even went as far as using my soap so she didn't have to leave the shower cubicle to get her own.

In the beginning, her attention frightened me, but within a couple of seconds, I realized she was hovering more like a protector than an arch-nemesis. I would have preferred that she maintain her distance, but if my options are only foe or friend, I'll always choose the latter.

"What is that?" I mutter to myself when a second lot of pings jingle into my ears.

I slant my head back when I realize the noise is coming from behind me. After balancing my bare foot onto the lidless toilet bowl, I peer out the tiny crack in the protective film covering my window. I can't hold back my smile when I spot Rocco standing in the warden's empty parking bay, so I set it free.

He hits me with a frisky wink, announcing he appreciates my excited greeting before he dumps a bunch of pebbles from his hand onto the ground. Once he's dusted off his hand on his trousers, he holds his index finger in the air, requesting a minute.

Within a second of nodding, the lights inside and outside of Wallens Ridge switch off, plunging the area into horrifying blackness. This isn't an unusual occurrence, and neither is the number of loonies the darkness encourages. We go through incidences like this every six to eight weeks. Usually, I hide in the shadows of my cell until the theatrics dull down. Tonight, I'm too curious to discover what Rocco has to do with Warden Mattue's sick mind games to play my usual hand.

The stress doubling the output of my heart doesn't last long. As fast as the lights dimmed, a set of headlights at the side of the lot flashes two times, alerting me to the fact there are some first responder trucks idling near the loading bay.

My confused gaze drifts back to Rocco in enough time to see him swiveling his index finger around his head while sticking out his tongue like a dog. When I fail to understand what he's signaling, he points to me, then hooks his thumb to the fleet of ambulances.

Does he want me to hurt myself? If he does, his plan is pointless. Wallens Ridge has an in-house doctor. The only people carted out of here in an ambulance are either corpses or the mental patients the darkness summons.

My mouth gapes open when the truth smacks into me.

He doesn't want me to hide from Warden Mattue's mind warp.

He wants me to participate in the theatrics.

When I mimic the expression he did earlier but with the finesse of a mental patient, Rocco grins a blinding smile.

I'm so excited I worked out his puzzle, I almost jump to his command, but then I realize I'm placing all my faith into the hands of a man I hardly know. That wouldn't be so risky if it were just my life on the line. I have to think about my son as well. He is so young, Juana's antics won't hurt him just yet, but I can't say the same in a couple of years.

You wouldn't know we were strangers only weeks ago when Rocco attempts to subdue the panic roaring through my veins by mouthing, "*Trust me.*"

I try to talk myself out of the immediate decision of my heart. I try to remind myself that six years isn't really that long, but before my objections can be heard by my heart, I mouth, "*Okay,*" to Rocco before I stuff Dillon's photographs down the front of my jumpsuit.

After picking up one of the Snickers bars Officer Edgar delivered to my cell after supper, I rip my teeth through it. My gnaws are so vicious, I make more mess to the front of my jumpsuit than I intend to do to the back. I couldn't see much of the action from my station in my cell, but what I did see was lots of spit, fangs, and soiled clothing.

I'm not willing to poo my pants to authenticate claims I'm crazy, but even mothers have a hard time telling the difference between chocolate stains and poop marks.

Once my jumpsuit is a right royal mess, and I've teased my hair out to replicate a woman on the brink of insanity, I sprint out of my cell to join the rest of the crazies throwing rolls of toilet paper over the industrial fans circling above our heads while screaming like banshees.

The foamy spit in the corner of my mouth gains me numerous eyes, so you can imagine how many I get when I try to bite an officer as if my fangs are filled with rabies.

He pushes me off him, grips my wrist in a painful hold, then pins me to the floor. While kneeling on my back like I weigh double what I do, he requests another two officers to hogtie me. This is terrible for me to admit, especially with how many women are being mistreated right now, but I wish I had considered messing myself up earlier. I have many eyes on me, but not a single one is peering at me with desire. All they see is a maniac, and the damage my shrieks are doing to their ears has them super eager to dump me into a system that cares more about profits than its patients.

In not even two minutes, I'm muzzled and carried out of my cell block. Not a word is spoken to me during the short walk through the underbelly of Wallens Ridge or when I'm tagged like an animal in the loading dock. It's eerily silent until I'm discarded, stomach first, onto a gurney in the first available ambulance.

"You've got yourself a live one," says the guard I tried to bite before he tosses a clipboard into the chest of a brute of a man with a clover tattoo on his left cheek. "Try not to bang her up too much during the commute. The warden has wanted to tap that for months. Her transfer to Oaks Valley may now give him the chance." He bobs down until he's an inch from my face. "They can't fight back when they're doped up on hallucinogenics. Half of them don't even remember being touched."

I attempt to crawl away from him when he uses the gap in my thighs to inappropriately touch me. He cups my vagina before his index finger hunts for my clit like he thinks I might be turned on by the prospect of being raped.

His fingertip barely grazes the slit in my pussy when his snicker switches to a whine. I can't see the man repeatedly stabbing him in the spleen with a pocketknife, but I do recognize his scent.

Rocco is killing the man who tried to devalue my honor, and for some reason, it turns me on more than it scares me.

When the officer slumps to the floor with a lifeless thud, Rocco locks his eyes with mine, winking when he sees no fret in them whatsoever. "Send a cleanup crew to the first ambulance." His eyes flicker before he drifts them to the man with the clover tattoo. "Smith says we need to move. They're bringing down another four."

Not having the time to untie me, he tosses me over his shoulder like I'm as light as a feather, then sprints us toward the last ambulance in the long line of many. My breathing turns ragged when my placement into a chair in the middle of the truck has me spotting an unconscious woman on a gurney. She's wearing a Wallens Ridge jumpsuit, and her hair is the same mousy brown coloring as mine. Come to think of it, she also appears to be the same height and weight as me.

"Who is she?" I ask Rocco after he removes the gag the officers stuffed into my mouth.

He uses his blood-stained knife to cut the rope digging into my wrists and ankles. Once he has my restraints dumped into a gym bag at his left, he peers at me like he finds my daftness cute. "Claudia Sánchez, meet the *new* Claudia Sánchez." I barely get a second to register my shock when he hits me for the second time. "Put these on." He hands me a pair of snug jeans and a plain white shirt.

With confidence always being an issue for me, I stray my eyes to the gentleman with the clover tattoo before slinging them to a brute sitting behind the wheel of the ambulance. The back of an ambulance is small. There's no way I can get changed without one of them seeing me.

Seemingly sensing my worry, Rocco clicks his fingers together two times. It has the men's eyes snapping shut in an instant. "Better?"

"Much," I reply, my voice stuttering with an equal amount of excitement and worry. "But what about you?"

I grew a child in my stomach. This could be presumptuous of me, but I'm reasonably sure Rocco has never dated a mother. If that is the case, I don't want to teach him about the mess motherhood causes the female anatomy in the back of a first-responder truck.

I'm just as confident I need a mental health check when Rocco's blistering grin causes heat to roar through my veins. He isn't smiling about the unease trickling out of me. He's grinning about the mammoth crack he placed between the fingers he used to cover his eyes.

He laughs when I tap my foot against his black boot before he spins around, granting me the privacy I'm unsure I still want. His laugh didn't solely mess up my insides, it ruined my panties as well.

While inwardly reprimanding my teetering moods, I store Dillon's photographs into a gym bag at my side, then change quicker than a flash of lightning brightens the sky. I'm not just eager to unearth the rest of Rocco's plan for my escape from a maximum-security prison, I also don't want him thinking I soiled myself for real.

"You good?" Rocco asks at the same time the hem of my shirt stops a good three inches *above* the waistband of my jeans.

"Yeah, I'm good… even with half my shirt missing."

After spinning around, Rocco drags his eyes down my body. He grins when he notices the stupid press of my thighs from his prolonged stare, and if I'm not mistaken, hungry gawk before he requests an update from his imaginary friend. "Did you come through for me, Smith?"

My bones jump out of my skin when an accented voice sounds out of Rocco's pocket a couple of seconds later. "The transfer has been organized. You can detour Oaks Valley. She's going straight to Drakes."

"Thanks, Smitty," Rocco replies with a playful rub of his hands before he signals for the driver to go.

As the ambulance chugs away from Wallens Ridge, Rocco gestures for me to sit in the chair next to the unconscious 'Claudia.'

When I do as requested, he hands me a cosmetic bag. It bruises my ego until I realize it isn't for me. "I'm not good with toners and shit, but I figured if you work your magic, the resemblance will be more authentic." He nudges his head to the woman strapped to the gurney at the end of his sentence. "She's cute, but she doesn't have your sexiness."

I'm stoked about his praise, but I'm also lost. "You want her to look like me?"

"Yep," he replies like what he's asking isn't a big deal.

It is.

It's a huge deal.

"Why? I want to get my son back. I'll never do that if I'm a mental patient at a prison for the criminally insane." I know about Drakes as does every female inmate at Wallens Ridge. It's where the warden threatens to send us if we don't keep our mouths shut on the many shady dealings he undertakes at Wallens Ridge. "This is a bad idea, Rocco."

"No, it isn't," he denies, his voice oddly nurturing even with me questioning his decision. "Claudia Sánchez will *never* be granted custody of her son because as far as the courts are concerned, she is *not* Dillon's biological mother."

"What?" I'm already seated, so I can't fall back into my seat with shock, but I would if I were standing. That's how much his comment shocks me. "I gave birth to him. I endured twenty-seven hours of labor with no drugs or support network. He is my son."

"I know that, Mama. We *all* know that." He scoops my hand in his before leaning forward in preparation to catch the tears he's convinced are about to fall. "But the world we live in isn't fair until we make it fair." Even though they're still dry, he swipes at my cheeks with the back of his hand before saying, "If you want your son back, we need to play the game Juana is playing." When I nod, understanding what he means, he smiles. Juana kidnapped my child. She stole him. And now I need to do the same. "You can't do what needs to be done behind bars, and there's no guarantee Dillon can hold out for six years."

His accurate statement has my tears super close to spilling. Dillon is only a baby now, but before I know it, he will be a toddler, then a child, then a man. I've already missed so much of his life. I don't want to miss more. Furthermore, Juana's manipulation has no age barrier. I saw her berate one of her nine-year-old granddaughters. It was brutal.

"Okay," I mutter out after a big exhale.

Rocco squeezes my hand. "I know you have no reason to trust me, but I'm being honest when I say I'd never risk you losing your son just for the hope of getting my dick wet."

It's the wrong time for me to smile, but I can't help it. You couldn't hear how much jest was in his tone. He's defusing the bomb sitting in my stomach with humor instead of violence.

It's another one of his extremely sexy traits.

Rocco's eyes bounce between mine when I say, "I probably shouldn't, but I do trust you. *Very much so.*"

He squeezes my hand again, exposing I said my last sentence out loud before he nudges his head to the unconscious woman. "You better get to work. We will arrive at Drakes in a little under forty minutes."

While nodding, I stray my eyes in the direction he nudged. The woman lying unconscious is very attractive, which has me feeling extremely conflicted. "Will they hurt her?"

Rocco shakes his head. "No, because just like the staff at Wallens Ridge, they'll be too scared to get within an inch of her."

"Promise?" I just told him I trust him, so I shouldn't be seeking assurance for his pledge, but I can't help but ensure my misery isn't pushed onto someone else. I did that once, and she ended up dead.

The heaviness on my chest slackens when Rocco says, "I

promise."

He winks at the relief flooding my face before he tells me he will be back in a minute. He can't go far. We're in an ambulance racing down the freeway with its lights flashing and siren wailing, but it's nice that he doesn't leave me curious. Juan did that all the time. I never knew where he was, and the one time I let my curiosity get the best of me, I stumbled onto something I wish I hadn't.

Things became extremely strained for us from that point. It wasn't long after that the daily beatings commenced. He thought he had to scare me into keeping my mouth shut, whereas I was willing to do it to save face. No blushing bride wants to admit her husband is having an affair, much less when it's with someone he's related to.

After involuntarily shivering, I set to work on alleviating the bags under the brunette's eyes with a healthy dose of concealer. I've never studied to be a makeup artist, but I learned a trick or two while attempting to hide the numerous bruises Juan left on my face from his mother. If you want glittery eyes and sexy red lips, I'm not the girl for you. But if you're seeking a flawlessly perfect face without a single blemish to be seen, look me up.

I almost have all the signs of tiredness removed from the brunette's face when Rocco returns to my side. I smile like a kid on Christmas morning when he holds out two pairs of shoes for me to pick from. One is a pair of Adidas running shoes, and the stilettos are a little fancier both in style and price.

When I point to the running shoes, Rocco asks, "With or without socks?"

"With, please."

I place down a bronzing stick when he pulls out of pair of socks from a plastic bag behind him. I've dressed myself since I was three, so you can imagine my surprise when he helms his campaign to cover my bare feet by bobbing down in front of me so he can slide the super comfy socks onto my feet.

Once he has the laces on the running shoes undone, he holds it in front of himself like I lost my crystal slipper at the ball. Something so simple shouldn't feel so dreamlike, but it does. I honestly feel so much like a princess, it is as if the last twelve months never happened.

"How do they feel?" Rocco asks after suiting me up. "They're not too tight, are they?"

I shake my head. "They're perfect. Thank you."

When I bend down to tuck my laces into my shoes so I won't trip over them—a trick I learned after an endeavor to get away from Juan one time saw me falling down the stairs for real—it brings my face to within an inch of Rocco's. I thought he was handsome from a distance, but I had no idea he is ridiculously good-looking. His green eyes are clever and curious, his lips are plump, and the straightness of his nose would have you convinced he's never thrown a punch in his life.

I guess you don't need to worry about breaking your nose if you knock out your opponent with one hit.

Heat creeps up my neck when it dawns on me that Rocco is assessing me as vigorously as I am him. He dances his eyes between mine before he rakes them down my nose and across my cheeks, then settles them on my lips. When my tongue instinctively delves out to wet my suddenly bone-dry mouth, he moans.

"Don't tempt me, Mama." He shuffles closer to me like he didn't just reject me. "I don't give a fuck about Clover and Marshall. I'll send them to hell in an instant if they see any part of you, you don't want them to see, but Smith... for some fucked-up reason, I'm kinda fond of him."

The moisture I wet my lips with ensures not a single strain is felt when they crack into a huge grin. I'm not smiling about Rocco's funny statement, it's Smith's reply that has me responding as if I'm a long-term patient at Drakes. "I'll be sure to remind you of that when I send you my bill. I had plans, Rocco, big ones, and you went and fucked them."

"Fucking a woman you've already fucked a hundred times isn't a plan, Smith. Some may call that a mistake." Rocco screws up his face, curses himself, then returns his eyes to mine. "Don't take that the wrong way."

"How could I?" I reply, my tone only partly angry. "We haven't fooled around yet, so I still have ninety-nine proposed instances to prepare myself for your *mistake*."

Okay, perhaps there was a smidge more anger to my tone than I let on. Can you blame me? I'm over here thinking I'm Cinderella while Rocco is counting down to an accomplishment couples with as much sexual tension as us could reach in a month.

"She's got you played," Smith barks out with a chuckle. "Welcome to the crew, Claudia. I can't wait to see you turn this boy into a man." My brows furrow when his unique accent is gobbled up by "Crank That" by Soulja Boy. It's a golden oldie, but the longer it plays out of the pocket of Rocco's jeans, the more it resonates with the teen Rocco once was.

"You wore the baggy pants and sideways cap, didn't you?"

"No," Rocco denies at the same time Smith shouts, "Don't forget the white-rimmed sunglasses."

Smith is laughing so hard, I can barely understand him, but I get an idea of what he's saying when the monitor next to the chair I'm seated in flashes up an image of what I am going to assume is a young Rocco. He has the same meaty lips and impressive height, but baggy clothes can't hide how skinny he is.

"Thank you, Smith. You can go now, Smith," Rocco growls while pulling out the cables on the monitor.

It's clear he's embarrassed, but he'll never admit it.

After swallowing my nerves, I murmur, "I would have totally tapped that."

"Me too," says a female voice from Rocco's pocket.

Her back up not only brings back the gleam in Rocco's eyes, it sees Smith disconnecting his female companion's connection to Rocco's cell phone. Her removal from the conversation plunges the back half of the ambulance into silence. It isn't uncomfortable. How could it be when Rocco is teasingly tracing a scar on my arm I got from the accident that claimed Juan's life?

I'm not exactly sure how I shattered the bones in both my arms. At the time, I wasn't in the right mindset to ask questions, and if I were honest, I'd also admit I was grateful for how frail my bones were. The breaks couldn't be set without surgery, so I had to stay in the hospital for weeks on end. Just the time away from Juana was a godsend, not to mention that's where I met Roxanne, and subsequently, Rocco.

Roxanne didn't have the capital to fund a legal campaign to have my charges squashed, but she pledged to support me no matter the outcome. That was more than I could have hoped for and more than I had been given previously.

Helping someone isn't always about money.

Sometimes all you need are words, and they're free.

My breath catches in my throat when Rocco drifts his finger from the three-inch scar on my right arm to the two-inch one on my left. Most men are turned off by the idea the woman they're crushing on is blemished with unfixable scars. That doesn't seem to be the case with Rocco. There isn't an ounce of disdain on his face. He actually appears as horny now as he was while staring at my lips.

I shake my head when he asks, "Did it hurt?"

"I don't remember the accident, but I'm reasonably sure even if I had broken every bone in my body, the pain wouldn't top childbirth."

When Rocco nods in agreement, I giggle. His expression would have you convinced he knows exactly what I'm talking about.

My throat becomes scratchy when I contemplate my assumption being accurate. My google search exposed that he recently turned twenty-seven. I'm only twenty-three and have been a mother for eight months, so it's pretty presumptuous for me to assume he doesn't have any children. He could have an army for all I know.

After swallowing to make sure the jealousy heating my veins isn't heard in my voice, I ask, "Do you have any?"

"Kids?" Rocco asks, speaking the word I was too chicken to say.

When I lift my chin, he shakes his head. "Nah. Not yet."

"So, you want children?" My tone is way too high for my liking. It can't be helped. Guys normally freak about the prospect of becoming a father. Rocco muttered his reply like he's open to the idea.

He contemplates for a couple of seconds before halfheartedly shrugging. "Maybe one day. More to prove I'm nothing like my father than to have a mini version of myself running around."

His reply both pleases and upsets me. I appreciate his honesty, but my heart breaks about his underhanded confession that his father is his monster. They're supposed to be our protectors, not our tormentors.

"Anyway, that's enough about the bullshit we can't change." He wipes the torment from his eyes like he can switch his emotions on and off like a light switch before he stands. "How about we concentrate on the things we can?" He hands me an overflowing dossier. "We need to lay low for a couple of days to make sure there are no throwbacks to our plan. We can either do that here or at my home in Hopeton."

When he peers at me, it dawns on me that he's leaving the decision of our location up to me. His endeavor to include me in his plan fills me with courage, but it isn't quite enough to get me over the line. "I'm happy to go wherever you feel most comfortable."

It was drummed into me from birth that I am to do as I'm told, so it'll take a little longer than an hour to reprogram that side of me.

A brick lodges in my throat when Rocco instructs the man with the clover tattoo to have a private jet ready to depart within the hour.

I've never been on a plane, much less a private jet.

After returning his eyes to mine, Rocco informs, "If all goes to plan, we'll look at moving in to remove Dillon by the end of the week."

Even if I were a novice to the cartel way of life, I still would have been able to decipher his message. Moving in on a target is the equivalent of Juana saying she's going to take care of someone.

Both have deadly consequences.

"Is *that* entirely necessary? I don't want anyone getting hurt." I don't want him getting hurt, but since that would be weird for me to express so early into our... friendship, I went for a broader response.

I shouldn't have bothered sugarcoating anything. Rocco's wink exposes he knows who my fret centers around. "You don't need to worry about me, Mama. The Sánchez crew is almost debunked—"

"But the ones left are clinically insane. They won't go down without a fight. Dillon could get hurt."

"He won't be caught in the crossfire because he will be with you, far *far* away from the carnage I'm going to direct your way."

I don't reply.

I can't.

I am completely lost as to what he means.

Rocco balances his backside on the gurney like there isn't an unconscious woman on it before he folds his thick arms in front of his chest. We're rolling down the asphalt at seventy miles an hour, but the only part of his body that moves during his reply is a tiny vein in his neck. "There are rules we're governed by... rules I cannot break no matter how much I wish I could." I nod, conscious it was rule-breaking that caused the Sánchezes downfall. "They won't stop me from helping you get your son back, but they will make it seem as if I am hunting you along with the Sánchezes."

"Hunting me?" I swallow to ensure my voice doesn't croak before asking, "Why would you hunt me?"

I want to inch back when he tilts in close, but I can't. There's too much honesty in his eyes when he says, "Siding with them is the only way I'll truly know how close they are to finding you. It's why India helmed the search for Dimitri's wife. Anytime Dimi got close, she pulled him in another direction."

It's another one of those torn moments. I'm incredibly grateful he's willing to put himself and his crew on the line for Dillon and me, but I'm also sad. Multiple times the past couple of weeks, I stupidly daydreamed about a blended family living in a house with a white picket fence and a dog as protective as Max.

It's quite ridiculous when you think about it. I was conjuring up a future with a man I've only known for days and sat across from a little over an hour. Now I get a week, if that.

I guess there was more to his comment about bedding the same woman more than a hundred times.

When he spots the disappointment on my face, Rocco discloses, "We went over *all* possible options multiple times the past couple of hours. No matter how many times we worked them, they all produced the same results. You either live without your son or without..."

"You," I fill in when words elude him.

His smile is only half its natural size when he jerks up his chin. "Most people have had enough of me by a week anyway, so in the long run, I'm sure you'll be grateful the decision was taken out of your hands."

"Doubtful," I murmur before I can stop myself. After wiping under my nose to make sure nothing gross is spilling, I fold my right ankle in front of my left ankle, then drop my eyes to my fancy new shoes. "How are you going to convince the Sánchezes to let you *hunt* with them?"

My eyes rocket up to Rocco's face when he chuckles. Emotions are taking up every inch of space in the ambulance. Now is *not* the time to be laughing.

I don't know whether to laugh or cry when he discloses the reason for his chuckles. "You know that pregnancy test you took?"

"The test that came back negative?"

He nods. "It was from a faulty batch. The blood Dr. Christina took earlier today will reveal you're actually a couple of months along."

I don't even nibble at the bait he's dangling in front of me. "You have to have sex to be pregnant, and I haven't had that in a *very* long time."

"And from what you disclosed earlier, it wouldn't have been good enough to remember anyway, so it doesn't count." He winks when I roll my eyes before he says matter-of-factly, "But Juana doesn't know that. As far as she is concerned, we're bumping uglies."

"Bumping uglies?"

He rubs his hands together while disclosing, "It's what Smith calls sex when he doesn't want his current squeeze to know what he's talking about."

"It is not," Smith interjects, confirming Rocco's claims that he's always listening. "What Rocco is trying to say is that we're going to convince Juana that Rocco helped you escape from prison because you're pregnant with his child and was unaware of your connection with the Sánchezes. When Juana advises him of your association, Rocco will be obligated by mafia sanction to return you to your rightful owner."

"That's when we will get Dillon out," Rocco fills in, his tone a cross between annoyed and hopeful.

Most of their ruse makes sense, but there are a few points I'm still confused about. "So Juana knows she isn't me?" When I point to the unconscious lady, my brows stitch, suddenly curious as to what they gave her that knocked her out for so long.

I return my eyes to Rocco when he says, "Not yet. I'll disclose how I switched Megan for you while bragging about how awesome I am."

"Which he'll do so well, you'll have no clue he's acting," mutters the female voice who backed me up earlier.

Rocco continues talking as if she never interrupted, "Juana knows nothing *except* that your pregnancy test returned a positive result this afternoon."

"That would have made her furious."

"It did," Rocco agrees. "Enough she put steps into place to fix the injustice."

I stare into his eyes for a couple of seconds before the truth smacks into me. "O'Doyle. She wouldn't leave my side in the shower cubicles."

"On my order. She'd do anything Juana asks to keep a roof over her brother's head and food in his stomach, so you can only imagine how far she'd go for the chance to get him out of her clutches altogether."

My hidden smile is heard in my reply, "You met Rhett." Rhett works the main gate at the Sánchez compound. He is a sweet as pie but so blinded to Juana's antics, it's almost as if he has Stockholm syndrome.

Rocco nods. "Years ago." When my brows pull together, he discloses. "We went to juvie together." He works his jaw from side to side before disclosing, "He has quite the fondness for you. He wanted me to tell you he's been keeping an eye on Dillon for you."

I appreciate the jealousy in his tone, but it isn't necessary. Rhett is gay. "We arrived at the Sánchezes at the same time. He had four siblings to take care of, but he still took me under his wing. I wouldn't have lasted a week without him." I'm not glossing things up to ensure Rocco upholds the pledge he made to O'Doyle. I'm being genuinely honest. If Rhett hadn't snuck food to me, I would have died of starvation.

Once I settle the upset making my stomach a twisted mess of confusion, I ask, "Can I ask something?"

"Of course," Rocco immediately fires back.

"If you have everything planned, why wait a week?" I really hope I don't sound like a bitch. I'm extremely grateful for everything Rocco and his team are doing, but I'm also worried. I've grown attached to Rocco remarkably fast, so I can only see that fascination worsening the more time I spend with him.

With Rocco stumped of a reply, Smith takes charge. "We need to learn how Juana operates. All reports we have on her are from years ago. If rumors are true, she hasn't left her compound since she took custody of your son."

"Since she *stole* my son," I correct, aware I'm taking my anger out on the wrong person but incapable of reeling in my annoyance. "And a delay won't change anything. Juana rarely does the dirty work herself."

"She won't have a choice when she discovers you're at Drakes," Rocco discloses, jumping back into the conversation. "No one but the patient's next of kin gets through their doors, and that's a rarity as it is. They don't even make exceptions for law enforcement."

Since I can't argue about the truth in his eyes, I remain quiet.

"I get that this sounds risqué, but I promise you it isn't," Rocco assures, wrongly believing my silence is because I'm worried he'll stuff this up. "If Juana leaves Dillon home when she goes to Drakes to see you, we'll plant people inside her compound. If she takes him with her, she'll bring him to your swap. Either way, we will get him." It dawns on me that he knows exactly where my worry stems when he adds, "We just won't get each other."

**16**

---

## ROCCO

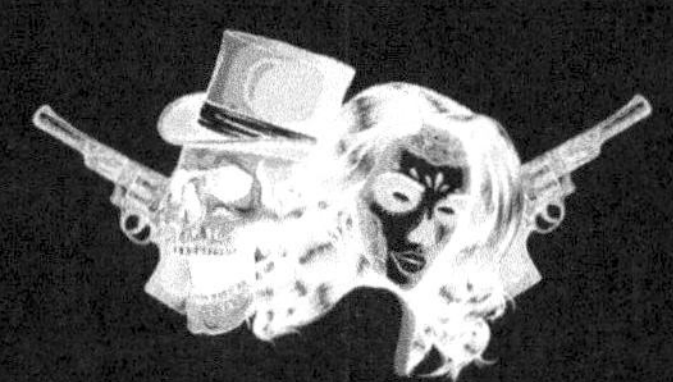

"*L*et her be."

It's been a long-ass day, and I'm tired as fuck, but Clover would need to snap my legs into pieces before I'd ever give up the opportunity of carrying Claudia in my arms. She's been quiet the past six hours. She didn't even inquire as to why the private jet we boarded after dropping Megan off at Drakes traveled two hours in the wrong direction before doubling back to ensure no sneaky federal fuckers were monitoring our flight plan. She just sat in the reclining seat next to me, deep in thought.

I'd be a lying prick if I said my ego wasn't stroked by her devastation. I'm stoked she feels the same immediate connection for me as I have for her, but it sucks that we can't act on it.

I'm not looking for a relationship. I have to get my own head space right before I can drag anyone else into the mess, but I would have loved the opportunity to get to know her a little better.

I guess it's just not meant to be. There's no way Claudia would ever pick me over her son, and there's no way I'd ever ask her to do that. For one, it would instantly change the way I feel about her, and two, it isn't her job to fix my father's screw-ups.

Just her being here for a week will test my limits. I've done so well hiding the shit from my childhood because I never surround myself with people long enough for them to see my bad points.

Roxanne almost had me on the hook last week. Our conversations made me so edgy, I nearly blurted out things I've never told anyone. Thank fuck the coke I snorted when she needed to use the restroom fixed the indiscretion, or who knows how much of a fool I would have portrayed.

I'm being bombarded with the same edginess now, but it's more because I have to explain to Claudia why she can't sleep in my bed than confess to decade-old secrets.

"Shh. It's just me," I whisper when Claudia balks about me pulling her into my chest. She crashed halfway from the private airstrip in Hopeton to my home. I'm not surprised. The sun is close to rising. Even I'm struggling to keep my eyelids open.

Once I have her nuzzled into my chest, I toss the keys for my ride into Clover's chest. "If she ends up wrapped around a pole like my last car you borrowed, make sure you perish in the wreckage with her because I don't want to waste a car *and* a bullet on your ugly mug."

Clover waggles his brows before he slips behind the driver's seat. I'm not short, but I feel like a midget when he pushes back the seat so far he's practically sitting where Claudia was only moments ago.

My back molars smash together when his quick churn of the ignition is chased by him flattening his foot to the floor. He usually rides a bike, so the rare occasion he gets behind a wheel sees him being a dickhead.

I wait for my taillights to disappear before I enter my home. The security system beeping in response to detecting an intruder sees Claudia stirring in my arms, but her eyes remain closed.

They only flutter open when I place her onto the mattress in the room Maddox and Demi used over a year ago, and even then, she only peers at me for the quickest second before she snuggles into her pillow and falls back to sleep.

The fact she feels safe around me should lower my desire for another hit of cocaine, but unfortunately, it doesn't. If I don't subdue the demons in my head with a mind-numbing concoction of some kind, Claudia will no longer look at me like I'm a hero. She'll think I am as revolting as the evil behind her incarceration.

Since I'd rather be strung out on drugs than be seen as a pedophile, I tuck Claudia in before making my way to my downstairs office. After punching digits into my security system to block everyone—including Smith—from the feed, I move toward my desk.

I've been around drugs since I was seven. Col never hid who he was from his children, and since I was a part of Dimitri's life from the moment we met, he never hid it from me either. I didn't snort my first line of coke until I was fourteen, but it's been my crutch ever since. I do drugs when I'm happy, sad, or suicidal. Fortunately, the latter hasn't been an issue for me since I killed my father. Before that, I thought about it more than I care to admit. I was confident hell couldn't be worse than anything I had experienced, so I wasn't scared of death.

The urge to do more than my standard three lines smacks into me hard and fast when I yank open the bottom drawer in my desk. With everything going on, I haven't had the chance to reflect on Demi's demise. Agent Machini's ruse was effective. She got Demi out as promised. She just didn't wager on Demi's brain bleeding out while thirty-thousand feet in the air. Reports say Agent Machini did every-thing she could, but her fight wasn't enough. They pronounced Demi dead ten minutes after an emergency landing, which was thirty minutes after takeoff. Her 'death' made front-page news in Hopeton, hence the reason my housekeeper placed a copy of the paper into my desk drawer. It just fails to announce her death was the day *following* her car accident with Maddox.

The already fatal beat of my heart doubles when I push aside a three-week-old copy of *Ravenshoe News*. A bright yellow envelope is stuffed behind it. My name is scribbled across the front. It isn't in a handwriting I recognize.

After dumping my favorite card to cut up lines of cocaine with onto my desk, I pull out the suspicious-looking envelope. Whatever is inside is light enough to convince me it could be empty, but the prospect doesn't ease my curiosity in the slightest. Without considering that Smith will most likely want to dust it for prints, I rip it open with the furiousness of a tiger in the middle of a mauling. My lips purse when I notice the single sheet of paper inside.

"No fucking way," I murmur to myself, shocked by what is disclosed in the document. It's a paternity test for a woman named Olivia Wilde. From what I've unearthed the past couple of years, that's the alias Tobias gave Ophelia when she 'died.'

If I had Smith's hacking skills, I could find out if the corporation backing the paternity claim was associated with Ophelia before she became Olivia, but since I don't, I take a mental note to look deeper into her legal woes *after* explaining myself to Dimitri.

I could ask Smith for help, but since I don't want to put him on the wrong side of Dimitri's wrath when the truth is exposed, I won't. Is it wrong of me to do? Probably. Do I give a fuck? Not at all. Fixing our mistakes makes us the men we are. If you don't have anything to fix, can you truly call yourself a man?

With my head thumping from tiredness, I toss the sheet of paper into the top drawer of my desk before opening the storage cabinet Smith organized for a micro freezer to be installed in. I know what you're thinking. You're calling me a fool for wasting thousands of dollars' worth of coke by storing it in a freezer, where it'll get moist and wet. In reality, the freezer is the best place to store cocaine when you live in a humid climate like Florida. Coke hates humidity, and a box filled with solid ice has none of that. Double bag that shit in a Ziplock baggy, and watch how long it stays fresh and ready to cut into lines for your friends.

I haven't touched the private stash in my house for months, yet it's in perfect cutting condition. I have three lines splayed out in front of me in an impressive eight seconds, and a Benjamin Franklin rolled up and at the ready just as quickly.

I'm about to devour my first line when the shriek of a woman in sheer panic booms into my ears. My heart leaps in my chest when I recognize the twang of the tormented cry. It's the same helpless groan of the woman who gave birth in a cold prison cell in the underbelly of Wallens Ridge State Penitentiary. It came from Claudia.

I race for the door so fast, not the slightest bit of disdain hits my veins when my abrupt movements force two lines of coke to fan across my desk. Cocaine can be replaced easily if you're me. A woman who fascinates me can't. It's taken twenty-seven years to stumble upon one, so I'm not going to risk another twenty-seven-year delay because running away from the demons of my past is more important than looking toward my future.

"Claudia," I call out when my entrance to her room has me stumbling onto an empty bed.

My neck jackknifes to the right when a faint voice trickles out of the attached bathroom of her room. "I'm in here."

She sounds really fearful, and I learn the reason for her fright when I push open the bathroom door. My pet iguana appears to be as taken aback by Claudia's bare legs as me. He's backed her into the corner of the bathroom like her toes are dinner. I can't say I blame him. Even with Claudia's chest heaving like she's endured a marathon, my cock is as hard as a rock. Her body—*fuck me*. I've never seen such a tempting sight, and I've been an invitee at auctions where some women were sold for over two hundred thousand dollars a pop.

I reluctantly drag my eyes away from Claudia's legs when she stammers out, "Y-you have a lizard in your house. A *very big* lizard."

The heaving of her chest doubles when I reply, "I do, but there's no need to fret. He's mostly herbivorous."

"Mostly?" she chokes out, her eyes widening. "What do you mean *mostly*?"

While stepping closer, I try my damnedest to keep my eyes on her face. In case you're wondering, I miserably fail. I'm so fucking hard, just walking is an effort. "It means he *mostly* eats plant matter, but he's had the occasional slip-up."

I realize she's more clued on about this lifestyle than first realized when she asks, "What types of slip-ups?"

After scooping George up by placing my hand under his belly, I answer, "Mainly unwanted fingers, but he's gnawed on the occasional set of toes." I grin like an ass when my comment sees her balancing her tippytoes onto the rim of the bathtub. Her leap from the floor to the bathtub is so agile, you'd swear she was a ballerina and not an inmate at a maximum-security prison. "I'm joking." I'm not, but she's too scared for me to share those stories just yet. "George loves belly rubs, shoot-'em-up movies, and long soaks in the hot tub."

I lick my lips before cracking them into a smile when Claudia mumbles, "Sounds like almost every man I've met."

"Pretty much." When I hold George in front of her, she sheepishly moves her hand toward the back of his head. "Don't approach him from above. That makes him angry. Either pat him while holding him or approach him from the front, so he knows you're not trying to dominate him."

I already knew she was strong, but it's proven without a doubt when she convinces George she isn't the enemy in under ten seconds.

"Don't get any ideas, bud," I grumble to George when he cozies up to Claudia's hand. "From what I've heard, she likes her men with less scales."

My comment has Claudia looking as desperate to scratch under my chin as she is George's. I don't mind. Iguanas are essentially big dogs. They recognize their owners, have great memories, and are affectionate when they don't feel threatened. George is just out of sorts because I've been absent the past couple of weeks. The lights in his enclosure are set to a timer, and my housekeeping staff keep him well-fed, but he gets pissed if he isn't allowed the run of the house at least once a week. He watches television with me and steals food from my plate when I'm not looking. He's a pain in my ass, but since I've had him almost as long as my drug habit, I put up with his shit.

Once Claudia has George almost comatose from her touch, I nudge my head to the hallway. "Do you want to put him to bed?"

She looks like I offered to fix the many injustices of her pinprick of a husband with my tongue when she nods her head.

"Well, here you go." When I attempt to hand her George, panic makes itself known with her beautiful face. "All his weight is in his tail, so he isn't as heavy as he looks." She takes a moment to gauge the authenticity of my comment before lifting her chin for the second time. "Hold him like you're burping an unsettled baby." I place him in her arm so his head is near her wrist, and the majority of his body swamps her forearm. "Just don't bounce him. He pukes like he's possessed when he is rocked too much."

I grin when she freezes like a statue before she commences a very straight, un-jarred walk toward the hallway. I could lead the way, but since that would steal the ability to drink in the smallest portion of her butt cheeks sneaking out the bottom of her panties, I'm not going to. The view is far too enticing to act as if it isn't. My tongue is hanging out of my mouth like a dog, and it's taking everything I have not to wolf-whistle.

"Oh... Jesus," Claudia whispers on a groan when her arrival at George's glass enclosure sees him scurrying off her arm.

The reason behind his early morning antics is exposed when I discover the latch of his enclosure wasn't fixed into place. It doesn't matter how small the hole, if there is one, an iguana will use it to escape.

"You good?" I ask while checking Claudia's arms to make sure George's claws didn't scratch her up too badly.

She smiles in a way that makes me forget my veins aren't laced with cocaine before nodding. "I'm just glad I was in the bathroom before he found me. I could have made a mess."

I throw my head back and laugh before asking, "Is that why you're without pants? Because you used the toilet?"

Claudia shakes her head. "I was planning to have a shower..." Not even half her reply leaves her mouth when her eyes bug out of her head. After bouncing her massively dilated gaze between mine for two heart-thrashing seconds, she drops her eyes to the teeny tiny shirt she's wearing as if it is a dress. "I'm naked."

"Not technically." She's wearing far more clothing than my wickedly devious head was hoping. "You have a bra, panties, and—"

"A shirt that leaves nothing to the imagination! Oh my god." In her panic, she darts into the wrong room to dive under the bedding. She's no longer in my guest bedroom. She is in the master suite. "I'm so sorry."

"For?" I ask while pacing into my room, truly confused.

Strands of her dead-straight hair stick to her face when she pops her head out of the plain black duvet covering my bed. "For... *that.*" When she nudges her head to George's enclosure during the 'that' part of her statement, I slant my head to the side and arch a brow, wordlessly announcing I'm still lost. "For... *ruining our sexual connection.*" Her last four words are whispers, and they see my popped brow becoming lost in my hairline.

"You think me seeing you *partially* naked..." even though she groans, I act as if she didn't, "... weakened our sexual connection?" When she briskly nods, I twist my lips. "Oh... then I guess I shouldn't have this, should I?" I grab at my crotch, unashamed that I'm outlining my erection to a woman like I'm a teenage boy who can't control his cock. "Or an irrepressible urge to see if your skin feels as silky as it looks." When her cheeks heat more with desire than disgust, I mutter, "Then there's the thirst to discover if your cunt tastes as good as it smells."

I hook her ankle when my name leaves her mouth in a husky moan, then drag her down the mattress. My tug exposes the lower half of her body from her toes to the sexy apex at the top of her thighs, but it keeps hidden the part of her body I was referencing when I expressed my desire to see if her skin is silky smooth. Her body is tiny and compact, but the little ripples in her stomach look like the perfect place for a man to rest his weary head after a tiring day.

"Did he truly never place his mouth here?" I ask while dragging the back of my hand down the plain cotton panties covering her delicious-smelling cunt, hopeful the slightest touch will tame the beast in my pants.

I don't want her thoughts anywhere near the prick she married when I burrow my head between her legs, but I'm too curious as to how he couldn't be interested in what Claudia was selling. Women have it all wrong when it comes to men giving head. They believe we only go down on them to get them off, where in reality, men like Dimitri and me do it because we fucking love the taste of a needy woman.

Claudia fights the urge to draw her knees together when I pull her panties to the side before she shakes her head. I growl at both her confirmation she's never been eaten out and the sexy visual of her cunt laying bare before me. She has a sexy, tight-looking cunt that has me craving her even more.

After taking in her glistening lips, throbbing clit, and the faintest strip of light brown hair running down the middle of her mostly bare mound, I raise my eyes to her face. "What do you say, Mama, should we fix the injustice?"

If her head moves a millimeter in the wrong direction, I'll punch out before a single syllable escapes her mouth. I don't have to beg for a woman's scraps any more than I'd ever force one to do something she doesn't want to do. If she wants to end this, I'll stop it right now. It will kill me, but I'll do it without her having any clue to the ache it will cause my nuts.

My brows pull together when Claudia asks, "Can I keep the bedding?"

It only takes a nanosecond to recognize where her fret stems. She doesn't want me seeing the faint white lines on her stomach that verify she is as kickass as both her personality and the nickname I gave her.

Although I'd rather show her exactly how hard her body makes me, I understand vulnerable people have crutches. Mine is cocaine. Claudia's is anything that will hide her body. Over time, crutches can be weakened. If the fact I'm bracing my knee between Claudia's bare thighs without an ounce of coke strumming through my veins isn't indication enough, I don't know what will convince you.

Usually, I don't hook up unless I'm off my face, and never once has it occurred in the bedroom of my private abode. I've fucked women here, but not once has it been in my bed.

This is my asylum, the place I retreat to when the sullied thoughts of my past become too much, but if Claudia's scent the longer I stare at her is anything to go by, it could soon be my safe haven as well.

# 17

## CLAUDIA

*I* pretended to stay asleep when Rocco placed me to bed to avoid precisely what I'm facing now. It took everything I had to ignore the sexual tension brimming between us in the private jet, which is quite pathetic when you consider how tense things should have been.

I had just escaped a maximum-security prison, placed a stranger's life in the firing line to save my own hide, then learned my time with Rocco, although blistering, will also be extremely short. I wasn't strong enough to comprehend such a diverse array of emotions, so I shut down instead.

Furthermore, my father taught me that you can't love a woman without beating her, and my relationship with Juan backed up his claims, so how am I to believe a stranger wants to help me merely because he believes I deserve a better hand than the one I was dealt?

I'm so damn confused. There's only one emotion that ranks more highly than it—the excitement that Rocco craves me as much as I do him. He didn't even bat an eyelid when I asked if I could keep the bedding hiding my body from his rapturous gaze. He merely nodded while peering at me with the same wanton-filled eyes he's currently drenching my vagina with.

I'm skeptical I can come even with a ton of stimulation, but you wouldn't know that from how my body reacts to Rocco's watch. My panties are soaked through, and he's done nothing more than drag the back of his hand down the moist material.

*It's just sex*, I remind myself while building up the courage to answer the silent questions Rocco is flinging my way. *And you want to have sex with him...* badly, *so what are you waiting for?*

When I nod for the second time, wordlessly expressing the thousand yeses screaming in my head, Rocco floods my nether regions with a flirty wink. Confusion bombards me when he removes the knee he wedged between my thighs to impede their frantic squeezes before he pivots and heads for the door.

I stop panicking that I made a horrendous mistake when his pace slows at a set of massive drawers nestled between the master bathroom and the double wooden doors that lead to the hallway.

He pulls a plain white t-shirt out of the third drawer before twisting to face me. "You need to watch what I'm doing. You can't do that with a chunky duvet wedged between us." My needy breaths fan my cheek when he scrunches up the shirt until only the neckline is seen, pulls it over my head, then releases it over my midriff top. Since he's a good eight inches taller than me, the hem of his shirt stops halfway down my thighs. "Better?" I barely notch up my chin half an inch when he adds, "Good. I'd rather you not hide your sexy body from me, but if a shirt is the only way I can make you comfortable enough to come on my face, I'm down with it."

*Sweet Mother of God.*

I am obsessed with his filthy mouth.

The moans I'm struggling to hold back emerge with a giggle when Rocco hooks my ankle to drag me down the mattress for the second time. After everything I've endured, I thought caveman antics would be jotted on my no-go list. Rocco has proven otherwise. I love how he can't seem to contain himself around me.

I face the same injustice when he removes his shirt and trousers before he kneels at the end of his bed. His quick bob steals the chance for me to ogle his body with the lengthy gawk it deserves, but what I saw exposes my vivid imagination isn't a myth. His body is just as good, if not better than I pictured while endeavoring to bring myself to climax the past three weeks.

"If you want me to stop, Mama—"

"You need to start before I can stop you," I interrupt, surprised by my lack of tact.

My impatience is understandable. An extremely attractive man who pledged to get my son back is kneeling between my splayed thighs. The heated breaths that expel from his mouth when he chuckles about my rudeness could get me off, not to mention the visual of him squeezing his cock in an attempt to keep it in his trunks.

Just the massive bulge in his underwear has me on the verge of climax, and I'm not ashamed about how desperate it makes me sound when I say, "But, yes, I'll stop you if I need you to stop." He's about to slice his tongue through the heat growing more rampant the longer he stares at it when a sudden desire to make sure this won't change anything between us pops into my head. "This won't alter anything, will it? We're just friends... *fucking*, right?"

"I guess that depends," Rocco answers without pause for thought.

"On what?" I ask just as swiftly.

He peers up at me, smirks, then says, "On how good you taste."

Before I can fire off another word, he tugs my panties to the side, stabs his tongue between the folds of my pussy, then drags it up to my clit. I fall back onto the bedding with a moan, certain I've never felt something as erotically satisfying as this. He doesn't just harden my clit with rapid-fire flicks of his tongue, he sucks it into his mouth, plays at it with his teeth, then circles it with his fingers.

"This changes *everything*," Rocco murmurs against my drenched pussy lips before he plunges his tongue inside me.

While moaning like I've never moaned before, I buck against his mouth, certain I can ride his tongue all the way to climax station. I'm shuddering, blubbering, and incoherent in under a minute, yet not the slightest bit of panic slicks my skin with sweat. I don't even cite an objection when Rocco creeps his hand up my stomach to grope my breast.

I'm so desperate for his touch, I curl my arms around my arched back to unlatch my bra. The growl he releases against my pussy when his hand slips under the polyester material of my prison-assigned undergarment almost sets me off. His shirt has ridden up to the wobbly half of my stomach, I'm rocking and rolling my hips without shame to ensure every inch of my pussy is mashed with his face, and I am cursing like I'm determined to cash in a one-way ticket to hell, yet I'm confident in saying this is by far the best sex I've ever had, and we're not even fucking—*yet.*

"Please," I murmur, wildly desperate to explore the intense tingling in the lower half of my stomach. I thought my toothbrush had gotten me off multiple times the past few weeks, but it shows how much I know about climaxing. The tingles I experienced those days were nowhere near as violent as the ones hammering me now.

"Why are you begging me, Mama?" Rocco asks before he flicks his tongue against the vehement rise of my clit. "You have all the control. If you want to come, come. If you don't, lay back and let me enjoy the delicious taste of your cunt."

His name tumbles from my mouth when the bowing of my back has him eating me more expertly. He stabs his tongue inside of me while his thumb firms my clit with precisely timed swivels.

"More," I beg a short time later, too blinded by lust to realize I don't have an ounce of control right now. All my power has been handed to this roguishly handsome man, and I couldn't be happier about it.

Grinning, Rocco spreads my legs wider before the delirious licks of his tongue cause me to lose my mind. I slide my fingers through his hair, holding his mouth to the lips of my shuddering pussy before chanting immorally wicked words into the humid evening air. I beg him to eat me faster before I tell him he needs to do this morning, noon, and night until I command otherwise.

Rocco doesn't glower about my bossy personality rearing its ugly head. He merely continues making me come undone with his talented mouth and fingers. He kisses my wet, hot center while sliding his index finger inside me. I moan a long, wistful groan, loving how he can make me feel so full with only one finger before rolling my eyes to the back of my head.

The sensation of him going to town on my pussy is almost too much, almost too perfect. It takes everything I have to remain lucid when I'm overwhelmed by a blinding orgasm. I cry out before clamping Rocco's head with my thighs. I don't want him to stop. I want this feeling to last forever, but I honestly don't think I can survive such a rush of euphoria. It feels as if my heart is being squeezed of every drop of blood, and the functions of my body are no longer mine to command.

While moaning like he is close to finding his own release, Rocco continues devouring, licking, and caressing my pussy until the absolute exhaustion making me a blubbering mess overwhelms me.

"You taste so fucking yummy. I look forward to doing that morning, noon, and night."

I'm so spent from his miraculous show of chivalry, I don't cite an objection when he tugs on my throbbing clit with his teeth for the final time before he crawls up my body. My eyes bulge out of my head when he shoves his underwear down his tattooed thighs. His cock is throbbing, pierced, and a massive drop of pre-cum is glistening at the tip. After hitting me with a frisky wink, he sheaths his cock with a condom he magically found somewhere between the floor he was kneeling on and his bed.

Anticipation of the greatness that is to come scuttles through me when he folds my knees until they're balancing on my heaving chest.

"You good?" His voice is breathless either from the image of his long cock prodding the opening of my dripping sex or from the banquet he just consumed. It could be a combination of both.

"I'm great." My two-word response doesn't weaken the honesty fueling it. My muscles are aching from the strain of a fantastic orgasm, but it will take more than a little rigidness to overlook how revitalized I feel. "And I have a feeling things are about to get even better."

A touch of insecurity plagues me when Rocco snaps off my panties. The wobbly skin mothers often refer to as a mommy pouch jiggles from his brisk movements, but I push aside the insecurities it instigates for unadulterated pleasure when he uses my distraction to his advantage. He jerks his hips forward, impaling me with an ardent thrust.

I call out, the sensation of being so full almost too much to bear. I'm not a virgin. I've given birth, for crying out loud, and I'm saturated front to back, so it shouldn't hurt as much as it does, but there's no denying it. The burn of being stretched is a bitch no matter the conditions.

"You good?" Rocco asks again, his tone more sincere than the throbs of his cock in response to the needy sucks of my pussy. It doesn't care about the pain. It is relishing being the fullest it's ever been. "Pull your knees in closer to your chest. It will open you up for me."

"If I loosen up anymore, your cock will poke through to my stomach," I blurt out before I can stop myself.

He laughs as if I am being funny. I'm not. I am dead serious. The head of his fat cock is already ramming my uterus. If he burrows any deeper, I won't walk normally for a week.

I take a minute to breathe through the tingles his laugh caused my insides before I flatten my breasts with my knees. The sensation ramps up when Rocco rests my feet on his tattooed pecs. Now, not only can he notch in the last two inches of his cock, my change in position also hides the wobbly part of my body I hate with my thighs.

Within a couple of pumps, the jiggles of my body are far from my mind. Rocco doesn't bury his head into my neck and pump in and out of me with no concern for my pleasure like Juan did. He continually adjusts our position until he finds the right angle for the crown of his cock to stimulate the sweet spot inside of me.

"That's better," he murmurs on a moan a couple of strokes later. "Even with you taking every inch of me, you're no longer suffocating my cock because you're hurting. You are sucking at me because you love my cock as much as I love the greedy squeezes of your cunt."

My feet slip on his sweat-misted chest when I arch my back, both loving and appreciating that he's as concerned about my pleasure as he is his own.

He growls out a moan when my push to get back into position adds to the rolling movement of my hips. "Do that again," he commands, his voice groggy.

He watches his girthy shaft slide out of my pussy when I push away from him with my feet before he grips my ass and drags me forward to impale me once more. Needy moans tear from my throat as we go turn for turn, driving each other crazy. He thrusts into me over and over again, fucking me slowly with perfectly crafted strokes, whereas my bounces are frantic and fast. It's the perfect combination that soon has my body teetering on the edge of another detonation.

Pleasure shoots through me when his fingers play at the wetness at the top of my opening. He's fucking me like I'm worth something, burning me up with his eyes, and now he's fondling my clit. I can't hold back for a second longer. I've reached a point where being reserved isn't an option. The urge to come is way too strong. So, with my eyes snapped shut and my back arched off the mattress, I come with a hoarse cry.

Ecstasy washes over me when Rocco adds to the waves pummeling my midsection by increasing the pressure of his thumb on my clit. He circles the nervy bud while whispering how he plans to keep it throbbing morning, noon, and night. "I'm going to fuck you in the shower, in the kitchen, and in the hot tub while George watches in disgust. Then I'm going to do it all again, but the second time, I'm going to fuck your virginal ass, and you will love it so much, you'll beg for me to do it again and again and again."

I shatter like glass, his confession triggering an avalanche of moans and frantic thrusts. I writhe against him, unsure why I'm turned on by the thought of him claiming me how no man has, but confident it's the cause of the pleasure sparking through me.

I've barely emerged from the clouds when Rocco withdraws his cock, flips me over until I'm on all fours, then re-enters me from behind. I fist the sheets while screaming. I'm not in pain. I am hollering my euphoria loud enough for the world to hear. His cock is commanding every inch of my pussy, and the thumb he tormented my clit with is placing the perfect amount of pressure on my back entrance. He hasn't broken through the seal of the tight muscle no man has previously breached. He's merely teasing me with the thought while also ensuring me I'll enjoy it as predicted.

"I'd teach you now what it feels like to have both holes filled at the same time if I hadn't promised Roxanne I'd be on my best behavior. She thinks that you're a good girl and that you are innocent." I feel his groan more than I hear it. "If only she could see you now. There's nothing innocent about any part of you. Your juices are coating my cock and your thighs, your ass has the marks of my frantic grabs, and the sucks of your cunt have me so fucking desperate to come, I'm willing to make a fool out of myself just to answer its pleas. That's unheard of, Mama. I've never achieved release without being coked-up. *Not since him.*"

His last three words are so quiet, I'm reasonably sure he wasn't meant to express them out loud. He's just too overwhelmed by our sweltering connection and too overcome with emotions. We always say stuff we don't mean when we're in unpredictable situations, and even someone who believes in fairy tales would have a hard time foreseeing a connection as seemingly unbreakable as this.

When worry he openly expressed himself slackens the pumps of Rocco's thrusts, I crank my neck back to peer at him before breathlessly murmuring, "Do it."

The sweat dribbling down his cheeks lands near the two dimples in my lower back when he shakes his head. "You're not ready."

I deny his assumption by pushing back. My jarring movement increases the pressure of his thumb on my back entrance. When it doesn't break the seal, I try again, my campaign only ending when Rocco's palm jumps across my left butt cheek. He isn't annoyed at my aggression, he's peeved as fuck he is giving in to peer pressure.

After coating his index finger with the juices of my climax, he presses it against my once forbidden hole. "If you truly want this, you need to relax."

My knees creep across the sticky sheets when he toys with my clit with his spare hand. His cock is buried inside of me, half his index finger is in my ass, and the other is teasing my clit. I'm too overstimulated to relax.

When I say that to Rocco, he asks with a chuckle, "If you can't take my finger, Mama, how are you going to take my cock?"

The naughtiness of his question sees me blindsided by another orgasm. As shockwaves of pleasure jolt through me, Rocco pushes his finger all the way inside of me. The sensation is amazing, and it has me unsure if the frantic rocks of my hips is to free his finger from my ass or to encourage it to go deeper. There's so much resistance and so much pain, but it's also riveting feeling so full.

Another orgasm begins to manifest when Rocco meets the thrusts of my hips grind for grind. He's arched over me, circling my clit with his finger while sliding his big cock in and out of my drenched pussy, but I'm unsure what's happening with the finger he slid into my ass. I'm reasonably sure it's still in there, but it doesn't feel like he's moving it. I could be too caught up in the tingles racing from the roots of my hair to my toes to recognize another blistering moment of desire, but I'm truly unsure.

I guess there's only one way to find out.

"Please.... I want... I need..."

"Say it, Mama."

"I need you to move your finger. To fuck my ass with it like you want to do with your cock."

I wait for shame to burn my cheeks.

It never comes.

The deep groan Rocco emits a mere second before answering my requests leaves no room for embarrassment. I'm barely coherent when he times the movements of his finger with the plunges of his cock. The sensation of having two holes penetrated at once is overwhelming. I scream out his name over and over again while waves of ecstasy bash into me on repeat. Pleasure bursts through me as I suck in ragged breaths. I feel like I'm drowning, and my lungs will never be completely full again.

As he tells me how sexy I am when I come, Rocco drops his

mouth to the curve between my neck and shoulder. I arch against him when his teeth graze the skin on my shoulder. I desperately want his lips on my mouth. I'll even sacrifice the removal of his finger from my no-longer virginal hole to get them.

"Kiss me."

With one of his hands gripping my throat, and the other curved around the wobbly skin in the lower half of my stomach, Rocco kisses me senseless while fucking me just as crazily. Our new position means he can't impale me as deeply as he did earlier, but the pulsating of his thick cock ensures I have nothing to worry about.

He's enjoying this as much as me.

Juan and I never fucked nor made love. There was no time for that. He rolled over after only a few pumps before grunting out a reminder about me needing to shower before falling asleep. He despised the smell of our intermingled scents so much, the times I forgot to shower saw him dragging me out of bed by my hair in the middle of the night and dumping my shuddering body under scalding hot water.

The stark difference between our exchanges and this one sees me doing something I never thought I'd do.

I take charge.

Rocco doesn't seem to mind. He drags his teeth over his bottom lip when I push him back until his back rests on the headboard of his bed, then he stabilizes the wobbly movements of my legs when I hug his hips with my knees. I become a little uneased about my plan when I realize how far I have to rise to brace the tip of his cock near the entrance of my pussy. Not only are my tits thrust into his face, but he'll have to take in the image of his cock jutting in and out of me by peering past my jiggling stomach.

I have no reason to worry.

Not an ounce of disdain highlights Rocco's voice when he cautions, "Take it slow, or I'll blow my fucking load right now. You're so goddamn sexy, Mama." My nickname comes out with a groan when I pull my knees out from beneath me to authenticate his pledge. "Fuck, Mama. Fuck. Fuck. Fuck."

As cum commences rocketing out of his cock, he stuffs in the final inch before he muffles my screams with his tongue. His possessive kiss has me coming undone all over again. I pant and shake alongside him before I collapse onto his chest in a blubbering, sweaty mess.

"Oh... god..." I pant into his chest several long seconds later, certain I'm a hair's breadth away from coronary failure. "That was amazing."

I glance up at Rocco with loved-up eyes when he pulls my sticky hair away from my face. I'm anticipating for him to remind me about good hygienic routines after vigorous activities, so you can imagine my shock when he winks at me, withdraws his still-throbbing cock from my pussy, snaps off and ties his condom, then rolls me onto my side so he can spoon me.

The rapid beat of his heart thumping against my back exposes he is as exhausted as me. It's been a crazy few hours, meaning I don't feel an ounce of shame when the soothing rhythm of his rising and falling chest lulls me to sleep in an embarrassingly quick ten seconds.

## 18

## CLAUDIA

When I wake a couple of hours later, it dawns on me that Rocco's nap isn't as revitalizing as mine. He's still holding me in his arms, except now my head is resting on his chest instead of his arm. His eyes are closed, but he's fisting his cock like he wants to strangle it instead of aiming to achieve the number of releases I did in the wee hours of this morning.

"Don't," he growls out in a bitter tone when I attempt to even the score between us by swiping my thumb over his engorged knob. Precum is pooling at the tip, but that's the only smooth part of his response to me touching him without permission. "I told you not to fucking touch me! You were *never* meant to touch me!"

I realize his anger isn't directed at me when he continues issuing threats after I've shuffled to the far side of the mattress. He grunts about how he should have killed someone years ago, and that he won't hesitate if he's touched again, all the while he grips his cock in what I'm sure is a painful hold.

My heart pains for him when a frightened groan escapes his lips a mere second before he whimpers for his Ma. "Help me," he begs, his voice on the verge of sobbing.

Confident I'd rather be hit than leave him defenseless to the terrifying throes of a nightmare, I return to his side of the bed before cupping his jaw with my hands. I rub away at the wetness sliding down his cheeks before peering at his tightly shut eyes. Although his face screws up in acknowledgment of our bodies' contrasting temperatures, he doesn't pull away from me. That assures me I'm doing the right thing.

"Rocco, it's Claudia. It's time to wake up, baby."

My words weaken the constrictive hold he has on his cock, but it does little to dampen the fury on his face. He appears angry at himself like he is ashamed of the thickness he can't control.

I learned a long time ago that sexual assault victims aren't responsible for the responses of their bodies during abusive situations.

It appears as if Rocco has yet to learn that.

"Rocco," I try again, my voice needier this time around. I'm not solely using our mutual attraction to my advantage. I'm also reminding him that despite our attackers wishing otherwise, consensual sex can still be enjoyable for victims of sexual assault. Take last night as an example. I loathed being touched so much, I was certain I'd never orgasm, much less multiple times. Rocco blew that theory out of the water. "It's time to wake up."

When I give his shoulders a gentle shake, his eyes immediately pop open. His pupils are swamping his usually alluring green eyes, and they're bloodshot like my arousal is the most potent drug on the market.

"Hey," I say when his eyes finally find me. He was too busy gathering his bearings to pay me any attention. I do the same anytime I wake up from a nightmare. The fact I was in a cell at a maximum-security prison shouldn't have offered me any comfort, but for some warped reason, it did. The Sánchez compound was a prison. It just didn't have any bars.

Conscious anger can be a go-to emotion for sexual assault victims, I don't take Rocco's snapped tone to heart when he barks out, "What are you doing in here, Claudia? Why are you in my bed?"

"I fell asleep here, in your arms, after we…" Yes, I can preach a good story, but I rarely remember the advice I blurt out when I'm feeling overwhelmed. "You know?" I lick my lips when a sexual flare clears away some of the murkiness darkening his eyes before I set to work on fully eradicating it. "I wanted to let you continue sleeping, but my stomach wouldn't quit growling."

"You're hungry?" He doesn't sound convinced by my statement, but relief is very much highlighted in his reply. "That's why you woke me?"

I nod, preferring to lie without words. "I almost went downstairs to help myself, but after meeting George and wrangling another less scaly anaconda last night..." I wink to ensure he knows I'm referencing his cock when I said 'anaconda,' "... I was too chicken. Who knows how many more scaly friends you have lying in wait for me?"

One lot of playful comments, and the weight on his shoulders fully lifts. He didn't forget about our blistering exchange last night. His terrifying step back in time merely pushed it behind the thick fog I'm slowly clearing with understanding yet playful commentary.

"Is there any food in your cupboards, or did someone hit the remote, and we've jumped from an episode of *Prison Break* to *Survivor*?"

Rocco's tongue peeks through his teeth about the overenunciation of my question before he drags his hand over his head. I don't miss the rattle of his hands, but I don't point it out either. "I have food." Sparks of the man I'm fascinated with break out of the dark cloud swamping him when he mutters, "I'm just unsure if it will satisfy your cravings or triple them." He grabs at his crotch like our flirty banter is responsible for his massive erection.

"I guess that depends," I say with a shrug after noticing his cock is pulsating more now with desire than rage.

"On what?" Rocco asks as he scoots closer to me.

I wait for the tension to reach breaking point before murmuring, "On how good you taste."

Just like he did last night, I don't wait for him to answer me. I push away the heavy bedding he could use to excuse his damp hair, circle my hand around his cock that's so big my hand appears dainty, then peer at him with please-let-me-take-away-your-pain eyes.

I've never offered to give head before, so I can't say I've ever been rejected—until now. Rocco doesn't straight up refuse my offer, he merely bookmarks it for another occasion, using the excuse he doesn't want me fading away before he's had his fill.

"What's your craving?" he asks after slipping off the bed and putting on a pair of black trunks. "I can make a mean omelet, but that requires a lot of dishes I refuse to clean." He slants his head before pursing his lips, wordlessly announcing I'll be on dish duty if I pick an omelet. "Other than that, I have bread, peanut butter and jelly, and gurgled coffee."

"Gurgled coffee? What the hell is that?"

"You know," Rocco replies while sheepishly grinning. "The coffee that makes the gurgling noises before it drips into the coffee pot."

I'm confident he's playing with me, but I can't help but reply, "Do you mean drip coffee?"

He shrugs. "Drip. Gurgle. Same fucking thing."

While laughing, I slip out of bed. I tug on the hem of the shirt he lent me when my wiggle causes it to ride up high on my thighs. This could be presumptuous for me to say, but I'm reasonably sure Rocco's abuse stems from unwanted oral stimulation. He used my hunger as an excuse for an interlude in proceedings, but the instant his eyes landed on my bare thighs, he commenced prowling to my side of the room like he has no plans for us to leave anytime within the next six hours.

Once he's within touching distance, I splay my hand across his tattooed chest. "Food first." You have no idea how hard that was for me to articulate. The yearning look in his eyes has my knees pulling together, much less the mess the massive bulge in his pants would have caused my panties if I were wearing any. "And since I'm technically your guest, I'm going with the omelet. Everyone knows guests don't do dishes."

After hitting him with the frisky wink he always awards me, I make my way to the door, grinning when he falls into line a few steps later. "Don't think this is the end of this, Mama. Your mouth and my dick have a raincheck that can be cashed in at any time."

I'd be a lying homewrecker if I say my pulse didn't quicken at the thought.

Dishes fall to the floor when the flirty behavior we've been exuding the past hour becomes too much to bear. Rocco clears the table with his forearm before placing my naked backside in the spot my empty plate was two seconds ago. His teasing touches and philandering comments have me soaking wet, so I won't mention how deliciously seductive it was watching him work his magic in the kitchen.

Despite of the scalding pops of sizzling bacon, he whipped up our breakfast wearing nothing but the trunks he slipped into when he scooted out of bed. He made omelets, grilled bacon, fried tomatoes, mushrooms, and potatoes. It was one of the most delicious meals I've ever tasted, but no amount of salivation could detract from the fact I was still seeking an even more scrumptious dish.

My desire to taste Rocco was the cause of many flirty touches the past hour. We kissed between flips of the bacon on the grill, ground against each other while waiting for the toast to pop, and I can't guarantee the omelets weren't spiced with more than salt and pepper when Rocco authenticated my claim I was sans panties by cupping my pussy.

The last exploit was almost our undoing. It saw the final omelet burned to the frypan and the smoke alarm activating, which in turn, saw Smith endeavoring to reach Rocco in any available form.

In case you're wondering, when push comes to shove, hackers can log into the computer panel in your refrigerator that tells you when your milk supply is low.

Remembrance of this freezes my hand halfway into Rocco's trunks. "Can Smith—"

"Smell a death threat from a mile out?" Rocco interrupts. "Yes, he can, so you don't need to worry about him."

He nips at my collarbone, my neck, then my jaw before he seals his mouth over mine. His kiss is as lush as the one we shared after our first 'date.' It warps my senses so much, even if Smith were watching, I'd still slip my hand in Rocco's underwear to stroke his big cock.

"You shouldn't be allowed to look like you and kiss the way you do," I murmur against his kiss-swollen lips when he reluctantly pulls back to peer over his shoulder.

He appears shocked by my compliment before cockiness overrides it. "I could say the same about you, Mama." He bites at my lip a handful of times before he guides me back until I'm splayed across his massive dining table. With how prominent lust is in his eyes when he rakes them down my body, the last thing I should do is nod when he asks, "Do you need the shirt?"

It's almost midday, and the sun is high in the sky, meaning it casts not a single shadow. I need coverage more than ever, so a slip-up in confidence is understandable.

"All right," he gabbers out, somewhat disappointed before he once again peers over his shoulder.

"What are you looking at?" I ask, too curious for my own good.

Rocco stops me from rising to a half-seated position by pushing down on my shoulder. "That," he murmurs a couple of seconds later, the need in his voice almost drowning out by the big dong of a grandfather clock I assume is in his living room since I haven't been given a guided tour of his home. "Morning, noon, and night, right?" My knees curve inward when a wickedly sexy smile stretches across my face. "Your wish is my command, Mama."

An unladylike curse word seeps from my mouth when he cups my ass, lifts my pussy to his mouth, then drags his tongue along the seam. His gaze never leaves mine, even when he circles his lips around my clit to suck it into his mouth. He watches me come undone, his heat as searing as the euphoria pumping through my veins.

I break eye contact when our hour-long foreplay sees me blindsided by an all-encompassing climax in an embarrassingly fast thirteen seconds. Its intensity and length force Rocco's tongue to work at double the speed it did while he lazily licked up the remnants of the greasy bacon from my fingers. He keeps the top of his dining table spotlessly clean before endeavoring to stretch my orgasm from one to two.

I get in on the act as well. After adjusting my position so I can reach him, I slip my hand into his trunks, then wrap it around his monster dick. I stroke him as hard and fast as the flicks his tongue does to my clit, all the while keeping my eyes locked on his face.

As a tsunami-size wave forms in the lower half of my stomach, I swipe my thumb over the crest of his cock, gathering a drop of sticky goodness beading there. I'm desperate to taste him. My mouth is drooling just at the thought of taking his big cock between my lips, but I'm also greedy. If my eyes are on his cock, they're not on his face, assessing and scrutinizing every expression he makes. I don't need to know all his secrets, but I do need to know not a single remnant of his nightmare is still clinging to his skin during our exchange.

Pump after pump, Rocco eats me more expertly. I bear down on his face, only needing the tiniest bit of stimulation to give me the final push for my second climax.

I'm on the very edge of hysteria when Rocco snaps out, "Stop." With me frozen and his fingers still deeply seated inside me, he stands, wipes the back of his free hand over his mouth, then yanks his trunks down his tattooed thighs. "I want to feel your squeezes." He groans when my body responds to the roughness of his voice by clenching around his fingers. "Yes, Mama. Just like that." He scissors his fingers, teasingly stretching me before he locks his eyes with mine. "Can I take you bare? I'm clean. Excluding my tatts, I don't mess with needles, and I had a full blood work-up when a bullet tinged off my shoulder last week. If you don't trust my word, I can get Smith to forward you the paperwork."

"I believe you," I mutter out before I can stop myself. At this point, I'd take a hooker's word that he's clean if it allows me to release the tension tightening in my core. Furthermore, he's not given me any reason not to trust him. "I'm also clean and have the Mirena in place, so no harm, no foul."

"Is that a yes?"

I barely bob my head half an inch when Rocco commences

replacing his fingers with the head of his cock. Aware he needs to go slow with so much girth, he slowly eases inside of me before he pulls back out. He inches in a little more with each stroke, his teasing pace only increasing once he's fully seated me. "You feel so good, Mama. So hot... and *wet*." He groans his last word more than he articulates it.

With a couple of strokes, my body begins to relax. The loosening of my clenched muscles allows him to take me deeper. Faster. Harder. He thrusts into me rhythmically, the movements of his hips precise and to the point. Within minutes, the deepness of his pumps causes his pubic bone to grind into my clit. The sensation is amazing. I've never felt anything as good as this.

When I say that to Rocco, he speeds up his pace. He drives into me on repeat while overloading my mind with naughty whispered thoughts. He serenades every part of me when we fuck—my body, my spirit, and my mind. I'm utterly and completely consumed by him. Our union is controversial, and it's happening at the speed of light, but it still feels right.

It's that confession that brings my orgasm to life.

"Yes, Mama. Squeeze my cock with your tight, wet cunt," Rocco grunts while maintaining the pace that drove me to hysteria.

While I ride the excruciatingly blissful wave, he tells me how good it feels fucking me bare, how this is his first time forgoing a condom, and that no matter what happens, he'll never do this with anyone else.

My muscles pulsate around him during his last confession. He moans about the tightness before he grips my ass tighter, then drives in even deeper. Wave after wave of pleasure bolts through me. I scream, pant, then beg for him to keep driving me crazy.

"It feels so good..." I shout my words, uncaring of who may hear me. This is too brilliant for a simple response. Too electrifying. And it becomes even more charged when Rocco finds his release.

The legs on the table bow when he buries himself in deep, then he grunts my name with a husky groan.

I thought his release would slow him down, but after pushing down on my knee, spreading me wider for him, he adjusts the rolls of his hips.

"I can't. Oh god, I can't," I huff out when the rim of his thick cock finds the sweet spot inside of me.

"One more," Rocco demands, his speed unrelenting.

Strands of hair stick to my sweaty face when I shake my head. "I'll die if I come again. It's not possible to orgasm so many times."

He discredits my lie by giving me everything I've ever wanted. He fucks me—hard. Deeply and relentlessly. Within seconds, I'm begging like I need to climax again more than I need air to breathe.

"More."

Rocco growls before he drags me to the very edge of the table. There's nothing between us now but the wild slaps of our bodies as he takes me to the edge all over again.

"Rocco…"

"I'm right there with you, Mama. Right… fucking… there."

He pumps into me over and over again before he seals his mouth over mine to muffle my screams while he spills his release inside of me for the second time.

19

———

## ROCCO

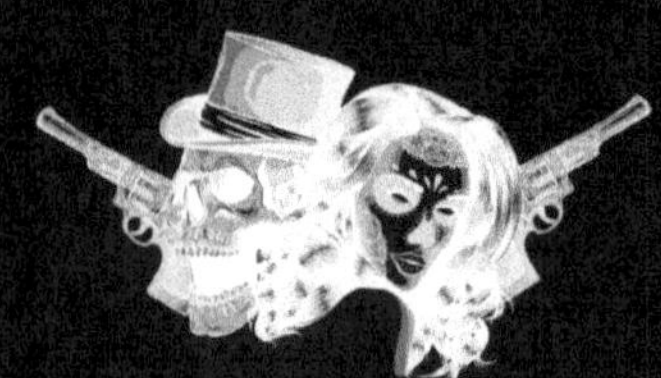

**M**y housecleaners will shit bricks when they see the mess Claudia and I made in the kitchen and dining room. We could have cleaned up at some stage the past five hours—Claudia has offered multiple times—but since that would have removed her spent self from my chest, I've continuously denied her offers.

I haven't had a moment of peace since I was eight—*until today*. We've lazed on the couch, watched a handful of movies, and talked about pretty much everything and anything. And I did it without once bringing up the reason I woke up drenched in sweat with a hard-on that could drill for gold.

I'm lost as to what happened this morning. I haven't had a nightmare in years, but I'm reasonably sure it was why I felt like I was drowning on air. I couldn't get enough oxygen, and no matter how many times I told myself my lungs will breathe no matter how heavy my panic becomes, I felt like I was suffocating.

Mercifully, Claudia seems none the wiser to the terror I faced this morning. She didn't look at me differently when I feasted on her scrumptious cunt or when I requested to forgo a condom. It's as if she has no inkling about how fucked in the head I am.

Since I'm eager to keep it just like that, I band my arm around Claudia's back before standing from the couch we're sprawled on. "Are you hungry, Mama? I'm not, but it will be a little improper for me to have dessert before dinner."

"Says who?"

Her question makes me laugh. It also exposes how confident she's becoming. Give me an hour or two, and I bet I can have her dumping the shirt she's refusing to hand over.

I walk us into the kitchen before placing her naked backside onto one of the barstools nestled around the island. "Ma never allowed sweets before dinner. She said it would ruin me." I open the fridge, groaning when I notice how paltry it is. There's plenty of salad, George wouldn't have it any other way, but nothing with enough sustenance for a rigorous all-night fuck session. "Takeout it is."

Claudia's brow cocks when she spots colored pencils and drawing pads in the drawer I keep the takeout menus in. "That's the Popeye tattoo on your *eighth* ab muscle, isn't it?"

I laugh at her underhanded and very much overemphasized compliment before lifting my chin. "Finlay is a mad artist. Almost every one of my tats is one of her designs."

"Only almost?" Claudia queries, extremely curious.

I dig the delivery pamphlets out before joining her at the island. "Almost." I lift my right arm to show her the script jotted down one side. It's similar to the passage she has for her mother on her rib. "This is the verse that's on my mother's headstone." I turn my left arm so she can see the caricature of Finlay halfway up my arm. "Finlay both drew and tattooed this design last year." I take a moment to drink in the absolute awe on Claudia's face before I twist away from her and roll my shoulder to ensure my mother's face isn't wrinkled. She died far too young to have wrinkles, whether in real life or in her portrait-like tattoo. "And this is the last photo I took of our mother. Finlay is great with cartoon characters and anime, but she struggles with portraits. It's why she changed her major. She's studying graphic design, fine arts, and new media with the hope she can get into anime creation."

I sound like a soft cock, but so fucking be it. I'm proud of how far Finlay has come the past two years. She still has a way to go, but not that long ago, she was a high school dropout. Now she's interning at a film company and a freshman in college.

My spin back around to face Claudia stumbles when she asks, "And your father? Is he marked anywhere on your body?"

"No, he is not," I reply matter-of-factly before tossing a bag of microwavable popcorn into the microwave, needing to distract myself before I blurt out something I'm not planning to tell anyone. "This should tide us over until the pizza arrives." I nudge my head to the den. "Why don't you go pick another movie for us to watch. I'll join you once this is done."

I don't give her the chance to deny my suggestion. I dial the number for a local pizzeria and squash my phone to my ear. My call is connected just as Claudia slips off her barstool and pads away from me. The low hang of her shoulders has me gripping my phone so hard I'm tempted to check the screen for cracks. I hate that even years after his death, my prick of a father is still fucking me over.

The frustration associated with it sees me tossing open the freezer and dragging out a bag of cocaine while ordering dinner. After requesting a large cheese pizza for Claudia and me and a side of salad for George, I toss my cell phone onto the kitchen counter before cutting an eighth of coke into lines.

The buzz I'm seeking comes in an entirely different manner when I toss open a junk drawer in search of a bill to snort the coke with. The box of condoms I snuck in the drawer while preparing breakfast is sitting untouched.

Claudia let me take her bare because I pledged I was clean. Although this is different, I still feel like a deceitful cunt. So much so, I slam the drawer shut before mopping up the lines of coke with a dishcloth instead of my nostrils.

Once I have the evidence of my almost slip-up hidden, I dump the bag of cocaine back into the freezer, snatch out a bottle of vodka in its place, then rejoin Claudia in the den.

Several slices of pizza and a handful of vodka shots later, we're halfway through the classic movie Claudia picked, and I'm itching for dessert. The sun has set, so technically, it is nighttime, so I'm not stepping outside the terms of the agreement we made last night.

I scoot down the couch until Claudia's head is closer to my chest than my stomach before taking a whiff of her hair. It smells of sex, and it ends any chance of me slowly hinting that I want to feast on her. I'm hard in an instant, and the recollection has Claudia's lips lifting against my chest before the faintest press of her thighs sends an electrifying jolt straight to my balls.

When I buck my hips to grind my rock-hard shaft against her thigh, she hums out a healthy moan. It's a sensual sound that has me thinking about sheet-clenching, sweat-producing, cum-exploding sex, and it isn't just my deviant head thinking it.

After rising onto her knees, cautious not to whack me in the nuts with her kneecap, Claudia places a trail of kisses from my tattooed pecs to the waistband of my underwear. Just like she's remained in my shirt, I haven't worn anything more than trunks all day.

It's a lazy exploration that has pre-cum seeping into the stretchy material of my underwear and my mouth salivating. I could hurry her along, but since this is merely a prologue of the greatness that is about to occur, I don't. Only fools rush in, and I am most certainly not one of them.

"Take what you need, Mama," I offer when Claudia lifts her needy, wanton-filled eyes to mine. She's reached the waistband of my pants, and despite the only light in the room coming from the LCD television mounted on the far wall, she can't miss how hard her appreciation of my body has made me. The head of my cock has stretched the band of my underwear, and the cotton material clings to my dick like cellophane.

My cock throbs when Claudia accepts my offer with a grateful grin before she shimmies my trunks down my thighs. Hot heat roars through me when she gasps about the boing my cock does when it springs free. It barely gets in half a bounce before she curls her tiny hand around my shaft and narrows her mouth toward the glistening tip. Her heated breaths almost have me wanting to make a fool of myself, so I won't tell you how impish her moan is when her tongue laps up the salty drop on the end of my cock, or I'll be a goner.

I stiffen with frustration when the movie we're watching switches to a dark scene just as Claudia is about to wrap her meaty lips around the crown of my cock. I don't want to miss a single immoral moment when she sucks me off for the first time, so I lean over to switch on the lamp.

Claudia snatches my arm back before I'm halfway there. "It's okay," she says, her voice equally nurturing and concerned. "I'm not him."

I stiffen for the second time, except this time around, my dick softens in the process.

*What does she mean she's not him?*

*Who the fuck is she talking about?*

The vodka I guzzled down with dinner burns my throat when the truth smacks into me like a cock-removing missile. Its scald makes my words super groggy when I snap out, "Of course I know you're not him! Why the fuck would you think any differently?"

I don't give her the chance to reply. I push her away from my crotch, yank up my trunks, then stand like I'm not shuddering a million miles an hour. As I rake my fingers through my hair, I fight the urge to vomit. I feel sick. Horribly and violently ill.

Needing air, I burst out of the den, sprint down the hallway, then break out into the outside patio. I'm practically naked, and it's cool today, but the briskness does little to dampen the fury burning me alive. It's so perverse, I push through the swinging door of Smith's kitchen before I even realize which direction I'm running.

With a piece of burned toast lodged halfway into his mouth, Smith drags his eyes down my almost naked form. I was too worked up to get dressed before my impromptu visit. Too assured my life is going down the fucking gurgler.

I didn't think Claudia was looking at me any differently. She also wasn't tiptoeing around me like I am a monster. Excluding my almost fuck-up, things were going great between us.

Well, so I thought.

I have no fucking clue what's going on, *except* how grateful I am that Smith is a fucking creep.

"I need access to the footage from my house last night."

After placing down his half-assed dinner, suddenly not hungry, Smith replies, "I don't have any footage from last night. You threw up blockers."

"Fucking bullshit, Smith. If you were out, how did you know about the smoke alarm going off this morning?"

He cocks a brow before hooking his thumb to the fence that divides our properties.

It isn't what you're thinking. We're not technically neighbors. His property backs onto mine, but with two pools, a mini putt-putt course, hot tubs big enough to fit a dozen people, and a massive pool house, there's more than a wooden fence between us.

Something on my face must expose how desperate I am because Smith comes to the plate remarkably fast for someone who's been seeking a way to exact revenge on me for ruining his plans with Ellie. "There may be a way I can work around the blockage." He stops, arches his brow, then drops his eyes to my briefs. "But I ain't doing shit with you standing around in your jocks. Put some fucking clothes on."

When I fold my arms in front of my chest, wordlessly announcing I won't return to my home without answers to questions I'm too afraid to ask, he nudges his head to the stairwell I breezed past during my sprint through his private abode. "There are clothes in my spare bedroom. I'm sure you'll find something to your taste."

We don't hoard clothes because we have an obsession with online shopping. We do it because we know there are fuckers in the world like us who have nothing. Time and time again, you hear about people leaving abusive relationships with nothing but the clothes on their backs. More times than not, those men and women are also fathers and mothers.

Although we can't shelter everyone, we have no hesitation taking in the ones we feel responsible for. They may have been seen as whores and crew members at one stage, but when they walk through the front doors of our homes, they're guests.

Once I'm dressed in a pair of dark trousers and a black button-up shirt, I join Smith in his office. It isn't a standard office with a big leather chair and a sturdy wooden desk. Twelve television-size monitors take up one wall, and another is lined with servers and computer equipment worth millions.

Smith's eyes lift to mine when I drag over a single-seated chair that has several strands of long blonde hair coating it before he asks, "What time did you lock me out?"

"I didn't lock you out..." My lie holds out for approximately twenty seconds. "Around four in the morning. I went down to my office for... you know." I sound as uneased as Claudia did when I woke up to her holding my cheeks and peering at me with worried, suspicious-filled eyes. That should have been my first clue she's stumbled onto something I'm not willing to share with anyone, much less the woman who's gripped me from the moment my eyes landed on her. "I logged back in just after breakfast."

"So, four in the morning until one-ish?" When I jerk up my chin, he jots down the timeline onto a yellow-lined paper. "Do you think the event we're looking for occurred before blackout, during, or after?"

"Fucked if I know," I mutter, truly confused.

I woke up feeling clammy. My skin was hot to touch, and my cock was throbbing like I hadn't sought release only hours earlier. Previous instances point to me having a nightmare, but I haven't had one of them in years, and Claudia was too laid-back and flirty for me to give it any real thought. If my dream was anything like the handful I had when Ophelia snuck into my bed, wouldn't Claudia have freaked the fuck out?

"Can't you just work your magic and bring up the footage?"

Smith shakes his head. "It doesn't work like that. I designed the system so you have *full* privacy. Look." I inwardly sigh when his log into the camera in my living room doesn't have him stumbling onto a half-naked Claudia. I'm pissed as fuck, and extremely distrusting, but that doesn't mean it's a free for all. "This is what I usually see."

"Every-fucking-thing," I say, groaning.

He nods before activating the program he specifically designed for me. "This is what is recorded when you activate dark-knight." I stuff my fingers into my ears when an ear-deafening pulse chases the darkening of his monitors. "Not only can I not see anything. I can't hear anything either," he shouts over the ear-piercing shriek. Once he shuts down the program that could cause permanent hearing loss, he locks his eyes with mine. "I could try to strip the noise from the file, but if I don't want to end up deaf, I'll need a more specific timeline than nine hours."

When I lift my chin, pissed yet understanding of his plight, a flurry in the far corner of his bank of monitors catches my attention. Claudia is moseying past the door of my office, her already sluggish pace slowing when she spots the line of cocaine that went to waste last night.

I guess that could be behind the return of my nightmares. I can't remember a day I've gone to bed the past decade without some type of narcotic thrumming through my veins.

"Bring up the surveillance footage from my office onto the main monitor."

"Rocco," Smith groans, anxious about my request. He has no issues snooping on Dimitri and me, but he draws a big fat line in the sand when it comes to women he doesn't know. "You watched her for weeks on end. If you don't trust her motives by now, why the fuck did you invite her into your home?"

I clip him up the back of the head before repeating my request, "Bring up the surveillance footage from my office onto the main monitor."

I hear his back molars grinding together as he does as asked. Since his main monitor is the size of most people's flat-screen LCD TVs, it shows every single crinkle between Claudia's brows when she stares down at the line of cocaine.

"If you're pissed she doesn't like that you're a coke-head, you need to add a ton more names onto your hit list. You're supposed to distribute the shit for Dimi, Rocco, not snort it."

"Shut the fuck up, Smith," I growl out in warning. I get he's concerned about my habit, but unless he's faced the shit I did in my youth, he has no right to judge me on it.

When Claudia brushes the line of coke off my desk like its dust, then takes a seat behind the Balinese piece of furniture, I move closer to the bank of monitors. She looks as good in my home office as she did in my bed. I just wish her exploration of my domain wasn't occurring with a whole heap of wetness in her eyes. Her cheeks are streak-free, assuring me my storm out didn't upset her too much, but there's no fucking doubt she's hurting. There's only one set of surveillance I've perused where her face was wearing the strains it's harboring now. It was in the minutes following Dillon's birth.

"Can you zoom in on what she's typing?" I don't have a lock code on my MacBook Pro. If you're stupid enough to break into my house and use my things, you can have full access to my shit because you'll be dead long before you tell anyone what you saw.

After coughing to clear his throat, Smith uses a game controller-type mouse to zoom in on my Mac screen. It feels like the world is crumbling in on me when he reads out each word Claudia types. "How can you help someone with sexually aggressive dreams." He stops, works his throat through a brutal swallow, then slings his eyes to mine. "Why is she looking up that?"

The concern in his question has me torn. I want to fold in two, but I also want to smear his desk with his brain matter to ensure he never once again looks at me like he is now.

"How the fuck am I to know?" I snap out, once again falling back on an old crutch I always use when snowed under—aggression. "You saw how fucking weird those Sánchez men are. Perhaps she's seeking ways to help them?"

I drag my finger under my nose and sniff, hopeful remnants of the bumps I took well over thirty hours ago are still lingering before forcefully closing Smith's laptop screen. When it fails to remove the image of Claudia seeking ways to stop me from unknowingly masturbating during the midst of a nightmare, I race to the bank of monitors.

"Where's the off button?"

I search around the monitor and behind it before straight-up attempting to rip it from the wall. What if she searches my name along with sexual assault convictions? Or worse, what if I murmured *his* name during my nightmare? Then, not only will my secret be out, everyone will know it was my father who fucked with my head.

I don't know about you, but I would have preferred to have been molested by a stranger. It would have been less shameful that way.

"There!" Smith shouts after pulling out a set of cords near his server towers. "It's gone. It's done."

When I let go of his monitor, it remains fixed to the wall by a single bolt. "And the tapes?"

His brows furrow before he shakes his head. "There are no tapes these days, Rocco. Everything is hardwired." When I step up to him, panicked out of my mind he has proof of how fucked in the head I am, he pushes out, "I activated dark-knight before I yanked out the cables. I can't see or hear anything. *No one* can." He gives me a moment to authenticate the honesty in his tone before he braces his ass onto his desk, then folds his arms in front of his chest. "What's going on, Rocco? Are you in trouble?"

"No." I brush off his claims with a laugh. "I just forgot about some risqué photos I uploaded of Claudia from last night. You know how bad the fog gets when I'm over envious with my cuts."

He doesn't believe me, but he pretends as if he does. "Then maybe that's a good reason to get off drugs?"

I mimic his stance before replying, "Maybe." With my veins drug-free, a ruse to get me out of this fucked-up situation pops into my head astonishingly quick. "I'll give it more thought after tonight's party."

"Party? What party?"

When I backhand his chest, some of the sweat drenching my

hand clears away. "Did Dimi not tell you? We're having a welcome home party for Fien. Booze, drugs, and hookers..."

"For a two-year-old? Sounds about right."

"The party isn't actually for Fien. It's for Dimitri's crew who worked tirelessly to bring her home." Fuck, Smith was right. I am more clued in when I'm not coked out of my head. "It starts at ten. You can bring Ellie if you want." I stop talking when he shakes his head. "Over already?"

A *pfft* vibrates his lips before he shakes his head for the second time. "But I can see that being the case if she stumbles onto the last two party favors on your wish list."

Happy for the focus to be on him, I say, "Prostitution is legal in a handful of counties in Nevada—"

"We're not in Vegas."

I continue talking as if he never interrupted me. "And with the dopeheads getting marijuana legalized, it will only be a matter of time before coke, E, and ketamine follow it."

"You're out of your fucking mind." Smith isn't anti-drugs. He's just anti-me taking drugs. "If that occurs, I'm moving back to Australia."

"Australia?" I ask, honestly confused. "I thought you were South African?"

"No," he draws out his one word as if it is an entire sentence. "My cock is from South Africa, but the rest of me is Australian..." he twists his lips, "... and German, Norwegian, Dutch, Korean." I wish he were lying, but he isn't. He has a bit of every nation in his DNA, including South Africa.

After rattling off a handful more countries, he plonks his backside into his chair, then raises his eyes to mine. I was hoping I had steered our conversation far enough away from my brutal meltdown for it to be a forgotten memory, but the worry in his eyes shows it will take more than a little shit-stirring for him to forget. "What do you want me to bring?"

"To?"

*To the admissions office of the psychiatric hospital I'll be forced to be a patient at when I try to off myself instead of living with the shame of what my father did to me?*

*To the massive burial site I plan to dump anyone stupid enough to share my secret?*

*Or to my father's grave where I plan to dig him up so I can kill him all over again, but I'll do it much more slowly this time around?*

My father's imaginary screams stop ringing in my ears when Smith answers, "To the party. I saw your fridge's inventory list this morning. You don't even have limes for my beer."

"That's because real men don't put limes in their beer, Smitty." I squeeze his shoulder, wordlessly announcing he walked straight into that one before saying, "It's all good. I'll head out and grab supplies now."

He curses under his breath when I snatch up the keys for his swanky new ride from his desk, but it has nothing on the sigh he releases when I ask, "What's your flavor this month? Blonde, brunette, or do you want a taste of Dimitri's favorite banquet?"

## 20

## CLAUDIA

*I* really stuffed up. I thought Rocco needed a minute or two to calm down. That after some quick breaths, he'd give me a chance to explain my unfortunate yet understandable blunder. I had no clue when he stormed out that he would be gone for hours. It's ten thirty at night, and I haven't seen hide nor hair of him.

I was so desperate to track him down, after researching a better way to handle the situation if it arises again, I walked through his house, calling out Smith's name. From the digital alarm clock in Rocco's room, Smith told me Rocco had urgent errands to run and that he'd be back soon.

That was over three hours ago.

The only good that came from my brief conversation with Smith was confirmation that Juana had called the warden at Drakes to request a visit with me. He scheduled her visit for late Wednesday afternoon. That's a little under forty-two hours. Smith has surveillance in both the Sánchezes' compound and outside of Drakes, meaning not only am I one step closer to seeing Dillon again, I may also have the opportunity to see him in real-time surveillance. I can't smell him or feel how soft his skin is via a monitor, but video footage would have to be better than grainy long-range images, wouldn't it?

After breathing out some of the heaviness on my chest, I pad out of the bathroom attached to my room. When I initially climbed the stairs to call it a night, I headed toward Rocco's room first. It only took smelling the combined scent of our skin mingling in the air for me to alter the direction of my course.

I fed George the untouched salad from the meal Rocco and I shared before I put my foot in my mouth, then I slipped into the shower. I'm not sure how long ago that was, but if the steam in the bathroom is any sign, I just had the world's longest head soak.

My already sluggish pace slows even more when the faintest trickle of music plays out of the downstairs living room. It sounds similar to the shoot-'em-up movie Rocco and I watched earlier today.

Rocco has finally returned, and I'd be a liar if I said I wasn't stoked about the prospect.

Once I've tossed on a pair of loose boyfriend jeans and a long-sleeve shirt, I gallop down the stairs. My hair is drenched and twisted off my face with a sideways braid, and my face is without a snippet of makeup, but I don't care. Apologies don't need glitz and glamor to make them sincere. They merely need to come from your heart.

I almost stumble off the last step of the elaborate stairwell. Rocco's return home wasn't a solo expedition. An army of men and women is in his home. They're chatting and drinking, and a handful of them are smoking cigars. The air above the living room is plumed with smoke, and the music I mistook as a shoot-'em-up movie is actually a horrible rendition of a rap song.

"Excuse me, have you seen Rocco?" I ask the first lady I stumble upon. She's wearing a super tight mini dress, and her face is perfectly made up with an array of products.

"No," she answers with a pout. "But if you find him, can you tell him Tasha is looking for him?" When she leans in close, my nose twitches with the wish to sneeze from the excessive amount of perfume she's wearing. "We have a raincheck that's due to be cashed."

"Oh..." I should say more. I just can't. I was endeavoring to do the same when I stupidly mistook the tightening of Rocco's thigh muscle as him freaking out about me touching him in a darkened room. Juan did the same, and the only way I could settle him was by switching on every light in our room. Since that blanketed Juan's issues instead of soothing them, I decided to try a different approach with Rocco.

Clearly, that was wrong of me to do.

When Tasha reads the heat burning my cheeks in the wrong manner, she pats her manicured hand on my forearm before she sashays away. I follow after her, but I don't make a beeline to the extensive collection of alcohol on the glistening bartop in the living room. I drag my eyes over the rowdy bunch, seeking Rocco amongst the riff-raff.

I wish my search weren't so eager when I find him in the den. He isn't alone. Not only has Tasha found him, so have another two equally attractive women. They're lounging across him as I imagine Roxanne did when she used him to rile a response out of Dimitri, but I'm reasonably sure Roxanne would have worn more than a bra for a shirt.

After taking a moment to wipe the riled expression from my face, I pace across the room to where Rocco sits. "Can I please talk to you for a—" He cuts me off by holding his index finger in the air before requesting for a blonde to continue with what she was saying. His dismissal drops my mouth like he just informed me he's married before it switches my annoyance to red-hot anger. "What I need to say will only take a minute."

He acts as if I never spoke.

His eyes don't even glance my way.

"Rocco—"

"In a minute, *Claudia.*" He spits out my name as if it is trash. "Can't you see I'm busy?"

"Yes, I can see that," I reply, my tone just as firm. "Apparently, cashing in all those rainchecks you seemingly hand out like candy on Halloween."

I got snarly to force him to respond, but all I get is my pissy attitude handed back to me on a silver platter. "There's no need to fret you'll miss out. My rainchecks don't have an expiration date."

I swear steam billows out of my ears when he has the audacity to wink at me. It isn't the wink he gave me when he protected me from a sexual sadist, nor the one he hit me with when he broke me out of a maximum-security prison. It is the same wink he awards a brunette with when she wiggles her fingers at him from across the room.

I thought he stormed out because he didn't want my help. I was so very wrong. He got what he needed from me, I gave it to him my very first twenty-four hours here, so now he's through with me.

I'd laugh about how pathetic I feel for falling for his trick if I didn't hurt so much. Juan at least waited a couple of weeks before he removed his cloak. Rocco couldn't even hold out for an entire day.

When I pivot on my heels and rocket out of the room, someone calls my name. A stupid bit of the hope inside of me is praying Rocco has come to his senses, but I soon learn otherwise when it dawns on me how unique the man's accent is. When I crank my neck to my greeter, I spot the face that belongs to the accented voice that comes out of every electronic product you could imagine. Smith is extremely handsome, although I'm skeptical his face usually holds this much worry.

"I'm okay," I lie to Smith before I dash through the hundreds of people hogging every inch of the floor space of Rocco's home.

When I reach my room, I yank off my jeans then slip under the covers on my bed. I won't cry. I refuse to give Rocco the satisfaction. I'll just quietly reflect on a telling day before falling into a hopefully restless slumber.

*Yeah, right.*

That idea lingers for around three minutes before it's replaced with a far more disobedient and jealous-provoking scheme. I had the gall to tell the head of the Mexican Cartel exactly what I thought about her when she prepared to pack me up and ship me out without so much of a goodbye, so you can be assured as hell I can match Rocco's game jab for jab.

My nostrils flare to suck in big breaths when I scan the wardrobe of clothes Rocco gave me unlimited access to earlier today. I throw a fist into the air when my hunt has me stumbling onto a risqué black dress a couple of minutes later. Its neckline is teasingly low, but the clingy material is cinched around the midsection. It's the perfect design for a mother seeking a sexy yet flattering look.

Once I've dumped my dress onto the bed, I move into the bathroom to fix my face. The endless supply of makeup in the drawers in the vanity shouldn't boost my assurance my ruse will go off without a hitch, but for some reason, it has that exact effect.

If I had noticed the cosmetics earlier, perhaps I would have caught on to Rocco's plan before I fell into bed with him. I guess everything happens for a reason. Rocco's swift change-up and surly attitude hurts, but in all honesty, if I could go back and erase the past, I wouldn't forgo last night and a majority of today. It was the first time in my life, I truly felt valued. That has to mean something, doesn't it?

When my confession wells tears in my eyes, I pray for my eyeliner to be waterproof before I set to work on clearing away evidence of a tiring day. Since my makeover has nothing to do with removing bruises and everything to do with causing a ruckus, I switch out my usual brownish-red lipstick for fire-engine red. It makes the plump lines of my lips more obvious while stealing the focus from the dullness of my eyes.

"Perfect," I murmur to myself while doing a little twirl. My dress fits like a glove, my makeup appears professional, and a few added accessories I found in a jewelry box in a set of drawers have tied the outfit together outstandingly well.

I feel so nice, I don't head straight for the den where I last saw Rocco. I mingle with the crowd while pretending I'm at the prom I never got to attend. There are as many eyes on me now as there was when I presented as a pizza delivery driver, but they linger longer this time around. Even a handful of the gawkers approach me with an offer to fetch me a drink.

I thank them for their kindness before telling them I don't drink. They laugh at me like I'm the headline act at a comedy skit. I understand why when I realize alcoholic beverages aren't the only mood enhancers Rocco's guests are enjoying. Even the host himself doesn't hold back. He snorts three lines of cocaine like his eyes aren't already glassy before he hands a rolled-up Benjamin Franklin to the brunette he winked at earlier.

I shouldn't be pleased when he balks about spotting my watch. However, I am. He isn't just embarrassed I witnessed his drug habit firsthand for the second time in such a short period, he's also stunned by the swiftness of my makeover.

I bet he thought I was crying like a baby in my room.

It's a pity for him, I'm stronger than that.

Feeling daring, I hold my hand into the air like a game-show model before doing a little twirl. It sees Rocco standing on a wobbly pair of legs. Regretfully for him, his drug-hazed head can't get him across the room fast enough. I've caught the eye of another man, and this time, I accept his offer of a drink.

I shake my head when the blond-haired gentleman says, "You can't be a local. I would have remembered seeing someone as beautiful as you before."

His flattery is more nauseating than nice, and it has me speaking before thinking. "I'm here visiting a friend. We met in prison."

"Prison?" He double-checks, certain he heard me wrong.

He didn't.

I nod. "Yeah. We served time together at Wallens Ridge. Have you heard of it?" I place my untouched drink onto the bar to pat his back when he chokes on his beverage. "Are you okay?"

I stop whacking his back like a psycho when Rocco enters my peripheral vision. Instead, I act as if we're flirting. It's a hard feat when the stranger is more interested in fleeing than hearing the story of how I became an inmate at one of the most gang-related prisons in the country.

"I'm joking," I push out with a giggle that makes me feel as if I am twelve. "I got you, didn't I?"

"You did," the stranger replies, still unsure. "But it wouldn't have scared me. I've dealt with far worse in the dating scene than a female inmate." I send a prayer to God for him to choke on an ice cube when he says, "I don't know how many times I've almost been trapped by single mothers. That should be the first thing on their profile." He fans his hand through the air like he's highlighting a massive billboard. "Looking for a replacement daddy for my fucked-up kid."

*Screw the ice cube, I'm going to take this asshole down myself.*

A squeak pops from my lips when an accented voice booming into my ear scares the living daylights out of me. "I wouldn't if I were you. He has undercover cop vibes all over him." When I glance over my shoulder, confused as to where the voice is coming from, Smith dips his drink at me in greeting. "Your earrings are wired with an earpiece," he explains after lifting his half-empty whiskey glass to his mouth. "As are my cufflinks." His equipment is so advanced, I hear the burn the whiskey causes his throat when he throws down the rest of his drink before it's gobbled up by the swish of his dark hair when he gestures for me to join him across the room by notching his chin up. "The pool comp is about to start. I need a partner. Interested?"

I nod, grateful for both his offer and assistance in not getting me arrested within thirty hours of escaping a maximum-security prison.

After removing my smile, I return my focus to the unnamed gentleman. "Since I don't have a profile as such, I guess I'll have to use an old-age approach to dating." I fan my hands through the air like he did earlier. "I'm a single mother *supposedly* seeking a daddy for my fucked-up kid."

When the crudeness of my reply sees him choking on his drink, I stomp the heel of my stiletto onto his polish shoe, spin to ensure the spike digs in nice and deep, then I saunter away. "Nuh-uh," I say to Rocco before holding my finger to his face like he did mine. "I'm busy, and from what I've heard, your rainchecks have no expiration date, so I have no reason to fret."

Smith tries to hide his grin with his whiskey glass. He shouldn't bother. Even if I hadn't sidestepped a stunned Rocco to make my way to him, I would have still seen it. It's too big to miss.

"He's going to fucking kill me," Smith mumbles under his breath when I loop my arm around the elbow he's holding out for me. "But it will be oh-so-fucking worth it if it forces him to pull his head out of his ass." He guides me into a massive game room next to the inground swimming pool before handing me a pool stick. "Have you played before?"

Unease twists my stomach before I shake my head. There is a massive billiard table in the Sánchez den, but it was rarely used for games. It usually housed bricks of cocaine, and on occasions, it was where prospective wives for the unmarried Sánchez crew were lined up to be scrutinized by Juana.

Neither her sons nor the men in her crew get to pick their wives. Juana takes care of everything from medical checks to ensure they're fertile to personal grooming the day they wed. She even took care of the honeymoon events no mother-in-law should be a part of.

Mistaking the disgust on my face as worry, Smith says, "It's fairly easy. I'm sure you'll get the hang of it in no time." He gives me a rundown of the basic rules before suggesting that I commence our game. "You're not aiming for any sequence during the break. That will be determined by which ball sinks first."

I wet my lips, nod, then mimic the pose I saw a redhead do when we entered the pool room.

"Close," Smith says with a chuckle when my attempt to smash the white ball into the colored balls sees the white ball flying off the table. "You don't need to whack the shit out of it to move it. Let the felt covering the table do its job."

After placing down his cue, he shows me what he means by leaning over me. I won't lie. He smells scrumptious enough to eat, but there's no sexual chemistry between us whatsoever. How could there be when bolts of electricity are surging across the room from an extremely angry and red-faced Rocco?

"Nice and *gentle*." Smith's last word comes out with a faint grunt when he slides the cue through our conjoined hand. I almost leap into the air in excitement when our hit sees the colored balls bouncing in all directions. We even manage to sink one. "We're big," he declares with a flirty wink before he unpeels himself from my back and heads for the part of the bar he placed his drink on.

Over the next hour and a half, I perfect my pool skills. Smith is a great teacher, and the couples we compete against are supportive of my flourishing talents instead of berating me. They don't even badger me when I hit the black ball more times than the colored ones.

I'm having so much fun. If I could dismiss Rocco's numerous scorning glares, I could have forgotten my attendance at this party was solely to get a rile out of him.

"Who's next?" Smith scans his eyes across the room, seeking another sucker to fleece of money. I suck at pool, but Smith's skills are so out-of-this-world good, even with me as his partner, he's making a killing tonight.

My heart falls from my chest when a rough voice across the room says, "We'll give it a go." Rocco stands from the chair he's been sulking on the past almost two hours before he offers his hand to an attractive blonde with adulterous curves and an insanely pretty face. "But how about we play for more than coin." I curse myself to hell when he rakes his eyes down my body so I can't miss the meaning of his suggestion. He doesn't want Smith's money. He wants his head on the chopping block. "Do you have any issues with that?"

His eyes are for Smith, but his question is for me.

I almost reply with a straight-up, *hell, yes, I mind,* but Smith stops me by whispering in my ear, "If he wants to play, Claudia, let him play. Running will only encourage him to chase you."

That's the issue. I stupidly want him to chase me.

After taking a moment to deny every objection my head throws up, I mutter, "I don't have any issues... because I know Smith will win." I lock my eyes with Smith, silently warn him he better bring the fireworks, then I hand my cue stick to Rocco's new friend. "Here, why don't you break?"

The way her dress clings to her body when she leans over the table already has my confidence faltering, so you can picture how badly it nosedives when her break sees her sinking three balls. She's either a professional or extremely lucky.

When I stray my eyes to Smith, curious to see if he recognizes her, my eyes falter halfway. Unlike nearly every male in the room, Rocco's eyes aren't on the generous curve of the blonde's backside. They're solely devoted to me.

His gaze is so searingly hot, it takes his female companion waving her hand into my face to break our eye contact. "It's your turn," she informs while handing me back my pool cue. "You're littles."

"*Yes, I am,*" I mumble to myself while moving around the table to aim for the ball Smith pointed out when I flicked my eyes to him for assistance.

It should be an easy shot. The ball is practically sitting in the pocket, but with nerves making me jittery, I'm concerned as hell I'll miss it.

"Yes!" Smith shouts when the ball pops into the pocket. "Now do the same with the four in the far-right corner."

After taking in the purple ball he's mentioning, I inconspicuously shake my head. There's no way I can direct the white ball to that side of the table without getting super close to Rocco. I'm already sweating standing at the opposite end of the mammoth felt-top table. There's no way I won't melt if he's only inches away from me.

With that in mind, I say, "I call seven."

"You'll never reach it. The angles are off. Four is a solid sinker."

I glare at Smith, aware he is right but also hating he can't just let this go.

He doesn't reply to my glower with words, but his stare is very telling. If I want to win, I need to move out of my comfort zone to do so.

While reluctantly sauntering to Rocco's half of the billiard table, I breathe out my nerves. Most players give me a clear path to make my shot, but Rocco doesn't budge an inch. His whiskey-scented breath fans my neck, and his bloodshot gaze scorches my body when I line up my shot.

His watch has me so worked up, my stick wobbles as much as my knees when he steps close enough to me, the polyester material of his shirt causes static with my dress. "What are you waiting for, Mama?" he whispers in my ear. "Take your shot."

It dawns on me that he's trying to distract me when the gentlest creep of his fingertips on my inner thigh has me missing my mark entirely. I don't hit a single ball, meaning I award Rocco two turns.

"He's got you played," Smith mutters in my ear when Rocco uses his first turn to block the pocket I was aiming for with one of his balls.

"We'll see," I murmur before I sashay to Rocco's side of the room. I'm not going to touch him as he did me. I'm merely making sure he hears how many flirty comments I can achieve in less than thirty seconds. If he's too busy glaring over his shoulder, he'll have a hard time hitting any ball, much less the white one.

"Have I told you yet how much I love you?" Smith whispers when my ruse goes off without a hitch.

The tip of Rocco's cue stick gouges the felt on the table when the man I propositioned asked me if my pussy is on the menu tonight as he'd like to order a double helping. He's drunk and way below my league, but his comment pisses Rocco off enough it takes me snatching his cue stick out of his hand and thanking him for the two shots for the stranger to realize how close to death he came.

While Smith sets to work on evening the score, Double-Dipping Dallas blubbers out an apology before he scurries out of the room like his pants are on fire.

Mercifully, my next two turns occur without me needing to encroach on Rocco's half of the room.

With Rocco's partner clearly a pool shark, it's been a ruthless game. It comes down to the wire. There's only one ball left on the table, and it's my turn.

"You've got this, Claudia. Double-check your angles, then take your shot." Smith's next set of words are solely for my ears. "If you want to bow out now, I'm down with your decision. Only you can decide how much shit you're willing to take."

His words affect me more than they should. Taking shit is a given in my life. I never had the choice to say I've had enough. I either grin and bear it or die. There is no middle ground.

Rocco's actions tonight hurt me, but it will take more than a bruised ego to override the many ways he's helped me. My actions have been mine the past three weeks. I'm free from the unfair incarceration that saw my son stripped away from me, and I am only days away from possibly holding him in my arms for the very first time.

I can hate Rocco's actions, but I will *never* hate him. He's given me way too much for that ever to be a possibility.

So, with that in mind, I place my cue stick on the table before shifting on my feet to face Smith. "I've had enough."

When Smith dips his chin in understanding, I dash out of the game room. Rocco's hand twitches like it's dying to shoot out and seize my wrist, but he holds back the desire. I want to say that's because he wants to respect my decision, but it's a little hard to do when he tells Smith giving up is the equivalent of losing.

"Only cowards forfeit because they know they're going to lose."

I could bite at the bait he's dangling in front of me, but what's the point? I've known from the start whatever I was hoping to get off the ground with him will only last a week, so why waste my breath on something that is inevitably going to fail no matter how much I wish it were different?

**21**

---

## ROCCO

*Farrkkk.* What the hell did I drink last night? My throat is on fire, my eyes are dryer than a desert, and my skin is both clammy to touch and scaly as fuck. It's obvious I'm dehydrated, which is shocking considering how much liquid I consumed last night. I didn't just deafen the nightmares of my past with numerous lines of cocaine, I drowned them with gallons of whiskey as well.

The deadly combination means I didn't have another nightmare, but I'm reasonably sure I made a dick of myself. Not only am I waking up with a spew bucket at my side, I'm on the couch in Dimitri's office, being glared at by him like I made a move on his girl last night.

*Fuck, I didn't do that, did I?*

I was off my face, and I am known for pushing boundaries when I'm shit-faced.

"Thirsty?" Dimitri asks from his babysitting station behind his desk. He's dressed like his day started hours ago, and the concerned crinkle his brows lost when Fien was returned to him is back with a vengeance.

I think I nod. I can't be sure. My brain rattles in my skull, but since it's doing that with every thump of my head, I can't be sure. "I'd kiss your feet for some *water.*" My last word is a gargled compliment to

Dimitri tossing a bucket of freezing water over me. It drenches me from head to toe and sees me leaping off his couch like I'm not hungover. "What the fuck, Dimi? I haven't seen you this pissed since..." I stop in just enough time. The last time he confronted me with this much aggression was when he handed me Roxanne's panties. I made it out of that exchange by the skin of my teeth, so I'd rather skip another shitfest. "What did I do?"

"Where would you like me to start?" He pushes off his feet and stalks across the room. "The number of drugs you distributed to narcs at your 'party for Fien.'" He air quotes his last three words, exposing he's as pissed as fuck I used his daughter to cover my tracks. "The fact you sideswiped three cars in the fucking driveway of my home. Or how about climbing into my bed to tell my woman how much you love her."

Confident his last point is the cause of his red-hot anger, I mumble, "It's not as deviant as you're making it out to be, D. I love Roxie..." when he growls, I talk faster, "... but not how you're thinking. She's my friend."

"After last night's fucking effort, your *only* friend."

I swipe my hand through the air, brushing off his claim without words before muttering, "Don't be like that, Dimi. You fucking love me. And so does Smith."

My brows furrow when he *pffts* at my statement. "I spent the morning cleaning up your messes *without* Smith's help because he was too busy talking your girl off the ledge."

Dimi doesn't talk smack when it comes to suicide attempts. He rode my ass the handful of times in my teen years when the ghosts of my past became too haunting to ignore, but I'm confident his reference this time around has nothing to do with Claudia attempting to end her life. She's too confident for that, too strong-willed. Just the way she hit back last night is a sure-fire sign. I was so fucking turned on by her snappy attitude, it took everything I had not to beg at her feet for a second chance. The only reason I held back is because the words she said to me wouldn't stop ringing in my ears.

*It's okay. I'm not him.*

They still frustrate me even now, and that annoyance is heard in my tone when I ask, "Did his chat work?"

"No," Smith answers on Dimitri's behalf. He's in the doorway of Dimitri's office, wearing the same getup he had on last night. The dark rims under his eyes expose he hasn't had an ounce of sleep. "I told her you're not usually the prick you portrayed last night, but nothing I said made any difference."

"I got a little cozy with some women before teasing her during a game of pool. It isn't the fucking end of the world, Smith. I didn't even touch the whores I invited." If I were honest, I'd admit the idea of touching anyone not named Claudia made me feel ill, but since honesty seems to be amiss for me of late, I keep my mouth shut.

"Not a big deal?" Smith asks, his voice a roar. "I guess dragging her out of bed at three in the morning to cash in your raincheck isn't that big of a deal."

*Shit.*

I'm certain things can't get worse until he adds, "But demanding her to do it in front of your guests who couldn't take the hint it was time to leave was. You told her to do as asked, or you were through helping her. That proving you're not fucked in the head was more important than helping her get her son back. It took Clover intervening to get you to stop, Rocco. Fucking Clover! He doesn't know the meaning of the word no, but even he knew the stunt you were pulling was wrong."

I want to defend myself. I want to tell Smith my actions aren't my fault, but I can't. My father fucked with my head, he made me hate myself in a way I never thought possible, but those demons should have been put to rest when I killed him. I can't continuously use them to excuse my fuck-ups, even with it being an easy out, and especially not to someone who has been hurt as badly as Claudia.

"Where is she?" When Smith folds his arms in front of his chest, replicating Dimitri's aggressive stance, I ask, "Come on, Smitty, how can I fix my mistakes if I'm not given a chance? I fucked up, so it's only fair I am given the chance to fix things." When my question is answered with silence, I get desperate. "You forgave Ellie for far worse."

"I haven't forgiven her."

He's a woeful liar. Even Dimitri hears the deceit in his tone.

"She's on a bus heading north." Smith looks pissed when Dimitri jots down details of Claudia's transport onto a slip of paper, but he keeps his mouth shut. He knows who runs the show around here. It isn't Smith. "When faced with either dropping her off at the bus station or driving her back to Wallens Ridge to finalize her sentence, Roxanne took her to the bus station." I sprint for the door when he discloses, "Her bus left an hour ago."

The closest bus station to Hopeton is in Ravenshoe. That means there's already an hour and forty-five minutes between us. That's far more than I'm comfortable with.

My race out of Dimitri's mansion comes to a dead stop when a Porsche Cayman skids to a stop at the bottom of the stairs.

"Get in," says Clover, the command in his voice leaving no room for argument. "I hacked into the LoJack system on her bus. They've planned a fuel stop a couple of clicks out of Merrickvale. If I drive like the race-car driver I was born to be, we'll reach the gas station a couple of seconds before them."

He flattens his foot onto the gas pedal a mere second after I slot my ass into the passenger seat of his car, and even quicker than that, I latch my seat belt into place. Clover has impressive driving skills, but I heard about the accident that almost claimed his life, so I'm not taking any chances.

We make it forty miles out of Hopeton before the question gnawing my insides blurts out of my mouth. "How bad was I last night?"

"Did you see your Buick after Maddox borrowed it?" When I notch up my chin, Clover mutters, "Worse than that."

Usually, I love his straightforwardness. Today, I fucking hate It. My Buick was totaled. It was a complete write-off. I can only pray I didn't fuck things up as badly with Claudia.

"You said some pretty dark shit last night, man." He wrings the steering wheel while muttering, "I was beginning to wonder if you were one of my many siblings."

Since the panic he knows my secret doesn't override my wish to reach Claudia, I don't respond how I usually do when ghosts of my past resurrect. "At least we got out. Other fuckers aren't so lucky."

Clover hums out an agreeing murmur before he devotes his focus back to the road. I don't mind. It gives me plenty of time to work out a plan of attack, and only a smidge of it focuses on how I can weasel my way back into Claudia's good books.

Three hours and fifteen minutes later, when Clover pulls into the dusty lot of a gas station, I thank Smith for coming to the plate for me even while pissed before disconnecting our call. My plan is messy, but aren't all the best ones? Only once you embrace the chaos do you appreciate its beauty.

"Are you not coming?" I say to Clover when he peels out of his ride and tosses his keys into my chest.

He shakes his head. "You're aiming for no bloodshed. I don't do that. It's not in my DNA."

He dips his chin in farewell before he heads toward the counter to purchase a ticket back to Hopeton. I watch the direction he walks for a couple of seconds before the quickest reflection in the tinted windows of the Porsche steals my attention. Claudia has just exited a block of outside washrooms. She's wearing baggy jeans and a shirt three sizes too big for her tiny frame, but she is still as sexy as hell.

The tingling sensation I experienced the first time I laid my eyes on her returns stronger than ever when she pauses partway back to the bus. Except this time, it's nowhere near my balls. It's in my chest, right in the spot I'm sure she felt my jabs when I bartered her son's well-being for my own selfish gain.

"Claudia!" I shout when the sweep of her surroundings has her spotting me.

As fear fills her face, she sprints for the bus, her fast pace only slowing when I band my arm around her waist and swing her in the opposite direction.

"Let me go," she screams before she diverts her pleas to the bus driver. "Help me. Please."

When his chivalry jumps to the absolute despair in her voice, I remove my gun from the back of my pants and aim it at his head. "Step the fuck back. This has nothing to do with you, *James*," I warn after taking in his name tag. "I don't want to hurt anyone. I just want to talk to her."

"Nothing anyone says will be honest when you're holding a gun to their head, son." James steps closer to me and a now-frozen Claudia. "Do you want her responses to be honest or drowning in lies?"

"I want the chance to explain," the drugs still filtering through my veins speak on my behalf. "But I can't do that with a shadow." When he takes another step closer to me, I flick off the safety of my gun and inch back the trigger. "I'll only warn you once, and you should know, I don't aim to maim."

"Don't," Claudia begs when James ignores my honest statement by taking another step closer. "He doesn't care about anyone but himself, so you need to trust what he says. He won't mourn your loss, but your wife will, James. She needs you, and so do your children."

Her words cut through me like a knife, but since they have James backing away from us, I act as if they don't.

When he reaches the steps of the bus, I commence walking backward. Since my arm is banded around Claudia's waist, she comes along with me. I don't have to worry about any overzealous Texan motorists intervening in my kidnapping. Clover has my back, and he won't issue a warning like I did. He shoots to kill, then asks questions.

I don't give Claudia the chance to outthink me like she did her husband. I place her into the passenger seat via the driver's side door before activating the remote-controlled child lock. She's trapped with me, but unfortunately, it will only be for another twenty-four hours.

**22**

———

# CLAUDIA

When the tires of Rocco's sports car kick up gravel on the edge of the freeway, memories of the accident that claimed Juan's life filter into my head. Rocco isn't shouting words at me like Juan did that day. He isn't throwing his fist into my stomach and face, but his silence is just as maiming.

He hurt me worse than Juan ever did when he used Dillon to rip my heart out of my chest. The guards at Wallens Ridge made me suck them off to eat. Rocco wanted me to do it to degrade me. That's why he carried out his atrocious act of self-righteousness in his living room. He wanted to bang his chest and act superior, and he did precisely that when he threw my nine-month-old son under the bus with me.

"I hate you."

My whispered confession sees Rocco's foot slipping off the gas pedal, but it doesn't award me the devotion of his eyes. "No, you don't. You hate that you can't hate me, but you don't hate me." My chin quivers when he mutters, "It's the same for your son. You hate that he ties you to the Sánchezes for life, but you will never hate him. That's why despite loathing everything about being pregnant, when push came to shove, you did *everything* you could to save him." A solemn tear rolls down my cheek when he confesses, "Juan's hand was on the steering wheel when you crashed because yours weren't. You removed them *after* directing his sports car toward the cliff face."

My hand shoots up to caress my head when a memory oddly familiar to Rocco's claim seeps into my mind. I recall feeling helpless and being mindful that no matter what I did, Juan was going to kill me. His mother just wanted me to rebirth her deceased son first.

"That's how I broke my arms," I murmur when the fog finally clears from the horrifying day.

Rocco nods before he drifts his eyes from the road to me. "When you hit the rock face, your head propelled forward so fast, you were knocked out on impact, but Dillon wasn't injured because your arms absorbed all the impact." He pulls over on the freeway like we won't get honked at before he folds my arms, so they replicate the way I placed them over my stomach on the night in question. "You broke your arms in multiple places because despite the pain you knew you'd experience, you weren't going to let anything or anyone hurt Dillon. You saved your son, so when I felt like I was drowning, I used him with the hope you'd save me the same way."

I choke back a sob when he confesses something I never thought he would. "My father molested me the week before my eighth birthday. I killed him when I found out on my sister's eighth birthday that he had done the same to her. Everyone thinks I killed him because he hurt my mother. The truth is, I did it because I didn't want anyone to know what had happened to me. If they know of my shame, they'll be worried I'll turn out like him."

My voice cracks when I deny the last part of his comment, "No, Rocco. The people who truly know you would *never* respond that way. And it isn't your shame. It is your father's. You did nothing wrong."

He wants to believe me. He just can't. "So you trust me with your son? Knowing what you know, you'd still let me be around Dillon?"

"Yes," I reply without hesitation. "Because I know you'd ensure nothing like that would ever happen to him." When he brushes off my claim with a shake of his head, I grab his hand in mine. "You would because you understand the pain associated with it. That's why you pushed me so hard last night. You wanted to make sure I remember what we were working toward was a gift, not a given. You embarrassed me to keep me humble."

"I embarrassed you because I didn't want you to look at me like you did when you thought I was imagining him touching me instead of you. I'd rather you hate me than ever have you look at me like that again."

"I wasn't thinking about him touching you…" I can't finish my lie. At the time, I didn't know exactly who his pain centered around, so I wasn't picturing anyone, but I did respond inappropriately considering I didn't know the full extent of his torment. "I'm sorry. I shouldn't have said what I did."

My eyes lift to Rocco's face when he murmurs, "And neither should have I. I fucked up, Claudia. Using Dillon to get back at you was wrong. I'm not expecting you to forgive me, but I do hope you believe me when I tell you how truly sorry I am."

Call me a fool, but I do believe him. Excluding him and Dillon, I don't have anything to lose, so when removing himself from the equation didn't have me fighting for him, he took it one step too far. It doesn't excuse what he did, and deep down, I'm still hurt, but if he truly weren't sorry about what he had done, he wouldn't have traveled hours to track me down. He would have just let me leave.

That should mean something, shouldn't it?

Since I believe it does, I say, "I accept your apology, but it will take more than words for me to forget why it was needed to begin with."

He nods, accepting my terms before he wets his lips. "I'd give anything to have the time needed to make it up to you, but unfortunately, time isn't in our favor. It's time for this Mama to go back to her son."

I bounce my eyes between his, utterly and wholly confused.

I have no clue as to what he's talking about.

I'm torn between smacking him out and kissing him when he mutters, "Juana is a textbook mafia boss. We could have gotten Dillon out straight away if I hadn't been so selfish." He wets his lips again, a sign he's badly dehydrated before he murmurs, "When it was determined you couldn't have both your son and me, I was so desperate to test the spark, I asked for a week. Juana's incompetence gave me an easy in. I got you for a week, and Smith got to tighten our plan to ensure there weren't any holes." His smile is both beautiful and tormented. "It took me losing you to realize you were never mine to begin with. I call you Mama because not only are you a sexy mama, you were born to be a mother. I shouldn't have kept you away from that for even a minute. It was selfish of me to do, and I plan to fix my mistake starting now."

Before I can demand further explanation, we're interrupted by flashing lights.

"Fuck," Rocco mutters in frustration when he realizes it's a State Trooper. After scraping his hand across his beard, he locks his eyes with mine. "I need you to mop up those gaga eyes, Mama. If he doesn't believe you hate my fucking guts, I'll have to kill him. If he's on the Sánchez payroll, that will make events tomorrow morning real fucking awkward."

"W-what's happening tomorrow?" I'm usually more clued on than I sound, but my stutter can't be helped. I'm equally lost and excited. It shouldn't be possible to have such contrasting emotions hit you at the same time, but there's no denying them.

"You're getting Dillon back tomorrow, but I need you to hate me to achieve that." Just before the State Trooper reaches his window, Rocco mutters, "We activated our ruse early. It's time to bring your son home."

Although my heart rate skyrockets, mercifully the tears that dropped down my face during Rocco's confession make my cheeks appear more an angry red than a pleased bloom.

"Can I help you, officer?" Rocco asks after sliding down his window at the Trooper's request. "Surely I wasn't speeding. I wasn't even moving."

"We had a call from concerned motorists about a disturbance at a gas station not too far from here. Your plates were forwarded to my office." He's lying. I know it, and so does Rocco. This Porsche doesn't have tags. "License and registration, please."

Rocco twists his lips before barking out a stern, "No. For one, I don't work for you, and two, I don't want to."

"Listen here, bud, just because you pay taxes does not make you my boss," the Trooper fires back, clearly on the ball with motorists using any excuse to get out of a citation.

It dawns on me that Rocco is following the script Smith is uploading to the dashboard in the Porsche when he follows it with the precision of a veteran actor. "I mentioned nothing about you working for me. You work for Juana Sánchez, who is a distributor of mine." He angles his head so the Trooper can see his face. "How do you think she'll respond when she discovers you pulled over her most notorious ally for a crock of shit claim that I caused a disturbance?"

When the law enforcement officer bobs down to issue Rocco a stumbling apology, it feels like my lungs can't get enough air. Rocco only knows half of his injustices. He doesn't just fatten up his monthly checks by accepting bribes from underworld associates. He also stands by and watches pregnant women be tackled to the ground by madmen before beating the puppies endeavoring to protect them.

He hit Max so badly, he fractured multiple bones in his back. He bragged about his accomplishment when he arrived at the hospital to take my statement before he told me the vet had put Max down. That's why I was so surprised when I spotted him outside of Wallens Ridge weeks ago. It could have been his doppelgänger, but just like my immediate connection with Rocco, Max was the best friend I never had growing up. I'll never forget him.

My thoughts stray from the past to the present when Rocco says, "That's what I thought you'd say." He dismisses the Trooper with a two-finger brush off before gliding his window back into place. The Trooper's eagerness to leave sees me wheezing down the tiniest breath, but the relief it gives my lungs is short-lived when Rocco asks, "What's going on, Mama?" I'm convinced he can read minds when he darts his eyes to the rearview mirror that shows the State Trooper is only feet away from his patrol car before he returns them to me. "You're safe. Juana won't touch you. She isn't allowed."

"It's not Juana," I force out through the panic clutching my throat. "It's…"

Smith overtakes my confession when words elude me. "That highway patrolman was the State Trooper who pulled Claudia over the night she was arrested."

I realize Rocco has read the non-doctored reports of my arrest when his head cranks back so fast, his neck muscles squeal in protest. When he spots the Trooper climbing into the driver's seat of his patrol car, he throws open his car door so fast, I'm certain its hinges are now warped.

I grab his hand before he gets partway out. Although he reads the pleading in my eyes in the correct manner, he's on a mission to fix *all* my injustices not just the ones he made. "I don't just want you not scared of me, Mama, I don't want you scared of *anyone*. He scares you." Since I can't deny his claims, I don't. "So I'm going to make sure he can't anymore."

I realize just how crazy my life is when I lift my chin with only the slightest bit of hesitation. After hitting me with a frisky wink to show his thanks I still want him to go to bat for me, Rocco signals for the Trooper to wait before he makes his way to him like they're about to have a casual conversation.

You can't screw a silencer onto Rocco's classic gun, so I know the exact moment he ends the Trooper's life for hurting me. The pop of his gun breaking through the silence teeming around me is quickly followed by Smith requesting me to slide into the driver's seat so I can guide Rocco, who is now seated in the driver's seat of the patrol car, to a woodland a couple of miles away from the freeway.

There's no doubt I've lost my marbles when I slip into the driver's seat without freaking out. The man I'm falling in love with killed for me—*again*—but once again, I'm turned on instead of panicked.

I signal right as Smith is requesting before calling his name. When he answers me with a murmur, I ask, "How long have you been listening?"

His silence is very telling.

It breaks my heart as much as Rocco's confession.

The shards the break nicked my throat with is heard in my reply, "He doesn't want anyone to know."

"I know," Smith eventually replies, his voice as pained as mine. "That's why I won't mention it until he tells me himself."

"You need to know, that may never happen. Until he learns that his father's shame isn't his, he won't stop accepting accountability for it."

Air whizzes from his nose as the whoosh of his head bob sounds out of the speakers in the Porsche's dashboard. "I know, and I'm prepared for that."

"So you won't tell anyone or use it against him?"

His huff this time around is more in annoyance than agreement. "It isn't my job to share his secrets, Claudia. He's kept mine, so it's only right I keep his."

Some could say I'm foolish for believing him, but I'd rather trust upfront than be a cynic. "Thank you." As fast as Smith's annoyance brewed, it disappears. He accepts my thanks with an appreciative hum before instructing me to turn down a dusty road. His laid-back response makes me smile, but it won't stop me from asking, "While I have you, can I ask another favor?" It takes him a little longer to grant my request this time around, but he gets there—eventually. "Can you leave us off the grid tonight? I don't want spectators for what could be our last night together."

I know what you're thinking. You are shocked I'm giving in so easily, but I did say only minutes ago that I need more than words to understand why Rocco hurt me the way he did. If our plan to get Dillon back has been solely pushed forward, tonight could be the last opportunity for that to occur, so I'm not willing to give it up for anything.

I just need to get Smith on board with my plans. "Please, Smith. If Rocco disagrees with me, I'll backflip on my request immediately."

He contemplates for barely a second before he replies, "I can unplug you... on one condition."

"What's that?" I ask, equally annoyed and curious.

*Who thought it would be so hard for him not to be a snoop?*

I realize I'm a little off the mark when he says, "I need you to convince Ellie that you didn't forfeit the game last night because you were interested in me. You did it purely for you."

My mouth falls open when the truth smacks into me. "Ellie was Rocco's partner during our match?"

"She was," he replies with a laugh. "And she's a little bit pissed about the proceedings."

"It was all innocent."

He makes an '*eh*' noise like he isn't convinced before saying, "I'd still appreciate it if you could have a word with her for me."

I begin to wonder if he can see me when my head bob has him sighing in relief. Rocco said he has eyes everywhere. I didn't believe him until now.

Before I can unearth which device he's using to watch me, Rocco scares the living daylights out of me for the second time today by pulling open the driver's side door of the Porsche. Once I've returned my heart to its rightful spot, I climb into the passenger seat before straying my eyes to the patrol car he parked a couple of spots back. "Shouldn't you bury him?"

Rocco screws up his nose before shaking his head. "The soil out this way is as hard as fuck. Besides, his murder has the Sánchez signature *all* over it. No one is going to look at me for this."

I shouldn't smile at his cheeky wink, but I do.

He floats his eyes over my face for a couple of seconds before nudging his head to my seat belt. "Put on your belt. I don't want you getting hurt."

I gleam about his protectiveness while securing my belt in my hand. Once I'm buckled in, he commences maneuvering us out of the narrow, winding road. We travel down the freeway for a good twenty or so miles before he calls Smith's name.

He calls and calls and calls his name until the anger on his face leaves me no choice but to intervene. "I asked him to unplug us from festivities tonight."

Rocco looks torn between fist-bumping the air and cursing me out. I learn why when he says, "I appreciate that you're giving me a chance to explain, but I don't think you should have done that. I don't have anything with me. If I'm not..."

"High?" I fill in when words elude him.

He nods. "I can't guarantee I won't have another nightmare. I don't trust myself when I have them, and you shouldn't either."

"I trust you, Rocco." I slip my hand into his before murmuring, "And why are you acting like all we're going to do is sleep? That's the last thing on my mind."

My tease has the effect I was aiming for. Any tension left lingering in the air evaporates when Rocco throws his head back and laughs.

I can only hope it stays away when I bare myself to him as openly as he did me.

I breathe out the nerves jittering in my stomach before taking in my reflection in the cracked vanity mirror of a one-star motel. With Juana aware of my imminent return, Rocco and I are spending our last night together at a motel on the outskirts of a town that borders Wallens Ridge. We dumped his Porsche two miles out, then walked to our accommodation to ensure our final hours won't be interrupted. Dimitri knows where we are, and Smith is monitoring every radio tower in the county. We have all our bases covered. We're just waiting for the clock to strike ten tomorrow morning.

After a final big breath, I step into the main area of our room. The tube lighting above my head is both unflattering and bright, meaning not only do my knees shake when I stop at the end of the bed as naked as the day I was born, so does my voice when I squeak out, "Surprise!"

I curse my ill-timing when Rocco slings his eyes my way. He's on the phone, ordering us dinner. "No, that's all. I'll pay cash when it's delivered." He doesn't give his caller the chance to reply. He places down the phone receiver, cursing when it takes him three goes to find the base since he can't take his eyes off me. "You should really warn a man before doing that. I need time to prepare my memory bank for the overload you're about to award it." His comment breaks my heart before it mends it. I love that he appreciates what he sees, but I hate that the only time he'll ever see it again will be in a memory. "You're stunning, Mama. So fucking... ugh! I can't find the right words."

I impede the bangs of his palm on his forehead by pulling his hand away from his head and straddling his lap. "Stunning works. I'm *totally* fine with stunning."

When he rolls me over without warning, the breaths of his husky laugh in response to my squeak fan my breasts before the prickles of his beard peak my nipples. He drags his face across the meaty globes on my chest, then down my stomach until he stops at the small section of flabby skin I'm paranoid about.

"You did so good, Mama," he murmurs against my goosebump-riddled skin. "You protected your son so well." When he raises my eyes, I'm shocked by the amount of lust in them. Shouldn't he be turned off by the stretch marks on my stomach instead of horny? "Both now and then."

My smile only reaches half its potential when a tap on our motel room door steals my focus. "Wow, that was quick."

After tossing Rocco off me like I'm a WWF wrestler, I snatch up the undershirt he dumped onto the bed before showering, slip it over my head, then mosey toward the door. Rocco's constant assurance that he'll get it comes too late. I pull open the door, frowning when I spot what is obviously a low-bottom gangbanger standing on the other side.

I thought he was the pizza delivery man.

"Two fifty," he grunts at me, unaware the white powder product he's selling isn't for me.

I sink to the other side of the room when Rocco digs a bundle of bills out of the wallet he fetched from the bathroom before he shoves it into the teen's chest. He hits him with a stern finger point before he snatches the baggy out of his hand, then slams the door in his face.

"The punk-ass fucker wasn't supposed to rock up until I texted him." He spins to face me. Nothing but shame is lining his face. "I ordered it before you…" He stops, swallows, then starts once more, "I am scared I'm gonna hurt you again."

His confession instantly lowers my annoyance. "Please correct me if I am wrong, but I'm reasonably sure the only time you've hurt me was *after* taking that." I nudge my head to the cocaine he just purchased during the 'that' part of my statement. "Were you high during our date at Wallens Ridge?" When he shakes his head, I ask, "What about when we… you know?"

Sparks of the Rocco I'm obsessed with shine brightly in his eyes when he shuffles side to side before he shakes his head for the second time. "That was the first time I had—"

"You're not seriously trying to say last night was the first time you've taken drugs."

"No," he instantly fires back, amused by the fury radiating out of me. "I've never had sex, fucked, made love, or whatever else you want to call it without being shit-faced. You were the first."

I'm too shocked to speak. It isn't exactly a virginal confession, but it's pretty close considering what he's admitting.

After taking a moment to settle the excited jitters in my voice, I ask, "Did you enjoy it enough to want to do it again?"

My ego skyrockets when he replies with a very convincing, "Fuck yes! As long as it's with you."

"Okay." I fold my arms in front of my chest to hide the shake of my hands before saying, "Then dump the coke into the toilet, and let's get down to business."

Juan would have beaten me until I was black and blue if I even insinuated that he had a drug problem. Thankfully, he and Rocco couldn't be more opposite if they tried. "All right. On one condition." When I raise a brow, wordlessly inviting him to state his term, he adds, "Your shirt goes down the S-bend with the coke."

"You'll clog the toilet if you stuff a shirt down there. It could cause it to back up."

"The smell will be *totally* worth you getting around in the buff all night."

His reply makes me smile, but it doesn't have me budging on my hell-to-the-no stance. I'm fine with getting naked—just! His numerous compliments every time he's seen me in the buff has boosted my confidence, but I've let him off reasonably easy for his stuff-up, so it's time for him to work for what he wants.

"Fine!" he gives in a couple of seconds later. "I'll flush the drugs, but your shirt *and* the bedding spend the night in the bathroom. For no reason whatsoever can you get dressed until the sun comes up."

His demand would have me sweating if there weren't so much eagerness in his voice. He wants this even more than I hope to one day see him clean.

After removing my shirt like I have the confidence of a catwalk model, I hold my hand out for Rocco to shake on our agreement. "Deal."

He swats away my hand, crowds me with his sometimes-overbearing frame, then tilts my head back. "Deal," he murmurs before he binds our agreement with a searing kiss.

Only once he has my mind hazed with lust does he disclose, "I don't have time to adhere to the terms of our agreement right now, though. The pizza place has a thirty-minutes-or-it's-free promotion, so I only have twenty-six minutes before I have to hide your fine ass with the bedding I want you to part with. I don't have time to mess around." I giggle like a schoolgirl when he tosses me onto the mattress before he kneels at the end. "As you know, I've *always* wanted dessert before dinner. Ma would never allow it. She said it would ruin me." He stares at my naked pussy before licking his lips. "I think she was right."

He crushes his lips with my aching clit then sucks down. The inviting warmth of his mouth combined with the roughness of his unkempt beard sends me crazy. When he pokes his tongue through the folds of my pussy, I call out, confident he could get me off by grinding his nose against my clit.

As my orgasm begins to build, I weave my fingers through his silky hair. I tug at it when he growls about how good I taste, then massage his scalp with my nails when he laps up my wetness like he can't get enough.

"You're so wet…"

He slips two fingers inside of me, hovers his thumb over my clit, then teasingly rubs my back entrance with his two leftover digits.

"So tight…"

I grind down on him, moaning when my unexpected movement causes the tip of his ring finger to dip into my ass.

"And so fucking dying for me to claim your ass, you're not ashamed to admit it."

His dirty words and magic fingers and tongue soon send me into a tailspin. With a moan, I arch my back and close my eyes. I'm so turned on about the thought of being claimed by him as no man ever has, I chant his brilliance into the crisp night air like there are no occupants in the rooms next to ours before succumbing to the tension coiling me tight.

My pussy clenches around Rocco's fingers as my body pulses with desire, and he watches every explosive jolt. "So fucking beautiful, Mama. So fucking perfect."

He continues eating me until I'm convinced I am about to die. The scent of sex infuses the air, and Rocco is only just getting started.

"Rocco…" I pant through the crazy, twisted feeling in my stomach, certain it couldn't be another orgasm forming so quickly.

Never once breaking our gaze, Rocco watches me over the fleshy globes on my chest while sliding his fingers in and out of me. Once he's certain he has me right where he wants me, he strums my clit with his thumb, sending me freefalling.

"Fuuuck," I scream, horrified by my potty-mouth but incapable of finding a better word to announce the sheer brilliance of our exchange.

While rocking against his mouth, grunting and moaning, I ride the long, blissful wave. It's a beautifully brilliant minute only dampened by the briefest knock on our hotel room door.

## 23

# ROCCO

*I* play the tough act well.

If you piss me off, I'll kill you.

If you mess with me, I'll kill you.

And if you hurt those I care about, I'll kill you.

But when a familiar creak sounds through my ears, I freeze like a fucking statue.

I didn't learn to run until it was too late. *He* had already hurt me. Just like I didn't realize what he was doing was wrong until he spoke those four little words no child should ever hear from their father, "Don't tell your mother."

What is it about those four words being spoken by a family member that paralyze us so much? Dimitri begged me not to tell my mom what happened when our stupid antics in the bathtub one day when we were six saw more of my blood spilled on the bathroom floor than water, and I didn't think twice about it. When Ms. Harcher made me pinkie promise to keep news of my solo at the Mother's Day fair in kindergarten from my mother, I thought I was the bee's knees.

I can't say the same when my father made me pledge similarly. I felt instantly dirty, and when no number of scrubs rid me of his scent, I acted out. My grades dropped off the chart, the scarce number of friends I had narrowed down to one, and I took the anger I should have directed at my father out on my mother instead.

To begin with, she thought I was rebelling because I was no longer an only child. I wish I had the courage to tell her that wasn't the case by doing the exact opposite of my father's command. It wouldn't have taken back what had happened to me, but it would have stopped him from hurting Finlay.

Alas, I have hundreds of mistakes to correct and not enough time to fix them all.

I wipe the riled expression from my face when I realize that the creak that froze me was the warped bathroom door of my motel room jutting open. Claudia breaks over the threshold, looking ravishing in nothing but her silky-smooth skin.

"Are you okay?" she asks while crawling into bed with me.

I dip my chin, only just holding back my smile that she doesn't glower about my gawk when her crawl up the mattress emphasizes the smallest curve in the lower half of her stomach. I love the imperfections of her body as much as her rocking tits. And don't get me started on the taste of her cunt, or we'll be here all day.

"Rocco..." Claudia half-moans, half-groans when I roll her over so I can spoon her from behind. I'm hard like we haven't spent the last several hours fooling around, and it's digging into her ass like I can take her ass without any prep work or lube.

Since I can't without hurting her as my father did me, I divert back to an old habit. "Can you blame me for a constant state of erection? Have you seen my girl? She's fucking gorgeous." I sense her smile more than I feel it, and if my intuition isn't leading me astray, she's grinning more about me referencing her as my girl than telling her she's beautiful. "Are you sure you want to go to sleep, Mama? The sun will be up in a couple of hours."

I regret my question in an instant when she replies through a yawn, "Today will be crazy. We'd be stupid to go into it like zombies."

Since I agree with her, I tug up the bedding I grabbed while she washed off the spunk coating almost every inch of her, then press my lips to her ear. "If I... *have a nightmare.*" I'm tempted to punch myself in the dick for the way I articulate the last half of my statement. "I want you to lock yourself in the bathroom."

Claudia shakes her head before she rolls over—which isn't easy considering how tight I'm holding her. She attempts to talk, but I push my finger to her lips before she can. "I ain't asking, Mama. I could hurt you."

I only discovered how violent my dreams were when I pinned Ophelia to my bed one night by her throat. I whispered in her ear that I was going to do to her what my father had done to me, and I almost got to the point of doing it. If she hadn't kneed me in the groin, I may not have stopped.

My nighttime ritual kicked in that very week. At first, it was just some Mary Jane, then I worked up to pills, alcohol, then subsequentially cocaine. I thought it was helping me handle the situation. In reality, it blanketed my issues.

The hole my father carved in my chest is still very much present, but it did fill in a little when I shared my confession with Claudia. It wasn't enough to extend the olive branch to those in my inner circle any time soon, but it has me considering looking at other crutches bar narcotics to get me past my issues.

My eyes float up from Claudia's fantastic tits to her face when she says, "I thought I would have exhausted you enough you'd be too comatose to move." She wets her lips before she glides her needy eyes down my body. "Clearly, that isn't the case."

After pushing on my shoulder so I roll onto my back, she shimmies down my body, then gets on her knees. Before I can consider how fucking stoked I am to have her pouty lips on my cock for the second time today, she has my dick in her mouth. When she swivels her tongue around the rim, I weave my fingers through her silky hair. She strokes me, licks me, and devours me like a hungry little nymph.

Within minutes, I use my grip on her hair to time the rhythm of her sucks. I feed my cock in and out of her mouth as if it is her cunt, occasionally causing her to gag.

"That's it, Mama. Gag on my schlong."

For the briefest second, she pulls back, raises her lips against the crest of my dick, then she gets back to sucking me off like she loves the idea of being asphyxiated by my cock. My skin heats at the thought, and my balls pull in close to my body as I rock my hips, giving her precisely want she wants—me.

The self-control I'm barely holding skids to oblivion when she commences massaging my balls. She grips them as well as her lips do my cock, and it is the sexiest thing I've ever fucking seen. There's no doubt in my mind her lips were designed for pleasure. They're so perfectly shaped that even while circling my shaft, she doesn't miss an inch of the skin stretched over my throbbing member.

My entire body twitches, and I feel moments from release, then one of Claudia's fingers slip toward an area even while off my head I ensure my bed companions steer clear of.

Even with it being an accidental slip that Claudia quickly corrects, I wait for the shame to come and the anger it usually instigates to develop.

It never arrives.

Claudia is peering up at me with too much awe for negativity to arise. She's taking me hard and deep while moaning the sexy little groans she did when I fucked her ass with my finger at the same time my cock claimed her cunt. I don't feel dirty or ashamed because she didn't touch me to hurt me. She's just so fucking horny, she can't control herself around me. She wants every inch of me as I do her.

"*Ohh...*" Her moans vibrate my dick when my desire to touch her becomes too much to ignore.

While fucking her mouth with precisely timed pumps, I angle her sexy ass closer to me before finding her clit. Her sucks turn frantic when I groan about how wet she is. She's drenched from front to back, meaning I face not an ounce of resistance when I slide my hand toward her back entrance.

As I place pressure on her puckered hole with two of my fingers, she grinds her aching clit against my wrist. I love her uninhibited response to my touch. She lets me touch her everywhere, and the free rein she gives me with her body sees me needing to issue my thanks.

I almost blow when my tug to have her pussy sitting on my face causes her lips to twist around my cock. I'll never imagine a ballerina twirl in the same manner ever again. My cock will forever harden while picturing the ballet-type movement her mouth did to my cock before she answered its flexes by taking him to the very back of her throat.

"Ah, Mama. My cum will slide down your throat in a nanosecond if you don't slow down."

I feel the smile she gave me earlier before her husky words harden my cock even more. "Isn't that the point?"

She doesn't give me the chance to answer. She licks me, sucks me, and drives me wild, and I return the favor. While she sucks me off like she's thirsty for my spunk, I eat her pussy like I haven't taken her bare three times in the past twenty-four hours. I push her over the edge, the movements of my mouth and grinds of my fingers merciless and without constraint.

Within seconds, Claudia is convulsing against my mouth. If the people in the rooms next to ours were asleep, they're not anymore. Claudia's scream would have woken them. She's hot all over, and the taste of her arousal on my tongue sets me off. Bursts of need rocket out of my cock. While grunting her name in a throaty moan, I coat her lips, tongue, and throat with my cum. The murky white streams only slow when my release stretches Claudia's climax from one to two. She murmurs my name while grinding her delicious cunt against my tongue.

We ride the sensation together for what feels like hours but is more minutes before we eventually fall into a sweaty, sticky heap.

Sleep soon follows, but regretfully, it isn't peaceful. I'm spent from a long night of fucking, and the erotic scent of Claudia's arousal is all over my face, but I feel *his* breaths on my ear and hear him lowering his zipper.

"Don't," I growl out, my voice closer to a child than a teen. "I told you not to fucking touch me!"

The frantic beat of my heart jumps between murderous and yearning when the voice that responds isn't close to the one I'm anticipating. "Rocco, baby, it's time to wake up."

It pulls me out of the dark long enough I'm no longer in the attic of my father's rental home. I am on the road that separated *his* house from Dimitri's, running with no shoes on my feet and soiled pajama bottoms.

This is usually when I suck in a relieved breath. I am not given the same reprieve today. I'm not only sprinting away from a madman who has fucked ideas on how to raise children, I am leading him straight to Claudia's son. He's sitting under a streetlight, babbling and cooing like he has no clue of the danger I'm directing his way.

I want to protect him, but I can't go near him. He could get hurt. But I can't leave him here either. He's just a baby. He can't defend himself.

I don't get the chance to comprehend how contradicting my responses are—I was a child when my father molested me, so I didn't have the means to protect myself either—my father has caught up to me. He's standing at my side, except his focus isn't on me. He has his sights set on Dillon.

"Go, Dillon! Run," I squeal, startling when I realize I'm no longer a grown man. It's the day of my eighth birthday party. I'm wearing the race-car-driver pajama pants my mom gifted me and clutching the top-loading Nintendo I begged out the ass for.

It's the day my father hurt me most of all.

My head cranks to the side when something cold touches my face. It isn't the tears I used to shed, nor shame draining the blood from my face. It's someone's chilled yet still soothing hands. They're cradling my face like nothing happening is my fault and that they'll love me no matter the outcome.

It reminds me so much of my ma's gentle touch. I recall how protectively she held Finlay in her chest the night she was born. Nothing but fear was seen in her eyes, but it wasn't strong enough for her to project that to her children. It was the proof I was seeking that I could have told her what was happening to me and that she would have protected me. That's what parents are meant to do. They're supposed to protect their children, not hurt them.

My father wasn't born a monster. He chose to become one.

I refuse to make the same mistakes as him.

Dillon is not my son, but at the moment, I am his only protector.

I won't let him down like my father did me.

"Stop!" I shout, my voice returning to what it once was. "If you fuckin' touch him…" When my error dawns on me, I pause. This isn't a negotiation. I'm straight-up telling him he will not hurt Dillon like he did me. "Get away from him!"

I shove my father so hard we stumble into my childhood bedroom. Fear engulfs me when I'm no longer towering over him. His large frame is squashing me into the mattress, and he's suffocating my teary sobs with a clamped hand over my mouth.

The thought of what he's doing to me races vomit up my esophagus, but I fight it back by replacing it with the tangy taste of my father's blood. I'm not the child he abused anymore. I can fight back.

I don't have a gun, nor do I have the strength to push him off me, but I do have one thing not even the shame he forced on me will ever take away from me.

I have the love and support of a good woman.

"Mama!" I scream at the top of my lungs a mere second before I'm yanked out of my nightmare by the softness of a pair of lips landing on mine.

With nothing but the sweet movements of her lips and the gentlest of nips, Claudia switches the sweat coating my skin from fear to lust. "I am right here, baby. I'm not going anywhere," she murmurs against my kiss-swollen mouth when my eyes slowly flutter open. "I promise you that."

After straddling my lap, she lines the head of my cock with her pussy, then slowly lowers herself onto me. We don't fuck like we have the past four or five times. We make love, slowly and rhythmically. We move together in sync, the harmony of our conjoined bodies once again convincing me she was made specifically for me.

I've never had an attraction so perverse I've wanted more than one taste, but I know without a doubt it would take more than a million exchanges with Claudia for me ever to grow bored.

Unfortunately, it wasn't meant to be. Dillon needs his mother more than I need peace, so once again, I'll sacrifice myself for the greater good. That is, after all, why I put up with my father's abuse for so long.

When his focus was on me, it wasn't on Ma or Finlay. I can't recall a single time he beat into my mother after my eighth birthday. It was a bruise he left on my cheek that pushed Ma over the edge, but it wasn't done in the manner she imagined. I tried to crawl away. He didn't appreciate my disobedience, so he slapped me with the very thing I was desperate to get away from.

"Stay with me, baby," Claudia breathes out groggily, stealing my devotion from my dark thoughts. "And let go of that shame holding you back because *none* of it belongs to you."

After raising my hand to her breast, encouraging further distraction from the nightmare still clinging to my skin, she tightens the walls of her cunt around my throbbing shaft. She massages my cock as she did my balls earlier, and she does it all while staring at me.

I thought I'd hate her watch so soon after a nightmare, that no amount of sexual attraction could detract from how dirty my father made me feel, but right here, right now, Claudia is making a liar out of me. I don't want to scrub my skin raw in the shower to remove my father's scent from my skin. I want Claudia's cum covering every inch of me like mine did hers before we went to bed.

"I need you to come for me, Mama. Coat my cock and body in your juices." I swallow harshly before speaking words I never thought I'd speak. "I need you to replace the rank smell of his cum with yours."

Claudia nods before she increases the speed of her thrusts. She suffocates my cock with her super tight cunt before she rolls her hips at the end of her falls. The grinding of our groins stimulates her clit, meaning it's hard and ready for me when I remove my hand from her hip to toy with it.

The vibrations zapping her nervy bud are heard in her voice when she murmurs, "I'm close... so fucking close."

I love her filthy mouth. It's only ever showcased during sex, and it exposes how wild I make her. "Then bring it to me, Mama. Take what you need from me while giving me *everything* I need."

Her nails stab into the headboard as she doubles her output for the second time. She rises and falls, rises and falls, rises and falls until the most beautiful fucking sight I've ever seen presents before me. My girl is coming undone, and I get to watch every fire-sparking moment.

As Claudia shudders through her umpteenth orgasm, I layer kisses on her chest, collarbone, and neck. Then, when she comes down from the high commanding all her attention, I switch my focus to her mouth.

Up until three days ago, I wasn't a fan of kissing. It was never something I sought during sex, nor did I crave it outside of the bedroom, but Claudia's mouth has me all types of conflicted. I'm forever torn on which part of my body I want them on the most.

More times than not, the end result is my mouth. She sucks dick like she was born to do it, and my cock throbs now just at the thought of my cum sliding down her throat, but my fucking god, can she kiss. She puts all her soul into her embraces, and they could pull the shortest man out of the longest trench.

Shockingly, I'll remember them more than the sugary goodness of her cunt every time I jerk off to her once she's gone.

## 24

# ROCCO

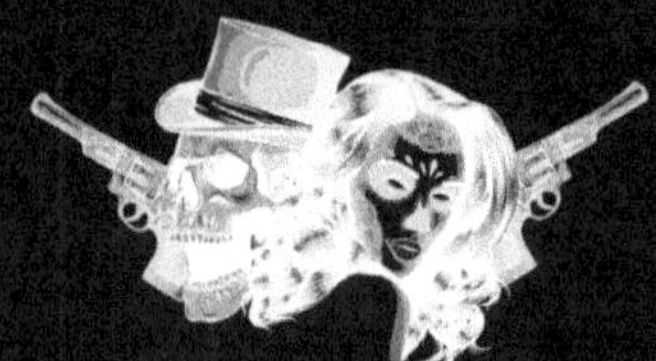

I've craved chaos as long as I have existed. I blame the desire for upheaval for the massive bullseye my eighth birthday party painted on my back. Ma didn't have the money for an extravagant party, so she did a villains and heroes party in the back-yard of our family home.

I was never going to be one of those kids that rocked up in a Superman or Joker costume. I went as Col Petretti, the man I hated but was stupidly hoping to piss off so much, he'd make my father face the punishment of my crime.

I don't know what it was about my fake Italian accent and the pillow I stuffed down the front of the black pants and buttoned-up shirt I had worn to Dimitri's mother's funeral that had my father looking at me differently. It could have been Col's laugh when he mistook my mocking rile as a compliment or the way the single mothers fussed over me when Col left to take care of some business.

Whatever it was, that party changed my life in an instant.

I was already fucked in the head from seeing my father beat my mother, but that night took me from a little unhinged to completely fucking psycho. I kill without remorse. I cut off men's tongues just for lying to me. Yet, here I am, standing with my arms folded in front of my chest to hide the rattle of my hands while struggling to find the words to explain that although our time together was brief, Claudia's influence in my life will shape my future from here on out.

I'm going to get clean, then I'll teach myself the shame that's kept me silent the past eighteen years isn't mine. It won't change anything from the past, and it won't fix me, but I'm hopeful if I ever come across someone as fascinating and beautiful as Claudia again, I won't assess her flaws before I assess her compatibility.

I've always joked that it would take a fucked-up woman to fix me. Only now do I realize it wasn't a joke. Claudia was dealt a shit hand. She's faced things no woman should ever face, yet she continues to defy the odds over and over again.

I thought her strength was because she was a mother.

I was wrong.

She's strong because she knows she deserves better, and I truly hope she finds what she's looking for when she lands in the country Dimitri has organized for Dillon and her to seek citizenship in. He's kept the details from me because he can't trust I won't jump on the plane with Claudia and Dillon and call it a day, even with him being my only true friend.

I have considered that multiple times the past couple of days, but the thought never lingers for long. For one, it isn't Claudia's job to fix my father's fuckups, and two, I much prefer believing she trusts me with her son than face the possibility she'll second-guess herself if my next meetup with Dillon was no longer a speculation.

"Don't," Claudia begs when I realize the best words I can give her are the exact words I've just given you. "I can't..."

A man who doesn't know her as well as I do would assume she means she can't give me up for her son. I know that isn't the case. One of the things that captivate me the most about her is that every laugh, smile, and tear she expresses belongs to Dillon. She doesn't do a single thing without him in her thoughts. She loves him with all of her heart, and that's the way it should be.

"Hey... none of that." I tug her close to me when I discover the reason for her request. Her eyes are filled with so much wetness, the slightest jarring movement could cause them to topple over. She hasn't cried since Dillon was ripped away from her. Not even when I used him against her did her eyes well with this much moisture. "You're about to see your baby boy, Mama. You are about to smell and hold him for the very first time, so how about you save those for him?" I bounce my eyes between hers when I say 'those.' "He's been waiting for this day as long as you."

Despite bringing it forward a couple of days, the premise of our ruse hasn't changed. Juana believes I knocked Claudia up with my kid. On the agreement she hands my child to me after his birth, I agree to have no association with Claudia whatsoever and no say in the punishment she will endure for her betrayal to her deceased husband.

What Juana doesn't know is that I turned Rhett. It wasn't hard when I showed him videos of his heterosexual brothers under Juana's watch. Even when victims don't have a voice, there are ways they can be represented. The representation this time around was Juana's inability to cut ties. She babies her children as if they're not grown adults, and the implementation of the devices she uses for that gave Smith an in.

The allegations alone could have removed Juana's title of a foster care mother, but since I placed a more lucrative offer on the table before Child Services could be informed of her sick misdemeanors, she voluntarily stepped down from the role.

She's well aware how lucrative the baby-making chain is. Many of its founders are. But Juana won't make as much as her acquaintances because she intends to keep all the male heirs her surrogates produce. Rebuilding the army of sergeants she lost after her husband died is taking too long. There's a five-year gap between Jeremiah and Dillon, so Juana has put steps into place to bridge the gap.

Once Claudia's womb is 'decommissioned' of my offspring, Juana will impregnate her with the sperm she extracted from her dead son after his death. If the children Claudia produces are girls, they'll be auctioned before birth. If they're boys, their births will be documented in Juana's name, and she will be their legal guardian.

I've seen some fucked-up shit during my time in the Italian Cartel, but not once have I stumbled upon someone as sick and demented as Juana. She's so desperate to relive her youth, she doesn't just steal her daughter-in-law's children, she also takes their placentas to authenticate the ruse she's recently given birth. The people in her hometown think her 'pregnancies' since Alej were God-gifted. They have no clue her swollen stomach and engorged breasts are compliments to the same mental condition Megan had last year.

When I cup Claudia's jaw, she fights her tears while murmuring, "Maybe you shouldn't participate in the exchange?"

"No," I say with a shake of my head. "It's the payment I'm making to ensure the safe delivery of my child that's forcing Juana to attend our exchange." When her brows furrow, confused as to what I offered Juana to push her out of her comfort zone, I add, "I told her she was the only one I trusted to bring my child into the world safely." The next part pains me to say, "Because she did such a stellar job raising her children, I told her I have faith she'll do the same with mine."

Claudia gags. It makes me smile.

It also makes me hard, but since Smith is gawking at us from his beat-up van, I'm going to act as if the zipper of my trousers isn't biting my cock.

My grin slips off my face when Claudia asks, "Will I have a way of contacting you?"

I shake my head. "It isn't worth the risk."

"Maybe not to you, but it is to me," Claudia mutters under her breath before she apologizes for her supposed selfishness. "I just wish there was a way around this. That it didn't have to end this way." A solemn tear tracks down her face when she whispers, "Everyone deserves a happy ending, Rocco, but you deserve it more than anyone."

I wipe away her tear along with the handful of rogue ones that toppled down when I tugged her toward me before I balance my chin on the top of her head. "One day I'll find my happily ever after... *it just won't be with you.*" With how tense things are between us, I shouldn't laugh when she socks me in the stomach. I was hoping a bit of humor would defuse the situation, and as usual, I was right.

I also wish things were different this time around.

It sucks being the good guy.

It's why I rarely step away from the villain status.

My chuckles end when Smith joins us at his makeshift command center. "It's time to roll out. Rhett is about to deliver Dillon's nanny her morning tea, and we have five minutes until handover."

I nod before shifting my focus back to Claudia. "Remember—"

"The safety is on the tang, and if I want my threat to seem authentic, I must both switch off the safety and curl my finger around the trigger." When I attempt to talk, she pushes her finger to my lips. "And you won't take it personally if I fire at you. I'm just not allowed to aim for your cock." I grin like a smug prick when she murmurs, "Which is a little risky considering how big it is."

"What did I tell you, Smitty? There's no faster way to a man's heart than to compliment his schlong." He pushes me off him when I curl my arm around his shoulders, tug him down, then mess up his hair.

It isn't the time for fooling around, but if I don't do something to repress the urge to beg Claudia to pick me over her son, I'll make the second most fatal mistake of my life. My first was believing my father molested me because I was a boy. My gender had nothing to do with it, and neither did the costume I wore at my eighth birthday party.

What Claudia said yesterday was true. Nothing I did was my fault. The shame I'm carrying is my father's shame, not mine.

It's taken me years to realize that, and I can see it taking me years to truly believe it, but it's a step in the right direction.

"Come on, Mama. Let's get you home."

I lead Claudia into the passenger seat of my ride before jogging around to the hanging open driver's side door. As far as Juana is aware, our agreement is outside of usual trade. That means there's no fanfare. It's a simple handover.

Smith hands me a bead listening device similar to the ones Dimitri generally utilizes, but it's midnight black instead of the usual clear color. "It's a prototype I want to test out. It has a similar program as dark-knight, but I turned it on its head. Even if the Sánchezes have blockers, we should still be able to communicate." When nerves screw up his face, he hands me a second listening device. "But keep this in as well just in case. I don't want to risk it."

*Him and me both.*

I thank Smith with a head lift, whereas Claudia uses words. "Thank you, Smith. For everything."

Her last two words seem about more than his assistance in getting her son out, but I don't have time to press her about it. Rhett is in my ear. Although he isn't directly talking to me, it's obvious he needs my help. Jose isn't the slightest bit eager for him to be in the main house minutes out from a handover that involves his once best friend.

"Send in that order I requested, Smith, and ensure Jose is aware I want it specifically tailored to *his* specifications."

Smith hums out an agreeing murmur before he closes the door of my ride, demands for the men responsible for extraditing Claudia and Dillon from the country without incidence to head for their stations, then re-enters his van.

I squeeze Claudia's hand, lessening the number of lint balls she's placing in the hem of her cashmere sweater with her fidgeting before I plant my foot onto the gas pedal.

We're barely a mile out when my request ends Jose's rant. After taking a call from an 'associate' of mine, he reminds Rhett he's nothing but a pawn for his mother to fuck with before he requests Frances to help him expedite the five hundred-thousand-dollar order Smith just placed on my behalf.

"Wait," Smith requests, his words not for me. Accented voices sound down the line before he gives Rhett the all-clear. "Remember, two drops for drowsiness. Three will make her sleep for an hour or two. Four will kill her. I don't recommend four."

As I take the street corner of the Sánchez compound, Rhett plops three drops of a sedative into Mrs. Haslow's tea. She's been the nanny at the Sánchez compound for over three decades. I don't know if she stays because she sees herself as the balance between good or evil or if she's as clueless as Juana's sons that the way they were raised isn't right.

When your father is the head of the Mexican Cartel, your mother doesn't need to remind you not to tell him anything. You're already too scared to be in the same room as him, much less confess something you have no clue is wrong, so perhaps they've never heard those four little words that would have clued them onto the fact they were being abused.

For the first time ever, I appreciate Smith's creepy snooping when the happy coos of Dillon sound out of the speakers of my car when Rhett enters the room to hand Mrs. Haslow her morning tea. Dillon's happy squeals make Claudia smile because they expose that he's a well-adjusted and content baby.

My eyes flicker between the security box at the front of the Sánchez compound and Claudia when Rhett advises us that the tea worked. Mrs. Haslow has passed out.

"I'll direct you to the safest exit point..." It dawns on me that Smith can see us when my arrival at the front gate sees him switching off the radio in my car.

The quick plunge into silence means the brutal bang of my heart is heard in my voice when I advise the new guard my name. I'd like to tell you my reputation extends this far out of Hopeton, but tell me one time the number two of an organization is spoken of above the commander when they're *not* rooting for the number one spot? It's a rare occurrence, and this time around, I'm more than happy for the focus to remain on Dimitri.

After instructing which way to go with hand gestures that show off the fancy new Glock on his hip, the guard pushes the button to open the electric gate. Mindful an increase in guns wasn't the only new security measure Juana took the past couple of days, I only squeeze Claudia's hand for the quickest second before I return it to the steering wheel.

I squeeze out my frustrations on the leather material when our drive past the distribution sheds fails to have me spotting Jose. I need him far away from his mother for my ruse to go off without a hitch.

"Fuck," I mutter under my breath when I spot him standing beside Juana at the steps of the main compound. All his brothers are there, and they're weaponed up like they're about to go to war.

"You need to fire at me, Mama." When I spot Claudia's head shake in the corner of my eye, I hurt her to save her from making a mistake. "Then say goodbye to your son because he's all but dead when she fucks with his head like my father did mine."

With Claudia's eyes front and center, Juana thinks her tears are in fear for what she is about to face. In reality, they're for what she's about to give up for her son.

Me.

Although I love how deeply I've imprinted myself on her in such a short period, I don't want her to feel conflicted. "Do what needs to be done to protect your cub, Mama, and don't *ever* be ashamed of it."

Her nod is non-existent, but I don't need to see it to know it exists. I can feel her protectiveness rising. It is as fast and insubordinate as the hardening of my cock. There's nothing more attractive than a woman who does not shy away from doing the right thing for her kids.

The gun stuffed down the back of my pants feels real fucking heavy when our arrival at the front stairs of the Sánchez residence sees Frances removing Claudia from my car in an unkosher manner. He doesn't open her door for her or offer her his hand. He drags her out by her hair.

I'm unaware what the words Juana speaks to Claudia are when Frances drags her to his mother's feet, but they fill me with so much anger, I can't hold back. "I thought we had an agreement." I float my eyes over the scrape mark going from Claudia's knee to her collarbone. It has me ropeable, but I've conned people into thinking I'm sane for over a decade. I can handle this. "I'm paying out the eye to ensure the safety of my child, so the least you can do is ensure I'm getting my money's worth while I am in the same fucking room as you." It dawns on me that Dimitri is listening in when he grunts about me impersonating his grumpy persona. "My kid is in her gut. If you toss her around, you're tossing around my kid."

"The fetus—"

"Fetus? You're calling my kid a fucking fetus!" Frances steps between his mother and me, unearthing he is the one I need to pay careful attention to when it comes time to taking Juana down. "I don't give a fuck what you do to her. I don't care if you beat her until she's black and blue, then pass her around to the men in your crew *after* she's given birth to my kid. But you won't do anything before. I don't give a fuck who you are, there's no fucking chance in hell I'll let any sick fuck's cock get near my kid that isn't mine."

That killed me to say. It made me instantly sick to my stomach, and it has me convinced my dick will never rise to the occasion again, but it has the effect I was aiming for. Not only does Juana look at me like I told her I nominated her for a Mother of the Year award, but she also commands Frances to help Claudia from the ground.

Once she's corrected Claudia's disheveled clothes and wiped away the tears she wrongly believes are for her, Juana locks her eyes with mine. "I won't lie. I researched you after your last visit." My skin crawls when she rakes her fingernails across my chest. She's old enough to be my grandmother but acting as if she wouldn't need to remove her false teeth to suck my dick. "I found nothing overly incriminating, but I knew there was something different about you. Something *unique*." She purrs her last word with a whisper. "I guess I was right." Her mouth is filled with so much saliva, strings of spit stretch between her teeth when she says, "Ma always is."

If I could stab her in the chest right now and not risk neither Claudia nor her son's safety, I would. Since I can't, I continue with my ruse. "You most certainly were, but since I have places to be and people to fuck, can we move this along?"

Juana doesn't look pleased by my crass tongue, but she hides it well. "Certainly." After demanding Jose to step forward with a brief-case, she says, "Your son or daughter will be delivered by C-section approximately three weeks before the due date to ensure—"

"No harm occurs to your incubator. I get it," I snap out, moving her along. I can hear Rhett's breaths as he races Dillon through the bushland surrounding us. He sounds like he's being chased. If that is the case, I need to get Claudia to their meet-up point as soon as possible. "As I told you yesterday, I don't care what you do to her. I just want my son."

"What if it's a girl?" This question didn't come from Juana. It came from Alej, and he expressed it like he doesn't fully comprehend what happens to his nieces, but it makes him sad anyway.

When I say, "She'll do, too," Alej's eyes shoot to his mother.

"See, girls are good. T-They can help."

Claudia's chest deflates as quickly as mine when Juana hits Alej up the back of the head. It isn't enough abuse for Alej to have the right to kill her, but if it were added to the claims of incest, Ezra, the Governor of Mafia Law, could disband the Sánchez chapter of the cartel, which would mean I'd no longer need to follow the rules. But since the only proof of incest I have is from a victim knowing a victim, I can't go to him with my claims. To out Juana as a sexual predator, I'd have to out myself as a victim.

I'm not willing to do that.

I don't think I'll *ever* be willing to do that. Then I catch Claudia's inconspicuous gaze, and my tough act fails again. If she can still look at me the way she does after I shared my biggest, darkest secret with her, perhaps those closest to me could as well.

I lose the chance to investigate further when Smith says, "Package has been received. Decoy is on his way. Prepare for carnage."

I've barely lifted my chin half an inch when Rhett races out the front door of the compound. The aftershave he doused his jaw in could explain his woodsy scent, but I'm praying like fuck Juana isn't as observant as she is weird when I notice the number of scratches on his arms and legs and the dots of blood on his shirt. You only get them after either gunning down an assailant chasing you through woodlands or when you were super close to the man who did.

"They... took... JJ," Rhett pushes out through big, tiring breaths. "I... chased them. They went... through the woodlands." His performance is so convincing it takes me nudging my head to the gun peeking out the back of my trousers for Claudia to remember this is a part of our ruse. "They went west... on Crocker."

When he signals for them to follow him so he can lead the way, Juana shifts her suspicious-filled eyes to me.

"Why the fuck are you looking at me? I'm too fucked in the head to take care of my own child, let alone one of yours. This ain't me."

With nothing but honesty ringing in my tone, she shifts her focus to Claudia. Her look is already murderous, so you can imagine how perverse it gets when I 'fail' to thwart Claudia's launch for my gun. I pretend to bat her away from me, but she's too fast. She yanks my gun out of my trousers, then points it at my head in the exact disarming motion I taught her this morning.

The Sánchezes are quick to come to my defense. Within seconds, half a dozen assault rifles light up Claudia's chest. It freaks me the fuck out, but some good comes from it. The panic roaring through my veins makes my threat sound super convincing when I scream, "If any harm comes to my baby, I will eradicate the fucking lot of you."

I don't make idle threats.

If I issue one, you can be assured I'll follow through with it without the slightest delay.

It's obvious the Sánchezes are aware of this. It only takes one warning for them to stand down, meaning I can shift all my focus to Claudia.

"You need to put down the gun, Mama." I walk toward her at an angle, assuring not only to place myself between the man itching for the chance to take her down but also getting her close to her getaway vehicle. "We talked about this. Ma will take care of you. There's nothing to worry about—"

"She took my son! She took him away from me." The pain in Claudia's eyes is so real, it cuts through me like a knife. "I want him back."

"JJ is not your son," Juana argues back as she charges forward at a rate faster than Frances can respond to. "He's my reborn son. He is Juan. I gave birth to him."

"No," Claudia denies with a brutal shake of her head that hides the shuffle she does toward the hanging open passenger door of my car. "JJ is my son. I gave birth to him at Wallens Ridge in front of you and the warden! That's when you took him away from me. I didn't even get to hold him."

It dawns on me that it isn't just the authorities Juana has lied to. Her sons are in the dark just as much. Their combined hiss is so loud, it almost drowns out Juana's denial. "Your son died during birth, Claudia. His umbilical cord was compressed during delivery. You didn't push him out fast enough."

I'm about to signal to Claudia that it's time to make her move, that she needs to leave before a mafia war commences, but my gesture comes too late. Armageddon commences when Jose mumbles, "That's the *exact* thing you said when Harmony didn't return from her doctor's visit. You said she didn't push Benedict out quick enough and that a compressed umbilical cord was the cause of their deaths." He takes a stumbling step backward when a truth not even Smith knows about smacks into him. "You gave birth to Jeremiah only a month later. You said he was above average weight because you had gestational diabetes." I've never thought I'd be profoundly impacted by a man crying, but Jose proves me wrong when he chokes out, "Is Jeremiah my son? Is he Benedict?"

I push Claudia into the passenger seat of my car and mouth for her to go when Jose aims the barrel of his assault weapon at his mother's head. I understand he's pissed, and I want to high-five him just for having the gall to stand up to his mother, but even if Jeremiah is his son, and his mother killed his wife to authenticate her claims she died during childbirth, they're not crimes punishable by death.

If Jose takes out Juana, he will be killed.

That isn't a maybe.

It is a fact.

Usually, I'd sit back and watch the carnage unfold with a smile on my face. I can't do that this time around. Juana is fucked in the head, but her unstableness feels pale in comparison to the expression that crosses Frances's face when he butts his gun to Jose's head. He's been waiting for this day for years, and he has no shame admitting it. "I told you he was up to no good, Mommy. He doesn't love you like the rest of us. He never has." He flicks off the safety and inches back the trigger while murmuring, "And now he'll die for his—"

He's interrupted by the revs of my sports car roaring to life. When it is quickly chased by Claudia planting her foot onto the gas pedal, he redirects his gun to my car instead of his brother's head. Aware he is the weakest link, I snatch his gun out of his hand and aim it at the back-side panel of my ride. I have the perfect shot. Those western movies you see where they shoot the person's gun out of their hand, I can do that if I'm willing to waste a bullet. I could also shoot out the tires of Claudia's getaway vehicle if I wanted to. It's the fact I don't want to that sees me shooting for the panel that's nowhere near the gas tank. I need the Sánchezes to think I'm pissed about Claudia's endeavor to flee me, and a macho showdown will do that.

I have a better understanding of Dimitri's delay a year ago when he was forced to aim for the cockpit window of the jet his daughter was in. Claudia is aware this is part of our plan, that I'd fire at her to ensure no one else did, but it still makes me want to fucking puke.

This makes it so final.

We're no longer racing toward the finish line.

We've crossed it.

"Fuck!" I curse into the cool morning air when the five bullets I pop into my car fail to slow Claudia down. Even when I shattered the back window to blur the shadow of her head behind the steering wheel, Claudia continued on course without delay.

If that doesn't prove to you how strong she is, nothing will.

I make sure my expression is murderous before spinning to face Frances. "Where are your fleet of cars? She's getting away!"

He gestures for me to follow him before he barks out orders to a handful of men who charged our way after hearing the discharge of my firearm. They guard Juana like she's a saint while following Frances's race to the transportation area I saw during my tour. Jose remains on the stairs of the compound, unmoving and unspeaking. His shock has me hopeful Juana will be sent to the courts to face her crimes without any input from me.

I dive into the passenger seat of the lead SUV, smirking when the keyless start fails to activate. Smith is controlling every vehicle in the Sánchez fleet. Although his delay will only last around twenty or so seconds, it will be long enough for Claudia to get a good gap between us. Her 'accident' near the end of her escape will see us lose another couple of minutes to check the wreckage for her body.

"Come on, you piece of shit!" Frances begs a mere second before Smith mutters in my ear. "Mama Bear is five clicks out from her cub. Send them west as planned."

Just as he finishes speaking, he disbands the program he placed on the Sánchez fleet. When Frances's car roars to life, he fist bumps the air before cranking up the volume on his radio. I feel like I've been thrust back in time when "Crank That" by Soulja Boy blares out of the speakers. Frances would have to be mid to late thirties, but he acts like a child when Juana places her hand on his shoulder from her position behind him and whispers, "Make Mommy proud, Frankie. You're such a big boy now."

I bob my chin when Smith mutters, "Fucking creep," in my ear.

This isn't your standard overbearing mother situation. Even with my father being the lowest of the low, I still believe he is a step or two above Juana. She even rivals Col for sickness when it comes to her family, and it's all the confirmation I need that I made the right decision when I placed Dillon above my own selfish needs. I can't change what happened to me, but I can stop it from happening to Dillon.

That, in itself, will make a life of misery bearable.

25

——————

# CLAUDIA

**M**y scalp is throbbing from where Frances ripped me out of Rocco's car by my hair, and the same madman is chasing me down, but neither of those points are the reason for the wetness hazing my vision. Driving away from Rocco was harder than I comprehended. He ran me through his plan multiple times this morning, but it was easy to skip the emotional upheaval when you're looking at details on sheets of paper. All I saw was the prize at the end. My son. I failed to realize how much my heart would break knowing the last time I'd see Rocco would be while he was firing at me.

I have a million memories of him stored in my head, but that one will forever remain in the number one spot. I'm not a sadist person who only looks for the bad in every situation. It's the fact I could see the heartbreak in his eyes before he took his first shot.

If he didn't care about me as deeply as I do him, he wouldn't have hesitated. He did because he's falling in love with me as I am him.

And now it's being cruelly stripped away.

"Two more miles, Claudia. You've got this," Smith encourages through the speakers of the radio when he mistakes my tears as excited ones. "A quarter of a mile up, you'll see a marker on a tree.

When you reach the marker, fully compress the gas pedal, then roll out the driver's side door." He must hear my sharp intake of breath because his campaign to ease my panic is immediate. "The bedding was recently laid. It is as soft as a cloud. If you time your exit, you'll be sweet." He sounds more New Zealand than Australian during his last sentence. "Ready?" He takes my hearty swallow as an answer. "Three... two... on—"

I throw open the driver's side door and roll out before all of 'one' leaves his mouth. My impact is jarring, but I suck up the pain. I gave birth without a single form of help. I can survive anything.

Rocco taught me that. He reiterated that exact thing many times the past twelve hours, and for some reason, I believe him.

While standing on my feet to gather my bearings, I suck in some big breaths. Rocco made sure there were enough landmarks in the terrain for me to find my way without equipment because if I want to stay hidden, I need to be completely off the grid.

When I find the air tower with the sunshine yellow dot painted on the side, I seek the new residential housing estate on its left. When I find it, I sprint straight down the middle of them. I'm seeking a private airstrip. A shipment for a rival is about to leave, and excluding the pilot, Dillon and I are the only two people on the manifest.

My race slows when accented voices overtake the drumming of my pulse in my ears. I've reached the cut-out Rocco placed into the wire fencing for me. How do I know it was him? He left strips of the dress and sweater I'm wearing dangling off the sharp edges of the wire, meaning not only will my skin be protected from the rough edges when I squeeze through the gap, the matching material will lead the Sánchezes to the same cargo plane idling in front of me.

I can crawl through the fence without concern because Gottle Enterprises means nothing to me. The Sánchezes don't have the same privilege. Henry Gottle, Sr. is the boss of all bosses. If Juana tries to step over him as she did her husband, she'll lose more than her cartel standing. She could very well lose her life.

The thought makes me smile. It remains on my face when I time the sequence of the guards' walk around the tower protecting the cargo jet's contents from Henry's enemies, and during my hopscotch through the infrared wiring Smith wired our motel room with this morning so I could practice my bounce routine.

I never thought weeks of balancing on a lidless toilet would come in handy.

Boy, was I wrong.

Some of the gaps in the electronic alarm system are barely the width of my ankle.

O'Doyle would have never made it through this maze without alerting armed goons to her arrival.

I don't get the chance to pat myself on the back for my stellar effort when I make it to the back of the cargo plane undetected. A red dot is highlighting my chest. It hovers over my heart for barely half a second before it treks up my chest, over the throb in my throat, then stops at my face.

Mindful the thudding of my heart is more in response to the closeness of my mate than fear, I mouth, '*Thank you*,' before darting between the crates stacked in the cargo plane, confident soothing the whimpers of my frightened child will fix the gaping hole in the middle of my chest.

## 26

## ROCCO

"Uhat are you waiting for? Shoot!"

In my mind, I salute Claudia when she mouths '*thank you*' before Frances rips his semi-automatic weapon out of my hand. I'm not scared he will hurt Claudia. Not only has she entered the cargo plane two of Dimitri's closest allies smuggled her son onto, only a fool would discharge their weapon on land owned by Henry Gottle, Sr.

I only butted my gun to Henry's head when things got a little heated between Dimitri and him a couple of weeks back, and I barely left with my life intact. Dimitri bartered a pardon on my behalf, and it was that negotiation that alerted me to the fact he was full of crap yesterday morning when he said Roxanne was my only friend.

He fucking loves me.

How couldn't he?

"I wouldn't if I were you." Frances's finger has inched his trigger back halfway. His bullets won't perforate the plane's shell, but he's so worked up with adrenaline, he's desperate to discharge some of the buzz clogging his veins. "We'll have a hard enough time convincing Henry to tell us where his plane will land as it is, but if you fire at *his* property, we won't stand a chance."

"T-This is Henry's property?"

After taking a moment to relish the stutter of Juana's words, I increase the crinkle running down her forehead by pulling back the scrub hiding the company name that owns this private airstrip.

She looks set to vomit. She isn't the only one. Bile scorches my throat when I strengthen our 'supposed' ties by treating her with the respect she doesn't deserve. "I'm just as pissed as you are, Ma, but I promise I will find her. I don't care if it takes two weeks or two years, she will *not* play us like this. You're Juana fucking Sánchez. The queen of the Mexican Cartel. I will not let her hurt you like this. You deserve better."

This isn't the first rant I've gone on the past forty minutes. I've played the cockhead ruse to such perfection I'm beginning to wonder just how much of my performance is an act.

After curling my arm around Juana's shoulders like she's delicate and fragile, I guide her back to the SUV Frances drove over the landscape like it wasn't capable of flipping over from hitting the smallest boulder at the wrong angle. "Let's go see if we can stop the plane from taking off."

I only make my suggestion because I know the entrance for the airstrip is on the opposite side to which we're standing. With the rough terrain, it's an easy ten-minute drive. Smith just advised the cargo plane is scheduled to take off in under a minute. We'll never make it in time.

*What a pity.*

"No!" Juana screams when the roar of an engine preparing to whizz down the runway whips up dust around us. "My son! You can't take my son."

I almost feel sorry for her when she whimpers the name of the child she lost at full-term. I thought Dillon was her replacement child for Juan. I didn't factor the idea she was pretending her stillborn child was still alive.

"Manny." She cries and cries and cries his name over and over again until she collapses into a heap in the backseat of the SUV.

"She needs urgent medical assistance!" When Frances looks hesitant, I back up my claims with a promise. "I'll take care of everything here, and anything I find out, I'll bring it straight to you. You have my word, Frances. I won't let you down." This embarrasses me to admit, but I cross my fingers behind my back before issuing my promise. Normally, I have no hesitation when it comes to lying. If it's for the greater good, they fly out of my mouth like water down a river. I'm not awarded the same feeling today. It makes me feel a little dirty. That could have more to do with the fact it involves Claudia, but I won't know that for sure until Frances leaves me the fuck alone so I can decompress the pain in my chest that has me wondering if I took a bullet to the heart. "Hurry, Frances. Ma needs you."

Like the soft cock he is, he bobs his head in rapid succession before he slots behind the steering wheel. He barely barks out a command for me to meet him at the house once I'm done before he treats the SUV like it's a dune buggy.

I pray for one of the front tires to find a hidden boulder before the deafening rumble of a plane soaring into the air steals my attention. I watch the plane Claudia and her son are in ascend above the clouds, aware I've done the right thing but hating the hurt associated with it.

This is why I should have remained the villain of my story. It's easy to act like you don't care than have your heart ripped out because you care too much.

Once Claudia's plane disappears, I scrub at my beard like I can brush off an exhaustive day with a scratch, then head to the truck one of Dimitri's interns hid for me earlier today. I don't need to talk to Henry to authenticate my ruse. Claudia wouldn't have made it onto his plane without his permission, but we couldn't let anyone know that. Not even Claudia. Admission that Henry helped Claudia could create a mafia war, which is the very thing we've been endeavoring to avoid since day one.

After climbing into a rusted F150, I ask the question that's been gnawing my insides since Frances and Juana left. "Did you get anything?"

I could elaborate on my question, but I don't need to. Smith knows exactly what I'm seeking because the sweetest murmurings of a mother meeting her son for the very first time plays out of the speaker of my phone a couple of seconds later.

It's a heart-tugging event that could only be more thought-provoking if I could see the smile I hear in Claudia's whispers. Smith warned me he'd most likely only get audio. Henry locks up his shit tight because all true gangsters know if you let a hacker in once, you'll never get them out.

"Pilot just announced wheels will be up in ten. If you put the pedal to the metal, you'll make it here with a couple of minutes spare."

Although he can't see me, I shake my head. "I told Frances I'd meet him at the compound. I won't be invited to the hunt if I can't follow orders for at least the first twenty-four hours."

"Once Ezra announces that the 'claimed' child in Claudia's stomach ranks higher than the Sánchezes' ownership of her, you won't need to worry."

"That hasn't happened yet, Smith, and until it does, I need them to believe I'm on their side. Furthermore, I don't trust them as far as I could throw them. Even if Ezra rules Claudia is my property, the Sánchezes won't stop hunting her because there's more to that family's craziness than a wish to return their sanction to its former glory." I want to tell Smith just how fucked in the head I believe they are, but I don't bother since it would be a waste of breath. "And Ezra's ruling will only last as long as Claudia's 'supposed' pregnancy. We have to follow the plan to the T. It's the only way I can guarantee Claudia and Dillon's safety. They must come first."

Smith breathes heavily out of his nose before he hums an agreeing murmur. "Do you want me to wait for you?"

I once again shake my head. "Nah. Head out. I'm a big boy. I can find my way home."

His silence is very telling. He doesn't want to leave me up at the plate, swinging the bat alone because he has no clue I've done precisely that most of my life. There's only one person who's ever gone to bat for me, and not even he could help me this time around.

"Let Dimi know I'll be back on deck tomorrow afternoon."

I wait for Smith to hum for the second time before I crank the ignition on the truck and head back to the motel Claudia and I bunked at last night. I've got a few hours to kill, so I may as well do it in a place where I learned to walk for the second time in my life.

The scent of sex permeates the air when I enter the room of a one-star motel a couple of miles from Wallens Ridge. If it weren't for the bedding on the bathroom floor, you wouldn't know anyone had stayed here. The cartel doesn't leave evidence, hence my return. I packed everything when Smith arrived at the crack of dawn to prepare Claudia for her risqué escape, but there's one thing I had to leave behind. If Claudia had seen it, every truth I ever told her would have been scrutinized.

I dumped the bag of cocaine into the toilet as requested. It just wasn't in the bowl as believed. I stored it in the cistern. It isn't that I wanted to be deceitful. I just couldn't risk being without supplies if my nightmares returned. I wanted Claudia to love me, not fear me.

Shame fills me for an entirely new reason when I dig the baggy of cocaine out of the cistern. The Ziplock bag protected it from the water. It's unsullied and ready to cut into lines.

I won't lie. The temptation is immense. The past twenty-four hours have been the longest I've gone without some type of narcotic thickening my veins since I was fifteen. That's a twelve-year addiction that's undone for one that only started a little over three weeks ago.

While pouring the cocaine into the toilet bowl, I recall the fear in Claudia's eyes when she stood in front of me fully naked for the very first time. It was on the opposite end of the emotional scale compared to the smile she released when she mouthed her gratitude only minutes ago.

She had everything to lose and nothing to gain, yet she still gave it her all.

Now I need to do the same.

I startle when the flushing of the drugs sees a thick, unretentive voice boom out of the earpiece in my ear. It isn't Smith. It's from a man who should be too busy settling his family into home life to worry about my fucked-up addiction. "That's step one. Now get your ass back here so we can commence step two."

"Dimi—"

I dart my eyes around the bathroom when his reply arrives with the glare of his beady eyes. "I wasn't fucking asking, Rocco. Put the plan into play, then your ass on a jet." His demand has barely left his mouth when the clang of him disconnecting his connection to my earpiece makes me jump.

When I fail to find any signs of a hidden camera, I mutter, "Can you see me?"

"Of course he could see you," Smith answers without pause for delay, proving he heard my conversation with Dimitri. "Do you really think he'd leave you up there swinging the bat by yourself? He personally oversaw every stage of today's ruse." I stop imagining him puckering his lips to kiss Dimitri's ass when he updates me on the private jet idling at an airport only a couple of clicks from the Sánchez residence. "I've sent coordinates to your phone, but you shouldn't have any trouble finding it. You can sniff out jet fuel as well as you can cocaine..."

His words trail off when I growl out his name in a snappy tone.

Usually, I'm all about the jokes, but today isn't one of those days.

"Too soon?"

I flip him the bird in the cracked mirror I'm standing in front of. When he laughs, I rip my shirt off my body like I'm a wannabe Magic Mike stripper before stomping on the little black button I thought wasn't quite the same size as its counterparts.

While Smith gripes about how much a camera button costs, I enter the main part of the room to remove the sheet that's soaked with the combined scent of Claudia and me before I make my way to the truck parked at the front. Mindful Smith is a fucking snoop, I snag the only shirt without buttons out of a gym bag on the floor of the truck before puffing out the same bag with the sheet. A piece of cotton won't stop my nightmares from returning, but I'm hopeful it will stop me from falling back on old coping mechanisms when they get too rough.

Claudia's scent doesn't just do weird things to my gut and balls.

It soothes the chaos in my head as well.

Smith's persona switches from friendly to professional when I arrive at the Sánchezes' property a couple of minutes later. He has a script at the ready, but his plan goes AWOL when our arrival corresponds with Ezra temporarily awarding Claudia's ownership to me.

His ruling pushes Juana into a mental psychosis episode. She's so unhinged, Frances has no choice but to call in professional help. Smith ensures that the doctor dispatched is from someone within our organization. She gives Juana a heavy sedative within minutes of arriving before suggesting she be placed on a thirty-day hold so they can assess her mental stability.

Frances immediately denies her suggestion, but regretfully for him, Jose is the eldest, so any decisions made about his family while their unit leader is out of action falls on his shoulders.

As you can imagine, after what he learned before Claudia's escape, even if it's only temporary, Jose is more than eager to take over the reins. It may be the only way he'll unearth exactly how warped his mother's reign has been.

Within minutes of Juana being wheeled into the back of an unmarked ambulance, Jose accepts Ezra's ruling before backing it up with a pledge that I can contact him for assistance at any stage.

His offer sees me leaving the Sánchezes' compound with lighter steps than I entered it with, but with my unease at a pinnacle. The Petrettis have proven time and time again that there's nothing more sinister than a family at war. They drag everyone else into their shit, and more times than not, the only people they take down are the innocents who should have been far from the controversy—the people like Claudia, Dillon, and Jeremiah.

"Does Isaac know Jeremiah isn't his son?"

Smith waits for me to close the door of my truck before replying, "No."

"Does Dimi think we should tell him?" I return Alej's wave before driving through the manufacturing sheds that are in full operation, even with their leader being transported to a mental hospital. "I get there's stale blood between them, but I think Isaac has the right to know, and it could smooth things over with them."

"I agree, but you know Dimi. He's as stubborn as he is rich."

"I would have said an asshole, but thanks for the head's up that the prick is listening." I stab in the coordinates Smith forwarded me into the GPS in the console of the truck before muttering, "God forbid he'd actually trust me. I guess I deserve it. I did hide a coke addiction from him for twelve years."

I barely hear Smith's sigh. My chest is rumbling too loudly with disappointment to hear anything else.

With my confession ending our conversation, my drive to the airstrip is done in silence. After parking next to the idling jet, I curl out of the truck and toss a set of keys to one of Dimitri's lackeys. "See you on the flip side, Smitty," I mutter before digging the listening devices out of my ear and dumping them into a bin next to the stairs on the jet.

I need a couple of minutes to decompress everything that's happened the past twenty-four hours. I can't do that with an audience.

My wish for privacy is thrown out the fucking window when my entrance into the private jet isn't greeted by a flight attendant eager to suck my dick. Dimitri is leaning against the bar. His thick arms are folded in front of his chest, and his glare exposes he's as pissed as fuck he is away from his family for even a minute.

"You didn't have to come, D. I had everything in lockdown."

"I know," he agrees, shocking me. Even if you prove without a doubt he's in the wrong, he never admits it, so not only am I stunned, I have no comeback whatsoever, not even a shit-stirring one. "But I'm not here to check up on you, Rocco. I'm here to make sure you'll still be here in another twelve years."

When it dawns on me what he's talking about, I curse under my breath before plonking my backside in the chair across from him. I thought he was here to make sure his family didn't face any repercussions for my actions today. I had no clue it was about my second worst secret.

I stop cradling my head in my hands when Dimitri asks, "What happened to snorting it off the tits of whores to keep your dick harder for longer? That's what it was always about, wasn't it?"

I want to tell him I snorted coke just to get hard, but since that would lead to a confession I'm not yet willing to make, I downplay my actions. "The shit is addictive, D. That's why we push out so many units per week." When my reply doubles the anger lining his face, I give him a truth to hide my lie. "We're not all superheroes like you, Dimi. Sometimes we need to snort kryptonite to feel strong."

I peer up from my balled hands when he murmurs, "Or sometimes we need the love of a good woman." His lips tug at one side when I bob my head in agreement. "Was Claudia that for you? Did she make your balls tingle and dick hard without a sprinkling of coke?"

"That and so much more," I reply with a chuckle, shocked about our conversation but glad we're having it. We haven't spoken like this in years. Dimitri was so focused on getting his daughter back, he didn't have time for anyone else. "When you know, you know. Right?"

He unfolds his arms, once again unable to maintain an angry stance while talking about family. We don't share an ounce of blood, but he is my brother. "Without a fucking doubt, so I'm curious as to why you let her go."

I look at him like he's insane. "I couldn't put your family in the firing zone so soon after leaving it."

"Bullshit," he fires back, his voice as loud as mine. "If you're in as fucking deep as you say you are, you would have done *anything* necessary to keep her."

Everything he's saying is true, but there's no way I can admit that to him. "You can't preach shit, Dimi. You pushed Roxanne away time and time again."

"Because I couldn't give her what she needed while searching for Fien! I couldn't keep her safe! You wouldn't have faced those same issues, Rocco."

"Yes, I would have!" I shout before I can stop myself. "I can't trust myself around her any more than she can't trust me with her son. I can't keep them safe because I'm the madman they should be afraid of."

Dimitri laughs like I'm joking.

I'm not.

"If my father had fiddled with more than my head when I was growing up, would you trust me with your children?"

The expression on his face immediately changes. "What are you saying, Rocco?"

"I'm not saying anything. I'm asking you a question. If he did, would you trust me with your children?"

I want to call him a liar when he bobs his chin. I want to tell him he's fucking insane before demanding him to remove his gun from its holster and shoot me in the head, but there's too much truth in his eyes. Too much confirmation. And that's excluding what he says during his nod. "Because if I had once thought you would ever turn out like him, I would have buried you alongside him long before I would have ever let you near my daughter."

His comment confuses me.

He's speaking as if he's always known my secret.

It dawns on me that that is the case when he confesses, "You talk in your sleep, Rocco. You have since we were kids. Nothing you said made any sense until I heard you calming Ophelia down after she woke up screaming." The murderous glint his eyes are never without softens when he mutters, "When you told her she had nothing to be ashamed about, I hoped one day you'd take your own advice, but I was never going to push you to do it." He smirks like the sadistic prick he is. "You took out the trash the following week, and your head seemed relatively screwed on ever since. Then—"

"Claudia entered the picture." My interruption halves the panic sitting heavily on my chest. I can't think about Claudia and have suicidal thoughts at the same time. It isn't possible. "She scared me."

Dimitri laughs like our conversation isn't as serious as it is. "Don't all the good women? If they don't have you running scared, they're not the girl for you."

It's the worse time for me to grin, but it can't be helped. That was one of Ma's favorite sayings.

When Dimitri slots his ass into the seat next to me, I barge him with my shoulder. "If only I hadn't fucked everything up."

"Has Fien's return home taught you nothing?" Although he's asking a question, I don't get the chance to answer him. "Nothing is lost if you're willing to fight for it. Your fight started today, Rocco. The motel where you flushed the drugs was step one. Thirty days of rehab will be step two." When I attempt a rebuttal, he cuts me off with an angry glare. "Thirty days is all I'm asking. If you give it your *all* for thirty days, I'll give you them for life."

I'm confused as to what he means until the shock rendering me silent exposes the faintest coo of a baby. I'm out of my seat in an instant. My eagerness to enter the room at the back of the jet sees me pushing open the door with so much force, its gust fans Claudia's hair away from her gorgeous tear-stained face.

She's standing next to a double bed, rocking an unsettled nine-month-old baby in her arms. When she spots me standing in the doorway, she smiles in a way that would have me agreeing to a lifetime of torture before she locks her eyes with Dimitri, who is standing behind me.

When I follow the direction of her gaze, Dimitri reiterates, "Thirty days, Rocco. Do we have an agreement?"

I drift my eyes back to Claudia, aware this is her decision more than it is mine. She has far more to lose than me. "What do you say, Mama? Do you think you could put up with my shit for a couple more weeks?"

She twists her lips to hide her smile before muttering, "Only weeks? We were planning years or perhaps even decades, but if you only want weeks, I guess we can handle that too."

I swagger toward her like the cocky prick I am when she gestures to me to come to her with a crook of her finger.

Once I'm within an inch of her, I realize my error. She isn't drawing me in to seal our deal with a kiss. She's adding a brutal demand to Dimitri's condition. A term I'm unsure I can fulfill without barfing. "But since I'm all new to this, and Dimitri exposed that you've had practice with Fien and Finlay, you're on diaper duty until I get the hang of things."

Dillon squeals like he's on a rollercoaster when the dump he did in his pants wafts up from Claudia wiggling his backside in my face. When I violently heave, confused as to how someone so cute could be the cause of such a horrendous smell, Claudia laughs, fists my shirt, tugs me in close, then seals her lips over mine.

I think the sweet taste of her mouth is to die for, but it has nothing on the six little words she whispers over my kiss-swollen lips when Dillon's spit-inspired babble has us coming up for air, "I trust you. I always will."

# EPILOGUE

## CLAUDIA

**Three and a half years later...**

My pulse thuds in my neck when I spot Rocco's car pulling into the front of the tunnel that separates our properties. Don't misconstrue. We've lived together since the day he broke me out of Wallens Ridge, just nobody knows that. Dimitri's agreement specified that if Rocco undertook thirty days of rehab to kickstart his road to recovery, he would gift me to him. There was no mention that I would be free during the process. That isn't the way things work in the criminal underworld.

The only person who can truly gift me to Rocco is Juana. Since she'd rather see me burn in hell, my placement in Rocco's life is unknown to those outside of his inner circle. If you include the many electronic forms he can hack, Smith visits Dillon and me daily. We've hosted dinner parties for Dimitri, Roxanne, Fien, and Matteo, and on rare occasions, Clover has enjoyed a beer around the firepit with Rocco.

Other than that, my neighbors believe I'm a widower raising her only child with the funds her husband left her. My groceries are delivered to my door, my exercise is done in the yard of the home Rocco purchased for us, and I haven't driven a car since I 'stole' Rocco's to flee him, yet I couldn't be happier.

I had only undertaken eleven and a half months of my original sentence when Rocco broke me out of a maximum-security prison, but it was long enough, even years later, I appreciate the freedom I wouldn't have had if it weren't for Rocco.

Furthermore, I'll never feel imprisoned in a home that's full of love, admiration, and an outrageously handsome man who dotes on my son as if he is his own.

Life is blissful, and I only see it growing when we share with Rocco the secret Dillon and I have been hiding the past couple of hours.

"Are you ready, baby? Dada is on his way."

Dillon peers up at me with his big blue eyes out in full force before he nods. He is a well-adjusted four-year-old who is respectful and has wonderful manners, but with an edge of Rocco's take-no-shit attitude.

Rocco has raised Dillon to be respectful to both himself and me. It's made him a little hotheaded when I want him to do something he doesn't want to do, such as brushing his teeth and going to bed, but you must take the good with the bad when you're teaching a child he has the right to say no.

Dillon's learning curve has been helpful for both Rocco and him. His innocence has proven to Rocco he wasn't to blame for his dad's sickness, and Rocco's wish to protect him since day one made me fall in love with Rocco at the speed of light.

It's been a crazy couple of years that I wouldn't change for the world.

"Hold your sign up high, baby," I request when the door in the basement of my home creaks open.

We live two doors down from Smith, but Rocco's plot of land is so large, the bottom right corner of this property's fence line juts up with Rocco's back left-hand corner. It made it easy for Rocco to order a tunnel to be dug like Dimitri's father did for all his compounds. If anyone were to test Rocco's motives, they'll witness him exiting and entering his property each morning and night. They have no clue he spends every night in my bed.

Rocco's act was so convincing the day I kidnapped my son, the Sánchezes truly believe Hopeton is the last place I'll ever visit.

Sometimes, hiding in plain sight is the best plan.

I realize it was wrong of me to activate dark-knight so I could plan a surprise when Rocco calls my name. He sounds panicked out of his mind, and it is proven without a doubt when his gold-dipped gun enters my visual before him. He also isn't alone. Dimitri, Clover, Smith, and a handful of men I've never met are also with him.

After swallowing the brick in my throat, I mutter, "We're in the den."

I don't breathe when Rocco asks, "Are you hurt, Mama? Did they hurt you or Dillon?"

"No. We're fine. We were just..." I stop, settle the nerves doubling the tension radiating from Rocco's side of the room before trying again. "Can you come into the den, please... *alone.*"

There's no way he will refuse my request when Dillon says, "Please, Dada!"

He'd walk over coal to get to him when he calls him dada.

Nerves take flight in my stomach for an entirely new reason when I hear Rocco flick on the safety of his gun before he returns it to the back of his pants. His guard is still up and ready to fight when he breaks over the threshold of the den, but they do little to slacken the shock that pummels into him when he reads the sign Dillon is holding out.

Once his eyes have scanned the words "Baby Shay No. 2 due July II," three times in a row, he snaps them to mine. They're filled with the panic I was anticipating when the digital pregnancy test announced we were expecting, but mercifully, his fret is barely seen through the pure admiration shining through them.

A tear topples down my face when Dillon scares the living daylights out of me by shouting, "Surprise! We're having a baby."

When Rocco seeks confirmation of his claim from my eyes, I nod. I only had the Mirena implant removed three months ago, so we weren't expecting this to happen so quickly, but as I'm slowly learning, everything happens for a reason.

"Are you happy?" I ask Rocco when he arrives at my side.

His smile is to die for as his blissful eyes bounce between mine. "More than you could ever understand, Mama."

I fall in love with him even more when he falls to his knees, presses a kiss to my belly, then squashes his ear to the area his lips grazed. He scarcely registers the increase of my pulse from his closeness to my pussy when Dillon asks, "Can you hear anything?"

After pushing Rocco out of his way with more strength than a four-year-old should have, he mirrors Rocco's pose. I giggle when his mouth falls into an 'O' five seconds later. All he's hearing is the gurgling of my stomach, but he acts as if his sibling just told him he or she will never speak a bad word about them.

As Dillon bounces off the walls, a specialty of his, Rocco stands, cups my cheeks with his hands, then removes the salty streaks marking my face with his thumbs. "You scared me, Mama," he murmurs once the mess has been cleared. "I thought they'd found you."

Even with Jose at war with his family, the Sánchezes haven't lessened their endeavors to find me. They've spent more money trekking across the world to authenticate claims of planted sightings than they have on their staff the past three years. It's seen their ranking slip to the very bottom position, but regretfully, their standing is still high enough for them to be protected by mafia law.

Rocco can't kill Juana like he did Warden Mattue when he found out he was the one who snatched Dillon away from me after cutting his umbilical cord. If he did, Dimitri's entire operation would slip down the totem pole like the Sánchezes did when Alejandro was murdered. Considering everything we have—including Rocco being clean for three and a half years—is thanks to Dimitri, neither Rocco nor I are willing to risk it.

Juana will face a jury of her peers one day. We just need to be patient.

"I'm sorry I scared you. I just wanted it to be a surprise." I lean in close to Rocco to ensure my next set of words are only for his ears. "Even when you are miles away, I can feel the heat of your eyes on me. They're so white-hot, I'm beginning to wonder if our child was conceived by immaculate conception."

I'm expecting for him to throw his head back and laugh or toss me over his shoulder, spank my backside, then demand that Smith put a child-hypnotizing program on the LCD TV screen in the den, so you can imagine my shock when he does the opposite. He doesn't request privacy. He invites a stranger into the strong unit protecting our home. He is the very last man I anticipated for him to invite. He asks Smith to make an urgent appointment with Ezra James, the Governor of Mafia Law, before locking his eyes with mine. "And place Claudia's name on the guest list."

I shake my head. "If he finds out you've been hiding me all this time, you could face your own hearing." I understand he's sick of hiding our relationship, and he'd give anything to shout the news of our pregnancy from the rooftops, but I don't want him to place his life in danger for it. "I can't do this without you, Rocco. I don't want to."

"You won't do it without me, Mama. I won't allow it. But you do need to trust me."

"I do trust you. I always have."

I didn't lie when I told him I trusted him. I not only trusted him to change our son's diaper, I trusted him to bathe him, care for him, and love him as if he is his own. And he has done that every single day for the past three and a half years. He would never hurt Dillon, so I have no choice but to place all my faith into his hands for the second time in my life.

I'm unsure if nerves or pregnancy are to blame for my nausea when I enter Dimitri's home for the first time. It looks different from the footage I've seen—bigger and far more impressive. It also doesn't seem as cold as I imagined. It's definitely a home. I just wouldn't go as far as saying it is a 'loving' home just yet. Dimitri is too dark for that. I guess it's part and parcel of being the leader of an organized crime syndicate.

"*Thank you,*" I mouth to Roxanne when she gestures for Dillon to join her, Fien, and Matteo in the playroom.

"It's okay, bud. I've got mommy covered," Rocco assures when Dillon hesitates.

Even with us being homebodies, he hates leaving me alone. I don't know if his neurosis stems from our nine-month separation or because he misses me as much as I do Rocco every day he goes to 'work.' We've only been apart a night or two at most, but with rumors forming about a Russian sanction hoping to set up shop in Hopeton, it could soon extend to week-long stints.

Perhaps that's behind Rocco's motives? If I'm not in hiding, we won't have to be separated for more than a day at a time. Dillon and I could travel with him as Roxanne, Fien, and Matteo do with Dimitri.

The excitement blistering through my veins is stripped when our arrival into Dimitri's downstairs office is met with a surly tone. "I fucking knew it." The man I'm guessing is Ezra stands before he folds his thick arms in front of his chest. "How long have you been hiding her? If my gut is anything to go by, from the very fucking start."

When Rocco jerks up his chin, agreeing with him, Ezra snaps his eyes to Dimitri. "And you knew about this?" When Dimitri fails to deny his accusation, he tosses his hands through his hair. "After everything you'd been through with your father, I thought you would have known better. This could end you, Dimitri."

"How could protecting the heir to the Mexican Cartel affect Dimitri's reign?" Rocco asks, his voice so loud I both feel and hear the rumble it causes his chest.

Ezra shifts on his feet to face Rocco. "You're not protecting an heir. You kidnapped him—"

"To ensure he wasn't abused. To stop him from being murdered like Col murdered Kaylee." I don't know who Kaylee is, but the mentioning of her name whitens both Dimitri's and Ezra's faces. "I removed Dillon..." Rocco pauses, swallows, then starts again, "... JJ from an unsafe environment to protect the integrity of the Mexican Cartel." Ezra isn't the only one shocked when Rocco hits him with information that would have taken years to unearth. "Juan was the only child born to Alejandro Sánchez before his death. He wasn't birthed by Juana Martinez. He was born to Alejandro's first wife, Johanna, who died shortly after delivery. Juan's birth was registered under the name of Arturo. Juana requested a change of name after she weaseled her way into Alejandro's life after the death of his beloved wife."

Smith places up evidence that corresponds with Rocco's claims onto the television-size monitor hanging on one wall of Dimitri's office. "During 1985 and 1992, Juana birthed four children. They were all girls."

My eyes snap to Rocco, certain I heard Smith wrong. Juana's children were boys. She doesn't have any daughters. Does she?

I realize just how deceitful Juana has been when Smith adds, "Records from Juana's hospital admissions correspond with the kidnapping of male infants from nearby hospitals." Newspaper clippings from dates very close to Jose, Frances, and Alej's births flash up on the screen. "We don't have evidence to back up our claims, but we believe Alej's disabilities made Juana trigger-shy. Although she was recorded as giving birth in 1992, no birth registration forms were ever submitted."

Rocco jumps back into the conversation. "It took us so long to unearth this because everyone believed Juana's psychosis occurred because of the birth of her stillborn son. It was only when I questioned why she guarded JJ like he was the heir instead of her eldest grandson, Jeremiah, did I realize we weren't digging deep enough." He peers at me with apologetic eyes before murmuring, "Juana wanted JJ so badly because he is the head of the Mexican Cartel. Rules state until an heir is of age, his custodian can fulfill his place. To this day, Juana has taken advantage of a privilege she has no right to claim."

I mouth that I love him when he hands Ezra undeniable proof that I am my son's true birth mother. Not only does he hand him the DNA test he organized years ago in case we ever reached this stage, he also shows him the footage the warden tried to hide from him years ago. It leaves no doubt that Dillon was born with a set of perfectly working lungs. He screams as loudly as I beg to hold him for just a minute when Warden Mattue hands him to Juana.

When Rocco stops to stand in front of Ezra, his cockiness leaps to an all-time high. "You threatened Dimitri with disbandment when for the past three and a half years he's been acting on the orders of the *true* Mexican Cartel leader."

When Rocco strays his eyes to me, Ezra follows the direction of his gaze. His voice is super groggy when he asks, "Is this true? Did you request for Dimitri to hide you?"

I nod without pause for thought. I'm not lying to save Dimitri's hide. I begged Smith the morning of my escape to reach out to Dimitri on my behalf. Rocco's recovery was happening in leaps and bounds, but when I found the cocaine he hid in the toilet cistern, I was worried he'd fall back to old ways painfully quick. I cared about him too much to sit back and watch him fall.

Smith promised he would talk to Dimitri, but I didn't know the outcome of the conversation until my entrance into the cargo plane had me stumbling onto a tall, broad Italian man with an extensive collection of tattoos subduing the wails of my son like he was nowhere near as dangerous as perceived.

After working his jaw side to side, Ezra cranks his neck to Dimitri. "I need a day. Two at most."

"Very well," Dimitri replies, his expression unchanging. He's either as cool as a cucumber, or he plays the role of a cartel leader well.

Ezra directs the quickest glance my way before he heads for the door. His exit from Dimitri's office slices the tension into tiny, much more manageable pieces.

"Was that true?" I ask Rocco once I'm confident we're free from prying eyes and ears.

Dimitri tells us to get a room when Rocco stands so close to me, I feel every inch of his impressive body—and I mean *every* inch. "Every word, Mama. Now you and Dillon aren't just umbrellaed under the Petretti entity, you can't be touched." My knees pull together when he whispers, "Except by me. Which is good considering you *really* like all the wicked things I do with my tongue."

When I push him away from me, faking that I have some sense of control when he's near, I grow worried I hurt him.

He folds in two before he falls to his knees.

"Rocco!"

I race to him, my pace slowing when he thrusts a ring box between us. As Smith chuckles about his dramatics, Rocco pops open the felt box to reveal a three-carat teardrop diamond ring. "If you say yes, Mama, this will be the only tear you'll ever wear."

I discover the reason our craft supplies were super low today when Dillon enters the room in a black tuxedo with a silver cardboard sign that reads, "Mama, will you marry my daddy?" My hand shoots up to cover my sob when he dumps his sign to the floor so he can join Rocco in kneeling.

He's only four, but he knows who he has to thank for every bit of happiness that beams out of me when I nod my head before whispering the faintest, "Yes," over the jubilant cheer of our closest confidants and friends.

# BONUS EPILOGUE
## ROCCO

*I* adjust my crotch to stop my zipper from biting my cock when my wife's sexy-as-fuck voice jingles into my ears. She's holed up in the bedroom of our hotel suite, resting her swollen feet from carrying our chunky butt of an unborn child around the streets of Vegas today.

My family wanted to go sightseeing, and how could I deny their one wish when my every wish was granted the instant Henry Gottle, Sr. acknowledged Dillon as being the true heir of the Mexican Cartel.

His title protects both his mother and him by a law not even someone as high-up as Dimitri can ignore. They're untouchable, and since my fucked-up head has finally realized I'm nothing like my father, I mean in all senses of the word.

No one will hurt my family—not even me.

"What did you say, Mama? I missed half of what you said?" I heard every word she uttered. I just love the sound of her voice so much, I'm willing to lie to ensure I get my fill.

The smile I feel more than I see assures me my ruse is about to be busted, not to mention the cocking of Claudia's brow when she enters the living room of our suite.

*Hot fucking damn.*

My woman was already fine before I got her knocked up.

Now she's downright fucking dynamite.

"I said…" she waits for my eyes to land on her face before continuing, "If laws protect India, what would happen if someone outside of the realm took her out?"

Even hearing her question for a second time doesn't stop it from stumping me. "Nothing but the retaliation of those in her corner."

"Who is…" She waves her empty hands through the air, wordlessly advising she isn't asking a question. She's stating a fact. "India has no one on her side and a ton of enemies who can't touch her because she's protected by mafia law." She points to a surveillance image of Maddox Walsh. "If he wants to kill her, why not let him?"

"Maddox isn't a killer," Smith discloses before I can.

Claudia silences us both by tapping on a death notice in a newspaper from almost four years ago. It was for an FBI agent who was slain in the underbelly of Wallens Ridge State Penitentiary. Although Maddox has never disclosed he was behind the murder of Agent Moses, every gangbanger this side of the country knows it was him. "You've lured India into a trap. You have her right where you want her, but you can only clip her wings. Maddox can wholly remove them."

When an impressive hum vibrates out of Smith's lips, I recall he's in the room with me.

"Smith…" He continues perusing the information in front of us like our meeting isn't face-to-face while humming out an agreeing murmur. His eyes only dart to mine when I finalize my sentence, "It's time for you to leave."

"What? I thought we were going over our plan until we made contact with Dimitri."

Dimitri and his family are on a cargo ship destined for Italy. It's a long story, one I'm sure you're already aware of if you read Dimitri's story, and one I'm not willing to repeat right now. My woman needs me, and I sure as fuck need her just as badly.

"We *were* going to do that, but plans changed." When the stupid fucker doesn't get the hint it's time for him to leave, I nudge my head to Claudia looking ravishing in a strapless maternity dress that showcases her swollen stomach to perfection. "I'm sure you'll find a way to reach me when Dimitri makes contact. Until then, adios, motherfucker."

I practically carry him to the door and toss him into the hallway. I'm not usually so aggressive, but since annoyance is heating my veins, my hotheadedness has reared its ugly head. I've been so caught up with this India bullshit the past four years, it took longer than it should to unearth Juana's scheme. If that isn't already bad enough, there have been a handful of occasions where I've failed to keep my word to Claudia.

Today will not be one of those days.

After setting the lock into place and activating the wireless dark-knight program Smith installed on my cell phone, I spin around to face Claudia. Her cheeks turn the color of the poppies on her dress when I murmur, "Morning, noon, and night, right?" When she sheepishly nods, I add, "I had you screaming in the shower this morning and woke you the same way from your midday nap so we could go sightseeing, so that only leaves one task on my hitlist today."

I drag my eyes to the window that shows the lights of the Las Vegas strip are super bright since it's dark outside before I return them to my wife. I grin when I spot the faintest press of her thighs. I fucked up years ago when I told Smith fucking the same woman a hundred times was a mistake. The more I have Claudia, the more I want her. She's more addictive than cocaine, and the sole reason I kicked my habit the first time around.

The therapist Dimitri hired to detox me in my home said men in my industry are more likely to relapse than standard johns.

I proved him wrong.

The first couple of days was a shitfest. I sweated like a pig, begged for my dead mother to save me, and told Dimitri multiple times that I hated him. The only reason I didn't relapse was because every single night without fail, Claudia rolled Dillon's crib into my room, climbed into my sweat-soaked bed, then held me until the shudders raking through my body subdued enough I could get a couple of hours of sleep.

She was a fucking saint, and I have no hesitation in saying I would not be here today if it weren't for her. This industry isn't for the weak, and since I was gobbled up and spat out before I officially became a part of it, it consumed me more than it should have.

I prosecuted before viewing any evidence and killed without remorse.

I still do that now, but only to the people stupid enough to put my wife, son, and unborn child on their radar. Then I'm there, waiting in the shadows, ready to protect them by any means necessary. I will protect them at any cost because protecting your family is a basic instinct of every man. Only the occasional few fall through the cracks.

I will not be one of them.

The abuse cycle of the Shay men ended the day I murdered my father, and it will stay buried long after I'm gone.

I promise you that.

The next book in the Italian Cartel Series is *Clover*. He is the hired hitman who is dark and mysterious. His book will be super spicy. You can download it here: Clover

**Facebook:** facebook.com/authorshandi

**Instagram:** instagram.com/authorshandi

. . .

**Email:** authorshandi@gmail.com


**Reader's Group:** bit.ly/ShandiBookBabes


**Website:** authorshandi.com


**Newsletter:** https://www.subscribepage.com/AuthorShandi

*If you enjoyed this book, please leave a review.*

# ALSO BY SHANDI BOYES

** Denotes Standalone Books*

## Perception Series

Saving Noah *

Fighting Jacob *

Taming Nick *

Redeeming Slater *

Saving Emily

Wrapped Up with Rise Up

Protecting Nicole *

## Enigma

Enigma

Unraveling an Enigma

Enigma The Mystery Unmasked

Enigma: The Final Chapter

Beneath The Secrets

Beneath The Sheets

Spy Thy Neighbor *

The Opposite Effect *

I Married a Mob Boss *

Second Shot *

The Way We Are

The Way We Were

Sugar and Spice *

Lady In Waiting

Man in Queue

Couple on Hold

Enigma: The Wedding

Silent Vigilante

Hushed Guardian

Quiet Protector

Enigma: An Isaac Retelling

Twisted Lies *

**Bound Series**

Chains

Links

Bound

Restrain

The Misfits *

Nanny Dispute *

**Russian Mob Chronicles**

Nikolai: A Mafia Prince Romance

Nikolai: Taking Back What's Mine

Nikolai: What's Left of Me

Nikolai: Mine to Protect

Asher: My Russian Revenge *

Nikolai: Through the Devil's Eyes

Trey *

<u>**The Italian Cartel**</u>

Dimitri

Roxanne

Reign

Mafia Ties (Novella)

Maddox

Demi

Ox

Rocco *

Clover *

Smith *

<u>**RomCom Standalones**</u>

Just Playin' *

<u>Ain't Happenin'</u> *

<u>The Drop Zone</u> *

Very Unlikely *

False Start *

<u>**Short Stories - Newsletter Downloads**</u>

Christmas Trio *

Falling For A Stranger *

<u>**One Night Only Series**</u>

Hotshot Boss *

Hotshot Neighbor *

<u>**The Bobrov Bratva Series**</u>

Wicked Intentions *

Sinful Intentions *

Devious Intentions *

Deadly Intentions *

9 781923 062825